WHISPER CREEK

Also by Allison Brennan

STAND-ALONE NOVELS

Beach Reads and Deadly Deeds
North of Nowhere

ANGELHART INVESTIGATIONS

Don't Say a Word
You'll Never Find Me

QUINN & COSTA

Make It Out Alive
See How They Hide
The Missing Witness
Seven Girls Gone
The Wrong Victim
Tell No Lies
The Third to Die

REGAN MERRITT

Don't Open the Door
The Sorority Murder

LUCY KINCAID

Missing
Cold as Ice
Cut and Run
Nothing to Hide
Too Far Gone
Breaking Point
Make Them Pay
The Lost Girls
No Good Deed
Best Laid Plans
Dead Heat
Cold Snap
Stolen
Stalked
Silenced
If I Should Die
Kiss Me, Kill Me
Love Me to Death

MAX REVERE

Abandoned
Shattered
Poisonous
Compulsion
Notorious

PREDATOR

The Kill
The Hunt
The Prey

NO EVIL

Fear No Evil
See No Evil
Speak No Evil

PRISON BREAK

Playing Dead
Tempting Evil
Killing Fear

FBI

Cutting Edge
Fatal Secrets
Sudden Death

SEVEN DEADLY SINS

Mortal Sin
Carnal Sin
Original Sin

MORENO & HART

Lost and Found
Frosted
Hit and Run
Crash and Burn

RIVER CITY

Mirror Mirror
Aim to Kill
Murder in the River City
Killing Justice

WHISPER CREEK

A THRILLER

ALLISON BRENNAN

MINOTAUR BOOKS
NEW YORK

This is a work of fiction. All of the names, characters, organizations, places, and events portrayed in this novel are either products of the author's imagination or used fictitiously.

First published in the United States by Minotaur Books, an imprint of St. Martin's Publishing Group

For information, address St. Martin's Publishing Group, 120 Broadway, New York, NY 10271.

Designed by Meryl Sussman Levavi

ISBN 978-1-250-39720-1

For Tosca and Bryan.

Thank you for letting me borrow Timber.

The world breaks everyone, and afterward,
many are strong at the broken places.
—Ernest Hemingway, *A Farewell to Arms*

WHISPER CREEK

PROLOGUE

He had to wait until the hail stopped and the family slept before he could access the barn. And still, he waited another hour just in case, standing in a thicket near Whisper Creek with a clear view of both the barn and the house beyond it.

This wasn't the first time he had sabotaged someone's property. It wasn't even the first time he had sabotaged this particular barn. Some people were too stubborn for their own good, and now he had to force their hand.

Time was running out. He'd thought for sure after John McKenna died last year that Ellen would have the common sense to do what was right for her family. But she was just as stubborn as her husband.

Guilt crept up his spine and he slammed that shit down. John died in an accident. An *accident.* Freak thing, not his fault, it shouldn't have happened.

He didn't mean for it to happen.

No one had needed to die.

He pulled out his flask and drank half the bourbon inside. Even the expensive liquor burned on the way down. He screwed the cap back on and slipped it into the pocket of his lightweight jacket.

Now, he told himself. *Stop stalling. Nothing has changed.*

He crept a hundred yards to the side door of the barn. No one locked their barns; there was no need. Some people secured their storage sheds or garages—equipment was valuable and far easier to steal, though theft was rare out here, where everyone owned guns and a truck could be heard a mile away.

Which is why he had come on foot.

He unlatched the door and entered quietly.

The barn wasn't silent. Sheep bayed in their sleep. A horse softly nickered. The rustle of hay as the dairy cows shifted. The creak and groan in the rafters as the wind whistled through.

The storm may have passed, but another was brewing in the northeast and would dump far more water into their valley than the first.

Now was the time to push Ellen McKenna. Hard.

He shifted the heavy backpack onto both shoulders, then climbed the ladder to the hayloft. Something rustled to his right and for a minute he thought it was the kid, sleeping in the barn as he himself had done with friends when he was little.

He shifted, a cat yowled when he stepped on its tail and bolted along a beam to the far wall. He sensed more than saw the dark cat run down tack shelves to the floor below. The sheep bayed loudly, and he really hoped they didn't cause a commotion. If the family heard, they might think a coyote had got into the barn.

But a minute later the sheep settled down, and he crossed to the loft door.

It opened above one of the gutters. Quickly, he removed and unzipped his backpack and extracted two cans of expanding foam. He looked over at the house sixty yards across the way. A faint light was on in the kitchen, but he'd noticed that it was on all the time. He didn't see or sense anyone moving inside.

Still, he worked quickly. He sprayed the foam into the gutter, leaning over to make sure the foam went down the hole of the downspout on both corners of the building. He then gathered straw from the loft and tamped it down onto the foam that was quickly hardening. It would take normally twenty-four hours to cure, but the warm air and humidity would accelerate the process.

When he was done, he closed the loft door, walked to the corner, crouching when the roof sloped downward. He removed a handsaw from his bag, knelt, and carefully cut a narrow strip through the wall that wouldn't be easily seen because it was behind the gutter. He then pushed hay up against the half-inch slit to conceal it. He repeated the process on the opposite side. The water from the next storm would seep into the barn from the now-clogged gutter, saturate the loft, the hay, the walls. The barn would slowly flood. Mold and mildew would grow quickly in the humidity. Feed would be contaminated. The barn would have to be fixed, if not completely rebuilt. The animals sold, or they'd have to pay to board them while the barn was being repaired. One more major expense in a long line of expenses that put pressure on the McKenna family.

This had to work. Time was running out.

Satisfied that the job was done, he left the loft. He hadn't wanted to use the foam because once the barn flooded, an inspection could reveal the sabotage. But by that point, the damage would be done and no one could prove *he'd* had anything to do with it.

As soon as he opened the side door, the cat he'd stepped on earlier ran out into the night, nearly tripping him. He swore under his breath, closed the door, and left the way he'd come.

When he reached his truck more than a mile away, he called in. "Done."

"If this doesn't work, we escalate. We only have a week."

"It'll work," he said, sounding more confident than he felt.

He didn't want anyone else to die, so he prayed hard that he was right.

CHAPTER ONE

Thursday Night

Rena Jones sat in the backseat of the King Cab pickup as the rain poured down like the sky had cracked open, pelting the top of the cab with a violent staccato beat. Her brother lay slumped beside her, his shirt soaked with blood and rain, his breaths coming in short gasps.

She pressed her trembling hands to the wound on his side. Her fingers were warm and sticky with blood, and no matter how hard she pushed, she couldn't seem to stop it.

"Brock," she choked, glancing at her husband, who was driving, his hands tight on the wheel as he navigated through unpaved back roads. Every bump and hole in the road had the truck bouncing and Sam grunting in pain. "We have to get Sam to a hospital."

"No," Sam ground out, his voice barely a whisper. His face was pale, jaw clenched, eyes pained. He was shaking, whether from shock or cold, she couldn't tell.

The windshield wipers were going full force, slapping rhythmically against the glass, but the rain was winning. Water sheeted over the truck like they were underwater.

Tears stung her eyes, hot against the cold. "But—"

"He's right," Brock said from the front seat, turning halfway toward her. His face was hard, but his eyes showed his deep fear. He loved Sam just like she did. It had been the three of them for so long. Ever since Brock walked into her life when she was eighteen and they fell in love. It was her and Brock and Sam against the world. Doing what needed to be done to keep them above water. The three musketeers. The three amigos.

"It's gonna be fine," Brock insisted. "A flesh wound."

"It's not a flesh wound!" she snapped. "He's losing too much blood. He needs stitches, a transfusion—something!"

"I'll be fine," Sam mumbled weakly. "Just . . . Let's get home. You can patch me up. Like last time."

Rena shook her head, throat closing. Last time was years ago, and the gunshot hadn't been this bad. That time, it had gone in and out of his upper arm. He still had the scar, which he'd covered with a tattoo of a cypress tree that reminded Rena of the one that grew out of the swamp behind their Mimi's house.

This time . . . there was more blood.

"This wasn't supposed to happen," she said, her voice low, furious. "Baldwin wasn't supposed to be home."

They'd been hired for four jobs. Four clean, silent entries. In and out, no one the wiser. Get the documents, break the computer, steal a few shiny things to throw off the scent. No one gets hurt. No one around to see them. The first two had been letter-perfect, no one suspecting the reason for the break-ins.

But this time? Tonight had turned into a damn nightmare and now they were stuck in the middle of a torrential downpour in an unfamiliar area in the middle of nowhere.

They'd entered through the back of the house after Sam disabled the alarm from the main box. He was so smart, her little brother. So damn smart. Her eyes burned, the deeply buried regrets that she should have done something, anything, to get Sam a real job, maybe even into college, rather than letting him follow her and Brock into a life of crime.

Intel had said Baldwin was in Dallas until Saturday, and he always took his German shepherd with him when he traveled. So, after Sam took down the alarms, they should have had all the time in the world.

But halfway through corrupting the hard drives, they heard three rapid barks from upstairs. A canine alarm. The dog sounded furious, then Rena heard a muffled voice.

Footsteps thundering down the stairs barely before they could register that they weren't alone in the house.

Baldwin, shotgun in hand, stepped into the doorway with surprise, anger, and fear in his eyes.

Rena had screamed. Brock fired. The dog lunged. Gunshots coming from her husband and Sam. The loud report of the shotgun going off once, pump, twice. The dog yelped, crumpled. Baldwin fell back, clutching his chest. Or was it his throat? It all happened so damn fast.

And then Brock was screaming, dragging Sam out the front door. Rena's ears still rang from the echo of gunfire. She wasn't even sure which one of them had hit Baldwin.

But it wouldn't matter who fired the fatal shot. They were either killers or accessories to murder.

Maybe he isn't dead. Maybe he survived.

God, she hoped he survived. Please, God, let him live. Baldwin *and* Sam.

The rain had started somewhere in that chaos, while she waited with Sam bleeding in her arms as Brock brought the truck around. Now it was drowning the world.

"Fucking road's flooding," Brock muttered, his voice faint but with a hint of panic.

Her husband never panicked, so she knew this was bad.

"The rain just started—" she said, but she could see the rising water now, remembered the storm last weekend that had kept them in town until Tuesday night. They were supposed to be done by now, but they'd been delayed because of the damn spring rain. The unpaved back roads were turning into rivers. Mud slid under their tires.

"We're trapped," Brock said. "There's no way through."

"Sam's bleeding out," she said, heart thudding. "Brock, we can't just sit here—"

"Fuck!" She jumped when Brock slammed his palm against the steering wheel, the sound cracking through the cab. "I'm sorry, okay? We don't have any other choice."

Before she could ask what he was planning, Brock swerved suddenly, tires crunching wet gravel, and they drove down a long, bumpy driveway. Trees loomed on either side, branches lashing at the truck from the wind. A flash of lightning illuminated outbuildings and a dark house. Brock killed the lights, then the engine.

Darkness swallowed them, but not silence. The storm outside raged, shaking their truck, tearing at her soul. They couldn't stay here, she knew. Sam would die. Her brother, her younger brother, her only brother. She couldn't let that happen.

A sob escaped her throat; she swallowed it.

"Do you trust me, Rena?" Brock said quietly.

She stared at him. The anger and fear in his eyes. And the love.

"Of course I do," she whispered. "I love you."

"We need to hole up tonight. Wait out the storm. We'll patch Sam up. Assess his injuries. Then finish the job."

She hesitated, heart hammering. "Okay," she said at last. "Where?"

"Stay here. I'll be right back."

Rena watched him disappear into the dark, every instinct screaming not to let him go. But she stayed. She held on to Sam's hand, whispered reassurances, tried to believe them herself.

The rain was so thick she couldn't see outside the truck. Then lightning flashed across the sky, lighting up the fields in stark white for a heartbeat before the dark came again. The trees writhed in the wind. Thunder rolled so loud it made her chest rattle. And she'd seen the dark house again in that moment of light.

She hoped it was empty; she feared it wasn't.

But they had no choice.

"You'll be okay," she whispered to Sam, brushing his damp hair back from his forehead. His eyes fluttered closed. "I've got you."

"I'm going to be fine, Rena," Sam said, his voice trying for *everything is coming up roses* but sounding more like *this is the end of the world.*

She hated this godforsaken rural county, this miserable state. The endless dark. The isolation. Out here, there were no sirens. No cell service. No one to save her brother.

And she couldn't stop thinking—what if Baldwin had a silent alarm? What if someone had seen the truck? What if Baldwin wasn't dead and could identify them? Or worse, what if he was dead and they were now murderers?

What if this was the beginning of the end?

"One more job," she murmured to herself. "Just one more. Then we're done."

But the words felt empty. If Sam died, money couldn't bring him back. Money would mean nothing to her without her family.

Ten minutes later, Brock returned, soaked and pale.

"I didn't hurt nobody," he said, breathing heavily. "But they understand."

She turned toward him slowly, her stomach sinking. His eyes were too bright. His voice too calm.

"Brock . . ." she said, warning in her voice.

He looked away. "We need to save Sammy. Help me get him inside."

She didn't move.

Because she knew.

He hadn't asked for help. He'd taken it.

And somewhere inside that farmhouse, someone now feared them enough to stay silent, at least for tonight.

They had crossed a line.

And Rena didn't know if they'd ever find their way back.

CHAPTER TWO

Friday Morning

Ellen McKenna watched her son Jake ride off across the field on horseback alongside their ranch hand, Mateo Delgado. Yesterday they'd discovered that the run-in—a simple, three-sided structure used to give cattle shelter from the elements—had been seriously damaged during last weekend's hailstorm. Overnight rain had caused part of it to collapse. With a brief break in the weather this morning, they planned to make repairs so the herd would have protection when the storm returned this afternoon.

The rain last night had been short-lived, but the already saturated ground couldn't absorb the sudden two-hour downpour. The narrow gravel road that cut through their farm toward the pasture still had standing water, leaving the surface pocked and muddy, but fortunately it hadn't been washed out. Jake and Mateo would also check for damage along the road, making notes and fixing whatever they could in the few hours they had before the rain was supposed to start up again.

She'd packed them each a full thermos of coffee and sandwiches in case the job took longer than expected. Their cattle grazed on the far side of their fourteen hundred acres, half of which was dedicated to their herd. There was plenty of high ground for the cattle to migrate to if the fields flooded. Most of their crops had survived the hailstorm last weekend, and though the ground was still saturated, the plants were thriving.

But they might not thrive if the fields flooded. They might lose everything.

They'd lost half their grapevines in the hailstorm, but it looked like the rest were going to flower. It would be the first year they had fruit on the vines.

It had been John's dream to create their own wine label, but it had never been the right time to start the vineyard. Three years ago, after a particularly good year for cattle, they planted a small, uneven twelve-acre plot bisected by Whisper Creek. It was the perfect soil for wine grapes, according to John, who'd consulted with his closest friend—a successful vintner—on the project. On one side, they planted Tempranillo, on the other, Sangiovese. But it takes three years, sometimes four, for the vines to age and flower.

This was the year, and John wasn't here to see it.

She looked up at the dark gray sky, thinking—believing—that her husband was watching over them, that he would see the first grape harvest. They wouldn't have their own winery—she'd have to sell the grapes this year and maybe next—but it was a start.

And someday, she would turn the old bunkhouse into a winery and bottle their own label—a label John had designed years ago.

Whisper Creek Vineyard.

"John, I miss you so much," she murmured.

Two and a half months from now, on July first, would have been their twentieth wedding anniversary. Now, she was a widow at forty-one.

It had been eleven months since her husband died in a tragic accident. Eleven months since her life had been shattered. She was still broken, but she'd put the pieces together as best she could for their four kids.

Some of those pieces still had wide cracks between them that she filled with work, because that helped. Being busy, being exhausted, thinking about the farm and everything she had to do to survive, all that helped her ignore the pain in her heart.

Running a farm was so much harder and more expensive without John. But she would *not* lose it. She *couldn't* lose it. It had been in the McKenna family for generations.

And she could feel her husband here, on the land. She saw him in the field, felt his presence in the house, heard his laugh when the wind flitted through the drafty barn. If she lost the farm, she'd lose her husband all over again, and she knew she would never recover.

She saw a white Ford truck turn up their long driveway. She recognized it immediately. *Verdacorp*.

She didn't need this today.

"Ellen?" Penny called out from the house. "Come in and eat."

"Just a minute, Grandma," she said.

Penny McKenna stepped out the side door, drying her hands on her apron. She squinted and saw what had caught Ellen's attention.

"Them again," she said, her jaw tilted up. "I swear, those good ole boys don't know how to take no for an answer."

"Grandma, let me handle it, okay?"

"I'll get the shotgun."

"I don't want to antagonize them."

"Maybe if you antagonized them some, they'd stop coming here and making you upset."

The truck stopped in front of the house. Across the yard, Lyla stepped out from the barn, and Ellen waved her back in. She didn't need her daughter in the middle of this; sometimes, Verdacorp didn't play nice, and she didn't want Lyla to get scared or worried. Penny, irritated, turned and went back into the house, muttering under her breath.

"I swear, those Robinson brothers need a good whooping and—" then the closing door cut her off.

Ellen walked to the edge of the porch, crossed her arms over her chest, and looked down at the two men in the truck.

Clive Robinson stepped out from behind the wheel. She pointed down the driveway and said, "You can turn your truck around and go. I have a lot of work today."

"Ellen, we just want to talk for a few minutes."

"Clive, we've known each other for how long? Twenty years? And have I ever changed my mind on anything I've set it on?"

"Ellie—"

"Don't call me Ellie." Only her husband and family were allowed to use that nickname.

"Ellen, I have some numbers for you to look at. We can make a deal today, and you can have a check on Monday."

"I don't want Verdacorp money."

"It'll help." Clive reached the steps.

"Do not," she said with a glance to his feet. He stopped walking.

"I know it's been tough for you here since John died."

"I'm tired of this, Clive," she said. "You've known John since high school. You know my family. And you're part of a company that is destroying farms throughout the valley."

"We're not—"

"Cut the bullcrap. I'm not buying what you're selling. Off my property, I mean it. I have work to do before the storm, and you're just wasting my time."

Tom Garza, who had come with Clive and had the finesse of a steer on roller skates, said, "We know you're struggling, and with these storms, you're gonna lose your crops and it's too late in the season to replant. You're barely holding on; we can save you."

"I don't need you, or Verdacorp, to save my family."

"Come now," Tom said. "The Coulters signed the land lease. You're the last holdout. You don't want to stop progress."

The Coulters? Millie and George told her just last week that they would never sign with Verdacorp.

"I don't believe you," she said.

But she worried. If the Coulters sold the right-of-way, that meant her land was in Verdacorp's way. They needed her to lease to them to connect the properties they already owned.

And it meant that all the conversations she and John had had with the older farming family were for naught. While they hadn't been ready to sell when John had made them an offer the month before he died, the Coulters had promised they wouldn't sell to anyone but the McKennas. Leasing a right-of-way for utilities—which included the underground mineral rights—would negatively impact the value of their land. And it would create problems for the McKenna property.

John had told her over and over, grow or die. She needed the Coulters' land.

"Ellie—Ellen," Clive said, "if you let me come in, we can sit down, have a cuppa coffee, and I can share a new proposal, one that will satisfy both you and Verdacorp."

"Does this new proposal have me selling or leasing any part of my land?"

"Yes, but—"

"Then the answer is still no."

The door swung open and Penny came out with the shotgun, which she could barely lift to her shoulder. Ellen feared if she fired it, it would knock her on her ass and she'd break a hip.

"Miz Penny!" Clive said warmly.

"You heard my granddaughter," Penny said. "Skedaddle, and don't come back. No means no, boys."

They didn't immediately move. Penny racked the shotgun.

Clive and Tom quickly climbed back into the cab. When Clive didn't turn the ignition, Ellen took the shotgun from Penny and aimed at the truck.

The truck came to life and they drove off.

Ellen had to smile, but still admonished Penny. "John told you five years ago you weren't allowed to shoot anymore."

"I wasn't going to press the trigger, but back in my day I was a sharpshooter."

"I've heard."

Ellen went inside, unloaded the shotgun, put the shells on the high shelf inside the door—out of Penny's reach—and propped the gun in the corner. "Avery!" she called up the stairs. Her older daughter was the only night owl in a house filled with morning people.

Bobby ran down the stairs, hand gripping the newel post as he swung around and headed down the hall, Whiskey, their yellow Lab, at his heels.

"No running," Ellen said automatically as she put her hand in front of Penny to prevent her from tripping over the dog.

"Sorry, Mom! Morning, Grandma!" Bobby grabbed a muffin off the cooling rack, ran out the kitchen door, down the steps, and out to the barn, Whiskey in pursuit as if this was a game. "I'm gonna look for Cleo!" he shouted over his shoulder.

"That boy," Penny said with a wide grin.

Ellen poured more coffee and grabbed a biscuit. Penny was an amazing cook, and while Ellen had repeatedly told the eighty-four-year-old that Ellen didn't expect her to cook, Penny dismissed her. They'd developed a comfortable rhythm where Penny made breakfast—she was up before dawn anyway—and Ellen or Avery made dinner.

This week, their schedules had been off. Storm prep last week, then days of cleanup after the weekend rain, and now more storm concerns, all while managing the fields and cattle.

Flooding was definitely a possibility. The ground was saturated, and while the levees would likely hold along the Red River to the north, the creeks that ran from the river all through the valley were already running high.

They could withstand an inch or two. The roads—all packed gravel leading in and out of their property—may be impassable because there were several sections damaged from last weekend's rain and hail. Just a little rain would cause the drainage ditches to overflow and create muddy spots where even four-wheel-drive trucks could get stuck. She'd had the kids stay home from school today because while Ellen could probably drive them to the closest bus stop two miles away, she worried about them getting home.

Jake usually drove everyone to school, but today he had to check on the cattle and fix the run-in. And she wouldn't have wanted him driving in the downpour that was expected before school let out for the day. At least once a year, someone got caught in a flash flood. It had happened once to John's brother Travis; he was lucky to be alive.

"Don't let Clive and that eejit he's been working with get into your head," Penny said. She sat down and began shelling peas. Ellen marveled that Penny could be so focused on her daily chores that she didn't seem fazed that they could be trapped here for a couple of days—or that their fields could flood and wipe out all their crops.

Not to mention the truth of what Clive had said. Their farm was struggling. She had crop insurance, like most farmers, but she didn't want to lose the entire season. They had the cattle—which was more than a lot of their neighbors had—but cattle prices were erratic, and this year already showed signs of stagnant prices. John had always brought in labor during harvest, but he did so much himself both at harvest and in the winter. Last season Ellen had paid out more than she'd earned; this year, except for the cattle, she would be in the same boat. Those animals might be the only thing keeping them afloat.

"Do you believe him?" Ellen asked Penny. "That the Coulters sold access rights to the utility company?" From what Ellen could piece together from the neighbors, the utility company was working with Verdacorp to buy narrow strips of land across the valley where they'd put up poles and cell towers, and Verdacorp would manage the mineral rights.

"I hope not," Penny said, "and I don't put it past Tom Garza to lie through his teeth."

"I hear a *but*."

"I haven't talked to them since before last weekend's storm," Penny said.

The Coulters and McKennas had been neighbors for more than a hundred years. Why hadn't they talked to her first? Had Ellen not explained the seriousness of the leases? The fine print that could damage their property as well as Ellen's? Why did they do it? Were they in financial trouble?

"I need to know if Tom is telling the truth," Ellen said. "Why would he lie when we can easily verify it?"

"Because he's a lying, cheating piece of horse manure."

Ellen had to smile. She loved Penny.

Penny put a hand on her arm, gave it a squeeze, her old fingers bony but strong. "You're doing good, Ellie. I know it's hard. But John would be proud of you. Pull up your bootstraps and be the woman my grandson married."

She blinked back tears. *Damn.* "I'm trying."

"It's not weak to ask for help, Ellie. I miss him, too."

Ellen knew she did; they all did. She needed a moment to collect herself before she went out again, so she headed upstairs. She didn't want her kids seeing her teary-eyed.

Two weeks would mark the one-year anniversary of John's death. It was getting harder and harder to be the strong woman everyone expected her to be. The pressure that Verdacorp had put on her neighbors and her family had been constant and soon would come to an impasse. And Travis—her brother-in-law—was part of the problem. He didn't see the issue with selling rights to a fifty-foot-wide strip of land that cut through their property. It wasn't the utility poles and lines and towers that bothered Ellen; she wasn't anti-progress. It was the fine print that gave the company mineral rights.

When she and John first discussed leasing right-of-way, they thought it was a good idea. They'd have needed money, money to grow and expand the farm even if they had to give up a strip of land. But as they researched, they learned about problems with the same proposal in the Panhandle: The utility company put up the lines, but sold the mineral rights to Verdacorp. Fields cut in half, fences put up, the ground destroyed putting in oil pipes and oil pumps. Animals cut off from their pastures, or forced to cut through uneven land, risking injury. And often the strip of land completely cut off easy access from one side to the other.

John knew Mitchell Robinson—they'd gone to school together. The Robinsons owned thousands of acres directly south of Whisper Creek Ranch. But the Robinsons and the McKennas weren't friends.

Two generations ago, Mitchell's grandfather and John's grandfather—Penny's husband—had been in a prolonged legal battle. The McKennas refused to sell a parcel that Robinson wanted to connect to another farm he'd bought, so Robinson declared that he owned the roads because they cut through his land. The McKenna family had an entire crop they couldn't get to market because Robinson had hired armed goons to block the roads. Then Penny had nearly lost her baby—John's father—when she went into labor because the men wouldn't let the doctor through. Robinson eventually lost in court, but it took months.

Sour grapes blossomed between the families, but over time they learned to be cordial again. They communicated only when they had to. Then, a decade ago, when Mitchell's father retired to Dallas,

Mitchell created Verdacorp and turned the Robinson ranch into a major agribusiness. Verdacorp fingers became entwined in projects all over north Texas and the Panhandle, and John hadn't been surprised when he learned they were involved in cheating landowners out of mineral rights.

Now, Verdacorp was buying up farmland right and left in Cooke and Grayson counties, overpaying so the McKennas didn't have a chance to compete. Verdacorp practically surrounded them. John had spoken to every family farm in the valley, large and small, and some stood with him. Some felt they could negotiate better terms. And some thought John was just being ornery, because of the history between the McKennas and the Robinsons.

Calmer now, with a mental list of everything she needed to do before the storm hit, Ellen was about to leave her room when her eyes grazed over her favorite picture framed on the top of her dresser. She and John were sitting on the porch, the sun setting and casting a warm glow over their faces. Her head was on his shoulder, her hand on her large stomach, John's hand on top of hers—she'd been pregnant with Jake then. They were so young, she thought. So full of hope and love and joy. Even with the hard work operating a farm, they had joy.

Ellen was not going to lose this land.

"I'll fight back, John," she whispered as she caressed the still face of her husband behind the glass. "This is our land, now and forever."

I miss you so much.

She pushed aside the tears and went back downstairs.

CHAPTER THREE

Ellen grabbed a muffin that Penny had just taken out of the oven.

"I'm going to make sure Lyla doesn't need help with the animals before I head over to the Coulters."

"Have you talked to the Mendozas?" Penny asked as she put another tray into the oven. A peach pie, based on the skins and pits at the top of the garbage and a pot of overripe peaches, from which Penny would make peach syrup, simmering on the stove. When she was worried, she baked.

"Not today."

"I called this morning to see if they needed anything, and Rose was short with me."

"I'm sure she's just busy." Not to mention that Penny didn't always realize that not everyone got up at four thirty in the morning. It was barely after eight now; when had she called them?

"I should check on them."

"Grandma, you can't drive anymore." Penny's license had been taken away five years ago when she couldn't pass the eye test, even wearing her glasses.

"I can see well enough to walk over there."

"It's nearly a mile. It'll be raining before you get back."

Ellen didn't want to say no to Penny, but the old woman—though healthy—often overdid it. If she broke her hip and they couldn't get to the hospital? Or fell and no one was there to help her get up? Ellen didn't want to even think about it.

"I'll call over there, okay?"

Penny didn't look happy, but she nodded curtly and went to wash the bowls she'd used to make the pie.

Ellen picked up the house phone and dialed the Mendoza house by memory.

No one answered. She left a message on the answering machine.

"Hi, this is Ellen McKenna. I just wanted to check to see if you needed anything before the storm hits. Jake and Mateo are in the field right now, but I can send them over if you need help. Let me know." She hung up.

"No answer?" Penny said.

"Grandma, they're probably doing what we're doing. They have dozens of sheep that need to be secured. If I don't hear back from them in an hour, Avery can check on them. She would love to spend time with Gianna."

"Avery can come with me," Penny said with a smile. "She has her permit and drives better than most young people today."

Living on a farm meant that all her kids drove on the property, except Bobby, because he wasn't tall enough.

"No one is driving on the road today," Ellen said. Why didn't Penny understand that the roads were crap? The last thing she needed was her eighty-four-year-old grandmother and fifteen-year-old daughter stuck in the mud, even only a mile away.

Penny scowled. It had been hard on her, moving back into the house where she'd raised her family. When John and Ellen had married twenty years ago, Penny and Milton had moved into the original house on their property, across Orchard Lane, where they had lived the first ten years of their marriage. They gave John and Ellen the larger house as a wedding present. Ellen had broken down and cried when they gifted her the keys. She'd never had a stable home; her dad had moved them all over Texas and Oklahoma, wherever he could find work.

Then, three years ago when Milton died, since Penny could no longer drive, John had insisted she move back into the house. Penny reluctantly agreed. It was an adjustment—especially in the kitchen—but Ellen loved John's grandmother. Her grandparents had never been a part of her life, and when she went to her own grandmother's funeral several years ago she didn't recognize most of her distant family or her family's friends. Her parents had divorced, her mom had a new family and lived in Oregon, and Ellen could count on one hand the times she had met her two half brothers who weren't much older than Jake.

"If Rose calls, let me know," Ellen said as she pulled on her boots in the mudroom. "After I check on Lyla, I'll ride over to the Coulters."

Penny gave her a look that essentially said *you're a hypocrite.*

Ellen didn't want to argue with her; she could reach the Coulters on horseback without even going on the road.

Sometimes, she felt like she had five children.

Ellen trekked through the muddy yard to the barn. The area around the barn was unusually wet; the storm over the weekend and the sudden downpour last night had saturated the ground. They had placed sandbags all around the base, so hopefully that would protect the foundation.

She walked over to the drainage ditch at the lowest part of the yard and scooped up the leaves, then used a push broom to clear more debris and mud. The drain looked clear, so when the rain came, it should be sufficient to handle the overflow and prevent the barn from flooding.

In the barn, her thirteen-year-old daughter, Lyla, had everything under control. The horses already had their blinders on and were secure in their pens. Their two dairy cows had been milked, and Lyla had strained the milk and poured it into glass containers, which would be labeled and stored in the refrigerator. Fresh milk lasted up to a week, and when Betsy and Susie were in full lactation, Ellen sold the raw milk to a farm in neighboring Grayson County that used it to make yogurt and cheese. They were both near the end of the lactation cycle, so Ellen wouldn't be making a large sale anytime soon.

Fresh hay and water had been distributed to all the animals, and Lyla had let the sheep and goats out to graze in the secure pen rather than the field, which would make it easier to corral them back into the barn. The chickens were out in their own pen, and Lyla promised to shoo them back into the chicken house as soon as the rain started.

Distant thunder told Ellen it would be sooner rather than later.

"Have you checked the sandbags?" she asked Lyla.

"Before Jake and Mateo left, we walked around the barn. There's a few spots that I need to repair. Jake hooked up the trailer on the tractor, so I'll get it done. There's a couple wet spots in the barn, I don't know why. Jake said he'd inspect them when he gets back, but for now I'm going to double up the sandbags on each corner."

Lyla was so dependable it was almost scary.

"Do you think there's a leak in the roof?" Ellen asked, looking up, her heart pounding uncomfortably. Reminding her that John had died here, outside this barn, when he fell from the roof. There was no way she was sending one of her kids up there to look.

"I don't know, I can—"

"Stay away from the roof." Ellen had hired someone to make the repairs that John had been working on when he fell. "I'll find someone to take a look."

Lyla nodded; her face suddenly sad.

Ellen rubbed Lyla's back, gave her a side hug, and kissed her head. Her kids had all been close to their father and missed him as much as Ellen.

She suppressed her own wave of grief because she needed to be strong for her kids. "Are you good here for about an hour? I'm going to ride over to the Coulters, but it won't take long."

"Yeah, I'm on top of it. The prep last week is making it easier this morning. Though I wish I knew how the water was getting into the barn."

"We'll figure it out when I get back." Ellen glanced around and said, "I thought Bobby was in here."

Lyla rolled her eyes. "He went out to look for that stray cat. Whiskey's with him."

"Whiskey's going to need a bath," Ellen muttered. The dog was not going to be happy being trapped in the mudroom, but if he was out in the wet fields, he was going to be filthy when they came back.

Lyla didn't like cats. Ellen never understood why—they'd always had barn cats on the farm. Her daughter tolerated them. Bobby, on the other hand, adored all animals, especially strays. He'd named the black-and-white cat he'd found Cleo.

But Cleo had become a problem. She'd shown up a month ago and started sleeping in the barn loft. Fierce and territorial, she hissed at their two longtime barn cats, Lilo and Stitch—neutered orange tabbies who now kept their distance from the stray. Still, every morning, Bobby climbed to the loft with food and water. Ellen suspected Cleo might be pregnant, but the cat wouldn't let her get close enough to find out. Bobby was the only human she tolerated.

Then, during the storm last weekend, Cleo had vanished. Bobby had searched for her every morning since. No matter how often Ellen told him Cleo could take care of herself, his worry only deepened.

Ellen picked up one of the radios that was charging in the small barn office. She was strict about the kids taking radios with them when they left the house. Their property was too large and there were too many potential hazards without a way to reach out, even if they were only going to visit Uncle Travis or a neighbor.

"Bobby, this is Mom. Where are you? Over."

She waited. A second later Bobby came on. "Walking along Whisper Creek. Cleo needs food and water and there are a lot of baby rabbits out here. Over."

She wanted to throttle her son. "Robert Matthew McKenna, you stay away from that creek. It's going to flood, and it won't take much more rain to send it over the top. Over."

He waited a bit too long for Ellen to be comfortable, then came back, "Mom, I'm worried about her. I can't let her get caught in the storm. Over."

"And I can't let *you* get caught in the storm. One hour, and do not go within twenty feet of the creek, understood? Over."

One. Two. Three. "Understood. Over." Bobby's voice sounded defeated.

Lyla shook her head. "That darn cat has been nothing but problems. And she's going to have kittens, you know it, and I'll bet you let Bobby keep them all."

"Yes, she probably is, and no, he can't keep them all."

Lyla rolled her eyes again and went back to her chores.

Ellen went over to Sir Lancelot's stall to prep him for the morning ride. She did have a soft spot for her youngest. After three relatively easy births, Bobby's arrival had been traumatic. Though only three weeks early and technically full term, labor was difficult—they rushed Ellen in for an emergency C-section when they couldn't detect a heartbeat. They got him out, but she was hemorrhaging so bad that they had to remove her uterus. After that harrowing experience, Bobby had been a complete joy in their lives.

Jake was so much like his father—responsible, steadfast, loyal. Avery, though Ellen hesitated to admit it, reminded her of herself as a teenager: book smart, boy crazy, and constantly testing limits. Lyla, like Jake, was dependable and had more common sense than any kid Ellen knew, though she was often too blunt. As Penny said, Lyla "didn't suffer fools." Ellen disliked the phrase "old soul," but if it fit anyone, it was her thirteen-year-old daughter.

And then there was Bobby. Kind, sweet, generous—he radiated love. He'd been their ray of sunshine after John's sudden death. So it certainly didn't surprise Ellen that he was out looking for a stray cat.

John would have done the same thing.

Ellen mounted Sir Lancelot, a beautiful gelding more than twenty years old, and headed across the field toward the Coulters' property.

Sir Lancelot had been born to one of John's horses the day John proposed to her—a memorable event made even more memorable when John had to rush home from their picnic and help his brother, Travis, with the delivery because the mare was struggling.

John had wanted to be a vet, and she'd studied to be a nurse. They shared one class their freshman year and it had been love at first sight.

Unfortunately, John dropped out halfway through his sophomore year because his dad died and John needed to take over the farm. Travis was only sixteen at the time, and John's mother wasn't well. Neither of John's uncles wanted to take over the farm—they'd both moved out of the area—so that left John and his grandfather.

Ellen would have dropped out with him, but John told her she should finish school. She graduated a year early, and they married a month later at the small church four generations of McKennas had been married in.

Until Jake was born, she worked as a nurse, and then to keep her license current she worked part-time at the hospital in Gainesville. But after Bobby's difficult birth and John's plans to expand the farm, she realized that she had grown to love Whisper Creek

Ranch as much as the McKenna family. She obtained her Certified Nurse Midwife license and took on two or three clients a year. She didn't charge much, but it was a needed service, especially in rural Texas. Her OB—a doctor she had both worked for and who had delivered all four of her children—asked her to check on some of his patients from time to time. Last week in the middle of the storm Jake had driven her up to the Sutton house in the hills above Rock Creek. Margery thought she was having contractions. She wasn't, but she was thirty-two weeks pregnant with her first child and worried about every twitch and turn. Plus, her last appointment revealed slightly elevated blood pressure, so they were monitoring her closely. Margery was young, her husband was deployed overseas, and her sister who moved in to help was just nineteen. Anyone in the same situation would be a bit nervous.

Ellen had Sir Lancelot walking at a brisk pace, not quite a full trot. The ground was too wet, and gopher holes were near impossible to see in the mud. The air was thick with humidity, the warm wind pushing at her back.

The Coulters lived directly west. They had four hundred acres and had sold most of their two hundred head of cattle years ago, keeping two championship bulls they leased for breeding, which could be very lucrative. Before John's death, he had been talking to the older couple about buying out their land, much as he'd done with the Mendoza property to the northeast, which they'd purchased the year before. But the Coulters hadn't been ready, and they assured Ellen they wouldn't sell to anyone else, which had given her hope.

Grow or die.

When John took over Whisper Creek Ranch, they had just shy of eight hundred acres. Now, with the Mendoza property, they were sitting on fourteen hundred acres. John's plan had been to buy the bulk of the Coulter Ranch and the bulk of the Baldwin property, which would put them to just over three thousand acres.

But now? Baldwin had sold to Verdacorp, and if what Tom Garza said about the Coulters was true, she wouldn't get that land, either.

There were some smaller farms north of their property that Ellen had approached who hadn't yet sold to Verdacorp, but the Robinson venture had already bought most of the farms both south and east of her property line. Ellen suspected that now they would move north and attempt to surround her. Verdacorp was willing to pay over market value and allow the landowners to retain five acres for themselves. If they bought up those farms, Ellen would be an island in the middle with no option to expand.

It took Ellen ten minutes to cover the near mile to the Coulters' house. She could have called, but felt it was better to talk to George and Millie face-to-face. They had been close to John's parents, and their oldest daughter had graduated high school with John's brother, Travis.

She dismounted and tied Sir Lancelot's lead to the rail on the side of the house. The wind suddenly picked up, then settled back down. Ellen knocked on the door.

Millie answered, smiled warmly. "Ellen! Dear, come in. It's getting windy out there."

Ellen took off her muddy boots and left them by the front door. "Thank you," she said and stepped inside.

"Coffee? I just made a fresh pot."

"That would be nice, thanks."

She followed Millie into the kitchen. George was sitting at the table, reading the news on a tablet. He smiled at Ellen. "How's things at your place?"

"Last week's storm prep helped. Jake and Mateo are out repairing the run-in that was damaged by hail."

"I fed and secured the bulls this morning. They were agitated, it's going to be bad."

Maybe, she thought. Animals had better senses about weather

than people. She hoped they'd done enough to prepare, but there wasn't much more that they could do other than secure the animals, shore up the outbuildings, and stay inside once the rain fell.

She sat across from George. He tapped on his tablet and she saw he was reading his email. The words on his screen were enlarged so it was easy to see Congresswoman Jeanne Clarke Culver's header across the top.

"Good thing email is free," he said. "Otherwise the weekly emails I get from this woman would be costing taxpayers a fortune. Did you see this? A letter about how to prepare for a storm. Like we haven't been preparing for sixty-some years."

Mille put a mug of coffee down in front of Ellen along with cream, knowing she preferred her coffee light.

"Now, George, she's just doing her job."

"I didn't get emails every week from Henry."

"Henry probably didn't even know how to use a computer," Millie said.

Five years ago, Jeanne had run for the congressional seat that her grandfather Henry Clarke had represented for twenty-some years after he retired because of his health. He died a year later. Ellen had taken Penny to the funeral. She'd gone to school with Henry and they'd been friends ever since.

"I need to get back pretty quick," she said, knowing how a conversation with the Coulters could turn into an hourlong gossip session, "but I had a visit from Clive Robinson this morning."

George and Millie exchanged a look, and Ellen's chest fell. "So, you *did* sell to Verdacorp?"

"Just the right-of-way," George said. "Not the whole farm. I told John I wouldn't sell the farm to them, and I'll stand by that."

A small blessing, Ellen thought. "Thank you."

"And they're just working with the utilities, many people sell the right-of-way for utilities. Better than the government coming in and snatching the land through eminent domain. The money is good, Ellen. You might want to think of doing the same thing."

She opened her mouth to speak, but George put up his hand. "I know your concerns, but we had a lawyer look it over, and there's nothing to worry about."

"I'm not selling a square foot to Verdacorp," Ellen said, sounding a lot harsher than she intended. She sipped her coffee to cover, then said, "I'm going through with the expansion."

"Do you have the money, dear?" Millie asked. "Clive said you were struggling."

Ellen wanted to wring Clive's neck. Was that what he was telling people? That she was struggling and therefore they should sell to Verdacorp because Ellen couldn't pay them a fair price?

"I have the money," she said, though it wasn't completely true. They'd bought the Mendoza property and had planned to plant it last year . . . then John died. This year, she was only able to get one fifty-acre plot planted with sunflowers, and they hadn't yet touched the pecan trees, which were a complete mess as they hadn't been harvested properly in a decade. She had hoped by next year she'd have half the old Mendoza property planted, which would on paper give her the ability to carry a loan on the Coulters' property.

"A lot of people are selling off," George said.

"The McKennas have farmed here for nearly a hundred and thirty years. I'm not backing down," Ellen said. "After harvest, I hope we can negotiate for the east half of your property. I'll plant winter wheat and move the cattle there."

George nodded. "That's a good plan," he said. "We can talk."

She hoped he wasn't just saying it to make her feel better.

"Can I look at your contract with Verdacorp?"

"I suppose so, but why?"

"I want to see the maps. Greg Baldwin showed me his, he's sending me a copy." Though she hadn't received it yet.

She didn't want to explain why. The bulk of her land was between Baldwin and the Coulters. She wanted to figure out what Verdacorp's plan was so she could combat it. It would also help her figure out who she needed to talk to next.

George got up. "I'll make you a copy right now," he said and left the kitchen.

"How's Penny?" Millie asked. "Still getting around all right?"

"She is. Oh, I almost forgot." She reached into her satchel and pulled out a paper bag of oatmeal raisin cookies. "She's been baking all week. She won't admit that the storm stressed her out, but looking at the number of pies and cookies we have in the pantry, she was clearly a bit anxious," Ellen added with a smile.

Millie looked inside and grinned widely. "Oh, George will be thrilled." She took three cookies from the bag, put one at George's spot, and one each for her and Ellen. "Um," Millie said after taking a bite. "Penny is the best stress baker." She laughed lightly.

George came back and handed Ellen a folder. "Here you go. If you have questions, call me. But I think this is a good thing, Ellen. It might be good for your farm, too—provide an influx of cash when you most need it." He picked up the cookie and smiled. "Thank Penny for me."

Millie got up and opened the refrigerator.

"Here, I made two trays of shepherd's pie, and I was going to freeze this one, but then dang forgot. Just warm it up tonight, it'll hit the spot."

"I won't say no to any of your casseroles," Ellen said, not wanting to hurt Millie's feelings by declining the food. She could hear Penny criticizing it in the back of her mind; Penny was getting catty in her old age, especially about other people's cooking.

I'll bet she used canned gravy, Ellen heard Penny say.

She said her goodbyes and left, securing the covered casserole in front of her. With the contract in her satchel, she trotted home as fast as she dared.

CHAPTER FOUR

Jake sat high in the saddle, silhouetted against a bruised sky that pressed low on the horizon. He did a quick head count, eyes narrowing as a gust of wind rustled the wheat in the distance, bringing in the distant scent of rain. The herd moved sluggishly, anxious. He didn't like that they'd be stuck way out here during a storm, exposed and vulnerable, but there wasn't much he could do about it now. This was the highest parcel on their property except for the main house, and they were safest here.

The southern boundary of the property had a rise—barely a hill, but high enough. If the low fields flooded, the cattle would drift uphill. They always did. That hill hadn't flooded since his grandfather was born. Still, that was history. Every storm was different, and the ground was already wet.

There was a run-in at the top of the knoll. They'd expanded and reinforced the structure several years ago, but a large section of the roof had been damaged by hail. Mateo was working to repair the roof while Jake focused on inspecting the cattle. The three-sided shelter wouldn't keep the herd completely dry once the wind kicked up, but it would offer some protection—especially from hail. That was the real threat. Last weekend, a dozen cows had been bruised from the pounding ice. No lasting damage, but Jake was glad they weren't going to market anytime soon so they would have a chance to fully heal.

Two troughs ran along the back of the run-in, one for water and one for feed. While the cattle primarily fed through grazing, they supplemented their diet with grains.

He scanned the edges of the field and spotted four cows clustered under a wind-raked tree, and a fifth one lying oddly apart from the others. Jake nudged his horse forward. He was about to raise his hand to wave them on when something about the fifth "cow" felt wrong. Too lean, too small, too still.

As he got closer, his gut twisted. It wasn't a cow at all. It was a dog, Timber. Greg Baldwin's massive German shepherd.

Jake quickly swung down from the saddle, boots hitting the muddy ground with a muffled thud. Timber raised his head weakly, eyes glassy but locked on Jake with recognition. His tail thumped once. He stood, but favored one leg and staggered.

"What happened, boy?" Jake asked, crouching low. Timber's thick coat was matted with mud and blood, dark smears streaking his muzzle and hindquarters.

Jake's stomach dropped.

"Easy now." His voice softened. "I need to check you out. Stay still."

Timber let him inspect the wound. "Good dog," Jake murmured as he carefully looked at Timber's leg. Embedded in the dog's leg were small, dark pellets—buckshot. Just a few, not too deep but wedged into his muscle. Painful, but not deadly if he got treatment.

Jake's mind flashed back five years, to Timber as a puppy chasing his brother Titan around Uncle Travis's yard. Back when Jake's dad was still alive, when Baldwin was still a fixture in their lives, before he sold out to Verdacorp. When Travis and Baldwin had adopted the two dogs from another farmer and agreed to get the German shepherds together for "playdates."

Jake reached for his radio. "Mateo, I've got Timber by the oak tree. He's injured—buckshot. I'm going to take him back to Baldwin's place."

"Hold up a sec, I'll be right there."

He was about to object, but then saw Mateo in the distance riding toward him at near full gallop.

Jake continued to pet the dog, who looked at him with both pain and hope. What asshole would shoot a dog? Jake tried to keep his anger in check, because both the dogs and horse were likely to pick up on his agitation and get nervous.

"You're a good boy," Jake told him. "Good, good boy. We're going to get you fixed up right quick, I promise."

Mateo arrived only moments later and dismounted. "What happened?" he asked, his face filled with the same concern that Jake felt.

"I thought he was a cow lying in the grass," Jake said, motioning to the four other cows standing under the tree only a few feet away. "Found Timber instead."

"Damn," Mateo said. "I should go with you; you might need help with him."

"Is the roof done?"

"Not yet, but—"

"Finish the roof," Jake said. "The storm isn't going to wait for us. Plus, someone needs to bring these four lazy cows back to the herd."

Mateo wanted to object, but nodded and said, "Okay, I'll meet you at Baldwin's when I'm done. Shouldn't take longer than thirty minutes."

"Thanks," Jake said.

"Want me to help you get him on the saddle?"

"No, I think he'll be nervous up there, and I don't have anything to safely secure him."

"All right. If you see anything weird, you radio me, got it? I'll be right there."

Mateo used his horse to urge the four cows back toward the herd and the run-in.

Mateo was more than twice Jake's age and had started working for the Whisper Creek Ranch more than a decade ago, around the time that Jake's little brother, Bobby, was born. Jake generally deferred to the more experienced ranch hand, but this time they had too much to do and not enough time. Over the last year that Jake had taken on more responsibility on the ranch, he had grown into his role. It's why he planned on postponing college.

He wanted to be a vet. But they couldn't afford it, and even if they had the money or he could get a scholarship, he couldn't leave his mom for so many years. He'd take classes at NCTC in Gainesville, a good two-year college, focusing on classes that would help him be a better farmer and a better businessman. They also had an equine program that sounded interesting, and Jake loved working with horses. He could go to NCTC and work on the farm at the same time. He'd think about vet school down the road.

Jake glanced toward Baldwin's house; a pale shape barely visible across the fields. Home lay in the opposite direction, beyond the pasture and crops. Had Timber been trying to get help? Heading toward their house—or to Uncle Travis's, who lived just across the road from them?

"Smart boy," Jake murmured. He tilted his water bottle, and Timber lapped it up, tongue flicking weakly.

They'd have to walk. Jake patted his thigh. "C'mon. We're going back to your house."

Timber followed, limping but determined. He wasn't bleeding anymore, which was good—if he were, Jake wouldn't have let him walk. But he was holding his own.

Something tickled at the back of Jake's thoughts.

Why hadn't Baldwin come looking for Timber?

Baldwin loved this dog—fondly calling him his shadow since both his daughters had moved to Dallas. One married, the other still in college. His wife had left the family years ago. Jake hardly remembered the woman, except for her perpetual sour expression and harsh voice.

He'd trusted Baldwin once. Jake's dad and Baldwin had talked about the McKennas' expansion plan, and Baldwin opened his fields to their cattle for grazing when they needed the extra space. They shared water rights to part of Whisper Creek, a stretch of which formed the boundary between their land. Baldwin wasn't a farmer—he showed horses. He didn't need all his acres and had long ago promised that when the McKennas could buy him out, he'd sell to them.

The McKennas needed Baldwin's property because it was rich in nutrients, having lain fallow for so long. Plus, they shared a large border, which made that plot a natural extension of the McKenna land.

Then Verdacorp had come calling. And Baldwin had sold to *them*, not the McKennas.

A dishonorable man, Jake thought. A man who couldn't be trusted to his word, which was something Jake's father had lived by.

A man is only as good as his word, son. Remember that.

His mom still talked to Baldwin; Jake avoided being in the same room.

The closer they got to the farm, the more Jake's sense of unease grew. The only sound was the wind whistling through the trees. Then, as the house came into view, he saw the front door gaping open.

Jake reached behind the saddle and pulled his rifle free.

As soon as the weapon was out, Timber froze and growled low in his throat, ears up, body taut.

"What happened here, buddy?" Jake whispered. He wished he had a lead—anything to hold the dog back. Something was wrong.

Baldwin's remodeled two-story house had a wide porch and tall windows. Fresh white paint, black trim, stained porch. Every detail seen to. A gentleman's ranch.

As they approached the porch, Timber began to whimper, a low, keening sound that made Jake's skin crawl. His fur rose, tail stiff.

Jake raised his rifle.

"Stay," he told Timber, his voice barely audible over the building wind.

Bloody paw prints trailed from the house through the open doorway. Something bad had happened here.

Jake stepped over the threshold, walking softly, his boots barely making a sound on the hardwood floor. The house smelled of pipe tobacco, the woodsy, almost sweet scent baked into the walls. He followed Timber's prints down the hall, past Baldwin's family portraits, to the library at the far end.

Greg Baldwin lay crumpled on the floor, a ragged red stain spread across his shirt, pooled beneath him.

Jake dropped to his knees beside him. He pressed fingers to Baldwin's neck. Nothing.

Then a flutter. A faint rise and fall in the chest.

"Shit," Jake breathed. He fumbled for his phone and dialed 911, voice shaking as he gave the address and told the dispatcher that Greg Baldwin was unconscious and bleeding.

"Gunshot wound. He's alive. Barely."

He looked back at Timber, who now stood at the door, watching with wide, mournful eyes.

"Who is this?" the dispatcher said.

"Jake McKenna, from Whisper Creek Ranch."

"Jake? It's Sally North. I've dispatched the ambulance, but I don't know the ETA, the main road leading out to your neck of the woods is still broken up from the hailstorm."

Jake remembered going to and from school this past week and how he'd nearly broken an axle going over the ruts.

"Send the sheriff," he said as he looked around the library. The file cabinet was open, papers strewn about. A painting missing. The computer gone. "Greg Baldwin was robbed and shot."

Timber walked in and now lay next to his master, his head on his chest, his brown eyes pleading for Jake to fix everything.

"Help is coming, Timber. Help is coming." Jake said to Sally North, "Sally, help me. What do I do?"

Jake listened to Sally and followed her instructions to the letter.

He didn't know if he had arrived in time to save his neighbor. He didn't like Greg Baldwin, but he didn't want him to die. He wanted to be angry with him, not grieving his death. Jake knew his daughters . . . and knew the pain of losing a father.

He didn't want Baldwin's girls to suffer as he had.

CHAPTER FIVE

Ellen arrived home less than an hour after she'd left to find Bobby sitting on the porch. His jeans were wet and his shoes were muddy. Whiskey lay at his feet, just as wet and muddy as her son.

She put aside her worries about George and Millie and sat on the swing next to Bobby. "You didn't find Cleo?"

He shook his head. "What if a coyote got her?"

"She's a smart cat. She's been on her own for a while. Maybe she wanted to have her kittens someplace else."

"But the barn is safe! I made her a bed and she had food and she likes me."

"Yes, she does."

"We *have* to find her."

He was on the verge of tears, and Ellen worried that if he found Cleo, she might not be alive. She didn't want him to be alone if that happened.

"I have work to do here, but I was going to send Avery to check on the Mendozas and see if they need help with the sheep. Maybe Cleo went over there."

"They're almost a mile away."

"But remember that old barn? Where they used to store their

equipment? If she got scared, that would be a good place for her to hide, it's dry and quiet."

"Our barn is dry." Bobby pouted.

"Take a cage. If you can find her, try to get her into the cage and bring her back. I'll look around here as I'm working."

He looked at her hopefully. "You will?"

"Of course."

"Can we go right now?"

"Ask Grandma if Mrs. Mendoza called back. If she hasn't, you and Avery can head over there—take the ATVs and a radio. Be back before two, I want you both home before the rain starts."

He jumped up. "Okay, Mom! Thanks!"

He ran toward the house and as the screen slammed behind him, she heard, "Grandma! Grandma! Did Mrs. Mendoza call?"

Ellen really hoped and prayed the cat was okay. Bobby was a tough kid, but when it came to animals, he felt deep empathy when they suffered. Her eyes burned thinking about what might have happened to the poor stray . . . and how Bobby might react.

Life and death were part of living on a ranch. She knew it, and ten-year-old Bobby knew it. But that didn't always make it easier.

═

It took less than ten minutes for Bobby to get Avery moving. Ellen reminded them about the roads and weather and made sure the radios were charged. As she watched them ride the ATVs on the long dirt driveway toward the gravel road, she wondered if maybe she should have gone with them. No, they were fine, she told herself. Avery was responsible, and Bobby would listen to her.

The house phone rang. A moment later, Penny called out, "Ellen! It's Jake."

She went inside and picked up the phone. "Done with the run-in?"

"Mom, Greg Baldwin was robbed last night. He was shot—they're bringing in a life-line helicopter right now."

She froze. "Greg? What? How?" A million questions cluttered her mind.

"I found Timber in the field halfway between Baldwin's house and the run-in."

"Oh my God, is he—?"

"He's injured. I'm going to borrow Baldwin's ATV and a trailer and take him to Uncle Travis. We should be able to remove the buckshot in his leg and bandage him up sufficiently until we can get him to a vet. I called Dr. Jim, but he won't be able to get here in time. Said I could call him and he'd walk me and Uncle Travis through any problems, but I think it's going to be straightforward, and Uncle Travis has some experience."

Ellen's head was spinning at the information. The poor dog . . . poor Greg. "Someone shot both Greg and Timber? You're sure?"

"Positive. Sheriff Perez is here. He wants to talk to you. Mateo fixed the run-in; says it'll weather the storm. He's going to bring my horse home when we're done here."

A second later, Rick Perez got on the phone. "Ellie?"

"My God, Rick, what happened?"

"Don't know yet. But this isn't the first robbery in the area. Two folks over in Grayson County had something similar happen, but no one was home."

"Who? I didn't hear about any thefts."

"The Pattersons, down just north of Whitesboro, were robbed Monday night, and the Trevino family over off Sycamore Creek was robbed Wednesday."

"They're okay? Of course," Ellen said immediately. "You said they weren't home."

"I didn't hear about the robberies until yesterday, since they were in Grayson."

Cooke and Grayson counties had similar demographics, and

the county line cut through farmland to the extent that unless you were a native, you didn't really know where one county ended and the other began. County Line Road and Farm to Market Road were roughly the boundary. Baldwin's property abutted the county line, not too far from the end of Sycamore Creek Road where the Trevinos lived.

"Ellie, you need to be careful."

"We have nothing of value here, other than livestock and farming equipment. What did they steal?"

"The Pattersons lost cash, electronics, paper—banking records and the sort. They're worried about identity theft and are working with their bank to lock down their finances. The Trevinos lost electronics and some jewelry. The Pattersons were robbed at night—they were visiting family down in Houston—and the Trevinos were robbed during the day while they were in the field. The thieves broke some stuff, making me think these are older teens who are just being jerks. But then Baldwin, well, this just feels different, even though the thief or thieves stole the same kind of stuff. I already have a call into Vance so we can compare notes, see if he has a suspect."

Sheriff Vance Jefferson was in Grayson; Rick was in Cooke.

"Is Greg going to be okay?"

"I can't say. He hasn't regained consciousness. But he's a tough old bastard, I'm putting my money on him."

Through the phone, she heard a helicopter in the background. She looked out the kitchen window; in the distance she could see the whirlybird over Greg's property.

"They shot him for what? Some collectibles?"

"Don't know what they got specifically, but all the damage was in his office. They came in through the back but left through the front, maybe because in the confusion of being confronted by Baldwin they were disoriented. They didn't touch his gun collection, which is worth a pretty penny and not even locked up. They tried to access the safe in his library, but it's still secure. His computer is broken on the floor, paper everywhere. You know the rumors."

She did. Greg Baldwin was considered one of the wealthiest landowners in the region. He had a gentleman's farm, had made his money in banking and investments and was semiretired, even though he was only in his fifties. People who didn't personally know him might think he had a lot of valuables in his house. He had nice things, but most of his money was in real estate, stocks, and horses.

"Ellie, I mean it. You need to be careful, hear me?"

She didn't respond. She thought about Bobby and Avery heading toward the Mendozas and wished she hadn't let them go.

"Ellen," Rick said. "You listening?"

"Of course. But Greg wasn't supposed to be home until Sunday."

"You certain about that?"

"We talked after the hailstorm, and he said he was leaving Wednesday to visit the girls in Dallas and look at a mare he was thinking of buying and would be back Sunday. I gave him a box of Penny's cookies for the trip."

"Hmm," Rick said. "Could be the thieves didn't expect anyone to be home, he surprised them. But that tells me they are local, because who else would know that he was supposed to be out of town?"

"I don't know the Pattersons," Ellen said, "but the Trevinos don't have expensive items lying around the house. What about Greg's caretaker?"

"I put in a call to him, but Jake said he doesn't live on the property and only stays in the apartment above the stables when Baldwin is out of town."

That was true. If Greg came home early, his caretaker would have left. "Still, call him because he might know why Greg came home early."

"Will do," he said. "Just keep your wits about you. I'm going to talk to the Robinsons, though they have more security than most folks in the area. Make sure they're aware that we have this situation. You want to reach out to the Coulters, Mendozas, and oh, the um . . . that new family at the end of the bend?"

"The Pritchards," she said.

"I haven't had a chance to meet them, but Ryan said they're friendly."

"They are. They have a couple of young kids; I'll make sure they're okay." She had planned to call them anyway about their storm prep. They'd moved up here from Dallas last summer in a back-to-nature move, and Ellen wasn't certain they were ready for all that Mother Nature could throw at them. "I'll ask Travis to keep an eye out as well," she added.

"Well, just, um, be careful out there."

"I will."

Ellen appreciated his concern, though she wasn't incompetent with a gun. She may not be the sharpshooter Penny was in her youth, but Ellen could hit what she aimed at.

"I can send Ryan over to help for the weekend."

She laughed; she couldn't help it. "You think that's a good idea?"

He chuckled. "Well, Avery's a good girl, and Ryan would be on his best behavior around you and Jake."

Avery and Rick's son Ryan had been inseparable for the last year. Young love. They were both good kids, but Ellen didn't really like how close they'd grown. She wanted Avery to see the world, go to college, walk a path where she found joy and purpose. Avery said she wanted to stay on the farm . . . which Ellen always reminded her when she slept past sunrise, which was every day that ended in *y*.

"We'll be fine," Ellen told Rick. "And no one, not even a thief, would brave the roads tonight. It would be suicide."

CHAPTER SIX

Avery pretended to be annoyed that she had to bring Bobby with her, mostly so he would remember that she was his big sister and he had to listen to her. But secretly, Bobby was her favorite. Of course, if he knew that he would abuse it, so she made sure he stayed in his place.

"Don't rev the ATV, you'll flood it."

"Slow down, there're ruts up ahead."

"Geez, Bobby, you're slow as molasses! Cleo isn't going to be sitting on the side of the road waiting for you to show up."

Avery was also worried about the cat. She'd helped Bobby look for her every day this week after school, up until dark. She was even late for her after-dinner FaceTime with Ryan last night. Ryan offered to help find the cat, which totally endeared him to Avery, but her mom said no, and Ryan's dad said no, and that was so totally unfair. It wasn't even technically a school night for the McKennas since they were all missing classes today because of the storm.

She was going to be sixteen in less than two months! She was smart and responsible and rarely complained about always being tasked to keep an eye on Bobby.

But no, her boyfriend couldn't come over because of some dumb reason that only their parents thought was valid.

She glanced back at Bobby. He was moving slow, his gaze going right and left, scanning the ditches and fields for the black-and-white cat. She slowed down as well, looking for Cleo, while calculating how maybe she could convince her mom to let Ryan come over before the storm to help. The Perezes lived just outside Gainesville, so it was a bit of a drive, and maybe if Ryan came this afternoon when he got out of school, he would be stuck all weekend. They could watch movies and maybe kiss—when Jake stopped glaring at Ryan. Was it Avery's fault that Jake and Ryan had been friends first? Or that Jake had caught them kissing after a football game months ago? He acted totally weird. Ryan would be seventeen the week after Avery turned sixteen—it was perfect. They were perfect.

She sighed, frustrated but dreaming of her future with Ryan, carving out their own little farm where she would grow berries and create her own label for jams, jellies, and syrups and sell the jars on the internet and to local stores. She had even written a business plan for her economics class that her teacher said was good—she'd gotten an A—and Ryan also loved the idea.

If only her mom would agree.

Maybe Gianna would have a good idea on how to get Ryan over for the weekend.

Though Gianna was four years older than Avery, they had been friends for seemingly forever. The Mendozas were practically family; Avery had known them her entire life. Avery went over at least once a week just to play games and talk with Gianna, who was lonely—eighteen months ago, when she was a freshman in college, a drunk driver hit her while she was crossing the street and now she was partially paralyzed from the waist down. She went to physical therapy twice a week and she wanted to go back to college this fall, but her parents hovered, worried she would be hours from home with no one to help her.

Avery had never been one to keep her opinions to herself, and she told Gianna she needed to talk to her parents and be totally honest. They didn't have to agree, she just had to explain how she felt and then do it. She was an adult. She already had a full scholarship, plus money from a settlement after the accident, more than enough for any help she might need while away from home.

But Gianna didn't want to hurt her parents. They were much older than Avery's parents because they'd had Gianna in their forties when they thought they'd never have kids. Avery understood that, too. She never wanted to hurt her mom if she could avoid it, but *still.* This was Gianna's *life*. She could do things, needed to do things. Gianna wanted to be a teacher, and there was no reason she couldn't do that even in a wheelchair. And she could walk short distances with crutches or a walker, and the physical therapist said with time she may even be able to walk without an aid.

Sometimes Avery didn't know why she was giving advice to a twenty-year-old. But after her dad died, Avery had started thinking about life differently. She couldn't explain it, and didn't try to understand. All she knew was that she wanted to live fully. She loved the farm, she loved Ryan, she loved her friends, and she loved her family. She wanted to give one hundred percent of herself to everything she loved.

She also loved Gianna and couldn't stand that her friend was unhappy and her parents still walked on eggshells because for eighteen months, Gianna had gone from nearly dying to being wheelchair-bound to walking a few assisted feet every day. They hovered and worried, and none of that was good for Gianna—or Carl and Rose, Avery thought.

Bobby slowed before they reached the long driveway that led to the Mendoza house. Though Whisper Creek Ranch had bought most of the Mendoza property, they had retained ten acres for their house, barn, and field for the sheep they still kept. Carl Mendoza had never been a farmer—he'd inherited the land from his parents, and had owned a hardware store in Whitesboro until he sold it last year when he retired.

Avery idled next to Bobby. "What's wrong?" she asked.

"Mom said I could check out the old barn, the one that stored all the equipment Mr. Mendoza let get rusty?"

Avery blinked back sudden tears. Bobby sounded just like their dad. He had wanted the Mendozas to sell years ago. They had let their land get overgrown and their equipment rusted to the point most of it wasn't even salvageable. When they'd finally agreed to sell, their dad had to take care of everything they had avoided for more than a decade.

Avery remembered how her dad would teach them not only how to care for livestock, how to plant, when to harvest, but the little things—how to keep the equipment in good repair, how to check outbuildings for dry rot and termites, how to care for the land and their home. He was so . . . *patient*. In how he spoke, how he taught, how he lived. Steadfast and diligent in making sure they all grew to love and care for their farm as much as he did.

Bobby tilted his head and looked at her, maybe sensing that she was upset, so she scowled at him. She didn't want to talk about Dad right now. He'd been gone nearly a year, and sometimes she had these overwhelming and raw feelings that made her sad and angry.

Bobby implored her with his big brown eyes and gestured down the overgrown path that led to the structure, which could be partly seen through the brush. "Please? Mom *said*," he reiterated.

She knew her mom had already okayed it, so she nodded, but added a dramatic sigh so he would understand this was a concession on her part.

After all, she needed Bobby to remember who was in charge.

"I'll check out the barn next to the house," she said. "Cleo wasn't scared of our sheep, maybe she made friends with the Mendoza sheep." She smiled, wanting Bobby to believe that they'd find her and everything would be okay. "Meet me at their house, okay? Thirty minutes, tops. Mom will have my hide—and yours, too—if you get caught in the rain."

Bobby smiled and waved as he turned down the muddy and deeply rutted road, a small cage tied on the back of his ATV. She really hoped he found Cleo, because he was probably the only one who could get that darn cat into the cage and back to their house.

Avery continued to Gianna's house. She parked the ATV between the garage and the barn and turned off the ignition. Thunder sounded in the distance and made her jump. A solid blanket of gray clouds covered the sky. The wind wasn't too bad yet, certainly nothing that foreshadowed the storm everyone was worried about. But Avery had been through at least a dozen bad storms that she vividly remembered, including the one last weekend. And Grandma was baking more than usual, which told Avery she was worried.

Grandma's motto was essentially, if you had enough food stockpiled, you could get through anything.

Avery left the casseroles in the ATV storage box and went into the barn. Immediately, she wrinkled her nose. Based on the smell, no one had let the sheep out this morning. They bleated at her rather frantically. Animals sensed bad weather better than people, but the McKenna sheep hadn't been as agitated as these.

She flipped on the overhead lights and saw that all the troughs were empty. It was nearly ten—had the family gone out and couldn't get back because the roads were already closed off? She doubted it, but maybe the sheriff's department had blocked them off preemptively. Flash flooding often came after a rain, and last night it had dropped buckets on them.

The Mendozas only had fifty sheep, all recently sheared—Bobby and Lyla had come to help two weeks ago because of Mr.

Mendoza's arthritis. Now, they all practically ran to Avery, bleating and crowding, seeking her attention.

She turned the water on to fill their trough, then went over to the alfalfa storage bin and, one at a time, tossed three bundles into the center of their large pen, which took up half the barn. The family no longer had horses, just the sheep, so there was plenty of room.

After, Avery looked in all the empty stalls for the cat. She didn't see Cleo.

Out of habit, Avery checked the doors to make sure they were secure so the wind wouldn't blow them in, then let herself out. She'd leave the Mendozas a note that she'd fed the sheep, in case they had gone into town for supplies. Even though they had a four-wheel drive, the roads were deeply rutted and troublesome. The county said they'd be out next week to fix Orchard Lane, the road they lived off of, but Avery had no idea about others in the area.

Maybe Gianna was here alone; Avery would have come over earlier to keep her company.

She glanced into the garage, and while it was dark inside, it looked like there were two trucks. Odd. Maybe they had family visiting.

She grabbed the casseroles, crossed the side yard, and walked up the ramp that had been built over the stairs for Gianna's wheelchair. She knocked on the kitchen door. All the drapes were still drawn, which suggested the family was away, but then why was their truck here?

"Mrs. Mendoza? It's Avery."

She listened and heard movement and voices inside, then suddenly the door opened and a man she'd never seen before stood there. He was tall with a thick beard and short dark hair.

She stepped back and held out the casseroles. "I brought these for the Mendozas." She smiled but it felt weird, like a grimace.

"That's nice of you," he said. "Come on in." He glanced down the driveway, as if looking for anyone she had come with, then he looked at her and smiled. It didn't reach his eyes.

"I'll just leave them; I have to get back and help my mom with storm prep."

Avery didn't know why she was so intimidated. Except . . . she'd never seen this man before, and why was he answering the door at the Mendozas' house? She tried to look behind him, but he was so big he filled the doorframe.

"I'm sure my aunt and uncle would love to chat." He stepped aside and motioned for her to enter. Now she could see Carl and Rose sitting at the kitchen table, coffee mugs in front of them.

Relieved, she said, "Oh, hi, Mrs. Mendoza. Mr. Mendoza."

Carl lifted his mug toward her and sipped. His hand was shaking.

Avery stepped in and said, "Grandma Penny made these casseroles since you might not be able to get out for a few days, you know how she loves to cook."

"Thank you, Avery dear," Carl said. "You can put them on the counter. Give Penny our best."

Rose didn't meet her eye. Something weird was going on. Gianna would know.

"I was also going to give Gianna this book," Avery said, pulling the paperback out of her jacket.

They didn't introduce her to their nephew. That was very rude—and the Mendozas weren't rude. *Definite* weirdness. Suddenly Avery just wanted to get out and tell her mom. But Bobby . . . he was going to meet her here soon.

She could find him before he got here, she reasoned. There were only two ways to get to the old equipment shed, through the field or by the road Bobby had taken.

"I'll just leave it here for Gianna," she said and dropped it on the table. It fell to the floor. She stared at it, then quickly picked it up and put it back on the table. "Have her call me, okay? I'll just get going."

Avery turned. The man blocked the door. She tried to smile and completely failed.

"I think Gianna would like some company," he said.

Rose shook her head. "Just let her go, please."

Rose was scared. Her voice quivered and Avery knew then that something bad was happening.

The man sighed, picked up the book from the table.

"Holly Jackson . . . I don't think I've read anything by her. Is it good?"

"Y-yes," Avery said. "It's a mystery?" Why was she speaking like a question? She needed to get out of here, now.

He handed it back to her. "Take it in to her. She's in her room."

Maybe Avery was reading way too much into the situation. Families could be weird, with a lot of drama. Even the McKennas argued, especially now that Mom and Jake were arguing about whether Jake should go to college.

Gianna would tell her what was going on.

She nodded slowly, left the kitchen, and walked down the hall to Gianna's room in the back of the house. The door was closed. She knocked.

"Go away!"

"G, it's Avery."

"Oh my God, come in!"

Avery entered. Gianna was in bed, and her wheelchair wasn't in the room. It was after nine, and Gianna hated lying in bed, especially after the accident. She said it made her feel like an invalid.

"Close the door."

Avery did so, put the book on her nightstand.

"Are they gone?"

"Your cousin?"

"I'm so sorry!"

Avery glanced at the door, then whispered, "What's going on?"

"Those people came in the middle of the night and they won't leave. One of them is hurt, he was shot! With a gun! And I don't know what's going on. The big asshole said they'd be out of here tonight, but he's probably lying. I'm scared, and they took my chair and my phone. Do you have your phone?"

Avery shook her head, feeling stupid that she'd left her radio with the ATV. But maybe . . . maybe she could get to it? Reach out to her mom, she would get help. "Who are they?" she asked.

"I don't know! They said if anyone talked, they'd hurt me. My mom is so scared, and Dad feels helpless, and I can't do anything to help because of these stupid legs!" She slapped at them under the comforter. "Go out the window and get help."

"But they might hurt you." Or worse, Avery thought.

"I don't care!"

"You don't mean that."

Then Gianna started crying and Avery sat on the edge of her bed and held her.

Avery swallowed her own panic. She'd seen that man's face. Bad guys didn't want to be identified. Would they leave them unharmed tonight as he'd told Gianna?

"And you don't know what they want?" she asked.

Gianna wiped her face with the back of her hand and shook her head. "They came in the middle of the night, during the storm. A man and woman carrying another man. They put him in the guest room and the woman has been with him most of the time. They forced Mom to help them. Mom thinks there's still a bullet inside and that's why he's not going to get better, at least not until they get it out. But this morning I overheard them all talking about how after tonight, they would disappear, but that *Sam*—that's the guy who was shot—needed a doctor. So, I don't know what they're going to do."

Avery didn't know what to do, either. If she was discovered crawling out the window, they might hurt her or Gianna's family. And if she got away, they still might hurt them.

"Bobby," Avery whispered. For the first time she felt truly terrified.

"Your brother?"

"He's searching for that stray cat who's been in our barn. She disappeared during the hailstorm and he went to the old equipment shed, but he's going to meet me here."

She bit her lip. Maybe she could get out the window and use the radio, *then* return before they figured it out?

"I'm going to get my radio, tell Bobby to go home and get help. I'll be back in less than five minutes. They won't even know I left."

Gianna bit her lip. "Be careful."

Avery slowly, carefully, slid open the window next to Gianna's bed. It was in the back of the house and couldn't be seen from the kitchen window, but she'd have to run around the backside of the garage to reach her ATV, otherwise they might see her if they were still in the kitchen.

The drop wasn't too far, and she slipped out the window and landed in the mud, barely noticing the sharp leaves of the holly bush scratching her arms as she brushed past them.

She ran around the back of the garage and considered just for a minute that maybe she should leave and get help. She didn't want to go back into the house. She didn't want to see that man ever again.

But what if they killed everyone before Ryan's dad, the sheriff, arrived? Avery would never be able to live with herself if her fear resulted in people she cared about dying.

Just make sure Bobby doesn't come here, Avery told herself. Tell him to go get help. That was the smart thing to do.

She rounded the garage to the narrow spot where she'd parked her ATV and ran right into the man who answered the door. He seemed just as surprised to see her, but then he narrowed his eyes and grabbed her arm. "I came out to make sure you came alone, and good thing." He held her radio in his other hand. "Don't be stupid, Avery, and this will all be over tomorrow."

Tomorrow? If she didn't come home, her mom would send Jake for her or come herself. She couldn't bear for anyone in her family to be hurt.

As if he could read her mind, he said as he half dragged her to the house, "You'll let your parents know that you're spending the night with your good friend Gianna, and then no one will bother us. Understood?"

She nodded, because she didn't know what else to say or do.

She was stuck. How was she going to warn Bobby?

CHAPTER SEVEN

Uncle Travis was waiting on the small porch for Jake when he drove up on the ATV, Timber strapped to the attached trailer. It had taken far longer than it should have to reach Travis's house because Jake didn't dare cross the muddy fields even on the ATV as the uneven terrain could have toppled the sled. As it was, he had to take it slow along the road because of the extensive damage from last weekend's storm.

Titan, Timber's brother, bounded down the stairs to greet Jake. He immediately went to the sled and sniffed Timber, then whimpered and paced.

Travis limped down the worn stairs. He looked angry and said, "What the hell happened, Jake?"

"I told you. Someone robbed Baldwin, shot Timber. I don't know much more than that."

"Is Baldwin okay?"

Jake shrugged and shook his head at the same time. "It doesn't look good, but he was alive when they put him on the medical chopper."

Travis shook his head as he approached the sled. He grunted

as he squatted next to the dog. Timber looked up at him with sorrowful eyes. Travis petted his head while looking at his bloody hind leg. "We'll get you fixed up, boy," Travis said, his voice cracking. "I'll help you get him inside, put him on the dining-room table. I already prepped the space."

"Uncle Travis," Jake said when his uncle unbuckled the straps. "I'll do it."

"I'm not a fucking invalid," Travis muttered.

Travis had been a medic in the Army. He'd been shot three times in the left leg while performing triage during a firefight and had an artificial limb below his knee. Travis helped on the farm when he could, but he couldn't walk far, especially in the field. It had turned him bitter, but he tried to hide it most of the time.

But Jake saw the bitterness, the anger, the sorrow behind his uncle's commanding presence. He'd have more sympathy if Travis didn't drink so much.

At least he recognized that carrying the hundred-and-fifty-pound dog would be tough and difficult on his leg. Frustrated, Travis turned and went back up the stairs.

Timber yelped when Jake picked him up. "I'm sorry, buddy. I know you're in pain." He carried him into the house, Titan at his side, ears and tail on alert.

Travis had put a sheet on the kitchen table, and Jake laid the dog on it. He tried to get up, but Jake held him down while Travis prepped a sedative. Running a ranch meant they often had to take care of their animals' needs—you couldn't call in the vet every time a horse or sheep got injured. It's one of the reasons Jake wanted to be a vet, he wanted to help people care for their working animals.

But it was more important to take care of his farm now, instead of other people's animals in the future. He wished his mom would understand that he didn't resent postponing college—or foregoing it completely. He needed to be here, at Whisper Creek, not just for his mom and their ranch, but for his dad's legacy.

His father would expect it of him. More, Jake expected it of himself.

"It won't knock him out, but it'll make him sleepy and take the edge off the pain," Travis said. "Stroke his neck, I'm going to put a muzzle on him."

Jake did as Travis said, murmuring soothing words while Travis put on the muzzle, then injected the animal.

Jake looked around, and his eyes narrowed when he saw several empty whiskey bottles on the bar that separated the kitchen from the living area. He didn't say anything. Since Travis left the Army twelve years ago, when Jake was six, he'd struggled with sobriety. He'd been better for a few years, until his brother's death last year. Sometimes, Jake thought Travis could justify anything he did, blaming his circumstances for his drinking. Yes, he was disabled and lived on disability, he couldn't do everything he wanted. But he wasn't worthless. Jake's dad had told Travis that over and over, but Travis just avoided his brother when he didn't want to listen anymore.

He'd started training dogs, something he was good at, including Titan, who had two years ago been certified as a service dog. Jake's mom was trying to convince him to start a business training service dogs, which were always in demand. But Travis had a hundred excuses as to why he couldn't do it.

Jake felt Timber relax shortly after being given the sedative, and then Travis said, "I need to shave the area, clean the wound, see what we're dealing with here." He motioned to a stainless-steel tray where he'd already laid out his sterilized tools. "Hand me what I need when I ask."

They worked in silence for the next thirty minutes as Travis shaved fur, cleaned the wound, and extracted each piece of buckshot from Timber's leg. There were six, one pretty deep, which started to bleed again as Travis dug it out.

Finally, he said, "I think I got them all. I'm going to dress the wound and then I'll need you to lay Timber on the extra dog bed." He motioned to where he had put a thick mat next to Titan's bed.

After, Travis brought water to where Timber lay. He wasn't trying to get up, but he was more alert now, watching them. It helped that Travis had raised and trained Timber the first six months of his life and saw him regularly, building trust. Travis poured himself a whiskey and sat heavily on the couch.

"As soon as the storm passes, I'll take him to the vet for X-rays, make sure we got all them buckshot. I have some meds here for him, but he still needs to be examined." Travis motioned to a chair. "Why don't you sit a spell?"

"Thanks," Jake said. He tried not to glance at Travis's hand, holding the whiskey glass. "But I need to get home. Mateo got the run-in fixed and the cattle should be okay where they're at, but there's still a lot of work to do at the house."

"I can come by, help some."

"I don't know how bad the road is going to get."

Travis didn't say anything. It wasn't that Jake didn't want his uncle to come over, but if Travis got himself stuck, it would put one more task on Jake's growing list.

"Did you talk to Sheriff Rick?" Travis asked.

Jake nodded. "He was there when I left Baldwin's place. They're investigating, apparently a couple other people have been robbed this week, just over the county line. Baldwin wasn't supposed to be home, Mom said. It really sucks. I hope he makes it."

"Me, too," Travis said. "Thank your mom for the stew she brought over last night. She looked tired. She works too hard."

Jake didn't know why the observation bothered him. They were all exhausted this week, but he didn't think it needed to be said. "She's good," he told his uncle. He squatted next to Timber and gently stroked his neck.

"She mentioned you claim you're not going to college."

Jake didn't want this conversation. "Not now," he said.

"Don't make the same mistake your dad did."

"Dad didn't make a mistake," Jake said, agitated. "He didn't have any regrets."

"You don't believe that."

"I do, because he told me. Why are you bringing this up?"

"Because your mom wants you to go to college."

Jake got up. "I have work to do," he said. "If you need anything, call us."

"I can take care of myself," Travis muttered.

Jake left, walked over to the ATV, and looked back at his uncle's house. He knew about Travis's struggles and frustrations, mostly because his dad had talked to him about them . . . and Jake had overheard conversations between his mom and dad over the years. He wished he could stay, because Travis acted like he wanted company, but he wasn't going to talk to Travis about college or his dad. Jake was eighteen. He was graduating from high school next month. He knew what he wanted, and that was to save Whisper Creek.

He wished he could explain that to Travis—and especially wished his mom would understand. He didn't like the tension that was between them, and he really hated that she had brought up the subject to his uncle.

Travis wasn't his father. He never would be.

Jake rode off a bit too fast on the ATV, swerved in the mud, then straightened and headed home.

Through the front window, Travis watched Jake leave, then drained the last of his whiskey and slammed the glass onto the table, the echo sharp in the empty room. Titan looked at him as if he could read his mind, and Travis reached out for him. "Good boy, lay down with your brother."

Travis motioned to the dog bed, and Titan hesitated, then sat next to the sleeping Timber, but kept his eyes on Travis.

Outside, the fading rumble of the ATV told him his nephew was finally gone. Good. He loved the kid, sure—but that smug, self-righteous tone? Too much like John.

And the self-sacrifice. Giving up his future for the past.

Like John.

John, the golden brother. The one everyone listened to. The one who never raised his voice but still made you feel small just by offering "helpful advice." Go to community college. Study a trade. Move to town. Find something new.

Travis didn't want something new. He wanted *before*. Before the war. Before he lost half his leg. Before his nights ended with too much whiskey and nightmares that woke him in a sweat.

He shut his eyes, breathing through the sudden spike of rage.

Damn, he missed his brother. Righteous or not, John was a good man who had raised a good family. He stared at the half-empty whiskey bottle across the room.

Stop it, he told himself. No more. What if Ellen needed his help?

Right, *him*. A broken man with a bum leg who drank too much because there was nothing else he could do.

Travis looked at Timber, an innocent dog who had been shot. He forced himself to be calm. The dog would get agitated, and Timber needed to rest and heal.

Dogs were pure souls who just wanted to be with their owners. A little praise and kindness, and they were loyal for life.

He sat down, leaned back, closed his eyes. His thoughts turned to Greg Baldwin. Who'd rob the guy? Why? Because people thought he was rich with the big, fancy house? Sure, he had money, but he put it all into the house and his horses and the stocks he traded. He didn't collect expensive shit.

Baldwin was a good man, even if he had the wrong idea about farming. He, John, and Travis had played poker with a couple other fortysomething men now and again. Not for much money—mostly for bragging rights—but those evenings made Travis feel almost normal again. Travis had made some money caring for his horses when Baldwin left for weeks at a time. Even with his messed-up leg, Travis could still ride, exercise the animals, groom and feed them. Besides, Josh Stuart, Baldwin's usual caretaker, was next to worthless. More of a drunk than Travis.

Ellen had suggested that Travis should board horses, that he had a knack. Board horses, train dogs, basically be a glorified pet sitter. While she was correct that he had a gift with animals, what if he was having a bad day and could barely walk? The horses couldn't wait to be fed and watered and exercised. What happened then? Would he have to call his sister-in-law to help?

Nope, he didn't want help from anyone. He hated collecting disability, but there wasn't much he could do and he needed the money. Even though he lived in this house—his grandparents' old house—for free. Even though his sister-in-law brought him food so he didn't have to shop or cook. It gutted him.

He wanted to do more, be more.

Stop wallowing in self-pity, get off your ass, and do something.

John had rarely gotten angry with him, but the week before he died, he and Travis had had a huge argument. John was disappointed in him. Travis knew it. But he couldn't face it.

And then John was dead.

Baldwin.

Jake said he wasn't even supposed to be in town.

Travis sat up. Was this another one of Verdacorp's schemes? They were unscrupulous, but he never thought that Mitchell Robinson would try to kill anyone.

And Baldwin had sold out to them, so what was the point?

The Robinsons and the McKennas weren't exactly the Hatfields and the McCoys, but they had been neighbors with multiple disagreements over generations. John would never have sold to Mitchell, but they hadn't been enemies. They'd even played football together in high school.

Travis forced himself up, ignoring the constant pain in his leg, and walked to the phone in the kitchen. He dialed Mitchell's number from memory.

Four rings later, he answered. "Robinson."

"It's Travis McKenna."

"Travis. How are you?"

"Fine," he said. "Someone shot Greg Baldwin last night. And his dog."

"I heard."

"Word gets around fast."

Travis tipped a little whiskey into a glass and sipped.

"The sheriff called to inform me, worried we might be targeted. I reminded him I have an excellent security system. What can I do for you?"

"He wasn't supposed to be home," Travis said. "And you play dirty, Mitchell."

"Watch your words," Robinson said coldly.

"He signed over damn near all his land to you."

"I have no grudge with Baldwin. You know that. And I don't resort to violence to get what I want. I've never had to."

"Good," Travis said. He didn't know why he was getting a bad feeling, but something just didn't sit right with him.

"How's Ellen?"

"She's still not selling."

"She's made that clear," Robinson said. "But things can change."

He ended the call without a goodbye.

Travis stared at the phone, his blood running cold.

What was Mitchell Robinson up to?

Was his family in danger?

He stared down at his useless leg and swore. Even if they were, he wouldn't be able to do one damn thing to help them.

CHAPTER EIGHT

Bobby searched every inch of the old equipment shed. His mom was right—it was a good place for Cleo to hide. Thick trees and bushes practically hid the large wood structure, protecting the space from the worst of the weather. And it was about halfway between his house and where the Mendozas lived. Not too far for the stray to wander. And there were probably mice for her to catch.

Still, he was super careful, because it was old and there were lots of sharp tools and even a broken tractor.

He knew, because he'd played on it before. He remembered when he was eight, when his dad bought the property, and he'd come with him to inventory the space. Little was usable, but his dad salvaged some of the tools and one small tractor that he brought home and fiddled with until he got it working again. They now used it for small jobs.

The storage shed was the size of a small barn and smelled like damp, moldy wood and ancient oil. Rusted tools hung on crooked nails, and piles of forgotten chicken wire made little metal nests in the corners. In the center, the tractor tilted to one side, the wheels on the right gone. Bobby crouched low, peeking under a warped workbench where an old tarp was bunched up like a nest.

"Cleo?" he whispered. "C'mon, girl . . . Let me take you home. You can come in the house."

His mom wouldn't like that, but he might not tell her. At first. He wouldn't lie—he never lied to his mom—but not saying something wasn't exactly a lie, right?

"Cleo, it's me—"

A sudden *clang* made him jump, something metallic clattering on a shelf behind him. Bobby's heart thudded in his chest before he saw a rusty can rolling lazily across the floor.

"Cleo?"

He pulled out his flashlight and turned it out, flashing the light toward the rusty can. Two rabbits froze in his beams.

He sighed and frowned. It wasn't Cleo.

Still, he searched the entire shed, carefully looking behind and under everything he could. He found more rabbits and a hole in the far corner where they could come and go as they pleased. Smart for the rodents—they'd be safe in here.

He walked back outside. It was late morning, but the sky was already darkening. The heavy clouds overhead pressed low, and the wind carried the sharp scent of rain and manure. Bobby moved around the perimeter, calling softly.

"Cleo? Hey, girl? You hungry?"

A bush rustled behind him. He froze.

Then—*squawk!* A pheasant burst out of the brush in a chaotic flurry of wings and feathers.

Bobby yelped, stumbled back, and landed on his butt in the mud.

After a moment of silence, he grinned and shook his head. He didn't get scared of much, but that one got him.

Pulling out the walkie-talkie clipped to his belt, he clicked the side button. "Avery? You there?" Static. He tried again. "Avery, I'm at the shed. No sign of Cleo. You see anything?"

Only more crackle and hiss. Bobby frowned.

"She's probably ignoring me again," he muttered. Or left her radio on the ATV when she went inside. Typical.

Avery pretended she didn't like him, but he knew she did. Still, whenever she was around her friends—especially Ryan Perez, her *boyfriend*—she acted like Bobby was just her annoying little brother. And Avery thought Gianna was awesome—she was older, had gone to college before her accident, and was very pretty. Bobby didn't really pay attention to that, but Jake's best friend, Andy, had said that Gianna was *hot*. Bobby had to ask Jake what that meant. He'd laughed and said that it meant that Gianna was beautiful.

Why couldn't Andy just say she was beautiful? Dad always said to say what you mean and mean what you say.

Bobby looked toward the horizon, where the three structures of the Mendoza property loomed in the distance. The barn, the garage, and their house. They looked hazy in the damp air. He wanted to keep looking for Cleo, but Avery told him thirty minutes, and he was already late. If he was much later, she'd tell their mom, and he might get in trouble. And if he got in trouble, he couldn't keep looking for Cleo.

Maybe Avery had found her? No, she would have told him because she knew he was super worried. And she was worried, too; she liked Cleo, even helped him look for her after school all week.

He climbed onto his ATV and fired up the engine, heading across the muddy field toward the Mendozas, which was shorter than going back to the road. Thunder crashed in the sky, and a few drops of rain began to fall, barely anything, but that meant it would start raining before two. And Mom told them they had to be home before the rain.

He was really worried about the cat, but he also didn't want his mom to worry.

He sped up and halfway across the field, the back wheels spun out.

"Aw, c'mon!" he muttered, rocking the ATV gently with the

throttle. No luck. The tires dug deeper. Jake was going to kill him. Bobby knew better than to take the ATV through the field after a rain, especially this field, which had been fallow for so long, and now he was going to have to leave it here. He was supposed to stick to the roads. Fortunately, he didn't have a long walk—the barn loomed in front of him, on the other side of a small creek that didn't look all that small anymore.

His boots squelched with each step, up to his ankles, every step heavier and heavier. He barely made it across the widening creek. He knew that it met up with Whisper Creek on the other side of the road, and that if this creek started really running, then Whisper Creek would get too high and flood. Which would be bad for his mom's vineyard that she walked in every evening because she missed Daddy so much.

He hoped it didn't flood. It would make his mom sad.

By the time he reached the barn ten minutes later, he was tired and doubly worried about Cleo.

The wooden door creaked as he unlatched it, pushed it open, and stepped into the dim interior. There was still alfalfa that the sheep hadn't eaten in the middle of their pen, and they moved around, agitated. Probably because of the thunder. They bayed and several walked over to him. He petted them as he passed. He liked sheep much more than goats, who could be mean and butt you with their hard heads and eat holes in your favorite shirt.

Avery said she'd search the barn for Cleo, but the cat only liked Bobby, so maybe she hid from his sister. He called for her, searched everywhere he could think of where a cat might hide, and Cleo wasn't there.

Why had she left their barn? How did she get out? Why didn't she come to him? Was she okay? Had she found a good, dry place to have her kittens?

Frustrated and sad, he knew it was time to get Avery and go home.

He exited the barn on the opposite end from where he'd entered and saw Avery's ATV parked just outside, in the gravel between the barn and the garage. Her radio wasn't in the holder, so why hadn't she responded to him?

The side door into the garage was partly open. He went to close it, then heard the door of the house close. He was about to call out hello as he came around the corner, but saw a man he didn't recognize standing at the base of the ramp that covered the stairs, smoking.

Bobby instinctively ducked back.

That wasn't Mr. Mendoza. And it definitely wasn't Avery.

But Avery was here. The man was probably a friend of the family.

Bobby peered around the corner of the garage. The man was big and looked mean. He bit his lip, hesitated, then edged back to the garage door and slipped inside.

It smelled like diesel and hay and something sharper, like antiseptic or maybe metal.

Two trucks were parked inside. One he recognized—it was the Mendozas' red Dodge. They had a handicap plate because Gianna was in a wheelchair. The other one was unfamiliar. Big and dark.

Careful to stay low, Bobby crept over to the unfamiliar truck. The passenger door was unlocked. He eased it open and peeked inside.

At first, he didn't see much, just a fast-food bag, a pair of muddy boots, an old thermos, but then his stomach twisted.

Stuffed into the side pocket of the door was a rag. It was dark red, crusted stiff. Could've been mud. But it didn't *look* like mud.

He stared at it, heart pounding, before slowly pushing the door closed with barely a *click*.

Bobby backed away from the truck. He looked at the rear license plate. It was white with blue letters and numbers and read *Louisiana*.

He didn't know the Mendozas had family in Louisiana. He thought they had always lived in Texas, like him. But people had family from lots of different places. His grandpa, his mom's dad, lived in Oklahoma. But that was just on the other side of the river even though he didn't visit much.

Maybe a friend? But it just seemed strange.

He needed to talk to his sister, but he didn't want to go to the house. Not if . . . not if something was wrong. He had to find out. Avery had her radio, so why didn't she answer him?

He quietly left the garage and ran over to the opposite side of the barn, careful to keep out of sight of the house while he did so. He squatted and stared at his radio, thinking. The creek was louder now, running through the trees and brush in front of him, though he couldn't see it.

What should he say?

Would she even answer?

His lower lip trembled as he thought that something might have happened to his sister. But he had to be strong. He had to be a man, like Jake was a man after their dad died last year. So Bobby raised the radio and clicked.

"Avery, it's me, I couldn't find Cleo. Did you? Over."

CHAPTER NINE

Bobby's voice crackled through the radio, making Avery jump.

"Avery, it's me, I couldn't find Cleo. Did you? Over."

She froze. The man stepped back into the kitchen, trailing cigarette smoke, closing the door behind him.

"Who's that kid?" he asked, squinting at the radio. "Who's Cleo?"

Avery forced a calm expression, though her insides twisted like a knot. "My brother, Bobby. He's looking for our cat."

The man narrowed his eyes at her, thinking. What was he thinking? What did he plan to do?

The radio beeped, then Bobby said, "Avery, what are you doing? Are you still at the Mendozas? I'll meet you there, okay? Over."

She reached out for the radio and almost had it before the man clamped a hand around her wrist and squeezed. She winced.

"How old is your brother?" he demanded.

"T-ten," she stammered.

"Shit. Fuck." He slammed a fist on the table, causing a water glass to fall over. Rose Mendoza caught it before it rolled to the floor.

"Where do you live?" he asked her. When she didn't immediately answer, he tightened his grip until she yelped. "I asked you a question, *Avery*."

"About a mile down the road."

"Who's at your house?"

"My m-mom." She blinked back tears.

"Okay, this is what you're going to do. You are going to tell your brother that you are spending the night here with your friend Gianna. Tell him to go home without you. If you say or do anything different, I'll first shoot your cute girlfriend, then I'll find your brother and break his neck. Do you understand me?"

Rose groaned and stifled a cry, and Carl said, "There's no reason to threaten anyone. We're cooperating. Please."

The man wasn't looking at Carl. He stared at Avery and repeated, "Do you understand me, Avery?"

She nodded. Cleared her throat.

He let go of her wrist and pushed the radio toward her. "You blow this, people will die."

She believed him.

Avery took a deep breath. Let it out slowly. Picked up the radio. Pressed the button. "Bobby? Um, I'm going to spend the night here. Go home. I'll see you in the morning. Over."

Half a minute later Bobby said, "Mom isn't going to like that. We have chores. And you promised to help me find Cleo. Over."

The man stared at her darkly, nodded once and motioned for her to respond.

"Mom will understand. I tried calling, but she's probably in the barn. The Mendozas need help with their sheep and, um, Mr. Mendoza's arthritis is really bad today and—"

The man pulled the radio from her grip and said to her, "Stop with the details because I don't know if you're trying to alert your brother or being truthful."

"If Bobby goes home and tells Mom that I said I talked to her, she'll get mad and call, maybe come over and—"

"I'll take care of that. But if I see your little brother, I'm bringing him here, and you'll have to deal with it."

"Okay, okay." She nodded frantically. "I understand!"

He handed her back the radio but with a warning. "Careful."

She pressed the button. "Sorry, I dropped the radio. Just tell Mom I'm helping and I won't be done before the rain starts, okay? I'll see you tomorrow. And if Cleo doesn't show up, we'll go look for her again first thing in the morning. Over."

A few seconds passed, then Bobby said, "Okay, if you *promise* you'll help me. Over."

"I promise," she said. "Over."

The man took the radio. "That wasn't so bad now, was it?"

"My mom's going to call," Avery said. "She's not going to be happy."

"And Carl and Rose are going to thank her profusely for letting you stay because they appreciate your help," he said smugly.

"Why don't you just leave before the rain starts? You won't be able to get out tonight, the roads are going to flood. They're already saturated, and the creeks are running high. It's going to be a mess out there. You'll be trapped."

"I have a plan, and you don't need to worry about it."

"But—"

"Shut up, kid," he snapped. Avery closed her mouth.

The woman who had been in the guest room since Avery got there, the one helping the man named Sam, who was bleeding in the bed, came into the kitchen. She looked angry and held up a prescription medicine bottle.

"You've been holding out on us!" she said to Carl and Rose. "You said the strongest pills you had were Tylenol. This is hydrocodone." She looked like she wanted to hit something. Instead, she grabbed a glass from the cabinet and filled it with water.

"Our daughter—"

"I don't care. My brother needs these. He's in a lot of pain. I asked, you lied."

She stormed out. Avery glanced at the man as he watched her

walk out. Maybe . . . She had an idea. Her mom was a nurse, she would know what to do with that man. But if they brought her mom over, would they hurt her? Hurt all of them? And if her mom came and didn't go home before dark, Jake would come looking for her and then they would all be in trouble.

Avery felt stuck, so she kept her mouth shut—for now. She needed to figure this out.

"Can I sit with Gianna?" she asked quietly.

"Go ahead," he said. "I nailed her window shut. But if you try a stunt like that again, you'll be staying here with them." He gestured to Carl and Rose.

When Avery got up, she glanced down and that's when she saw that the Mendoza's ankles were zip-tied to the chairs.

She ran down the hall to Gianna's room and slammed the door shut. "We're going to find a way out of this," Avery said with a lot more confidence than she felt. She hugged Gianna tightly as her friend cried. "I promise, Gianna, we'll find a way."

At least Bobby was safe.

For now.

With narrowed eyes, Brock watched the teenager bolt down the hall. He didn't trust that girl. He admired the fact that she'd snuck out the window, that was bold, brave, *and* stupid, but he couldn't let anything like that happen again.

His phone rang. He stepped outside to answer it. The air was wet and warm; the wind was light, but it would get worse. The dark skies promised to drop buckets on them today. He wished he'd never taken this damn job.

He glanced at the window. What was he going to do with all these people? They would certainly give his description to the cops, but the truth was, he had no record and didn't live in the area. He,

Sam, and Rena would go back to Louisiana and disappear for a while. Keep a very low profile.

It wasn't ideal, but while he had committed a lot of crimes, he wasn't a killer. Baldwin was an exception. He had shot at them first, so Brock didn't feel guilty about it.

Though he wished the dog hadn't been hit. He was only doing what dogs were trained to do.

"Yep," he answered his phone.

"I'm going to say this once, Mr. Jones," his boss said. "Last night was a grave error. Do not make another one."

Brock scowled. Who was he to threaten him?

"You told me no one would be home."

The man ignored him. "Do you have all the documents?"

"Three. You need to get those people out of the house tonight. You promised."

"There's a storm brewing, Mr. Jones. The roads will be impassable tonight."

"I don't control the fucking weather and neither do you."

Silence. Brock tensed, but he wasn't going to back down. Last night was on his boss, not on him.

He almost told him that Sam had been shot, that they were out of this, going home right now, but then he knew he wouldn't get paid the rest of what was owed him. Half up front, half when the job was done. He needed the second half, another hundred thousand. He'd need it all so they could get Sam help and lie low for a while.

"I'll get them out of the house," he said. "I will call you when it's clear. Don't screw this up, Jones."

Before Brock could say another word, the line went dead.

CHAPTER TEN

Friday Afternoon

The rain started at noon, a light drizzle, but when Ellen looked north she saw darker clouds.

Avery had better not be late. This was going to only get worse.

She walked back from getting the mail at the end of the driveway, lucky that the postal truck had been able to get through this morning. Mostly, she had wanted to get out of the too-warm house, clear her mind about the Coulters selling a prime strip of their land to the utilities, knowing full well Verdacorp would be mining the land. There had to be a catch. She'd glanced through the contracts and there was a restrictive clause, but that didn't make sense with what she knew about other sales in the area.

She needed to call her lawyer. Maybe he could make sense of what was going on with Verdacorp and the recent land sales.

She flipped through the mail. Bills. A card from her father—he always remembered her birthday by calling her, but sent the card late. There'd be a hundred-dollar bill inside, his standard present for every birthday and Christmas. He worked hard, even at sixty-five.

Drank just as hard. He was a sad man, had never remarried, and when she left for college he just worked and drank.

It saddened her, but he rejected every offer she'd made to move to the ranch. There was an apartment above the old stables they could have fixed up for him, but he always said no.

A fancy invitation from Congresswoman Jeanne Culver, for a BBQ at her family ranch outside Gainesville for Memorial Day. At $250 a person. Ellen regretted voting for her five years ago, she certainly wasn't going to give her a dime of her money. She ran as a friend of farmers, but voted with agribusinesses like Verdacorp. She hadn't done anything overtly awful, but Ellen didn't trust anyone whose largest donor was the corporation trying to buy out every farm in the valley.

And a letter from the University of Texas. Addressed to Jacob Milton McKenna. He'd already been accepted; he'd already turned it down. She was still angry about it, so what was this? Acknowledgment that he'd turned down a scholarship?

Tears burned as the steady drizzle fell. Her son had already sacrificed the fun of his senior year to work the farm, now he was sacrificing his dreams. It hurt, dammit. Her son should never have been in this position.

She'd just returned to the house when she heard a vehicle and turned toward the driveway to see Jake riding the ATV he'd borrowed from Baldwin.

She watched as he parked it in their equipment shed, then he walked over to her. "How's Timber?" she asked.

"Uncle Travis got the buckshot out of his leg and cleaned him up. He'll keep watch over him. Have you heard back from the sheriff? Is Baldwin going to be okay?"

"I haven't heard, but Rick will call when he knows something."

She handed him the letter from UT. She hadn't opened it. He didn't, either, instead stuffing it in his back pocket.

"You talked to Uncle Travis about this," he said, patting the letter.

"I was frustrated. I shouldn't have."

"I made my decision."

"It's the wrong decision."

He shook his head. "I'm doing what Dad would have done."

"You're doing what your dad *did.* He left college for this place. That's not the same thing."

"You can't run the ranch on your own."

"I'll find a way. You are my son. I don't want you giving up your life for a struggling farm."

"Is that really what you think I'm doing? Is that what you think Dad did? Did you think less of him because he dropped out of college to help the family?"

"Of course not. Why would you even say that?"

"Because I have weighed my choices. I know I can leave and you would support my decision. I need you to support the decision I freely made to stay."

"And if I lose the farm, you will have nothing. No land, no degree, no future." Her voice broke. She didn't want to get angry or upset with her son, but she was both.

"You won't lose it, especially with me here. Mom, I'm not changing my mind, and I don't want to argue about it every day."

She hated that they were in this position. If John hadn't fallen from the roof and died, Jake would be planning for college instead of the harvest. He would be planning for a career. A future. Meet a girl. Get married. Have kids. She saw his life as it could be and wanted it for him.

"I'm good with my decision, Mom. If you can't be, then I don't know what to say."

She had so much to say, but didn't know how to say it. Then Lyla came out of the barn and called, "Jake! There's a leak and I can't figure out where it's coming from."

He raised his hand in acknowledgment, then said to Ellen, "Is Mateo back yet?"

"I told him to make sure that Greg's horses were fed and watered and secure in their stalls. We won't be able to get over there again today, and until the girls can make arrangements for the livestock, we need to take care of them."

"Okay."

"Then he's going to check on his place, make sure there's nothing that needs attending, and he'll come back here. I told him if Miriam wants to stay here tonight, they can stay on the pullout in the family room." Since Penny moved in, they had lost their guest room. "But I doubt she will."

Mateo and his wife lived in a two-bedroom house on the farthest parcel of McKenna property. It had been used as a bunkhouse for dozens of years but had fallen into disrepair. Mateo had fixed it up and lived there for free with his wife, Miriam, who was a substitute teacher. They had a twenty-three-year-old son who was in the military.

Jake said, "I'll take a look at the leak. I may have to put in a temporary fix if I can figure out where it's coming from, because we don't have time for a major repair. Where's Avery? I could use her help."

"She and Bobby went to check on the Mendozas. Carl has been having a tough time lately." She lowered her voice, not wanting Penny to overhear. Not because she was keeping secrets from her grandmother, but because she didn't want to have another conversation about Verdacorp right now. "I saw the Coulters this morning. They sold right-of-way for utilities, but there's a consent clause where they have to give explicit permission to exploit mineral rights. So, there may not be a problem, and after I talk to the bank next week, I'm going to make them an offer on their property. I think they'll take it. But I need to study the maps first. If the utilities cut through the parcel we need, it's not worth it."

"Baldwin didn't have a clause like that."

"I don't know, maybe he did. He told me they weren't going to bury a pipeline or drill, but I haven't seen the contract yet. I warned him about the hidden clauses in other contracts I've seen."

"He should never have sold to them in the first place," Jake said. "And he sold the farm, not just right-of-way. You and I both know if Dad were still alive, he would have sold to us."

Ellen put her hand on Jake's arm. "I know you're angry. I am, too. But we've been friends for years, and if there is any restrictive covenant in the contract, then that's good for us."

"He promised to sell *us* the land," Jake said, his jaw tight.

She understood how Jake felt. But Greg had been so kind and helpful to her and her family after John died. She couldn't hold a grudge, even though she was angry about what had transpired over the last two weeks.

Penny stepped out onto the porch and rang a cowbell. It was too far a distance for her to shout, but the bell was plenty loud enough.

"I'll see what she needs," Ellen said. "You go help Lyla, and use Mateo when he returns."

She watched as Jake headed toward the barn, wishing they weren't arguing about college. She wanted what was best for him, and how could giving up his dream of being a vet be best?

John gave up his dream.

Her husband had never regretted it, he'd told her. Then again, John had always embraced life as it was handed to him. She admired him for his ability to see the good and potential in every problem. To face every obstacle and find a solution.

But their son . . . She wanted more for their son.

Ellen shook away her melancholy and ran into the house, stepping into the kitchen dripping wet. Penny was stirring the stew she had started earlier. "You'll all need a hot meal tonight," she said, frowning at the puddle of water Ellen had left in the entry. "I'm warming up that shepherd's pie Millie gave you." Penny shook her head. "That woman makes barely edible food, I swear I don't know who taught her, 'cause her mama was a great cook."

Penny did not praise lightly.

"You rang the bell?" Ellen said as she wiped the water off the laundry room floor and tossed the rag into the laundry bin.

"Yes. Margery Sutton called. I said you'd call her right back."

Ellen adored Margery, but every twinge was cause for panic. She still had nearly eight weeks before her due date. But stress wasn't good for her or the baby.

She dialed the number from a list they kept by the phone.

After one ring, a voice said urgently, "Hello?"

"Susie?" Ellen said, recognizing Margery's younger sister.

"Ellen, thank God."

"What's wrong?"

"Margery is spotting. I want to take her to the hospital, right now, but she said to call you first."

It was more than thirty minutes in good weather to get from her house up off Rock Creek Road to Gainesville, where the hospital was, but right now it could take nearly twice that. There were medical services in Whitesboro, but they wouldn't be able to handle a premature baby and would automatically transport her to Gainesville.

Plus, the roads were so bad from the hailstorm over the weekend that getting a very pregnant woman out over the bumps and potholes until she reached the highway would be problematic. And getting back would be next to impossible, at least for the next day or two.

"Is she actively bleeding?" Ellen asked. Light spotting was normal during pregnancy.

"Just a second," Susie said.

There were voices in the background, then Margery picked up the phone and said, "Ellen? I'm sorry to bother you."

"No bother. Tell me what's going on."

"I didn't even want to call . . ."

Ellen bit back a comment. Margery had called her nearly every day for the last two months. But if five minutes of conversation could keep Margery calm, that was fine by Ellen. Ellen had gone with her to her last OB/GYN appointment two weeks ago. They had an ultrasound and all the blood work was good. The only mild concern was a slightly elevated blood pressure, which is why Ellen really wanted to keep the soon-to-be mom calm.

"Just tell me how you're feeling."

"I took a nap this morning, I swear I'm so tired and the thunder last night kept me and the dogs up."

"I understand that." Whiskey didn't like thunder, either. He always tried to get under her blankets during storms. Ever since John died, Ellen let him.

"So, about nine I went down for a short nap, not even an hour. And when I woke up, there was blood in my panties."

"How much? The size of a quarter? More?"

"About a quarter. And I know it's normal, I read everything you gave me, but I just feel . . . well, super tired and crampy."

"You're carrying around an extra thirty pounds. That would make anyone tired and crampy," Ellen said, trying to make light of it, but mentally going through the checklist of potential problems.

Susie was talking in the background, but Ellen couldn't hear most of what she said, except for, "Just ask her."

"No," Margery said to Susie, not Ellen.

Ellen knew what Susie wanted, but this was the worst day to leave the farm. It was too far to travel on an ATV, but her truck, even though it was a four-wheel drive, could easily get stuck up at Margery's place, or anywhere along the route.

Still, they were in a flood watch, not a flood warning, and while the skies were dark, it was barely raining for now.

If she waited, it would only get worse. Flash flooding was the primary problem, but she'd keep the radio tuned to the emergency station.

"Margery, just to be safe, I'll come up there and do an exam, check your blood pressure."

"You do not have to do that. Don't listen to my sister."

"If there is something that needs to be taken care of, it's better that we know now, right? There's probably nothing wrong, your ultrasound showed a healthy baby, and your labs are normal. But I'll just check a few things, okay?"

"I would appreciate it. I know the weather is awful and you have kids and a farm and—"

"My kids are fine, Jake's eighteen now. We have everything under control here, I promise you." More or less, Ellen thought. "I'll be there in thirty minutes."

"Thank you, Ellen, I really appreciate it."

"Let me talk to Susie for a sec."

Susie got on the phone and Ellen said, "Make sure she's hydrated. Dehydration is a serious problem, especially in the last trimester. And small healthy meals, as often as she wants, okay? Her stomach is shrinking as the baby grows, but she needs to eat."

"I'm on it. I just— I'm worried. Maybe I shouldn't have insisted Margery call, but—"

"It's okay. I'll see you soon."

Ellen hung up and Penny said, "Do you actually think something's wrong with her or the baby?"

Penny's tone sounded like Margery was just complaining.

"No, but she's nearly thirty-three weeks pregnant with her first baby, and her blood pressure was slightly elevated at her last appointment. Avery and Bobby will be home at two. If they're not in the door by two-oh-one, call over there. You should be able to reach me on my cell phone, but if not, Margery's number is on the board." She pointed to the list.

Penny sighed, but didn't comment.

Ellen went upstairs and grabbed her medical bag, plus a

comprehensive midwife reference book in case she needed to look something up.

By the time she went back outside, the rain was still coming down slow but steady. She put her things in the front of the truck and was about to leave when Jake waved at her from the barn. He looked concerned.

"Mom! You need to see something."

CHAPTER ELEVEN

Jake crouched on the west side of the barn and pressed his hand to the soaked wood. "It's wet. The whole thing. Must've started last night with the rain. But it should've drained by now."

Ellen joined him, brow furrowed, eyes narrowing at the dark streaks bleeding down the boards. "We cleaned the gutters not two weeks ago."

Jake nodded slowly. "And replaced them last year. There shouldn't be a problem, but . . ." He trailed off, his voice tight with unease. "I think something's blocking the downspouts. I just cleared out the debris"—he motioned to a pail he'd brought down from the loft—"but the water's still not draining. Maybe an animal built a nest in there."

It seemed improbable, but not impossible.

"Rats? We haven't had a problem with the feed. And I don't think a bird would build a nest inside the drain."

"I don't know. I just know something's wrong. It's backing up and forcing water through the seams. We'll have to cut off the two corner downspouts."

"That'll make a mess down here," Ellen said, already picturing the muddy flood pooling near the foundation. "But we don't have a choice. If we don't, that wall will have to be completely replaced." She didn't want to think about the cost—in time and money. "Still, two hours of rain shouldn't have soaked through like this."

Jake stood, brushing his muddy hands on his jeans. "That's the thing. The water's not just hitting the wall. It's inside. It's in the barn." He hesitated. "The hay in the loft is damp. If it starts to mold . . ."

Ellen's stomach sank. Mold would spread fast—and not just in the hay. The entire loft could become a breeding ground for rot. "We need to move it as soon as possible."

"I was thinking, if we get a break in the storm, I'll climb up to the—"

"No." Her voice cracked through the rain like a whip. It was louder than she meant it to be, sharper. Too sharp.

Jake blinked. "I won't go up on the roof, Mom," he said gently, reaching for her arm. "I promise."

She nodded, throat tightening. "I'm sorry. I shouldn't have snapped."

But the words felt heavy on her chest.

She couldn't forget. She would never forget.

John had fallen from this roof—an accident that should've left him with bruises and maybe a concussion. But it wasn't the height that killed him. It was the way he landed. His neck had snapped. One second he was alive, patching the barn roof, and the next he was on the ground, broken and dying.

She had seen him fall. Heard his body hit the hard ground. Had sprinted toward him as time folded in on itself, her breath stolen by the impossible. Her husband. The love of her life. The father of her children. She reached him as he struggled, held his hand as he took his last breath. Cried when his body stilled. It had happened so fast . . . but felt like an eternity.

It was the worst day of her life. The kids weren't home, thank

God. Uncle Travis picked them up from school early. But when they saw his face, they knew. Something had shattered in each and every one of them the day John died.

She blinked rapidly. She didn't want to cry; she didn't think she had any more tears after eleven months, two weeks, three days of living without John.

"Mateo should be back soon," Jake said, his voice soft. "We'll cut the downspouts, then go up to the loft. Not the roof. Just the loft. We'll see where the water's getting in."

Ellen nodded. "Okay."

But her eyes drifted down the gravel driveway, squinting through the haze. The rain had grown heavier, its rhythm relentless on the barn's corrugated roof.

"What's wrong?" Jake asked.

"Nothing," she said. "Avery and Bobby are at the Mendozas. They're supposed to be back by two, just with this rain maybe I should call over, have them come back now."

"They're fine. Avery is smart. She'll call if she thinks they can't get through."

"I know. And I wouldn't worry about it except I need to go check on Margery Sutton."

"Is there a problem?"

"Probably not, but she's having some concerns and I need to check on her before I can't get there at all. You can take care of things here?"

"Of course," Jake said. "And if Avery and Bobby aren't back by two, I'll go get them."

"Be careful. The creek is already running high."

"Roger that."

Whisper Creek cut through their property and went under the road that separated their ranch from the former Mendoza property and other farms. The bridge—basically, a reinforced section of the road—had been replaced three times since Ellen had married into the McKenna family. It should hold, even if the creek rose over it, but if it did, they wouldn't be able to cross it, effectively cutting them off from the Mendozas—and from Bobby and Avery.

It was just after twelve. "I hope to be back by three, I'll call if I'm later than four."

She went to the truck and headed for the Suttons' place.

She passed Mateo as he clattered up the drive on horseback, hunched in his saddle, Jake's horse trailing behind him. His rain slicker clung to him like plastic wrap, soaked through despite its promise of protection. She waved at him, and he lifted a hand in greeting, then focused on navigating the horses through the mud.

While Jake was a responsible eighteen-year-old, she was glad Mateo had made it back.

Ellen turned onto the road and considered stopping by the Mendozas to check on her kids. But as she passed the driveway and saw the lights from the house in the distance, decided that the delay could mean the difference between her making it back before the storm, so she continued on her way to the Suttons.

CHAPTER TWELVE

Tom Garza didn't understand why any of this was *his* problem.

He hadn't hired the bimbo who fucked up the contracts. But it wasn't like Mitchell Robinson would admit that he let his dick influence his business decisions.

Jerk.

But the jerk paid well, real well, and thus Tom sat down with Mitchell's obnoxious, spoiled daughter Presley in her office—yes, the nineteen-year-old had her own *office* on the Robinson ranch complete with state-of-the-art equipment, video game systems Tom's kid would have died for, a fully stocked mini-fridge, and a movie screen that came down from the ceiling with flair.

Presley Robinson was smart, sassy, and beautiful, and she knew it.

She popped a bubble with her gum and said, "This will be fun. AI is the best. Whaddya want me to say?"

"I just need them out of the house for a couple hours. Their daughter lives in Frisco, something about car trouble, being stranded."

"Specifics, Tom," she said in a condescending tone. "Like, I have her name and number but you need both old farts out of the house? We need to have a good reason."

"The daughter—"

"Grace," Presley said with an eye roll.

"Grace is worried that they won't be able to get home during the storm, so they should pack a bag and stay the night."

"Good, but still, why would both of them need to go?"

How the hell did he know that? He was divorced, he would have used any excuse to get away from his wife. Maybe George Coulter was the same way, leave the wife at home and help his daughter. Tom didn't know these people—he'd moved up here from Houston two years ago to work for Verdacorp. He'd quickly put the farm outside Willis that he'd grown up on in the rearview mirror as soon as he turned eighteen and got his first job in the city. He hated country living.

"Family dinner," he said. "Her husband is Chris, their kids are little, like eight and six. They would love to see their grandma and grandpa. That'll work."

"Do they call them Grandma and Grandpa? Because I called my grandpa Papa, so that's kinda important."

Again with the eye roll and attitude. How did Mitchell put up with this shit?

Well, maybe because Presley was his only kid. A spoiled daddy's girl who could do no wrong.

She sighed, typed rapidly on her computer.

"I got it. Grace and Chris have two boys, C. J. and Frankie." She scrolled, reading rapidly, a half smile on her face. "God, these people! They post everything online. Their lives are a fucking open book."

"Do you even need me?"

"Well, duh, as soon as I'm done, you're going to have to make sure they're gone. I'd send out my drone, but not in this weather. It cost over ten thousand dollars."

Spoiled. Rotten. Brat.

Tom just nodded. "Okay."

"Grandpa and Mimi." She leaned back, closed her eyes, popped her gum.

Her neck looked good enough to strangle.

A minute later she abruptly sat up. She put on headphones, plugged her phone into her computer, typed on the keyboard.

This wasn't the first time that Presley had called someone using an AI voice modulator, so they thought they were talking to someone else. All she had needed was a sample of the subject's voice, and AI did the rest.

It was fascinating, and damn scary. Tom made sure his son knew that if he ever called asking for help or money or for him to do something completely out of character, that he needed to hang up and call him directly. Presley and other scammers could clone the number, fake the voice, but they couldn't reroute a phone call.

Yet. He was certain if it was possible, Presley would figure it out. Why couldn't she use her power for good?

Because she's Mitchell Robinson's spawn, he thought.

Presley drank half her Red Bull, then typed on the keyboard. Tom couldn't hear the Coulters' end of the conversation, only what Presley said.

"Hi, Mom," Presley said. "How are you? . . . Stew? Sounds great. Yeah . . . Well, I have a little problem. Chris had to go down to Conroe and help his parents, and I got into a fender bender . . . I'm fine, the boys are fine, but my car can't be driven, and C. J. has indoor soccer early tomorrow morning. I know how much you like to watch the games . . . No, I don't want you getting up at four to come, it's a mess up there. Is there any way you can come down tonight? I'm making my famous lasagna! . . . Ask Daddy, *please*?"

Presley looked at Tom and winked. A half minute later, she said, "Hi, Daddy! Did Mom tell you? . . . Yes, I promise, we're not hurt at all. I mean my wrist is a little sore, but it'll be fine . . . The boys would love to see you . . . I don't want you coming down if it's already pouring up there . . . Really? . . . Sure, stay the weekend! Chris won't be back until Sunday night . . . Great. I can't wait. Love you, Daddy!"

She hit a button on the computer and laughed.

"That was *so* easy! They want to leave within the hour to make it out before the roads close. Even said they should have thought of it before!"

"They have two bulls. They have no one to feed them."

Presley shrugged. "They'll figure it out." She waved him away. "Go, watch their place, call when they leave."

Tom got up and left. Dammit, this wasn't going to work. They'd call the McKennas, most likely, the oldest kid usually came over to help when they needed it. But . . . that should be okay, he thought as he crossed through the large foyer to Mitchell's office. The bulls would already be secured in the barn, so Jake or Ellen wouldn't go over until morning.

By then, they'd have the contract and no one would be the wiser.

He knocked on Mitchell's door and waited until he heard "Come in."

Mitchell's grand office was intimidating. Dark wood, hunting trophies, a desk half the size of a king bed. The marble floor of the foyer gave way to a room with hardwood floors around the perimeter and a vast, plush burgundy rug in the center. Two-story windows on either side of a stone fireplace looked out to the vast Robinson property—green grass, white split-rail fences, and a man-made lake that was stocked with trout. Today, of course, it was gray, the rain coming down steadily, the lake barely visible in the distance.

Clive was sitting across from his younger brother. Clive was actually a pretty good guy; Tom liked him. Five years older than Mitchell, but he didn't have the business gene in the family. Mitchell was practically a clone of his grandfather. In looks, personality, and business acumen—the good and the bad. Their dad? Had no business sense at all, but unlike Clive, he didn't know it.

"Did Presley take care of things?" Mitchell asked.

"Yeah. An hour, give or take."

"Let me know when they leave," he said.

Tom glanced at Clive. He didn't want to go out alone, it was miserable out there and he'd like the company.

But Clive made no move to get out of the comfortable leather chair.

"Okay, boss," Tom said and left.

Mitchell watched as Tom closed the door. He leaned back and said to Clive, "He doesn't seem to be fully invested."

"He is," Clive said. "He just spent the last hour with Presley, she can wear anyone down." He laughed. Mitchell didn't find it funny. "Mitch, you know how she is. She's brilliant and makes all of us peons feel dumb."

His daughter *was* brilliant. Mitchell just wished she was still in college. She had been expelled for a prank. No one got hurt, but it embarrassed the university, and she was asked to leave. Mitchell got her into another college—he had many friends in high places—but then she tells him she wants to take a "gap year."

"A year to work for you, Daddy, and teach myself. And we can travel and do fun things!"

She didn't so much ask him as tell him what she was doing. He didn't think she would ever go back, but he found it hard to deny his daughter anything. Her mother left them when she was six and maybe he indulged her, but she deserved it. He was building this legacy for her. Clive was content being second, and Mitchell had no sons to leave his business to. And even if he did, Presley was his firstborn and undeniably intelligent.

"Where's Nicole?" Clive asked.

"I sent her down to the house in Dallas. She and Presley had a disagreement and I don't have the energy to mediate."

He would have to find a way to move Nicole along. Presley had called her stupid to her face, and Nicole was not having it. Truth was, Nicole *was* dumb, and just because she was gorgeous and wild in bed didn't mean that Mitchell would tolerate her mistakes.

He should never have trusted her with the documents. Just because she had a background as a legal secretary didn't mean she actually knew what she was doing.

But he needed to wait, because until he had all the contracts back in his possession, he couldn't cut her loose. She might get angry and talk.

He'd send her to Europe, hire someone to seduce her, let her break it off with him. It was the only way to ensure his girlfriend remained silent.

Though even now she probably had no idea the seriousness of her mistake.

"Now, Clive, you were telling me where we are with Ellen McKenna."

"She's not budging. She's more stubborn than John."

"That's not the right answer."

"I don't know what to tell you, Mitch. I've been working on her for months. Hell, I got Travis to talk to her, and that was not easy. I had to lower our ask to only that two-hundred-acre plot between our land and the Coulters. He got on board, and she told him no."

Mitchell was aware of the compromise, one he didn't want to make, but it was the minimum area he needed to complete the project.

He would lose the contract if he didn't get that plot of land. Of course, he'd offered to buy the entire property—it would be satisfying to take the land that his father could never purchase. But he only needed those two hundred acres.

He *had* to have those two hundred acres.

"What does she want?" Mitchell asked. "I've offered well over market value. I've offered for a small parcel."

"According to Travis, she wants to grow."

"Explain."

"Grow or die, it was John's motto and she's zealous about it," Clive said. "She has over a thousand acres now that she bought out most of the Mendoza property. She wants to double that."

"There's no way."

"Well, Baldwin was going to sell to her, and so were the Coulters. The Coulters still can, but it won't be contiguous since we have their eastern half. Both those properties would have given her well over the thousand more she wants. There are a few other small farms on the north she could offer for, but the land isn't ready to farm, and it's too dense for cattle. She'd have to put in a lot of time and money."

"Double?" Mitchell didn't understand why, after the death of her husband, Ellen McKenna would want to work herself to the bone to achieve next to nothing and for land that she had married into.

"Travis would be happy to sell off ninety percent of their land and just have horses, but he's not going to push her."

"He's not on the deed?"

"No, it's all in her name."

"And her children would inherit," he said thoughtfully.

Clive tensed. "Don't go there."

"Don't be ridiculous. Of course not," Mitchell lied. True, he didn't want to hurt anyone. But he had to find a way to convince her that selling to him was the only way to survive.

"Look," Clive said, leaning forward, "we follow through with my plan. It's going to work."

"It's too slow. I need that plot."

"I have an idea," Clive said. "She wants to grow; we help her grow. She sells us those two hundred acres, we sell her part of Baldwin's property we just bought, eight hundred acres. We keep the acres we need, give her part of what she wants, everyone is happy."

"I'm not happy," Mitchell said, but it was an idea. Maybe the only way he could salvage his plans—plans that were two years in the making. "But she needs to make the decision before five o'clock Sunday. We're down to the wire. I need everything signed, sealed, and delivered by Monday morning."

"Okay. I'll talk to Travis—"

"No. Talk to Ellen directly."

"She won't talk to me. I was there this morning and Penny ran me off with a shotgun."

"For shit's sake, Clive, that old woman can't hit the broadside of a barn. Go to Ellen, offer her the trade. She's getting a great deal—I mean, it's a fucking steal and I hate offering it. But we're out of time. Draw up the contract and let me see it first, then get her to sign it."

"Okay. Sounds good." Clive rose.

"Clive," Mitchell said sharply.

"Yep?"

"There is no other alternative, understand? Ellen McKenna will sign that contract. If I have to go over there myself to convince her, I will."

CHAPTER THIRTEEN

The drive to Margery's house took less time than Ellen expected. Even with the rain falling steadily now, a gray mist hugging the trees, and the low water crossings threatening to swell, she made good time. That, she told herself, was a good sign. The dirt and gravel roads were rutted from last weekend's hailstorm, and wet from the rain last night, but she hadn't needed the four-wheel drive, not even on the steep driveway that climbed up through the cedar trees to the small house Doug Sutton had finished building just before his deployment.

Ellen parked under the carport next to Margery Sutton's old Bronco and grabbed her waterproof bag. Her boots hit the wet gravel with a crunch. Before she could knock, the door opened. Susie stood there, barefoot, her long blond hair pulled back into a messy braid. Her expression was tight.

"She's been having these cramps since last night. Nothing regular. But she says she just doesn't feel right. And then the blood—it freaked me out more than Margery."

Ellen gave her a reassuring nod. "That's why I'm here."

She was glad she came. She liked Susie, but she was definitely more high-strung than her older sister. If Ellen could get them both to remain calm, that would go a long way toward alleviating many complications.

Inside, the house smelled like lavender and cinnamon—someone had been baking or maybe trying to soothe nerves. Faint instrumental music that Ellen couldn't identify floated through the speakers. Margery lay on the couch, curled on her side, her hand pressed low against her belly. Her pale hair clung to her forehead and she looked more tired than usual. But she smiled when she saw Ellen.

"I'm so sorry I got you out in this bad weather," she said.

"Better safe than sorry," Ellen said, setting her bag on the coffee table. "Let's see what's going on."

She knelt beside the couch, her tone gentle but firm. "Tell me everything. When did the cramping start?"

"Last night, around two in the morning, I woke up to pee—I swear I have to pee every hour on the hour."

Ellen laughed. "I remember those days."

"It wasn't sharp or anything, just a little tight, maybe? I went back to sleep and a couple hours later got up to pee and the cramp came back."

"Where specifically is the cramp?"

"Mostly my lower back, but then this morning it kind of radiated around my lower belly." She rubbed her hands under her belly to illustrate. "And then after breakfast, that's when I had the spotting. But it hasn't come back."

"Spotting is normal, but not continued bleeding. You know the difference?"

"Yes. The book you gave me explained it well. It was spotting."

"Okay." Ellen nodded, slipping on a blood pressure cuff. "Any headaches? Blurred vision?"

Margery shook her head. "No. Just tired."

"Good." She took Margery's hand and gave it a light squeeze

before inflating the cuff. While the pressure dial climbed, Ellen spoke low, almost conversational. "Baby moving well?"

Margery smiled, her eyes lighting up. "More squirmy than usual. I can't wait to meet Bump."

Margery was the first woman Ellen had worked with in years who hadn't wanted to peek at the baby's gender. Ellen liked that. She hadn't looked with her first, but the others? Yeah, she had wanted to know. Sometimes she wished she had just been surprised, because there were so few good surprises in the world anymore.

Ellen released the valve and watched the numbers drop—140 over 90. Higher than Ellen wanted, but not in the danger zone. She made a note in her logbook.

"Let's check your other vitals. Then I'll want to do a quick exam."

Margery nodded. Susie hovered near the kitchen, arms crossed over her chest, trying to look calm but clearly fighting the urge to ask a hundred questions. Ellen caught her eye and offered a calm, practiced smile.

"Can you bring Margery a glass of water? Or something with electrolytes if you've got it?" she asked.

"Yeah—yes, of course." Susie turned to the fridge like she was grateful for something to do.

Ellen checked Margery's pulse, respiration, then used her Doppler to find the baby's heartbeat. The galloping rhythm filled the living room, strong and steady.

"There's our little one," Ellen said, and Margery let out a happy sigh, a smile on her lips.

She moved methodically, palpating Margery's belly, feeling the firmness of the uterus, checking for any signs of early labor. No contractions she could measure yet, but the tightness could be Braxton Hicks.

When Susie returned with a glass of Gatorade over ice, Ellen guided Margery to sip slowly, then helped her sit up so she could take her weight and temperature properly.

Ellen made notes in her small, leather-bound book, flipping pages back to compare earlier measurements. This was the third visit in two weeks where Margery's blood pressure had edged upward. Not dangerous yet, but not trending in the right direction.

Still, the blood tests had been normal, and the urine test done two weeks ago at her last appointment showed no sign of protein that would be a clear indicator of preeclampsia.

"Okay," she said gently, sitting on the ottoman across from Margery. "Your blood pressure's a bit high. It's not alarming, but I want to keep an eye on it. Baby sounds great, and there's no immediate sign of labor, but I'm going to hang out for the next hour or so, just to watch."

Margery nodded, eyes wide but calm. "You think it's preeclampsia?"

"It might just be stress," Ellen said carefully. "Or the weather. Or nothing at all. But we won't guess. We'll watch. And I'm going to leave a message for Dr. Patel, just as a precaution, so he can decide if he wants any labs drawn or a hospital check later. I'm pretty sure if your blood pressure doesn't increase, he won't want you out on the roads today."

Margery looked half-panicked. "I don't want to leave. There's a flood watch in effect, and we have to cross Rock Creek to get to the highway. It floods all the time."

"And being calm means not thinking about things like floods or driving in this storm. Right?"

"You're right. Sorry."

Ellen smiled reassuringly, then called Dr. Patel. He didn't answer, but she didn't expect him to. She left a message.

"Hi, Ron, it's Ellen McKenna. I'm with Margery Sutton right now—she's a couple days shy of thirty-three weeks. You last saw her two weeks ago in your office. She's having some intermittent cramping, low back pain, and fatigue. Her BP is 140 over 90, pulse normal, her last urine test showed no proteinuria, fetal heart rate strong, no signs of labor at this point. I'll be monitoring her vitals every fifteen minutes for the next hour. Neither of us want her to be out in the storm, unless you say we absolutely need to get her in. Let me know what you want to do."

She hit end, then turned back toward the living room. The rain still whispered against the windows, steady but not dangerous yet. She wanted to go home, check on her family, make sure that Avery and Bobby made it back safe. Make sure Jake didn't do something dangerous like climb onto the barn roof. Make sure Penny wasn't overdoing it in the kitchen, and that Lyla had eaten lunch.

But for the next hour, she could be here for Margery.

She sat back down, asked about what she had been eating. Susie had kept a good log. "She doesn't eat a lot at one time, but she eats often!" Susie said with a laugh.

"That's very normal, and actually good for her and the baby. Her stomach has shrunk as the baby has grown."

"I'm craving pickles. Isn't that so cliché?" Margery said.

"Probably salt. Too much salt is bad, but too little salt is bad, too. Have a pickle whenever you want. What might be good is a bean salad, tossed in olive oil and a good red wine vinegar. Garlic salt and pepper maybe."

"I can do that!" Susie said. She went back to the kitchen, relieved, it seemed, that she had something productive to do.

Ellen asked, "How's Doug? Have you talked to him lately?"

Margery shook her head. "He was supposed to call me yesterday afternoon. He didn't know when he'd be able to, he usually has a window he can call, and his night is my day. But he didn't call, and I didn't get a message. So of course I had to look up where his aircraft carrier is now, and it's still in the Mediterranean and everything seems fine, but . . ." She shrugged.

"You're worried."

She nodded. "He's really good about calling me, and he emails almost every day. But I haven't heard from him at all in two days . . ."

Which, Ellen thought, was why her blood pressure was elevated.

"Listen to me, Margery," she said firmly. "You are worried about Doug, and that is normal, but your stress is not good for the baby or you. If your blood pressure spikes, there's no choice but to go to the hospital. So for now, we are going to think only positive thoughts. We are not going to think anything bad; we're not going to read anything sad. No news, no social media, nothing but focusing on growing this beautiful baby."

"You're right, I know you're right."

"Good." Thunder rolled through the sky and Margery jumped. "Hey, it's just a little storm," Ellen said.

"Little?" Margery raised an eyebrow.

"Honestly, you're in the best place in the valley. You are on one of the highest hills, you have a generator if the power goes out, and you have a wood-burning fireplace."

"Doug really thought of everything," she said, smiling.

"You found a good one," Ellen said, then thought about John.

She had found a good one, too. And now he was gone. She remembered being young, pregnant, full of trepidation and deep joy. John worked hard, but he was with her every night, giving her back rubs, going downstairs to get her a dish of ice cream in the middle of the night, telling her he loved her every single day.

Dear Lord, she missed him.

But she didn't want Margery to see that she was melancholy, so she forced herself to smile and wrapped the cuff around her arm again.

"Let's see if we can get those numbers to come down, okay?"

Susie brought them all sandwiches and Margery a large glass of milk, which she'd asked for. "I don't even like milk, but it's all I seem to want," Margery said.

"Other than pickles," Susie said, and they both laughed.

Her blood pressure was exactly the same, which was actually good. It wasn't going up or being erratic.

Still, Ellen willed it to go down, just a bit, so she could leave and make sure her own family was safe.

"I'm going to call home, tell them what I'm doing and when to expect me."

"You can't stay?"

"I'll stay for a while, but I need to get back before I can't get back."

"Oh. Yeah, I'm sorry—I know you have kids. You didn't have to come."

"I wanted to," Ellen assured her. Then she stepped out onto the porch and phoned home. She was grateful to hear a ring. Cell service was always spotty during storms, but with the Suttons on a hill, it helped.

Penny answered on the third ring. "Hello!"

"Grandma, it's Ellen."

"How is the Sutton girl?"

"She's good. Elevated blood pressure. Worried about her husband, who she hasn't spoken to in two days. I'm going to stay for another hour or so."

"Keep the radio on. The weather reports are coming in fast and furious."

"I will," she said. "Are Avery and Bobby back yet?"

"No, I haven't seen them."

Ellen looked at her watch. It was one thirty. "Like I told Jake, if they're not home by two . . ."

"I'll call over there, have them come home right now."

"Thank you." She breathed a sigh of relief. She should have done that herself, but she also knew how much Carl and Rose appreciated Avery's help with the sheep, and her friendship with Gianna. After the accident, most of Gianna's friends stopped talking to her. It was as if they thought paralysis would rub off on them. And having to leave college had been so hard on the young woman. Growing up, Avery had adored Gianna, the pretty older girl who always had friends and dates and got a scholarship for college. Gianna was kind, but Avery wasn't in her peer group. Then after the accident, Gianna realized that Avery was the only friend who had stuck. Ellen hadn't had to tell Avery to stay in contact, she'd done that all on her own.

Ellen then asked, "Has Jake finished in the barn? He and Lyla need to eat."

"Everyone's still in the barn. I popped Millie's shepherd's pie into the oven to warm. It doesn't smell as good as mine, just saying. But I have stew for tonight, and I baked an apple pie."

"Grandma—"

"I can't sit still. Storms make me antsy. Oh, and the Pritchards called. What's the wife's name again?"

"Abigail."

"Right. Abigail. She wanted to know if we knew of someone who would come out to fix their generator, which they can't seem to get working. They called everyone in the phone book and no one will come out until Monday."

That didn't surprise Ellen, locals knew that this area would be cut off because Mule Run always flooded during storms.

"Can you ask Mateo to go over there? They have three little kids; they're going to need the generator tonight."

"They don't know what they're doing," Penny grumbled, her admonition of "city folk" moving into the rural community loudly unspoken.

"They want a simpler life for their kids," Ellen said. "I like them. They just need a year or two to get used to it."

"I'll talk to Mateo *after* he and Jake are done with the barn."

"Thank you. I love you, Grandma."

"Love you, too. Drive carefully."

"I'll call when I'm heading back."

She ended the call and watched the rain fall, straight and steady. How much longer did she have before it would be too dangerous to drive?

She went inside. "Susie, do you have a radio?"

"Sure." She went to the kitchen to retrieve it.

Ellen put on the local weather station and kept the volume low, just loud enough so she could hear it. She checked Margery's blood pressure again and was relieved that it had dropped to 135 over 80.

Now, it was heading in the right direction.

Penny McKenna checked on Millie's casserole and wrinkled her nose. She didn't want to feed bad-tasting food to her family, but she also couldn't waste it, either. That would be a greater sin. Gravy . . . yes, she'd warm up some of her own gravy, which would at least make the shepherd's pie edible.

She walked into the well-organized pantry—that was all Avery, not her. The girl had even labeled the shelves to make things easy to find. Avery enjoyed helping Penny can—they made jams, syrup, canned whole fruits, pie filling, gravy, and more. Avery had even made Penny pretty little labels for Christmas two years ago: *From Grandma Penny's Kitchen* was printed on the top, with enough space to write what was inside and the date of canning.

There were several jars of gravy left, so she took one and used the jar opener her grandson John had bought her years ago. She used to be strong enough to open anything in the kitchen, but these days her hand just didn't grip as it used to.

She dumped the gravy into a saucepan and turned it to low. Then she was rinsing the jar when she glanced at the phone.

She needed to call Rose and have her send Avery and Bobby home.

She dialed the number. It took four rings before Rose answered. "Hello?"

"Rose? It's Penny."

"Hello, Penny."

"Can you send Avery and Bobby home? Ellen had to go up to Rock Creek to check on the Sutton girl, and the rain is coming down hard, and she's worried that little bridge between your place and ours will flood and they'll get stuck."

"Oh. Bobby left; he's on his way. He was going to tell you that Avery is going to spend the night. She's been a big help."

Penny frowned. "Did she ask Ellen?"

"No, she told Bobby."

"When did he leave?"

"Not long ago."

Penny sighed. It wasn't her place to make these decisions. "Avery needs to talk to Ellen. She can't assume this is okay."

"I'll have her call."

"Her cell phone. She's up at the Suttons. I'll keep a lookout for Bobby." The boy was probably still out looking for that cat, and Penny hoped he didn't get himself stuck. Still, he had nearly thirty minutes until his two PM curfew.

"Okay. Thank you." Rose hung up.

Penny stared at the phone. Rose didn't sound like herself. Usually she was chatty—far more chatty than Penny preferred—and it was Penny who had to find an excuse to hang up.

She looked out the window. The rain fell in steady drops. If the ground wasn't already saturated, the water would be more welcome.

It was going to get worse, she thought as she went back to the stove and stirred the gravy.

Thunder rolled in the distance and Penny frowned. That boy had better be back sooner rather than later.

After Bobby got off the radio with Avery, he sat against the barn wall for a long time trying to figure out what to do.

Something was wrong, but he didn't know what. He didn't know why Avery was lying to him about helping with the sheep, because she wasn't in the barn doing anything. And he didn't know who that man was.

It started to rain, so he went into the barn, where it was dry. He climbed up into the loft and sat there, staring at his radio.

He didn't know what to do. His dad would know. His mom would know. His brother and sisters and even his grandma would know what to do. But Bobby was scared and worried. He didn't want to leave his sister, but he didn't want to stay and have that man find him. Because he knew, deep down, that something super weird was going on and he needed to get help.

He couldn't use the radio because the man might hear him. Going home seemed to be the best option, but what if Whisper Creek flooded the road and no one could get back to help Avery? Then his sister would be trapped here with no one.

He laid back in the hay and closed his eyes. His dad always said that when you had a hard decision to make, you should shut off the world. Close your eyes, get rid of all the junk in your head, and focus on your problem. If you're quiet enough, calm enough, and say a prayer, the answer will come.

Bobby didn't know if that would work. He didn't sit still all that well—his teacher always told him to stop fidgeting. But his dad was the smartest person he knew and if his dad said it would work, then Bobby had to try. He didn't know what else to do, so he closed his eyes, said a prayer, and waited for an answer.

CHAPTER FOURTEEN

Gianna's bedroom door opened abruptly, and the hulking man stood there, his eyes hard. "Avery," he barked.

Gianna yelped and Avery jumped. She hated that she was scared, so she steeled her expression and looked him in the eye.

"What?"

"You need to call your mother and say anything you need to say so that she tells you it's okay for you to spend the night. I don't want any surprises. No parents showing up here, no more little brothers on the radio. Understand?"

"Did my mom call?"

"Some woman named Penny. Her mom"—he pointed to Gianna—"talked to her, said she's your grandmother?"

He said it as an accusation, as if Rose had lied to him.

Avery nodded. "Yeah, she lives with us."

Why hadn't Bobby told her? He should have been home by now. But Avery didn't say that. She didn't want this guy to go out looking for him.

"Get up," he said. "Now."

She got to her feet slowly and he grabbed her arm, pulled her out of the room and down the hall to the kitchen.

Carl and Rose looked scared, tired, and very old, as if this ordeal had aged them a decade.

The stranger pointed to the kitchen phone mounted on the wall. "I'm going to remind you, Avery, that if you give any hint that there are any problems here, and your mom shows up? She's a dead woman. Do you understand me?"

Avery's stomach twisted, and she nodded. She went to the phone, was about to dial, when he grabbed her wrist. "Her cell phone. She's up on Rock Creek Road, your grandmother said. What's up there?"

"I—uh—I don't know."

"You're lying."

Avery really drew a blank. Rock Creek . . . Who lived there? Then it hit her. But if she told him the truth, he'd know her mother was a nurse and might make her come here and fix his friend Sam. Avery was torn. She wanted her mom, but she didn't want her mom to be hurt.

"What?" the man demanded.

"A friend. The Suttons. They live up there," she said. "I don't know why she's there, maybe she brought them some food or something? My grandma bakes a lot when there's bad weather."

He stared at her and she didn't think he believed her, but he let go of her wrist.

Avery dialed her mother's cell phone.

Three rings later, she answered. Tears burned behind Avery's eyes. But she worked to keep her voice calm. The man had his face near hers, so he could hear both sides of the conversation. His eyes bored into her. She swallowed.

"Hi, Mom. It's Avery."

"You're still at the Mendozas?"

"Yeah. They'd like me to spend the night. Mrs. Mendoza talked to Grandma, but Grandma said I have to ask you. Please? I've been helping Mr. Mendoza with the sheep and Gianna is having a difficult time right now."

"I don't like this."

"I know, and I wouldn't ask if it wasn't important."

"Send Bobby home right now. I can pick you up on my way back from Margery's."

The stranger grabbed her upper arm and squeezed.

"Really, Mom?" she said. "You don't need me for anything, and Gianna needs me. She really does or I wouldn't ask."

"I don't like feeling manipulated, Avery," her mom said.

"I'm not, I swear."

Silence. The man squeezed her so hard she yelped.

"What?" her mother asked.

"Sorry, I hit my elbow on the counter."

"Fine," her mom said with a sigh, and Avery could hear the tension in her voice. Her mom had a lot on her mind, and Avery wondered if there was something wrong with Margery and the baby. Because why else would her mom go up there now, when the roads were such a mess?

"Thank you!" She was about to hang up but her mom continued. "But stay put. This storm is getting worse. Maybe this is for the best. Margery's blood pressure is elevated, and I'm thinking of bringing her to the house so I can keep an eye on her tonight. If Rock Creek floods, she won't be able to get to the hospital if the baby comes early. I'll give her your bed."

"Okay," she said. "I love you, Mom."

"Love you, too, honey."

She hung up.

"Who is Margery?" The man asked.

"A friend."

"Why is your mother there? This Margery, she's pregnant? Who is your mother?"

"Um, Ellen?"

"What does your mother do?" He raised his arm as if to hit her.

"She runs the house. The farm. My dad died last year and now my mom does everything. I don't know what you want from me!" Her voice ended in a cry.

He stared at her, then he let her go. "Go back to your friend."

Avery ran back down the hall and slammed the door shut.

The rain had been falling steadily for over an hour, soaking the tall grass in the field near where Tom sat in his truck, engine off, heat fogging the inside of the windshield. He rubbed it with his sleeve so he could better see. Across the road, the Coulters' house stood half-shrouded behind a row of leaning oaks, the gravel driveway turning to mud under the rain. Tom could barely make out the porch from where he sat, but he knew what he was looking for.

He sipped coffee from the thermos he had filled early this morning before he left his house. His shirt clung to the back of his neck from being caught in the rain earlier, and the north Texas humidity preventing him from drying.

His phone buzzed once. A text from his son: *Can we play* Ghost Recon *tonight?*

Tom exhaled through his nose, thumbed the screen but didn't type a reply.

"Not if Mitchell keeps jerking me around out here," he muttered.

He frowned. His kid was growing up too fast. His mom did her own thing and dated a lot, so Tommy spent most of the time at Tom's house in Gainesville, where he also had friends in the neighborhood. Tom wished he could be home more than he was, Tommy was fourteen. He was a good kid, but soon he might not want to play video games with him anymore . . . once he turned sixteen, got his license, and discovered that girls were a lot more fun and interesting than the Xbox.

He sent a belated response.

Whenever I get home, game on. But I might not be back until tomorrow. Mrs. Willis is bringing over dinner for you tonight, if you need anything let her know.

Tommy sent him a thumbs-up emoji and Tom pocketed his phone.

This job—it had started as just a side gig, going out with Clive as he sweet-talked—or strong-armed—landowners. Sometimes, Tom had to do other things, things he didn't particularly like, but he was paid well. But then Mitchell had started talking about "leverage" and "opportunities," and now Tom was spending his Friday afternoon sitting in a field like some cut-rate private eye, waiting for a couple old folks to leave their house so Mitchell could send in his goons to steal from them.

He didn't like it. He didn't like anything he had to do, but he did it anyway, because what choice did he have? This was his job. This is why he got paid the big bucks, he thought, anger rolling over him.

Tom had the sinking feeling that all the favors, all the errands, all the little things he'd done at Mitchell's request—some legal, some not so much—were stacking up like a row of dominoes. And when too many stood in a row, what happened? They fell. And then where would Tom be? Would Mitchell hang him out to dry? To take the blame? Yep, yep he would.

Well, Mitchell Robinson would be *very* sorry. Because Tom knew things, many things that would get that arrogant jerk and his bratty daughter in hot water with the police . . . or the FBI. If Tom went down, they'd go down harder.

The sound of an engine snapped him to attention. Across the road, the Coulters' ten-year-old Ford pickup roared to life. George Coulter was behind the wheel, his wife, Millie, beside him. They both looked happy, but nervous. No surprise. No one wanted to be out in this miserable weather, especially a couple old folks who were closing in on seventy.

The truck bumped its way down the driveway and turned south

onto the road, heading toward Callisburg, where they'd cross over to Gainesville, then take the interstate down to the Dallas area. Their daughter lived in the suburbs.

Tom felt like shit. He'd helped trick them into thinking their youngest daughter wanted them to visit for the weekend. They'd know something was up when they got there and their daughter wasn't expecting them. They'd know that someone had pretended to be her. Then what would happen? Would they come home? Call the police?

But at least they had nearly two hours to get the contract before anyone was the wiser. Two hours was more than enough time.

Tom waited five minutes. Then another five. Rain tapped on the hood like impatient fingers.

He finally turned the key in the ignition and rolled slowly across the road, tires sliding on the wet gravel before finding traction. The Coulter place looked more charming than tired when he was close up. All the little details—curtains in the windows, trim neatly painted. The plants that had decorated the porch when he was here last week with Clive to witness the signing of the contract were gone—likely moved into the house or barn before the storm hit.

He parked behind a rusted tractor, no longer a tool but a yard decoration, and climbed out. The rain hadn't let up. It soaked into his collar the second he stepped from the cab. The air was thick and heavy around him as he moved around the house, checking windows, peeking inside. Nothing. The place was still and empty. Even the chickens were quiet, having been put into their hutch early, the dark gray sky tricking them into believing it was dusk.

He stepped up onto the porch, staring at the door like it might open on its own.

He didn't want to be here. He wanted to be home, on the couch, losing to his kid in a video game.

He took out his phone and dialed.

Mitchell picked up quickly.

"It's clear," Tom said. "They're gone. You can send whoever you're sending."

"Good," Mitchell said, and the line went dead.

Tom walked back to his truck, kicked the tire, swore when his toe came back throbbing. He climbed into the driver's seat and hit the steering wheel hard with his fist.

Everything Mitchell Robinson was doing would only work if Ellen McKenna sold him two hundred acres that she was not going to sell. Tom knew it. Clive knew it. And Mitchell knew it, even though he lied to himself that he could convince her.

Time was running out, and Tom hoped—prayed—Mitchell didn't do something stupid.

He drove off, glancing in his rearview mirror at the little farmhouse and barn. He turned toward the Verdacorp main office, on the edge of the Robinson property. He'd rather wait there alone than at the Robinson house until Mitchell called for him. As he would, sooner or later.

"This is all gonna come back and bite me in the ass," he grumbled.

CHAPTER FIFTEEN

Avery glanced over at Gianna sitting in her rocking chair, a handmade quilt over her damaged legs. She'd always been a little jealous that Gianna had a television in her bedroom, but felt bad about that now. Gianna couldn't do everything Avery could—she couldn't run, could walk only with help, and was always in pain. She deserved to have the luxury of a television mounted above her dresser.

Now, she hoped to distract her friend from what was happening.

"Wanna watch something on TV?" she asked. She tried to keep her voice light, but it cracked slightly at the end.

Gianna didn't answer right away. Her eyes flicked toward the curtained window, the one they hadn't dared to touch since being locked in. Then she looked at Avery.

"No," she whispered. "They're going to kill us."

Avery's stomach flipped. Her chest tightened as if someone had cinched a belt around her ribs. "They're *not*," she said emphatically. But the words felt like a lie. She wanted to believe the man was telling the truth, but she was just as scared as Gianna.

Gianna's voice rose, trembled. "We *saw* them, Avery. They're not gonna let us go. We can identify them."

Avery's throat burned. "We're going to get out of this. I promise, we'll find a way." She said it like a vow, as if the sheer force of her will would give her an idea to escape.

Then the bedroom door slammed open, the knob banging against the wall leaving a mark. Avery prayed her mother hadn't decided to come by, that Bobby had gone home, that no one else was going to be trapped with these dangerous people.

The broad man with the hard jaw and dark eyes stood in the threshold. Avery jumped, and Gianna whimpered. They both instinctively shrank back. He slapped zip ties against his palm. Avery stared at them, sickly mesmerized. She knew what was going to happen and was helpless to stop it.

Tears spilling freely, Gianna cried, "Please don't hurt us."

"I'm not gonna hurt you," he said flatly, "if you behave."

He stepped into Gianna's bedroom, looming like a thundercloud. "If everything goes smooth, we're outta here in a couple hours."

Gianna sobbed harder.

He frowned and pointed at Avery. "You. Come here."

"What are you doing?" Avery snapped, trying to sound strong, but her voice trembled. She forced herself to stand, legs wobbling. She *would not* cry. She had to *act* strong, no matter how scared she was.

"I have an errand, it won't take long, and I'm not leaving you two free to pull any stunts."

An *errand*? Avery's heart pounded. If he left—*if*—maybe she could reach a phone. Or scream. Or—

He spun her around and snapped the zip tie around her wrists, tight enough to sting. She gasped as he pushed her down onto the hardwood floor

"Ow!" Her tailbone struck hard, pain shooting up her spine.

"Sorry," he said in a tone filled with humor. He grabbed her ankles and cinched them together. She winced. "You'll be fine," he said.

Then he moved to Gianna, who cried softly as he bound her in the same way, but let her remain sitting in the rocking chair. He looked at her with a hint of concern, which surprised Avery. "You're okay, right?" He actually sounded like he cared.

Gianna nodded, still crying.

"I'm not going to hurt you, girl, not if you behave. I told you that earlier, and I mean it. But this"—he motioned to their bound limbs—"is just in case either of you gets an idea while I'm gone that you can sneak out. And I let your parents go sit in the living room, so they're a little more comfortable. I'm not a monster."

"Did you tie them up, too?" Avery demanded.

He grinned. "Yeah, I did, they're fine. But you're not going to be here alone. My partners are staying behind. Remember, one of my people is hurt, and I can't risk bravery and stupidity at the same time. Got it? If you try anything, you will be hurt. That, I promise. This is almost over."

Gianna nodded, trembling.

Avery didn't flinch. She glared at him with more hatred than she thought she had in her soul.

He smirked at her like she amused him, winked, then stepped out and pulled the door shut.

Avery stuck out her tongue at the door. It was stupid, but made her feel a little better.

Then she turned to Gianna, whose face was wet with tears.

"We're gonna get out of this," Avery said again, her voice low, firm. "I promise."

Brock stepped into the bedroom, quietly closing the door behind him. Rena sat cross-legged on the queen-sized bed, talking to Sam, holding a damp cloth to Sam's sweaty forehead.

"How is he?" Brock asked.

"His fever's climbing," Rena said. "The pain meds helped, but the buckshot's still in there. He needs a hospital, Brock."

"I know." His jaw clenched.

"I'm good," Sam croaked, flashing a wan grin. "I'm just lying here for the view."

"You're not good," Rena snapped, brushing a strand of hair from his clammy face. "You're playing tough, but it's only going to get worse."

Brock paced a few steps, stared out the window. The trees outside dipped under the weight of the increasing rain. He had to go, but he was nervous about leaving Rena and Sam here alone. What if someone else came to the house? What if that kid's mother calls and no one answers?

This was all going south fast.

"Everyone's tied up," he said finally. "I just need to collect the last contract and deliver it to Robinson. Then I'll call, you get Sam ready, and then we're gone."

Rena's eyes narrowed. "What do we do about everyone here?" She motioned toward the door.

"They stay tied. Someone'll be by tomorrow when the girl doesn't come home. Cops, maybe. But by then, we'll be far out of Texas."

"We should leave now. Forget the contract. Forget the money. I don't care anymore."

Sam said, "We can't, sis. I agree with Brock, we finish the job. I can go now. We don't need to stay here. I'll just lie down in the back—"

"No," Brock said. "It's too risky, and you're better off here in bed. I know where I'm going, I'll circle back here and get you both. One hour, ninety minutes, tops."

Rena reached for his hand. "One hour. Promise me."

He nodded. "If I call you, and I *don't* come back, you take their truck and drive south. Get Sam to a clinic where nobody asks questions."

"I'm *not* leaving you behind."

"You *will.* If it all goes sideways, I'll give Robinson up, throw him to the wolves if I need to. But you don't stay. I need to know that you and Sam are safe."

A beat of silence.

"Rena, say it. Say you agree with the plan."

Her lips trembled. Finally, she nodded.

He leaned in, kissed her on the lips. What he'd give to be home, with Rena in his arms. Or playing card games with Sam. He should *never* have taken this job. But the money . . . Damn, the money was so good. He'd worked for Robinson a few times over the years. Nothing like this had happened. The jobs had been simple, breezy, in and out, get paid.

This job was supposed to be simple. It had been anything but.

"One more thing. The redhead—Avery? She's smart. Dangerous-smart. Don't trust her. Keep this door open. Listen. But don't untie anyone. I mean it. No matter what happens, no matter what they say."

Rena nodded again. "Hurry back," she whispered as he walked out.

Bobby huddled in the hayloft, his damp hoodie clinging to his skin, breath shallow as he peered through the knothole in the barn wall. The rain had started as a drizzle. Now it drummed steadily on the barn roof.

He should have gone home. He *should* have left when Avery told him to go home. He had come to that conclusion after thinking hard about what he should do. He had been about to leave when he heard the stranger on the porch and, from Bobby's vantage point in the barn, he watched as the angry man was talking about doing one more job or something like that. Then he'd leave.

As soon as the man left, Bobby could go inside, and find out what was really going on.

What if he hurt his sister? What if he took her?

Bobby didn't want anything to happen to his sister.

The man had been on the phone for only a few minutes, then he went back inside and Bobby decided to wait it out. He *should* go home, but if the man really did leave, Bobby had to be here to help Avery and the Mendozas.

And he was terrified to leave the barn for fear that someone would see him and he'd be trapped in the house with everyone else. At least from his vantage point he could keep an eye on everything and when the stranger left, he would go help them.

Then suddenly, the sound of a diesel engine roared to life.

Bobby flinched, his heart pounding so hard in his chest it hurt. He leaned closer to the hole and saw the black truck pull out of the garage, churning mud behind its tires.

He waited until he didn't hear the truck anymore, then he climbed down the ladder as fast as he dared, his feet slipping on the slick rungs.

Avery's ATV was right there, between the barn and the garage. Carefully, he opened the door . . . the wind pulled it from his hand so roughly that his palm was raw. He winced and looked down at the angry wet scrape. He shook it out, hoping the pain would go away fast. He looked both ways, saw no one, and ran the ten feet to the ATV.

The key wasn't in the ignition.

He checked the rear compartment where they often put keys for safekeeping.

Not there, either.

"Dang it," he muttered.

He had to make a choice: go home on foot through the mud and rain, risking running into the black truck coming back from wherever it had gone . . . or risk sneaking into the house.

He chose his sister.

Bobby crept around the garage, sticking to the shadows. The rain soaked him, his socks squishing in his boots. They were supposed to be waterproof, but the rain came down through the openings around his ankles. Still, he kept moving toward the house. He didn't want to walk across the porch because if someone else was inside, they might see him.

He reached the back windows, stood on tiptoe, and was still too short.

Bobby ran back to the barn, grabbed a wooden crate, carried it back to the first window. Climbed onto the crate, peered inside.

A large bed, unmade. Dresser with clutter. A desk and a chair and a rocking chair and a pile of yarn. Mr. and Mrs. Mendoza's bedroom, he thought. No one was there.

He brought the crate over to the second window, climbed up, and saw Gianna's face practically right there. He tapped on the glass.

Gianna turned, surprise on her face. It was her bedroom, he realized, and she was probably freaked out seeing him in the window.

He smiled, then he saw Avery on the floor and became confused. She had her hands behind her back and he realized she was tied up.

Avery jerked; her eyes wide.

He mouthed, "Are they all gone?"

She shook her head frantically, then turned, eyes darting toward the open bedroom door.

Bobby squinted through the rain-spotted glass.

A woman stepped into the hallway, directly into his line of sight. She froze when she saw him.

Her mouth fell open in surprise—then rage.

Avery screamed, "*Run, Bobby! Run!*"

He jumped down from the crate, his foot slipping. Pain flared in his ankle as he hit the mud, but he shook it out as he scrambled to his feet and sprinted around the back of the garage, then behind the barn, and into the muddy fields. He thought he heard a shout behind him, but then he only heard the rain and thunder and the hammering of his own heartbeat.

He didn't look back.

CHAPTER SIXTEEN

As the rain poured onto the barn's corrugated metal roof and the wind whistled through tiny cracks in the structure, Jake stared at the horizontal slits in the western wall of the barn and realized that someone had deliberately cut them. They were flush with the gutter, so because the downspouts were clogged and the gutters filled with debris, the water flowed directly into the barn through one-foot-long, half-inch-high slits—two of them in each corner.

Jake squatted and ran his fingers around the rough wood, which had been cut recently. On purpose. Jake couldn't fathom who would do such a thing.

The hay up here was not just damp; between the rain last night and what had come in today, it was saturated. He didn't know if he could salvage any of it, except for maybe the hay bales closest to the edge of the loft.

He called down to the floor of the barn. "Mateo! I need a couple two-by-fours and my toolbox."

"What'd you find?" Mateo asked.

"Someone cut holes into the barn wall."

"You sure?"

"Damn sure," Jake muttered.

He cleared the hay out of the way. Mold and mildew grew fast in humid northeast Texas. Most wouldn't be salvageable. The only food they had for the animals was the alfalfa in the bins below, which would be gone in a couple of days. After he fixed the holes, he'd ask Lyla to help him pull out any hay that was dry. They'd stack it in an empty stall for now, until the loft could be dried out and repaired.

Their livestock could graze when the rain stopped, but farm animals needed both grazing and feed. This would cost them out of pocket, because their insurance wouldn't cover the hay. And their high deductible would make fixing the barn costly.

He kicked a bundle of ruined hay. Dammit! It was one thing after another.

"Jake?" Lyla's voice came from below. "You okay?"

He didn't want to upset his sister, though Lyla was the least likely to get upset about anything. She was so even-tempered that Avery made it a game to try and rile her up.

"Just angry."

"About?"

What did he say? His parents had never lied to him about anything, opting to keep him included in the good and bad of running a farm. And it would come out anyway, he just didn't want her to worry.

"I think someone cut through the wall here. I'm going to fix it."

He heard Mateo say something, but not what he said. Then Mateo called, "I got the toolbox on the pulley!"

Jake walked over to the ladder, then stopped. The floorboards were mushy.

How long had the water been seeping through? How much damage was there?

He squatted near where he had pushed away the hay. Touched the unfinished wood. It was damp and soggy.

The entire loft was going to have to be replaced. He hoped he'd caught the damage before it seeped into the walls, otherwise they'd have far more repairs than he expected.

This was something he and his dad could have done with Mateo's help. They'd made major repairs before on the barn, the house; ever since Jake was ten he'd been able to handle most repairs with some guidance. He liked working with his hands. But his dad had done the bulk of the work. Could Jake do this alone? Even with Mateo and Lyla—who was far handier with tools than Avery or Bobby—Jake didn't think they could fix such extensive damage without professional help.

Which meant more money out of pocket. Money that they couldn't afford to spend when they were barely breaking even.

He went over to the pulley and hoisted up the heavy toolbox. Mateo climbed the ladder, saw that Jake had moved all the hay to the side. "Most, if not all of it, has to go," Jake said. "Those"—he gestured to a smaller stack of bales near the edge of the loft—"are dry, but I'll have Lyla go through them to make sure."

"That's nearly three-quarters of the hay wet?" Mateo said in disbelief. He inspected it, shook his head. "Damn."

Jake picked up a two-by-four, his hammer, and a box of nails. He blocked first one hole, then the others. It didn't take long, but it was a temporary fix. When the storm passed, he would need to check the entire wall for damage. Maybe he could replace just a few boards, and not the entire wall. Ditto for the loft. It might not all be ruined.

"What do you think happened?" Mateo asked.

"Someone came in and cut holes in my wall," Jake said bluntly. "Sabotage."

"You think?

"Yes, I do!" Jake didn't want to get angry with Mateo, he had worked on the farm almost since Jake's birth. He was practically family. He breathed out. "I'm sorry."

"Hey, it's okay, I get it."

Lyla called up, "I finished with your horses, Jake. Mom isn't back yet."

He looked at his watch. "It's only been thirty minutes," he said, standing on the edge of the loft. "If the animals are secure, go on inside."

"I want to help."

"You have. Go get your lunch, then come back and you can go through the hay that we might be able to salvage. Okay?"

"Fine. But you need to eat, too. Mom made me promise to get you to eat."

"We'll be in in a few minutes," he said.

Reluctantly, his sister left.

Jake checked his work and made sure no more water was coming in. "Seems to be good," he said. "Let's get a quick bite, then I need to inspect the creek and the drains."

"I'm not going to object to eating," Mateo said and followed Jake down the ladder. "But Penny asked me to go over to the Pritchards' place, they're having some trouble with their generator. I'll get back as soon as I can."

"Eat, then go. And you have your own house to worry about."

"Miriam has things under control."

"We're okay here, now that I have the holes plugged," Jake said. "If I need you, I'll call."

"If you're sure," Mateo said, sounding skeptical.

"I'm sure," Jake said, a little irritated. He wasn't his father, he didn't have the experience and there were some things Jake was still learning, but he was capable of taking care of this land. Mateo sometimes made it seem like everything Jake did was wrong, without actually saying it.

Or maybe that was Jake projecting his own doubts on Whisper Creek Ranch's longtime employee.

He opened the door and Mateo put a hand on his shoulder. Jake tensed. He didn't want any more criticism.

Instead, Mateo said, "Jake, you have a lot on your shoulders and you're handling it well. But it's never a sin to ask for help."

"I know," he said. "I appreciate it. But I think we have it under control here."

"You do. But if something else happens, call me. My loyalty will always be to the McKenna family."

When they stepped out of the barn, Lyla was standing on the porch watching a white truck bounce over the increasingly rough road, heading toward the house. Penny stepped out and stood next to her.

Jake glared at the white Verdacorp truck.

He strode over to the vehicle before Clive Robinson could get out. When Clive tried to open the door, Jake pushed it closed. He didn't care about the rain or wind; he wanted Clive gone.

Clive rolled down his window. "Jake, please. It's just me. I need to talk to your mom. I have an offer I think she'll agree to, something that will satisfy everyone."

"We're not selling. We've told you and Mitchell that over and over."

"But you want to expand your farm?"

Jake knew there was a catch, there had to be.

"Come back after the storm and talk to my mom."

"The offer is only good this weekend."

"Then the answer is no."

"You don't even know what it is."

"I don't care."

"Eight hundred acres—half of the Baldwin property we just bought—for the two hundred acres between the Coulters' place and our pasture. That's a four-to-one ratio."

Jake laughed, he couldn't help it. "I don't believe you."

"I have the contract right here."

"I know there's a catch, because there's no way in hell Mitchell would give us four times more land than he's getting. And you want us to sign tonight, without a lawyer? Do you think my mom is stupid?"

"I think she's one of the smartest women I've ever met. I like your mom; I don't want to screw her or your family." Clive reached over to the passenger seat and grabbed a folder. "Where is she?"

"None of your business."

Clive frowned, looked out at the dark sky and swirling wind.

"When she gets back, give her this. Have her call me *tonight*." He thrust the folder at Jake. He grabbed it and stuffed it under his jacket to keep it dry. "I know my brother can be a bit of a dick," Clive said as he turned the ignition. "He tried to buy the whole farm when all he really wants is two hundred acres to give us a contiguous set of parcels. It's a win-win, no tricks. So, think about it, have Ellie call me, okay?"

"No promises," Jake said. He marched up the porch steps and stood with Mateo, Lyla, and Penny as they watched Clive turn around and drive back the way he came. Their driveway was a mess, the gravel sinking into the mud. He hoped his mom got back soon.

"What did he give you?" his great-grandmother asked.

"He says they want to trade half of the land they bought from Baldwin for two hundred acres of ours—the section where our cattle currently graze."

"A trick," Penny said. "I don't trust any of the Robinsons, not even Clive."

Jake agreed with his great-grandmother, but he couldn't figure out how they could cheat them out of their land. His mom had a good lawyer, and she already knew about most of Verdacorp's sneaky clauses. "I'm going to put this inside with Mom's papers."

"I was coming out to get you," Penny said. "It's after two, and Bobby isn't home yet."

"Did you call the Mendozas?"

"Avery is spending the night, Bobby left an hour ago. I'm getting worried."

"I'll call over there," Jake said. He wasn't worried yet—the road wasn't flooded, and Bobby was probably still looking for the cat, though he should have come home when Mom told him to.

"Oh, and I talked to Millie a bit ago. She and George decided to visit their youngest daughter down in Frisco for the weekend and hoped you or Mateo could feed and water their bulls and chickens tomorrow and Sunday. Said they'd be home early afternoon."

"That's kind of last minute," Jake said. He'd watched the Coulters' animals many times, but they always gave him plenty of notice when they needed him.

"My guess is they don't like the look of the storm and wanted to get out before the roads were cut off."

Mateo said, "I can go over there after I fix the Pritchards' generator."

"No need until the morning," Penny said. "Millie said the animals were taken care of for the day."

Jake said, "If you can do it in the morning on your way here? I don't know what the fields are going to be like, whether I'll be able to take a horse or an ATV over there."

Mateo nodded. "Will do. I'm going to grab some food and head out, then." He went into the house.

Jake was relieved he didn't have to leave the house. He was worried about the break-in at Baldwin's place, and that the thieves may come here. They didn't have anything of value, but maybe the thieves didn't know that. He was the man of the house, and he took that responsibility to heart.

Not to mention that the barn had been sabotaged and they had their own animals and land to care for.

"Lyla, take an ATV and check the level of Whisper Creek," Jake said. "I'll call over to the Mendozas and find out when Bobby left. I may have to drive over there and get him." If Bobby got the ATV stuck again, Jake would take away his privileges. He'd spent more time fixing the ATVs after Bobby rode them than anyone else, and only two weeks ago he'd driven one into a ditch and Jake had to hook up his winch to get it out. There was a deep dent in the front bumper.

"Will do," Lyla said, sounding more excited than she should.

"Don't take any risks," Jake warned her. "But if the creek is past the third mark on the pole, the low pasture will flood." He didn't have to tell her that it would only get worse because the rain showed no sign of letting up.

He went inside to call the Mendozas.

Travis checked on Timber, then poured himself another whiskey, brought it outside, and sat heavily in the padded rocking chair on his porch. Titan followed him, laid at his feet, watching him. Concerned.

"I'm okay," he lied as he scratched the dog between his ears.

Dogs loved unconditionally. Feed them, speak kindly, shelter them, and they were loyal for life. He didn't need people when he had a dog.

He stared out at the muddy yard. The field of wildflowers that started to pop out again after the hailstorm was drenched, flowers of every hue pressed into the ground, choked and dying. The rain was destructive, coming straight down, the gray clouds dark, fierce, angry. It wasn't cold, he could sit here all day and night if he wanted, just watching the storm move in and move out.

He'd done it before.

He sipped his whiskey, reached down to itch the leg that was no longer there, and swore. Drank more, because being drunk was the only thing that erased the phantom itch.

He knew it could have been worse. He knew he could have been dead. Or lost his entire leg instead of just the half below the knee. Or both legs, like a buddy of his who'd stepped on a land mine and was unlucky enough to have survived.

That's what Travis thought, but Chris was a better man. Chris had no legs, but moved around better than Travis. Last year, a couple months before John died, Travis had gone down to Houston to spend the weekend with Chris and his family. Chris, whose wife didn't leave him like Travis's had; Chris, who had two kids before losing his legs and three more since; Chris, who had to be in pain 24/7 but didn't drink or complain. Chris had gone to college and now taught U.S. history in high school and said he had never been happier. He laughed as he wheeled around in his "sports chair" as he called it. His upper body strength enabled him to navigate short distances on crutches.

Chris was a good man who had been given a bum rap and hadn't let it stop him.

Travis scowled. Damn fucking pity party. Chris would be so disappointed in him if he saw him now.

John would also be disappointed. Would be? He had been, and then he was dead, and Travis couldn't prove anything to his perfect brother. John would never know if he turned his life around.

So why even try? Why did he even care?

Because Jake looks at you not with pity, but with disgust.

His nephew hid it well, but Travis saw the truth in his dark eyes that were so much like his brother's. He was a drunk, and Jake knew he wouldn't change.

He didn't *want* to change. He just wanted to be left alone with his dog until he died.

Travis drained his whiskey and slammed the glass down on the handmade wood table. His grandpa had made this before Travis had been born. Cut, sanded, built, all from wood in the yard and his own hands.

Usually, Travis could hear any approaching vehicle before he saw it, but the storm was loud, masking the engine of the Ford truck. So, when he saw it turn the bend he stared as if he was hallucinating. Until he recognized Clive Robinson.

Titan's head came up as Travis tensed. The dog watched, ears alert, looking as if he might attack. Travis had never trained Titan to be an attack dog, but he was a German shepherd, and they were naturally protective. Travis had trained him to be a service dog, to help him if he fell, to bring him his pain meds when he couldn't walk. To remind him to eat when he rarely felt hungry.

Travis didn't move. He watched as Clive pulled the truck almost up to the porch. The house itself was on a small knoll, mostly safe from the flooding in the fields. His grandparents had lived here for nearly twenty years, after Milton and Penny had given the big house to John and Ellen when they got married.

Travis had moved in when Penny lost her driver's license and moved in with John. He hadn't wanted to, but John convinced him. And maybe, Travis realized, he would have died in that pitiful apartment in Dallas. At least here, he could die in a slice of paradise, on the land he grew up on and still loved.

Clive was drenched as soon as he stepped from his truck. He frowned as he trekked up the stairs to where Travis sat. Titan watched him, unmoving. Clive smiled at the dog. The dog didn't smile back. Neither did Travis.

"You'd better go home before you won't be able to make it home," Travis said. "Because you're sure as hell not staying here, and Ellen will kick you out faster than boots hit the saloon floor on payday."

"I dropped off a contract for Ellen to look at, but she needs to sign this weekend. We need it Sunday night so we can file first thing Monday morning."

"Ellen isn't selling to you or anyone," Travis said.

He had pushed Ellen to sell right-of-way to Verdacorp because it would have given her the money she needed to keep the farm. But she didn't want to, and she had good reasons—well, some good reasons, and some reasons that were just stubborn. But he respected his sister-in-law, and if she didn't want to sell, he would back her play.

"We need the two hundred acres between the Coulters' house and our property line."

Travis frowned, thought. "That square that abuts Privett Road?"

"Yes."

"That's part of our primary grazing land. Why do you want it?"

"It connects our property to our right-of-way through the Coulters' property. Mitchell, kicking and screaming, has agreed to trade eight hundred acres from the Baldwin property for that two-hundred-acre parcel."

Travis laughed. "You want me to believe that your cheap-ass brother who would sell his soul for a deal would give Ellen four times the land? And Baldwin's property is choice—"

"Yes," Clive interrupted, one eye to the north, where lightning sliced across the dark sky. A roll of thunder followed quickly.

Clive pulled a folder out from under his jacket and handed it to him. "This is a copy of what I gave Ellen. Read it. Look at the map. You'll see it's on the up-and-up. We need that land."

They *needed* it? "Why?" Travis asked. "You sound desperate."

"Like I said, it connects to the Coulters' land, and to other parcels we have. Talk to her. Convince her. You were on board last year."

Slowly, Travis nodded. "I was, until Verdacorp started dicking around with our neighbors. Until you started overpaying for land that John and Ellen were trying to buy. And then pushing her to sell not a week after John was buried."

"That wasn't me," Clive said, having the good sense to avert his eyes.

"Yeah, Clive, it was," Travis said. "You and Mitchell are a team, brothers, partners. You went too far."

"I'm sorry about that."

"Tell Ellen, not me."

"I have. She's so stubborn, you'd think she was born a McKenna rather than marrying into the family."

"Must be why John fell so hard for her," Travis mused.

"Are you going to help?"

"No."

"What? Dammit, Travis!"

"I'll talk to her tomorrow, see what she's thinking, look at the contract, and give her my honest opinion."

"Which is?"

"I don't have one yet. I need to read this"—he held up the folder—"and make sure you're not trying to screw her over."

Clive stared at him, then gave him a nod. "Okay. Thanks. Remember, I need this signed before nine AM Monday."

"I heard you the first time."

Travis watched Clive run back to his truck and drive off, mud and water spraying out from his tires on both sides of his dirty truck.

He stared at the papers in his hand. Glanced down at Titan, scratched him again between his ears. The dog relaxed when the truck was out of sight.

"What are the Robinsons up to now?" Travis asked Titan.

Titan didn't respond. He probably thought the exact same thing Travis did.

The Robinsons were up to no good.

CHAPTER SEVENTEEN

Ellen stood on Margery's front porch and watched the rain fall hard on the ground while she talked to Dr. Ron Patel. He'd called her back twenty minutes after she left her message. Margery's blood pressure was still elevated. He didn't think she needed the hospital, but asked Ellen if she could stay a few hours to monitor.

"I can't," Ellen said. "My kids are home with my grandmother, and if I don't leave now, I may not make it back before Whisper Creek floods."

"How difficult would driving be right now?" he asked.

"Not too bad. But in an hour? I don't think I'd make it, let alone if I stay any longer."

"Do you have room at your house for Margery?"

"I was thinking about that earlier," Ellen said. They could always make room, even if she had to put the kids on the floor in the family room. "If Margery goes into labor and Rock Creek floods, she won't be getting out for a couple days. I'll bring her to my place and keep an eye on her."

"Is there any chance your property will be flooded? I hear the rain isn't going to let up until tonight."

"The farm is at risk, but our house is raised—we'll be okay. We have plenty of food if we're trapped for a couple days." She really hoped it didn't come to that.

"Call me later and let me know how she's doing."

"Thanks, Ron."

Ellen ended the call, then turned to find Susie standing in the doorway.

"It's bad, isn't it?" Susie said. "Is Margery going to be okay?"

Ellen wanted to reassure her, even though she couldn't make promises. Still, Margery was young and healthy, and the baby's heartbeat was strong.

"Everything is going to be fine," Ellen said. "But, like I said to Dr. Patel, if Rock Creek floods, you'll both be trapped here. If Margery wasn't pregnant, it wouldn't be a big deal—you have food and a generator. But now? It could stress her, and stress could cause her blood pressure to spike."

"Are you sure you can get through to your house? I mean, you can stay here, we have plenty of room."

"If we leave soon, we'll get through. Go pack a suitcase for you and your sister. I'll explain everything to Margery."

"No," Susie said. "I'm staying. I can't leave the animals, especially if the road floods and we can't get back up here. I'll be fine."

"Are you sure?"

"I trust you to keep my sister safe."

Ellen smiled and squeezed her arm to reassure her as they walked back inside.

"I'll pack her bag," Susie said and went down the hall to the bedrooms.

Margery looked up from where she lay on the couch, concern and confusion on her face. Ellen sat next to her and explained everything Dr. Patel had said, and that there was more than enough room at her house for Margery.

Margery was surprisingly calm about it; in fact, she seemed relieved, which told Ellen that this was the right choice.

═

Ten minutes later, Ellen eased her truck down the steep, muddy driveway. Rain lashed the windshield in relentless sheets of water, the wipers barely keeping up. The roughly paved, part gravel single lane turned to a slick ribbon as Ellen navigated the narrow road. Cypress and pine towered above them on each side. Margery sat beside her, one hand resting protectively on her belly, the other clutching the handle above the door, her knuckles white.

The entrance to the recreation area to the east, that spread from the road to the river, was blocked off with a rusty gate. There were so many trails and wonderful day trips to hike in this area, many with stunning views of the river, but today the paths would be dangerous and mudslides into the river a real threat.

They continued down the road and Ellen was able to pick up the pace a bit as it both widened and straightened and turned from mostly gravel to mostly paved. Moments later, as the trees parted, Rock Creek came into view.

Here, Rock Creek was more an inlet off the Red River, a wide branch that ended at the raised road, shored up by large rocks. It was a pretty good fishing spot, according to Travis, though Ellen wasn't one for fishing. She didn't have the patience.

Rock Creek was massively swollen. When she arrived less than ninety minutes ago, it had been moving swiftly beneath the road through a concrete culvert. Now, the water had risen threefold, a churning brown mass that had spread wide. The banks had long since vanished, trees emerging from the water along the edge. It frothed and surged, touching the road.

The culvert was no longer enough to channel the creek. Water pooled and roiled as it funneled into the narrow pipe, and the overflow surged toward the edge of the pavement, mere feet from breaching the roadbed. The roar of the water thundered through the closed windows.

"Oh my God, Ellen!" Margery gasped, her voice high and tight. "Are we going to make it?"

"Yes." Ellen didn't let herself blink. "It hasn't topped the road. We're going now. Remember what Dr. Patel said—remain calm, Margery. You *have* to stay calm."

But her own hands were clammy, gripping the steering wheel too tightly. She eased her truck forward. The tires slipped slightly on the wet incline, and she instinctively let off the gas. Then gently, slowly, she guided them toward the crossing.

The bridge was nothing more than a wide cement slab laid across the culvert—a country solution across virtually all the creeks in their valley. Here, it was raised and strengthened because Rock Creek often rose.

On either side, the creek surged just beneath the road. A fallen tree, its gnarled limbs stripped of leaves, shot under them in the current like a torpedo. Another slammed against the downstream side of the culvert, wedging at an angle, creating a partial dam.

Ellen's throat was dry. She felt the subtle vibration of the flood beneath them as the car rolled over the slab. The sound of water filled her ears, louder even than the rain.

"Hold on," she muttered, not just to Margery. She had to keep her wits about her.

Midway across, the wind gusted hard from the northeast, rocking her heavy truck. The water lapped at the very edge of the road now. A stick, a branch—no, part of a fence post, barbed wire sticking up—skimmed the road's shoulder and vanished beneath the car as they passed.

Margery whimpered beside her.

"Almost there," Ellen said. "We're okay, Margery. We're okay."

A hard bump jolted them—the back tire dipped into a pothole

hidden beneath a puddle—and for a split second, Ellen felt the wheel tug sideways. She clenched her jaw, corrected the drift, and accelerated gently.

Then they were over. Just like that, safe on solid road again.

Ellen exhaled. Her shoulders slumped an inch, her pulse still racing.

"You okay?" She glanced at Margery, but her gaze rested on the generally quiet inlet behind them that now roared like a river.

"Is it worse farther down?" Margery asked, her voice trembling.

"Rock Creek usually floods first when we get this kind of rain," Ellen said. "So we should be okay for now."

"But this is a main road and it's going to be underwater in minutes. How are we going to get to your house?"

"The other creeks cut through farmland; they have more space to spread out." Which wasn't going to do her crop any favors, but right now that was the least of her concerns. "But I'll drive as fast as I dare."

She turned off Rock Creek Road and headed west, leaving Rock Creek behind them. The road was riddled with water-filled divots and scattered branches. The rain was so dense now it felt like driving through a car wash, the wipers unable to keep up, forcing her to drive slow.

She just prayed Whisper Creek wasn't as bad, or they wouldn't make it home.

CHAPTER EIGHTEEN

By the time Brock turned off the crappy, unpaved main road and onto the crappier, rougher, mud-and-gravel drive leading to the Coulters' farmhouse, the storm had fully arrived. Sheets of rain lashed the windshield in relentless waves, the wipers doing little more than smearing the water from side to side. Thunder rolled low and deep, like distant artillery. A jagged fork of lightning tore the sky open just as the house came into view—a homey silhouette hunched against the horizon.

He pulled up close to the porch, tires crunching over wet gravel, and killed the engine. The rain drummed fiercely on the roof of his truck. Brock sat for a moment, watching the house. No lights. No movement. The place looked deserted.

But after what happened with Baldwin, he didn't know if he trusted the word of Tom Garza anymore.

Still, it didn't look like anyone was home. No truck in the carport. The chickens were locked tight in their hutch. He couldn't hear them over the wind and rain, but he imagined they were as annoyed as he was.

He didn't want to be here. But he wanted the money more than he worried about the consequences.

He stepped out into the storm, boots splashing in the rising puddles, the bottom of his jeans immediately soaked. The slicker he put on to run up the steps to the covered porch did little to protect him from the rain. He slid it off onto a sturdy wood chair by the door. All plants and lighter furniture were gone; the charming farmhouse now looked stark and abandoned.

The screen door screeched as he pulled it open, the wooden door behind it locked.

But he was hired because he was good with locks. Sam was good with security systems. He didn't have Sam today, and it wouldn't matter if he were here. The old Coulters didn't have an alarm.

Fifteen seconds later he was inside. He didn't worry about anyone seeing him, no neighbors were in line of sight. He shut the door firmly behind him, let his eyes grow accustomed to the dimmer light indoors.

It smelled like old wood and something faintly medicinal—liniment, maybe. Something his grandma used to put on her arthritic joints. He paused in the doorway, dripping, heart ticking a little faster than usual. Not fear. Just alertness. Awareness. The kind that comes from doing things you aren't supposed to be doing, in places you're not supposed to be.

He moved through the front room, boots creaking against the worn hardwood floor. A floral-print couch. Two modern reclining chairs in front of a television a quarter of the size of his. A TV too small to watch a football game, for sure. A china cabinet filled with fading family photos and a porcelain Jesus. An entire wall of portraits through the years, of weddings and births, of school milestones and family gatherings.

A folded flag centered on the mantel, framed by two photos: one of a handsome young man at his high school graduation with his mom and dad—the Coulters—on each side, and two young girls standing in front. The other of the same young man in uniform, the standard military portrait with the American flag in the background.

Above the memorial was a framed cross-stitch that read: *As for Me and My House, We Will Serve the Lord.*

A lot of clutter, but clean and neat. A house in order, of quiet routine. A family that had come and gone and left two old people with just each other and a few farm animals.

This job should be easy.

Brock walked toward the study, the one room he'd been told to search. He was to leave no trace—no drawers left open; no items disturbed. The Coulters were old. If they ever noticed the contract was gone, they'd just assume they'd misplaced it. That was the idea. No alarms. No questions. They'd ask for a copy and be given the *right* copy—the one they were supposed to have been given in the first place.

Brock didn't know how the contracts had been screwed up; he'd simply been hired to retrieve them. He only worked for Mitchell Robinson on occasion, whenever Mitchell needed a light hand and no trace back to him.

He should never have brought Rena and Sam along this time. They'd joined him only infrequently, when the job wasn't dangerous. And he thought this job would be a piece of cake. Four houses, four days, two hundred thousand bucks. And, sure, he had needed Sam's electronics skill in two of the homes. But he could have done it differently, without putting the two people he loved in this world at risk.

It had been anything but easy, anything but safe. And now his brother-in-law had buckshot in his gut and if he died, Brock might just kill Mitchell Robinson. Not because it was his fault, but because Brock loved his brother-in-law, he loved his wife, and life wouldn't be the same without Sam.

He pushed his growing grief aside. Sam wasn't dead; he would make it. They had a doctor back home in Louisiana who, for the right price, would fix Sam and look the other way, no gunshot reported to the authorities.

Brock carefully, discreetly searched the small den. This was all business. A rolltop desk, a three-drawer filing cabinet, a bookshelf filled with farm manuals and old copies of the *Farmers' Almanac*. The Coulters were orderly people: he opened the filing cabinet as the best bet for the contract. In the top drawer were records for their two bulls: breeding contracts, folders on every cow sired, health records, and more. He glanced at the bottom line—he had no idea studs could make this much money. It might be something to think about, because he wasn't going to work for Mitchell Robinson anymore.

The second drawer had insurance papers, bills, and right there in the front, a folder labeled *Verdacorp*.

Brock took it out, laid it on the desk, and opened it, careful not to let the paper crinkle too loudly. He knew no one was home, but . . . habit.

Because sometimes he robbed people quietly while they slept.

He studied the contract and frowned.

This wasn't the original.

Text, letterhead, that was right. But it was a cheap copy with an odd faint gray line running down the middle. The paper felt different, too. Too smooth. Like it came out of a home copier.

He glanced at a low table to the left of the desk, where a copier sat, the steady orange light telling him the device was asleep.

Well, shit.

Brock pulled out his phone and hit the last number who'd called him.

"Robinson."

"It's me," Brock said. "We've got a problem. The original isn't here."

A pause on the other end. Rain pelted against the windows.

"Are you sure?" Mitchell's voice was sharp, almost accusatory. "They only signed it last week. They have the original."

"I'm looking at it. Signatures are a copy. Paper doesn't even feel right."

Another pause. Then: "Tear the place apart."

"What?"

"You heard me," Mitchell said. "There's a safe. Has to be. They probably put it away after signing. Find it. If that paper ends up in the wrong hands, my business is done. I'll lose everything. Do you understand? I don't care if you rip out the goddamn floorboards. Because remember: if I don't have all four original contracts in my hands before five PM tomorrow, you get paid nothing."

The call ended.

Brock stared at the phone for a moment. That fucking asshole.

Fueled partly by anger, Brock methodically took apart the house. Fast but careful, so he didn't miss any possible hiding place. Pulled books from shelves, overturned drawers, peeled back rugs. He searched closets, cabinets, the pantry. Looked behind picture frames, under mattresses, inside the crocheted piano bench. In the master bedroom he pulled every drawer and checked the backs for false panels.

Nothing.

The house began to feel tighter around him. The storm outside screamed louder. He realized how much noise he was making. How, despite the thunder, each clatter of a drawer echoed like a gunshot.

No safe. No hiding place. No contract.

Back in the study, Brock ran a hand through his damp hair, breathing hard. The storm hadn't let up. The windows rattled in their frames now. A tree branch scraped along the siding like fingernails inside a coffin.

He pulled out his phone again and redialed.

Mitchell answered on the first ring. "Tell me you found it."

"There's no safe," Brock said, voice low. "No sign of the original. I don't think they kept it here."

Silence. Just the crackle of static.

Then Mitchell spoke, his voice harder now. "A contract doesn't disappear, Brock. If it's not there, then someone took it. And if someone took it, we're exposed."

Lightning lit up the room in stark, electric white.

"Maybe they gave it to someone. Like their lawyer or one of their kids."

"Maybe," Mitchell said, voice cold. "Maybe they did just that. I'll find out who. Be ready when I call."

Brock felt something cold crawl up his spine as the line went dead.

CHAPTER NINETEEN

Mitchell Robinson sat hunched at Presley's command post. His daughter treated the vast desk and expensive wall of monitors as her kingdom. The soft glow from the screens casting long, pale shadows across the room. He asked her to show him all the surveillance cameras. They had a security office attached to the stables, manned by one of his employees. That was to protect *his* property.

These cameras faced out, always watching the perimeter. His neighbors. His future empire.

He had enlisted his daughter Presley to help him go over the security feeds because he needed to know what happened today, before he found out that George and Millie Coulter had done something with their original contract. Mitchell was a smart man—about business, about land, about the desires of others—but he didn't have the technical skills of his daughter. While he understood the basics and what could and could not be done, he couldn't make it all work. The drones. The security cameras. How to make things go forward and back and enhance them. So, he relied on Presley. She might have the technical skills, but he was teaching her how to *see* things the way he did. Every detail mattered.

Quickly, he looked at all the footage in real time. The winding road through his property, the gently sloping fields, the tree lines that marked old boundaries. The dense foliage that bordered Whisper Creek, the slender trickle of water that united the Robinsons' land to the McKennas'.

The creek that had started the feud more than a hundred years ago. A feud he didn't think anyone remembered. Except him.

He wouldn't forget, as it had been pounded into him from every Robinson who came before him.

His father had been a stupid man. He never had vision. He'd never expanded, never turned a profit. After Grandfather died, Mitchell's dad had run the farm into the ground. He drank too much, whored around, spent money like drinking water. Mitchell didn't understand why his father rejected the land, turning it over to the laborers who Mitchell also employed, but without the free rein they'd had under his dad.

Because the land was in his blood. He wouldn't let just anyone work for him. He had the best workers in the field, the best equipment, and fetched the best prices. He had expanded because he had to; his father's ill-thought-out plans had devastated the once healthy soil. And then he created Verdacorp ten years ago, got the farm out of debt, and expanded.

Because farming was suffering, shrinking, prone to price fluctuations at the will and whim of the government.

He had to change tactics, and realized he had a head for business—better, he had a head for the business of land and all the land had to offer.

His grandfather and his great-grandfather would have been proud.

Mitchell didn't care what his worthless father thought, now a drunk living in a house Mitchell had bought him down in Dallas, with a full-time nurse because Theodore Robinson had drank himself into every health problem imaginable, and Mitchell didn't want to see him. Clive went down to visit once a week, but

Mitchell had no use for the pathetic, stupid old man who had nearly lost their legacy.

He pushed thoughts of his father aside because they always angered him. He vowed to be a man his daughter could be proud of. He had wanted more children, he'd wanted a legacy. He had Presley, a daughter worthy of him, but he needed to find a wife who could give him two or three more children. He'd thought Nicole had been the one. He had been wrong.

He focused on the camera feeds that Presley expertly managed.

To the north, the cameras offered a sweeping view of the McKennas' land and parts of the Baldwin acreage. He couldn't quite see either of their houses—trees and terrain and distance kept them obscured—but he had a clear view of their cattle herds and the southernmost edges of their crops. Enough to know when someone came and went. Enough to make guesses about routines, planting issues, harvest yields.

By this time tomorrow, the Baldwin property would be his. The paperwork was done. The deal would close at precisely five PM, and as soon as the ink dried, Mitchell planned to install a full perimeter of cameras. He already had the posts and gear ready to go in his equipment shed.

Baldwin didn't even need to survive, because the contract was signed, sealed, delivered . . . effective Saturday, April 30, 5 PM.

"I need to see all the angles pointing to the Coulters' property," he told Presley.

She popped her gum—a habit he despised, but the one time he commented on it she only popped it more—and tapped a few keys. The screens split, expanded, shifted to show three angles of the Coulters' property. Their house was the closest to his own, though still nearly a mile across two hundred acres of pasture and scrub that the McKennas owned—and he wanted. Needed. He would buy it, trade for it, do anything to have it.

No one understood that those two hundred acres were the

lynchpin in this business deal he'd been cultivating for two years. He wasn't lying to his brother: without it, they'd lose everything.

With it, they would be kings.

"I need the middle camera," he said. "The one that shows the barn and most of the house."

Click, click, click. Now that was the only feed showing, taking up the bulk of the screen, the high-definition camera catching the corner of the old farmhouse and barn. Though the recording was in color, everything looked gray because of the rain and storm clouds above. Like seeing the world in black-and-white, the occasional burst of color almost unreal.

He'd paid extra for the zoom on that one. State-of-the-art optics that could pull in a license plate from a quarter mile. He had tested it.

Mitchell enjoyed watching the land, but what he truly relished was watching *people*. The way they moved, the subtle patterns in their behavior. That was where the real power lay. Several months ago, he'd noticed the Perez boy, the son of the sheriff, sneaking onto the McKenna property late at night. So, he watched, curious. And his theory held: it didn't take long before he witnessed the teenager, Avery, meeting him under the oak tree, for a midnight picnic and a kiss.

Did Ellen know what her daughter was doing in the middle of the night? Innocence was all Mitchell saw, but he could make it far more titillating . . . if he needed to cause a rift between the McKennas and the sheriff.

Which might be sooner rather than later.

Mitchell didn't need to see everything. Just enough to know when to press, when to pull back. The land was just an important piece in a bigger game. What mattered most was control. Long ago, he'd learned that the best way to control something was to watch it without being seen, and act when necessary.

"Rewind in high speed," he told Presley. "I need to see everyone who visited the Coulters from now back to when they signed the contract last week."

She rolled her eyes; he ignored it. Fortunately, she did exactly what he asked. Yes, she was spoiled, but she was also smart because Presley was his daughter, through and through.

It took him a few minutes to adjust to watching the world in reverse.

Backwards a man exits the house and gets into a dark truck, which then drives away in reverse. Brock. He was inside for nearly an hour. A job that should have taken minutes, but the Coulters had done something with the original contract.

And he hadn't found it.

Another man walks around the house in the rain, then backs into his car, which drives away in reverse as well. Tom, making sure the Coulters were gone and no one was inside.

A truck drives up in reverse and comes to a stop. George and Millie appear outside; Millie moves from the chicken coop, unsecuring it—watching this backwards was a bit unnerving, and Mitchell reflected how human minds were designed to only look forward. Because of course he knew she was shutting the chickens into the hutch before they left for the weekend. They were protected from the rain because of the awning, but tonight they wouldn't be protected from predators who might dig under the fence, so they had locked them into this chicken house. This confirmed to Mitchell that they did intend to be gone overnight.

While Millie was at the chicken pen, *George walks backwards from the barn,* likely ensuring their two bulls were secure and fed. *They both make two trips from the truck into the house, carrying items back inside.*

Time passed, light barely changing because of the dark skies, but it was enough to remind Mitchell he was turning back the clock.

Sometimes, he wished he could turn back the clock and make different decisions, different choices.

But time didn't work like that, and the video camera gave a tainted illusion of what might have been. What could have been.

A woman on horseback gallops back in reverse, arriving at the house. She dismounts and walks backwards into the house. Moments later, she walks backwards out of the house and gets back on her horse, which trots away in reverse.

"Presley," Mitchell said. "Slow it down and show me that woman on horseback again going forward."

"Whatever you say, Daddy," Presley said.

Why did his daughter always sound so damn condescending?

But the video showed forward motion now and he saw the woman ride up to the Coulter house from the field. From the McKenna property.

Without being asked, Presley paused the video on the best view of the woman. She was blurry but Mitchell knew who that was.

Presley typed rapidly on the keyboard and the image became a bit clearer.

Ellen McKenna.

Could *she* have the original contract? Why would the Coulters have given it to her? Sure, they were friends, the McKennas and Coulters had been close since the dawn of time, Penny's sister married a Coulter and moved out to Amarillo back before Mitchell's dad had been born. The Robinsons knew everything about the McKennas and every family who had married into it.

Why would they have given Ellen the original contract? By accident? Because she asked? Why did she want it?

This was the worst thing in the world to have happened.

"Daddy, what's wrong?" Presley asked.

He didn't answer her. Because *everything* was wrong.

He had to get it back. At any cost.

CHAPTER TWENTY

Bobby ran and fell. He got up and kept running, which was really hard to do in the mud. But if he couldn't run fast, neither could anyone else. When he dared look back, he didn't see the crazy-eyed woman anymore, but tripped and fell again, his clothes completely soaked and now muddy. He scrambled up and kept moving forward, even though he'd lost a boot in mud that now went almost to his knees. Even though he was so wet he felt heavy and exhausted.

Then he reached Whisper Creek and realized he couldn't get home.

The creek cut through the valley from the Red River, usually only a trickle when it hit their property. Though years and years of rain and storms had cut a trench through the valley, it was usually easy to cross.

Not today.

The creek was now ten feet wide and he couldn't tell how deep. He could swim pretty good, but the water was moving fast, and he knew better than to go into any water that was moving this fast. There could be a flash flood, trees could fall and hit him, he could get trapped in the culvert under Orchard Lane.

He could die.

As he watched, rain falling all around, the creek continued to grow, spreading closer to him. He couldn't go back to the Mendozas; though he desperately wanted to help his sister he had no idea what to do. But there was one place he could go that should be safe. A shelter that had withstood far worse storms than this one.

He walked parallel to the creek, but far enough from the edge that he wouldn't accidentally fall in. He kept one eye on the water as he walked as fast as he could to the equipment shed where he had first looked for Cleo.

His bottom lip trembled as he lost his other boot. He was cold, wet, sore, hungry. Avery was in trouble and he couldn't help her. His mom was probably super worried about him, and what if she came out and got stuck in the creek looking for him? And he hadn't even found Cleo! What if she ran up a tree and couldn't get down?

He shook his head. He would not think bad thoughts. Avery was going to be okay, his mom was too smart to get stuck in the creek, and Cleo had found shelter.

It was taking *forever*, he thought, as he passed his ATV, now buried so deep in the mud he could barely see the seat. But food . . . he always had snacks in the storage in the back.

He unclipped the cage that he'd brought in case he found Cleo, and under the cage, in the storage box, were a couple apples, a can of cat food, a jug of water, and a bag of popcorn Grandma had given him. He put everything in the cage to make it easier to carry. They'd get wet, and wet popcorn was gross, but it was better than not eating anything.

Bobby kept walking, moving slower and slower as the water and his fatigue weighed him down. The creek was noisy, the water creeping closer and closer to him. He kept moving, thinking he should be at the shed by now. He couldn't have gotten lost, he knew all these fields, but everything looked different in the rain and he could barely see more than ten feet ahead of him.

And then he saw it, practically when he ran into it. He was

overjoyed. The ground was saturated, but he'd climb into the loft. There was old hay there, he could find something to sit on, maybe something to dry off with, like an old horse blanket. But even if there was nothing, at least he would be out of the wind, and he could bury himself in hay for warmth and to help get dry.

In his wet socks, he climbed up the ladder to the loft, balancing the cage carefully. He slipped twice but finally made it up, his heart racing. The wind shook the old wood outbuilding, but it had withstood worse storms, including the pounding hail over the weekend. It was mostly dry in the loft, except for one steady drip in the far corner.

He took off his socks and squeezed out the mud and water as he looked around. There really wasn't much here. Mostly tools and some wood crates. He took off his jacket and hung it on a protruding nail. He squeezed the water from his shirt as best he could, and his radio fell out of his waistband.

Then he had an idea. Why hadn't he thought of it before?

"Dumb, dumb, dumb!" he said out loud. His voice was scratchy and he drank a little of the water, then coughed to clear it.

He couldn't communicate on the channel his family used because the bad guys who had Avery and the Mendozas might hear. But he *could* change channels and find help from someone else.

Avery talked to her boyfriend, Ryan, on Channel 9. It was the strongest channel, because he lived down in Callisburg. They talked when Avery was grounded and couldn't use the phone, usually because she broke curfew. Bobby wasn't positive that he would be able to get through because rain and stuff messed with the radio waves, but he had to try.

"Ryan, Ryan Perez, this is Bobby McKenna. Are you there? Please answer me. Over."

Nothing but static.

Bobby tried again. "Ryan, it's Bobby. We're in trouble. Please answer. Over."

Static.

Tears burned, but Bobby tried again. And again. And again.

Rena ran back to the house in full panic. She'd chased the kid so far in the storm that she thought she wouldn't be able to find her way back; then the house came into view suddenly and the mix of relief and fear nearly brought her to her knees.

The kid got away. Hell, he could have climbed a tree and she wouldn't have noticed because the rain was coming down so hard she could barely see two feet in front of her.

She burst into the kitchen, bringing in a blast of wind and rain. She slammed the door shut and picked up her cell phone. Dialed Brock. Willed him to answer.

He didn't.

"Call me," she said into his voicemail and then ended the call and went to Sam.

"Hey," Sam said. "You're drenched. What happened?"

Sam didn't look great—pale, with dark circles under his eyes, blond hair matted to his head—but he was sitting up and there didn't seem to be fresh blood coming through his bandage. That was a relief.

He still needed a doctor.

"The brother, Bobby, who Avery told to go home hours ago, he was peeking in through the windows. He can rat us out. We have to leave. But Brock isn't answering the phone!"

"Shh," Sam said. "It's going to be okay."

"No, it's not. It's not okay! You're hurt, you need a doctor, we have four *hostages*! We've never had hostages before. This is so much worse than anything we've ever done. I don't know what to do."

Her cell phone rang and she yelped before she grabbed it. "Brock?"

"What happened?"

She told him. Then, "We have to go. I'll take their truck. Where?"

"There's an empty house; the people are gone for the weekend. I double-checked, it's safe. Go there, I'll meet you. I have one more thing to do." He gave her the address and directions.

"Meet me now. Please. I don't care about the money or anything, I just want to go home."

"I'll be there, an hour or two. It'll take fifteen, maybe twenty minutes from where you are, because the road is a mess. In fact, bring the redhead with you, just in case."

"No."

"Yes, Rena, you have to. We need the leverage just in case something goes wrong. And if it wasn't for her and her brother, we wouldn't be in this situation, would we?"

Rena didn't want to take a hostage with her. But what did it matter? Look at what they'd already done!

"Okay. We'll leave now. Don't be too late, please."

"I love you, Rena."

"I love you, too."

She ended the call. "We have to go," she told Sam.

"I heard. It's going to be okay."

"Just because you keep saying it doesn't make it true."

She grabbed a blanket from the bed and helped Sam out to the truck. It was a nice Dodge Ram Crew Cab with four full-size doors and a spacious backseat, a wheelchair lift folded up on one side. She settled Sam in the back, gave him the blanket, and turned the ignition, setting the heater to low. "I'm going to get the girl."

"I'll stay here," he said with a touch of humor. He gave her a small smile that she couldn't return.

She went back into the house and to the bedroom. Opened the door and stared at the two girls. She cut the zip ties around Avery's ankles and said, "Get up."

"Why?" Avery asked.

"Because I said so."

"Where's my brother?"

Rena shrugged. "Don't know, don't care. We're leaving. Just in case your brother was able to find someone out there."

Her lip quivered and Rena tried not to care. She tried not to think about what might happen to a ten-year-old boy in the middle of this storm.

"Get. Up," she repeated and showed the girl her gun.

She complied.

Rena took Avery to the truck and told her to climb into the driver's seat. Then she climbed into the passenger seat, cut off the zip ties on her wrists. The girl had rubbed her skin raw.

"Put your hands on the steering wheel. Both of them."

She did.

Rena took out fresh zip ties and tied first one hand to the steering wheel, then the other. "You're driving."

"I don't have my license."

"I don't care. I've been driving since I was fourteen, my guess is so have you."

Rena pulled the gear and put it in reverse. "Now, go. Or I swear, I'll shoot you in the head and toss your body into the ditch."

Her voice was serious, and as Rena watched Avery, she knew the girl believed her. She could see it in her eyes, the way they darted around, looking for escape. The resignation. The fear-filled hate.

Rena had never killed anyone before in her life.

But there was a first time for everything.

CHAPTER TWENTY-ONE

"Ryan! Your radio is squawking!"

Ryan had just gotten in from school when his mother yelled at him about his radio. He wished he hadn't even gone, most of his friends hadn't gone because of the storm, but because he lived in town he didn't have an excuse to skip.

"Thanks, Mom."

He ran up the stairs to his room and hoped it was Avery. He worried about their farm because Avery and her family were concerned, especially after the hail damaged their vineyard. He'd wanted to help them, but his dad said no. After all his lectures about being a good neighbor and helping people, he wouldn't let Ryan miss school to help the McKennas.

". . . please answer. Over."

It wasn't Avery, but the voice sounded familiar.

He grabbed his radio off the charger and depressed the talk button. "Who's this? Over."

Silence, then in a rush, "Ryan, is that you? This is Bobby McKenna and we're in trouble and I can't call home and I need you to call my mom and get help."

He didn't say over, but Ryan heard the click telling him that Bobby was waiting for a response.

"Bobby, it's Ryan. What happened? Talk slow, you're crackling. Over."

"Avery is in trouble. She's at . . . There are bad people . . . a gun. I lost my boots and am hiding in the old equipment shed near . . . Mendozas' house. Call your dad and . . . be careful because they have a gun. Over."

Ryan's head was spinning. "Bobby, I only caught part of what you said. Avery is in trouble? Where, is she? Over."

"The Mendozas. She and Gianna and Gianna's family. There are bad people . . . Avery is tied up. Call your dad! Over."

Ryan said, "I'll call my dad and I'm coming up right now. I'll call your house. You stay where you are, okay? If it's safe, I mean. Stay so someone can come get you. Where, exactly? Over."

"The Mendozas' old equipment shed. My mom and Jake know where it is. It's safe, but I'm wet and cold and I'm worried about Avery and I can't find Cleo anywhere. Over."

He was still looking for the stray cat?

"Okay, I'm calling your mom, stay there. Over."

Ryan pulled on his heavy-duty boots and ran back down the stairs, cell phone in hand. "Mom! I'm going out."

"No, you're not," she called from the kitchen.

"Mom, Bobby McKenna is trapped in a barn and they need my help."

She stepped in the doorway, drying her hands on a rag, giving him the once-over. "Are you lying to me?"

"I wouldn't lie to you. I'm calling his house now, but he called me because he couldn't reach anyone. He said that there's something weird going on at the Mendoza house." He didn't want to tell her about the gun, but he knew that if she found out he had withheld information from her, she'd call it lying and ground him for weeks.

"I'm calling your dad. The roads are a mess out there, and Rock Creek has flooded."

Rock Creek *always* flooded, but the McKennas didn't live anywhere near there. "I won't go near it. But yeah, tell Dad that Bobby says there's a stranger with a gun at the Mendozas' house."

"You are not going there," she stated.

"No, I'm going to call Jake and help him get to Bobby. Please, Mom, they need help, and you know it'll take too much time to get a deputy up there with everything else going on with the storm."

She sighed. "Keep the emergency radio on in your truck, and I swear, you'd better take every precaution on these roads. Don't go to the Mendozas, I know you want to, but stay away. You keep in touch."

"If you reach Dad, have him call me and I'll tell him everything I know, but I need to go, I'm worried about Bobby and I don't know why he couldn't reach his family."

"Do you want me to come with you?" She glanced behind her into the family room where his three younger sisters were doing homework and watching television at the same time.

"No, I don't know how long it will take." He gave his mom a quick hug. "I'll be careful, I promise. I'll call you."

And he left before she could think twice about it. He had a lot of autonomy because he didn't usually get into trouble, so he capitalized on that now. This was an unusual situation, however, and his mom could have stopped him. He was glad she hadn't.

As soon as he was in his truck, wipers moving full force against the torrent of water, he called the McKenna house.

The phone rang. And rang.

═

Jake called his mom from the corner of the porch, pulling the long kitchen cord out, as he watched the driveway, willing his brother to show up.

"Hello?" His mother's voice was clipped, tense.

"Mom, it's Jake. Bobby's not home and no one is answering at the Mendoza house. I'm going over there."

"No, stay put. I'm not far." The cell reception crackled on her end.

"Where are you?"

"Just about to turn onto Orchard from Ranch. I have to go slow."

"The creek is high, Mom. You might not get through."

"I'll get through."

"Call me as soon as you know what's going on. I can look for Bobby."

"He has to be at the Mendozas," she said, as if willing it to be true. "I'll call. And—"

Then the line cut off.

Dammit.

Lyla ran up to him. "Whisper Creek is at its banks. But it looks like the water is diverting east, not west. That's good, right?"

Partly, Jake thought. At least better than the alternative. The bulk of their pastures were west of the creek. But if it flooded to the east, they'd lose the sunflowers and half the wine grapes, not to mention, depending on the severity, Baldwin's property could flood.

Not your concern, Jake thought. It was Verdacorp's concern now.

But he thought about Greg's horses. He still had the ten-acre parcel with his house and horses, and there was no one there to make sure the horses were safe.

He hadn't heard from the sheriff if Greg's caretaker was there. Mateo took care of feeding and watering the horses this morning, but the storm had to be agitating them.

Jake looked back down the road, willing Bobby to drive up. He could have gotten the ATV stuck again—how many times had Jake had to pull Bobby out of a jam?

"Jake, what's wrong?" Lyla asked.

"Just worried about Bobby. Mom is on her way back and will stop at the Mendozas."

Lyla frowned. "She needs to get home fast. The creek is going to flood the road. She won't be able to get through."

"Mom knows." He put his arm over Lyla's shoulders and squeezed. He didn't want her to worry. He had enough worry for both of them.

Penny called out, "Jake! Ryan's on the phone."

"Avery's not here," he said, irritated.

"He asked for you."

Jake didn't want to talk to Ryan. They were friends, sure, but ever since Ryan started dating Avery at the beginning of the school year, things were just weird.

He went inside the house. "Ryan? It's Jake. I'm in the middle of—"

"Bobby called me over the radio, over the channel Avery and I use. He said that Avery is in trouble at the Mendozas' house, that there's something going on there, that a stranger is in the house and has a gun. Bobby is trapped in the old equipment shed on the other side of your creek."

"You talked to Bobby?" Had Jake not heard the radio? He didn't always have it on him when he was at home, but Lyla would have heard it in the barn.

"I don't know why he didn't reach out on your family channel," Ryan said. "Except that maybe if he's right, and there's someone with a gun at the Mendozas, he has Avery's radio. I'm on my way now, I told Bobby to stay put. I can help you get to him."

"Where are you?" Jake asked.

"Just coming up to the Sorenson Ranch. Visibility is crap."

"It'll take you at least another ten minutes to get here, probably longer. Our road is partly flooded, and Whisper Creek is about to breach to the east."

"That's where the equipment shed is," Ryan said.

"I'll get Bobby."

"I can—"

"Do you have your radio?"

"Channel nine."

"Okay, let me know when you turn onto Orchard, and I'll let you know if we need help, otherwise I'll see you at the house."

"What about Avery?"

"My mom is on her way to the Mendoza's now. I'll call and warn her that something weird is happening over there."

Jake hung up and called his mom.

But she didn't answer.

CHAPTER TWENTY-TWO

"I won't be long," Ellen said to Margery when she drove down the Mendozas' driveway. She went as slowly as possible, but her truck bounced quite a bit and she was pretty certain Margery was uncomfortable, even with the pillows all around her. "You okay here?"

"Yes," Margery said with a half smile. "I don't want to go out in the rain more than I need to."

Ellen pulled up as close to the side door as possible, but she'd be soaked even walking ten feet.

The Mendozas' truck wasn't in the garage, and the door was wide open, which seemed unusual. She wondered if there was an emergency, but if there was, Avery would have called. She saw an ATV belonging to either Avery or Bobby parked on the side of the garage, which irritated her. It should have been stored in the barn or garage since Avery was spending the night.

Still, she was getting an odd feeling that something wasn't quite right. Maybe Gianna had a medical emergency . . . but Avery would have called her. For all the times they butted heads about trivial things, Avery was a responsible teen.

Ellen jumped out of the truck and ran through the mud, up the ramp, and stood under the porch. The wind pushed the rain into her back.

She pounded on the door, looked through the window, her hands cupped so she could see in the semi-dark.

"Rose! Carl! It's Ellen!" She shouted to be heard over the rain that pounded on their roof. "Hello!"

She listened, heard nothing.

Where could they be? The barn? All four of them? Gianna's wheelchair wouldn't make it through the mud, and she couldn't walk over the uneven surface.

She tried the door; it was unlocked.

She opened it and went inside.

"Rose? Carl? It's Ellen McKenna. Are you here?"

"Ellen!" She heard a voice in the back of the house. "Ellen, help!"

She ran down the hall and opened Gianna's door. The girl was in her rocking chair and as Ellen approached, she saw that her wrists were zip-tied to the armrests.

Ellen ran over to her. "What happened?" She looked around for scissors. "Gianna, where's Avery?"

"I thought they were going to kill us, three people broke in last night, and, and, and they left with Avery!"

Ellen's blood ran cold. "Where's your mom and dad?"

"The living room, maybe? That's where they said they tied them up. I haven't seen them all day, I'm so worried!" Gianna was crying.

"I'm going to find scissors and I'll check on your parents."

Ellen ran down the hall, past the kitchen and stopped when she glanced into the guest room and saw blood on the white sheets. There was a lot of blood, bandages, scissors, prescription drugs. What the hell was going on?

She grabbed the scissors and went to the living room.

Rose and Carl were tied and gagged on the coach. Carl had a bloody gash on his forehead that had dripped and dried down the side of his face.

Ellen pulled the gags from their mouths. "Gianna," Rose said breathlessly, her voice a scratchy whisper.

"She's okay." Ellen cut their binds.

"I'm sorry. I'm sorry. I had to lie, they would have h-hurt Gianna."

"Where's Avery? Where did they take her?"

"I don't know," Rose said as she stood. Her knees gave way and she collapsed. Ellen barely caught her before she hit the floor.

"Stay here, I'll untie Gianna and bring her to you."

Ellen went back to the girl's bedroom, trying not to think about where Avery was and who had her and why.

She cut Gianna's binds off and asked where her wheelchair was.

"They took it so I couldn't leave," she said.

Ellen looked in the other rooms and found the wheelchair shoved into the master bedroom. She brought it and helped Gianna get into it, then wheeled her down to the living room.

As soon as Rose saw her, she burst into tears, resting her head in Gianna's lap.

"It was after midnight," Carl said. "We were asleep. A man—he pulled us from bed and tied us to the chairs in the kitchen."

"Did they rob you?"

He shook his head. "I don't think so. We have nothing worth much. They were waiting for something, waiting to do something, but I don't know what."

"How many?"

"Three. Two men and a young woman, she was between twenty-five and thirty. The younger man was injured, bleeding. He was shot—that much I overheard."

"You must have heard something else! What are their plans?"

He rubbed his head. "They were hired to steal something, and whoever they stole from was home when he wasn't supposed to be."

"Greg Baldwin," she said, realizing that the people who had her daughter were the ones who had shot her friend and left him for dead.

Rose said, "They got stuck in the rain last night and came here to wait it out, that's what we thought, but then they stayed in the morning. I heard one of them say they had one more job."

"The big guy left first," Gianna said. "And then Bobby was here, he came back and saw us through the window."

"He came back?" Ellen was confused.

"Avery told him to go home, over the radio. She said she was spending the night and he needed to go right home, but I guess he knew something was wrong. He came back, looked in my bedroom window, and then the woman saw him and chased him. But she came back pretty quick and said they had to leave before Bobby told anyone they were here."

Bobby. Her son. He was okay, but where was he? He wasn't at home when she talked to Jake. Was he hurt? Lost? Out wandering in the storm?

"Why did they take Avery?"

"I don't know!" Gianna said, holding her sobbing mother. "The woman—her name is Rena!" she added quickly as she remembered. "Rena. That's what the injured man called her, and he was Sam. I can't believe I just remembered that."

"What did she say?"

"They needed Avery just in case."

Ellen pulled out her cell phone but couldn't get reception, so she went to the kitchen phone and dialed 911. It rang and rang and rang. Someone would answer eventually, but when? People were probably calling in from all over the region because of the storm.

She hung up, dialed Rick Perez directly.

He answered on the fourth ring and told her to wait.

Several minutes later, he came back. "Ellie? You still there?"

"Yes."

"It's a mess out here. We just shut down County Road 371 at Mule Run, and 122 is completely impassable. I hope you don't mind one more mouth to feed tonight."

She rubbed her temple. "What? Are you stuck up here?"

"Not me. I got a message from Ryan, that he was up helping Jake because Bobby is stuck in a barn or shed or something. It was garbled, and I have two missed calls from LuAnne. She might know more."

"Rick—listen to me. Please. I'm at the Mendozas and they were held captive by three people last night. I think they're the people who shot Greg. One of them was injured. They left separately, one in their truck, and the people who have Avery are in the Mendozas' truck. Rick, they have my daughter!"

"You're at the Mendozas now? Are they okay?"

"They were tied up when I got here, Carl has a head injury, but he says he's fine. I can't stay. I have Margery Sutton in my truck with signs of preeclampsia, I need to get her in bed and resting. Bobby is out in the storm; I don't know where. I guess Jake and Ryan are looking for him? I have to get home!"

Ellen was near tears over fear for her kids.

Carl came into the kitchen. He looked older than she'd ever seen him.

"Go," he said. "I'm getting my shotgun and handgun. If they come back, I'll kill them."

"Are you sure you're okay here, the three of you?"

"Yes," he said.

"Thank you." She went back to Rick. "Can you get here?"

"I don't know," he said. "I have one deputy up that way because Rock Creek Road flooded, he's blocking the exit at the highway. He has to stay until the emergency crews can block it off. I'll send him to your place as soon as he can get there, but it'll be a while, he's going to have to come in from the south, and if he can't get through you're going to be on your own. I'll try to get up, but we have three serious accidents down here between Gainesville and Callisburg. How's Whisper Creek?"

"I don't know yet."

"Be careful, Ellie."

He ended the call.

She turned to Carl. "Are you positive you're okay? You all can come to my house, we always have room for more." It would be crowded, but safe.

"I talked to Rose. She wants to stay. This is our *home*. And I couldn't do anything to stop them."

She rested a hand on his arm, then spontaneously hugged him. "They came in the middle of the night, Carl. You didn't have warning. Keep all your doors locked, and Rick will send a deputy as soon as he can."

"Go find Avery. I'm sorry I couldn't protect her."

Guilt watered his eyes.

"I'll find her. Thank you."

She ran back out and climbed into the truck. Her phone beeped, indicating she had a message. She looked; Jake had tried calling her nine minutes ago.

She didn't want to scare Margery, so she told her the bare minimum, trying to minimize the danger, but she must not have done a good job because Margery looked terrified.

"We'll get to the house and you're going to take a nap and relax," Ellen told her. "Penny has been cooking all day, we'll fix you something."

She listened to Jake's message, but it was garbled, so she called him as she turned the truck around and headed toward Orchard Lane.

"Mom?"

"The people who shot Greg Baldwin have Avery," she said. She quickly told him what she learned from the Mendozas. "And Bobby is out there somewhere."

"He's hiding in the old equipment shed. I'm on my way to get him."

Thank God, she thought.

"I'm coming home," she said.

"Hurry, Whisper Creek is backed up, you won't be able to make it over the bridge much longer."

"I'm already on my way. Three to four minutes and I'll be at the bridge."

"I'm looking at it now, I have to cross to get to the shed, but I don't know if I'll be able to cross back."

"Just let me know when you have Bobby, and don't do anything dangerous. Please. If you can't get back across, go back to the Mendozas and stay there."

"Not when Avery is in trouble. If I can't cross the bridge, we'll walk along the bank and cross over at Baldwin's property line, or I might be able to get to Uncle Travis's place if I go the long way."

When Baldwin had bought the property years ago, he'd had engineers come out and put in a ten-foot pipe to go under part of his farm, to divert Whisper Creek into a seasonal lake. The McKennas had been furious at the time because the creek used to meander back to their property and helped with irrigation on the southern portion of their crops. But, ultimately, it had helped manage the seasonal flooding and Baldwin had allowed them to tap into his lake during dry spells. The project had an added benefit of creating a land bridge over the creek.

She had a million questions, but she trusted Jake. "Be careful."

"Did you call Sheriff Perez?"

"Yes. He can't get up here, the roads are closed at Mule Run. I have to find Avery. I have no idea why they took her or where to start looking, but I have to find her."

"We will. I'll be home as soon as I have Bobby."

CHAPTER TWENTY-THREE

The rain had turned the road into a stew of glistening rock, dangerous potholes, and slick mud, making it extremely treacherous.

Avery had finally figured out all the players as Rena cried half-hysterical into the phone. Rena was married to the asshole who had restrained her in Gianna's room—his name was Brock, and he'd told Rena to take a hostage.

Her.

Sam was in the backseat. He was Rena's brother, Avery was pretty certain. He had a bullet in the leg, which wasn't too bad since he could walk, and another in his side, which was bleeding through the bandage wrapped around his abdomen. It was bad, and Avery wondered if it was already too late for him.

Avery blinked and stared through the windshield as the rain came down in sheets. The wipers couldn't keep up, the rubber blades hissing with every frantic pass. Her fingers clenched the steering wheel hard, but it wasn't like she had a choice. The plastic teeth of the zip ties bit into the soft skin around her wrists, already sore from the first time she'd been restrained. She was literally tied into the ten and two position on the steering wheel. She could barely feel her fingers anymore.

"Okay, okay! We're on our way," Rena was saying. It was clear that the storm was screwing with the cell phone reception, because for the last five minutes Rena kept saying *what* and Brock repeated himself. "Will you be there? We have to go. We have to get out of here. I don't care about those stupid contracts, I don't care about the money, I just want to go home!"

He must have given her a positive response, because she pocketed her cell phone and wiped her snotty nose with the back of her gun hand.

"Do you know where Privett Road is?" Rena demanded.

"Y-yes," Avery stuttered.

"Go there."

"It's—it's a long road."

"Just get to it and I'll tell you which way to go."

"It doesn't go anywhere. If you want to get to the highway, there's a faster—"

"Shut up. And don't fuck with me. My brother needs help. I just want to get out of this fucking state."

She decided to stop talking. She'd find out soon enough.

"I'm okay," Sam said from the back. "Sis, I'm okay."

"You're not!" Rena said and tried to force herself to stop crying.

"I can take you to the hospital in Whitesboro. It's not even thirty minutes away, I can—"

"Shut up!" Rena screamed. She was losing it. Maybe she had already lost it. Maybe she would just kill Avery with the gun she had in her hand as soon as they got to Privett Road.

She had to figure a way out of this.

"Just drive," Rena said, marginally calmer. "Drive. Nothing stupid, because if you get us stuck, we'll be able to get out, but you won't."

Avery believed her. She slowed down as standing water rushed over the gravel road. They could be caught in a flash flood and Avery would be dead. They rolled through it, water splashing up on both sides like a ride at an amusement park.

But there was nothing fun about this.

Rena hadn't told her which way to go on Orchard, so she'd gone left, away from her house because she suspected that Bobby would have headed home, and Avery didn't want them to come across him in the rain. She didn't want her brother in any more danger than he already was. Plus, while their house wasn't visible from the road, their driveway was wide with a wooden archway that proclaimed *Whisper Creek Ranch, Est. 1898.* Avery didn't want Rena to see it and think that they could hole up there. Not with her great-grandmother and family inside.

Then, at the county road that intersected Orchard, she turned right because that was toward town, toward civilization. They'd first pass Greg Baldwin's place, then they'd go through the heart of Verdacorp land. Maybe someone would see her driving the Mendozas' truck and become suspicious. Maybe Gianna had already gotten out of her zip ties and called Sheriff Perez.

Maybe.

Maybe she was already dead.

Rena nodded. "Good, good. Keep it steady. Don't get cute."

"I'm not," Avery said, her voice dry, raw. Her heart hammered as she slowly sped up now that they'd passed through the low spot on the road. "I'm just trying not to crash." The truck hit a deep divot in the muddy gravel road and Sam grunted from the backseat.

"Be careful!" Rena screamed.

"I am!" Avery yelled back.

She risked glancing in the rearview mirror. Sam's head was slumped against the window, his face a mask of pain. He looked over to his sister. "I'm okay, Rena."

He kept saying that, but Avery knew he was anything but okay.

"Are you sure you don't want me to take him to the hospital?"

Rena hit her in the head with the gun and Avery saw stars. She swerved and almost drove them into the water-logged ditch. Rena grabbed the wheel and jerked them back onto the road.

"Just take us to Privett Road and I'll tell you where to go from there."

Rena didn't know where Privett Road was, maybe Avery could trick her, drive all the way to . . .

"Stop!"

Avery slammed on the brakes. The truck skidded over the waterlogged dirt road and nearly rolled into the ditch. Her heart pounded hard in her chest.

This was it. Rena was going to push her out of the truck and shoot her in the back.

Rena was looking at her phone. "Turn right in a half mile. That will lead us to Privett Road, then we're going to turn right."

They were going in a giant circle. Did Rena know that? There were only two houses on Privett before they reached Orchard Lane again. The Coulters on the east, and the Sudduths on the west.

Avery pressed the gas, but the truck didn't move. They were stuck in the mud like it was glue.

"What the hell?" Rena said.

Tears burned behind Avery's eyes. "We're stuck."

"The truck has four-wheel drive. Use it!"

Avery took her hands off the wheel, showing Rena that she couldn't reach the gear shift.

Rena scowled, then put the truck in four-wheel drive. Avery gently pressed the gas. Nothing happened at first, the engine roaring over the sound of the storm. After the tires spun for a half minute, they finally gained traction and they were moving again. She pulled out of the muck and drove slowly down the road.

Avery was shaking, the fear of the unknown was almost as terrifying as driving in this storm. On both sides of the road the ditches were filled with water, the water falling faster than they could drain. Soon the roads would be flooded and they'd really be stuck. Or caught in a flash flood and drown.

Then she spotted headlights approaching fast from the opposite lane. A blue Ram truck came into view, then slowed down as it got closer. The road was narrow enough that two cars could barely pass, and in this weather they had to be doubly careful not to drive into the ditch.

Avery's heart leapt into her throat. She couldn't see the driver through the rain, but she recognized that truck.

Ryan.

"Just drive," Rena growled. "Drive straight, drive slow, give no sign of anything to that driver, understand? Eyes forward, don't even smile."

Avery nodded. She couldn't speak through the lump in her throat.

As Ryan passed her on the left, they were both going not much more than fifteen miles an hour. Their eyes met briefly.

Ryan did a double take. Confused at first, then recognition.

Then the moment was gone. He had passed them. His taillights blinked red. Rena turned around in her seat.

"Was that someone you know?" she demanded.

"N-no," Avery stuttered.

"Fuck," Rena muttered and twisted in her seat to look out the back. Avery glanced into the mirror and saw what Rena saw.

Behind them, brake lights flared.

No, Ryan, Avery thought, but didn't say. She didn't want him to be caught up in this mess. At the same time she willed him to follow and tried to think about how she could use this to her advantage.

Rena swore and glared at Avery. "Son of a bitch! He's turning around."

She grabbed the wheel and jerked it. Avery's hands, still clamped to the steering wheel, burned as the zip ties cut into her wrists.

The truck swerved violently off the road and Avery screamed. Tires tore through wet gravel, then mud, then the world dropped out from beneath them. They crashed through a rotted fence and tumbled down a muddy slope into the waterlogged ditch. The truck slammed into the water nose-first, buried at a forty-five degree angle. Avery's head cracked the steering wheel. Pain flared across her forehead. The airbag didn't deploy.

She coughed, dizzy, disoriented, the roar of the water and pounding rain filling her ears. Thunder rocked the truck and Avery moaned.

Rena was climbing into the backseat. The two front doors were held shut by the water pressure, but the driver's side back door was only partly blocked.

"Sam! Come on!" Rena shouted. She pushed open the back door, climbed out, partly in the ditch and partly on the slope. She yanked her brother across the seat and out. He stumbled, fell to his knees, got up and scrambled up the slope with Rena.

Avery blinked water out of her eyes. They were going to leave her here. They were going to leave her tied to the steering wheel to drown.

Ryan.

They were going to carjack Ryan, maybe kill him! Because he saw her and recognized her and came to help.

Rena didn't look back. She half dragged Sam out of the cab and up the slope, her boots slipping in the mud.

Then she was gone.

Avery jerked against the wheel. The ties wouldn't budge. Her hands were frozen, her fingers numb, her wrists bleeding and raw. Water poured in, covering her feet, moving up her legs. The truck groaned, the engine sputtered, then it died.

Through the pounding of the rain, she heard squeaking brakes and the blare of a horn. It seemed to go forever.

Ryan.

Then she heard a gunshot.

Ryan knew better than to get out of his truck, but Avery was in that ditch, and the truck was half underwater. What if she was unconscious?

He'd glimpsed two other people inside. Who were they? He recognized the truck—it belonged to the Mendozas. But the two people were definitely *not* the Mendozas.

So he put on his hazards and stopped his truck in the middle of the road, ten feet from where she'd gone over.

He had encountered no other vehicles since he crossed County Road 122; no one was stupid enough to drive on the unpaved roads saturated with water and marked with deep ruts.

As he stepped out, he saw two people coming up the bank.

"Avery!" he called out before he realized the woman wasn't Avery.

The woman had a gun in hand, and she pointed it at Ryan. "Keys."

"They're in the truck," he said, keeping his hands in plain view, not wanting this woman to think he had a gun. "Where's Avery?"

The woman didn't answer him. "Move away from the truck."

The man looked sick and he was bleeding. Oh, God, was Avery in the truck bleeding? Was she hurt? Worse?

"Now!" the woman screamed and fired the gun at his feet. She didn't hit him, but he moved away from the truck.

The woman opened the passenger door, helped push the man inside, then slammed the door shut. She ran around to the driver's side and climbed in. Thirty seconds later they were driving off.

Ryan watched until he was certain they weren't coming back, then he ran to the ditch and looked at the truck stuck in the muddy water at a sharp forty-five-degree angle, only the rear wheels of the truck bed visible from the road.

"Avery!" he shouted.

He didn't hear anything at first. The water in the ditch was rising—either because one of the many creeks that cut through the valley was filling it, or the drainage pipes couldn't keep up with the rainfall. Or both. Either way, if the ditch filled, the cab would be completely underwater and Avery would drown.

If she was unconscious, she may be drowning right now.

He screamed her name again and scrambled down the slope slick from rain. He slipped, swore, and thought he heard "Help!"

Then he saw her. She had her face against the window and when she spotted him she looked both terrified and relieved.

"Ryan! I need help!"

The two front doors would be almost impossible to open between the water pressure and being pressed against the ditch.

"Can you climb over the seat? I'll get the back door!"

"I can't!" she said.

"Are you hurt?"

Maybe he heard wrong because the windows were up.

"My hands! They're tied to the steering wheel."

He looked at the steering wheel, but the visibility was so bad he couldn't see much of anything inside, plus the windows were fogged up.

He slipped and fell into the water, stumbled and his hands hit the side of the truck. The truck shifted toward the passenger side and Avery screamed.

It took all his strength to pull open the back door against both water pressure and gravity. The truck was aimed down into the ditch, but now was also listing a good twenty degrees toward the passenger side.

He put his body between the door and the frame. It hit him as gravity forced it down, but he held it open with his body.

"Avery, are you okay?"

"Ohmigod, I thought she shot you," Avery cried. She held the steering wheel tight. Her wrists were red and bloodied. "I can't get out."

"They took my truck," he said. He looked at the water in the front; it was up to Avery's waist. "I have to lean over and cut the ties. Hold on."

He pulled his knife from his pocket and had to let go of the door in order to climb over the seat far enough to reach the steering wheel. As soon as he leaned forward, the truck slipped forward another foot and Avery screamed.

Then they stopped moving. The water was up to Avery's chest. His heart thudded so hard he could barely hear the rain anymore. He reached out and sawed through the zip tie on her right hand, wedging the knife between her wrist and the steering wheel. It took a good ten seconds, but it broke.

As he shifted to get the left wrist, the truck tilted more to the right. He screamed when he almost dropped the knife. He squeezed his hand tight around it, nicking his palm.

He waited a second until the truck stopped moving, then cut through the second zip tie.

"Are you hurt?"

"No," she said.

He didn't know if he believed her, but they really didn't have time to argue about it.

"I'm going to get out and hold open this door. You need to climb over the seat and come out this way."

"Okay." Her teeth were chattering and she was as pale as a ghost. Both of her wrists were still bleeding.

He grunted as he pushed open the door. They were lucky that the truck had tilted toward the passenger side because there was no more water pressure forcing it closed, but the door was heavy and he was still fighting gravity.

As soon as it was open, he once again put his body between the frame and door. "Now, Avery."

Awkwardly, she climbed into the back. As she did, the truck fell completely on its side and Avery slipped down into the muddy water and Ryan heard a thud as she hit the other side. More water rushed in and now was also coming from the driver's side as the truck sunk farther into the muck.

"Avery!" Ryan didn't dare move from the opening because the

door would slam shut and he wasn't certain he'd be able to open it again. But if she didn't surface, he would have to.

She broke through and gasped. She reached for the handle above the door and used it to pull herself up. He grabbed her biceps with one hand and held the door with his other hand and his body. He strained and pulled her up, and she used the handle for leverage.

As their weight shifted, so did the truck, threatening to completely roll over.

"Hurry!" Ryan yelled, not sure Avery could hear him.

She pulled herself up, grabbed the top of the door with her other hand, and came through the opening. She fell into the ditch with a splash and hit her head on the undercarriage of the truck.

"Avery, get up! Get out of the ditch! The truck could fall back."

Blood streamed down the side of her face as she awkwardly climbed up the embankment.

Ryan pulled his body away from the frame and the door slammed shut with finality.

He walked along the side of the truck and jumped to the edge of the ditch, then crawled up the side to the street. He and Avery lay side by side.

She was crying.

"Are you hurt?"

"We could have died." He hugged her, then they sat up. She sniffed, holding on to him. "I'm sorry," she said.

"Nothing to be sorry about."

"They could have killed you."

"They didn't. Are you okay to walk?"

"Yeah."

He examined her face, wiped blood away from her scalp where she hit her head on the truck. There was a huge bruise on the side of her cheek and he touched it lightly. Relief rushed over him.

He kissed her, then helped her up. "Can we get to your house through the fields?"

"We need to stick to the road as much as possible," she said. "The fields are too wet, it'll be really hard to walk through them, and I don't know if the creek has flooded yet. If it has, we'll really be stuck."

Ryan looked around. "They went south, probably toward the freeway."

She shook her head. "They were heading to Privett Road."

"Really? Why? They won't be able to get through to the freeway."

"That's what they said, that's where we were going when I saw you. They didn't tell me where, but there's not a lot of places they could go. There's a third guy."

"When we get to a phone, I'll tell my dad, he'll find them. Where's the closest house?"

"Greg Baldwin." She pointed north. "About a mile up to his driveway, then a quarter mile to his house from there. I know my mom and Greg had a falling-out, but he'll help."

"Greg's in the hospital, in a coma. He was shot last night. You didn't know?"

She shook her head. "I was at Gianna's all day. Is he going to be okay?"

"I don't know," Ryan admitted. "But we can break in if we have to, get to a phone and call my dad."

They held hands and started walking in the middle of the dirt-and-gravel road, the water up to their ankles. The rain continued to beat down, the lightning and thunder battling it out in the sky, and Avery told him everything that had happened since she arrived at Gianna's and faced a burly man named Brock.

CHAPTER TWENTY-FOUR

Brock wasn't at the house off Privett, and Rena had lost her phone in the crash. The reception had been so bad, what if she got it wrong? What if it wasn't this house? What if she was supposed to turn left and not right?

She was in a near-full panic, but she had to get it together. For Sam.

Rena left him in the truck to make sure that the house was empty. She didn't know if she had the courage to take another family hostage.

The door was unlocked, so she let herself in. This was definitely the right house. Brock had done a number on this place—everything had been gone through, drawers still open, file folders tossed about, pictures off the hooks in his search for a safe.

She went back to the truck and helped Sam inside. He was fading and even he wasn't saying that he was fine anymore. Because he wasn't fine, and they both knew it. In fact, he wasn't saying much at all, only his occasional grunt or groan confirming he was alive.

She helped him into one of the bedrooms and stripped off his wet clothes. The bullet wound had broken open again, blood seeping through the bandage. She took the bandage off, it had gotten wet and disgusting. She found a first aid kit in the bathroom and cleaned the wound, dressed it, and then put him in bed naked, piling on the blankets. She brought him water and offered to make him something to eat. He said he wasn't hungry and closed his eyes. For a minute she thought he'd just up and died, but as she watched, his chest went up and down, up and down.

She put her head down on the bed next to him and stifled a scream. Everything had gone to hell.

And Brock wasn't here.

Five minutes later, when she was certain Sam was still alive and just resting, she went to the living room and found a house phone. She dialed Brock's cell phone number.

He didn't answer. But she was calling from a strange number, so he might not answer.

She left a message.

"It's me. We're here. Where are you? I need you, Brock. I need you."

What else could she say? That she'd nearly killed two teenagers? That the redhead might be dead? That she hated herself and hated him as well? That she wished she never heard the name Mitchell Robinson?

Instead, she hung up, went to the kitchen, and looked for something healthy to cook for when Sam woke up.

Brock listened to his wife's message. Her voice was full of frustration and deep fear that pained him.

He was the one who got her and Sam into this. He needed to find a way out.

Mitchell Robinson walked into the Verdacorp office, where Brock had been waiting for him. Waiting for more than fifteen minutes before the bastard came in.

"Am I keeping you from something?" Robinson asked dryly.

Brock pocketed his phone. He would call Rena back when he was alone.

"What do I need to do?" he asked through clenched teeth.

"Ellen McKenna has the Coulter contracts. Get them."

Brock stared at him, incredulous. "And how the hell am I supposed to do that? They have a house full of people, a bunch of kids."

Screw it, he thought. He didn't need this.

"I have a plan," Robinson said with an unpleasant laugh. "We'll use the storm to our advantage. In fact, as soon as you get dressed, you can leave, get the file, and be back here in less than thirty minutes, if you're smart about it."

Get dressed?

Brock looked down at his jeans and flannel shirt. What did Robinson expect him to wear?

"I don't understand," Brock said. "What is the plan?"

Robinson ignored Brock and picked up the desk phone, dialed. A moment later, he said, "Get the utility truck ready. I'm sending Mr. Jones over to the garage to pick it up in five minutes."

He put the receiver down, looked Brock up and down. "The uniform might be a little tight, but I think it's close enough. This way." Robinson left the office, then turned back when Brock didn't immediately follow. "Now, Mr. Jones. We don't have all day."

CHAPTER TWENTY-FIVE

Ellen got Margery settled into Avery's bed and took her blood pressure.

"You must be frantic about your kids," Margery said, reaching out toward Ellen.

"Shh," Ellen said. "You need to remain calm."

She *was* worried, about all of them. She hadn't heard yet from Jake about Bobby; Avery had been taken by the people who had shot Greg Baldwin; and Lyla was in the barn, working alone to prevent water from flooding the horse stalls. Had she known about the water damage this morning, she could have taken the horses to Travis's place, or to the Coulters' barn. But it was too late now. Lyla had to keep the barn as dry as possible.

In the back of her mind she thought that the barn had had so many problems over the last year and she should have been on top of it, but that realization was buried under her fear for her children.

"I don't know how you do it." Margery rubbed her stomach in a slow, circular motion. Ellen blinked back sudden tears. She remembered carrying Avery for nine months and two weeks—she was late, she was nearly ten pounds, and had kicked at her sciatic nerve periodically just to keep Ellen on her toes. Or, rather, on her back because when she hit just the right place, Ellen couldn't move for hours without pain.

And when she arrived, she was chunky and beautiful, with a shock of red hair and John's warm hazel-brown eyes. None of the other kids were redheads, but Penny had been overjoyed because she had been a redhead before her hair turned snow white, long before Ellen had met her. So they named her Avery Penelope and while Penny said she didn't have favorites, she always did small, extra things for her namesake. Like making a special picnic for when Ryan came over in the middle of the night.

Ellen's eyes burned. Avery thought she didn't know that Ryan sometimes came over after everyone went to bed and they went out to the old oak tree to talk and make out. She'd never confronted Avery about it, because the kids were good kids. She could see the tree from her bedroom window and seeing Avery and Ryan just sitting holding hands, looking at the stars, reminded her of the long summer nights when she and John had done the same thing.

"Rick knows," Ellen said, clearing her throat to force back her emotions. "Avery's smart. They're not going to hurt her, because they need her." Ellen had to believe that. She had to believe that Avery would find a way to escape, or that Rick would find them, save her daughter.

But the fear clawed at her heart. She'd lost her husband, how could God take her daughter, too?

"Margery, your blood pressure is too high. You need to relax. You're safe here, your baby is safe. Close your eyes, keep your feet elevated slightly"—she adjusted the pillow under her calves—"and don't think about anything except the fact that you have a growing baby who needs you to be healthy and calm. Okay?"

"I'll try."

"I'll be back in a bit. I'm going to call Susie and tell her we're safe."

Ellen went downstairs and called Susie. Penny was watching her, but not talking. When Ellen ended the call, she said, "What?" She didn't mean to snap. She pinched her nose to force back tears and took a deep breath. "I'm sorry."

"What are you sorry about?" Penny asked. "You're worried. I'm worried. We won't sleep until all our chicks are back in the nest."

"I need to do something and I don't know what to do!"

That she hadn't heard from Jake worried her as well. Maybe he couldn't call, but he had a radio.

Still, Jake and Bobby were together by now. Avery was alone, with strangers who had hurt the Mendozas and tied up a disabled girl and shot Greg Baldwin. If they were willing to shoot a man—and his dog—would they really restrain themselves with a teenage girl?

A sob escaped and she bit it back. Penny came over to her and gave her a fierce hug, then dropped her arms. "Go see Lyla," she said. "She's still in the barn. I'll fix Margery something."

"Where's Mateo?"

"He's still at the Pritchards' place. He called when he got there, said their generator needs repairs and they are having trouble getting their cows into the barn, so he's going to be a while." She shook her head. "They're nice folks, but they don't know much of anything about raising dairy cows or mechanics. They think having a farm is like gardening."

"Abigail has a green thumb," Ellen said with a small smile. "I've never been able to grow tomatoes like hers."

She was glad Mateo was able to help them. Even though she would have preferred that he was here, helping Jake with Bobby, or Lyla with the barn, or just being here with her because she couldn't stop thinking about where Avery was and if she was going to be safe.

"And earlier? Millie called. Said they were visiting their youngest down in Frisco. Something about an indoor soccer match or car problems, I don't really know. But they asked Jake to care for their bulls and chickens tomorrow. With all this going on!"

"They didn't say anything to me this morning about a trip," Ellen said. "When Mateo calls, ask him to take care of the Coulters' place in the morning before he comes here. Jake might not be able to get over there if the fields or roads are flooded."

Mateo lived on the other side of Privett, on a small parcel that the McKennas had owned for generations, used primarily for grazing before the winter wheat came in. It was a straight shot to the Coulters' place, as long as Privett was passable.

"If the rain stops by then," Ellen said, looking out the window. It wasn't even five and it was near dark. The rain fell without letting up, a steady, constant thrum on the roof. Was Avery out in this? Was Jake driving Bobby home?

She needed to do something. "You're okay checking on Margery?" she asked as she put on her jacket, hood, and a fresh pair of boots, since the pair she'd worn earlier was still wet.

"I'll feed her, sit with her, keep her calm. You check on Lyla. Make her come in and eat."

"I will," Ellen said and reached for the door. Whiskey jumped up from his bed in the corner of the kitchen and Ellen said, "Stay."

He sat down and watched her with sad eyes.

The wind pushed Ellen from behind as she walked through the muddy yard to the barn. Jake had laid out plywood across the worst of the yard so they could more easily walk to and from the barn.

The lights were on inside and when Ellen stepped in through the side door, she called out, "Lyla?"

"Mom! You're back."

Lyla left one of the stalls and came over to her. She looked tired, her dark hair pulled back and her big green eyes bloodshot.

"Grandma said you haven't eaten."

"There's water coming in from the foundation and I don't know why." Lyla motioned for her to follow to the side of the barn under the loft. "Jake fixed the holes up above, cut off the drainpipes, but there's water coming in here."

Lyla turned on a brighter work light on the wall and pointed to the floor where the wall met the cement foundation. She had sandbags all around, but pulled one aside and showed Ellen what she meant. "What can cause this?"

"I don't know," Ellen said as she squatted and touched the pooling water. She could practically see it spread. She pushed on the wall; it was soft and rotting. It was going to have to be replaced.

She put the sandbag back. They had the entire barn surrounded by sandbags not so much to keep it from flooding—the water wouldn't rise higher than an inch in their immediate yard because they were on a slight rise—but because standing water could seep into the foundation, causing dry rot and structural problems.

The barn had been standing on the same foundation for generations. It had been repaired, updated, modernized, but it was the same basic structure. Maybe there was something seriously wrong with the foundation, or it had cracked. But wouldn't they have seen signs of leakage over the years? Cracks that had gotten worse over time?

"I'll have to hire a structural engineer or contractor to take a look," Ellen said.

"Do you think—" Lyla began, then stopped.

"Go on, what were you going to say?"

"The loft was sabotaged," she said bluntly. "Jake said it was, that someone had cut holes in the wall, right next to the gutter so the water would get into the loft when the gutters were clogged. Maybe someone did something like that near the foundation and we haven't found it yet."

Ellen was still having a hard time wrapping her head around the fact that a stranger—or, worse, someone she knew—had come onto her property for the purposes of damaging her barn. But Jake wouldn't jump to that conclusion without evidence, and it was clear that something was going on.

"I hope you're wrong," Ellen said, "but we can't discount the possibility."

"Do you think the animals are okay in here?"

"Yes. Even if someone did structurally damage the barn, it would take a lot more water than tonight, and much stronger winds, to take down this barn that fast."

Lyla was still concerned.

"I'll bring someone in first thing next week, okay?"

Lyla nodded.

"I brought Margery Sutton home with me because her blood pressure is elevated and she wouldn't have been able to get out with Rock Creek flooding," Ellen said. "I need to check on her. But you've done everything you can for the animals. Come in, eat, and later we'll come out and check the sandbags."

"Okay," Lyla reluctantly agreed.

Before they could turn off the lights in the barn, they went off themselves. They stepped outside and the house was dark.

"You start the generator to the barn, I'll take care of the house," Ellen said. She put up her hood and ran across the plywood Jake and Mateo had laid earlier over the mud, to the far side of the house where the generator was hooked up, fueled, and ready to go.

Penny stepped out on the porch, saw that Ellen had it taken care of, and went back inside. Was her grandmother really going to come out into the rain and risk falling in the mud to start up the generator?

Yes, yes she would, Ellen thought, grateful that she was here to take care of it. Penny may be a spry eighty-four, but a gust of wind could push her down.

Ellen had the generator up and running and was about to go inside when she heard Lyla scream.

She turned and ran toward the barn.

"Lyla!"

She found Lyla in the mud five feet from the generator, holding her hand. "Are you okay?" Ellen asked, squatting next to her. "Where are you hurt?"

"It shocked me! My arm feels numb."

Ellen inspected her arm, didn't see any damage, but Lyla's arm hung awkwardly at her side. "Does it hurt? Is it broken?"

"No, just numb, I can't feel my fingers."

Ellen walked over to the generator. At first, she couldn't see anything unusual, but then realized that there were copper wires where they shouldn't be, loosely wrapped around the engine.

This wasn't an accident.

"Mom?" Lyla said.

Ellen went over to her daughter and helped her up. "Go inside, I'll fix this."

"What happened?"

"There's some wires that shouldn't be here. The numbness will go away, but go inside. Now."

Lyla obeyed, holding her right arm.

Ellen went into the dark barn, straight to the tack room, where she knew there were work gloves.

She went back and carefully removed the extra wires. Then she inspected the rest of the generator and didn't see anything wrong. Still, she was worried. She didn't want to turn it on in case something else was damaged.

She went back into the barn and removed four gallons of fresh milk from the refrigerator. The rest would go bad overnight without refrigeration, but there wasn't much she could do about that. She didn't even know if they would have room in the refrigerator for these gallons, considering how much cooking Penny had done this week.

She was at the top of the stairs when she saw lights coming down the driveway. She turned, hoping it was Jake, then sighed when it was only a utility work truck with the Cooke County logo on the door.

Idiot, she thought. They should have been out during the week to repair the roads after the hailstorm, there was nothing they could do now until the rain stopped.

She went inside and put the milk on the counter, then waited for the county employee to tell her things she already knew.

CHAPTER TWENTY-SIX

The water was higher than he'd expected.

As soon as Jake crossed Whisper Creek—now a churning, mud-slick ribbon overwhelming the low spot of Orchard Lane—he knew he wasn't getting back that way. The current had swallowed half the road already and every second that passed made it more dangerous. One bad slide, or more likely hydroplaning, and the truck would be dragged down into the drainage ditch or thrown into a tree. Or worse.

The rain lashed the windshield in frenzied sheets, wipers barely keeping up. Branches whipped against the side of the truck as Jake turned onto the overgrown, unpaved road that led to the rotting equipment shed, headlights bouncing off thick bushes and towering cypress trees.

He gripped the wheel tighter. Bobby was out here alone. Trapped. Scared. Ryan had said he was in the storage shed, but what if Bobby left, tried to walk home? What if he was on the ATV and got stuck in the creek? Or thrown off in a ditch? Every bad thing that could have happened to his little brother ran through Jake's head.

Jake couldn't even call this road a driveway. The path was a mess of roots, stones, and axle-deep mud. Parallel impressions in the mud were deep, caused by years of heavy equipment coming and going. The tires spun more than once, and the truck groaned in protest, slipping sideways before finally catching enough traction to crawl forward. Jake cursed as he lurched over a sunken dip that nearly swallowed the front end. A wall of rain blurred everything beyond the high beams.

The trees parted at last, revealing the sagging silhouette of the old equipment shed. It hunched against the storm like a wounded animal.

Jake exhaled a shaky breath. He hadn't realized how tightly he'd been holding his chest until now. He pulled in as close as he could—there was no room to turn around, only a wall of brush and storm-thrashed trees. The branches beat the shed's siding like they were trying to claw their way in. Lightning cracked nearby, followed by a roll of thunder that vibrated through the cab of the truck.

Jake stepped out; boots instantly swallowed by standing water. Not just mud—liquid dirt, thick, cold enough to bite. His flashlight beam shook as he trudged toward the shed, ten feet feeling like a hundred. Each step threatened to trap him in the muck. And if they had to walk out of here . . .

He didn't finish the thought. They might be stuck here all night.

No. Mom needed him, he would get back to the ranch as soon as physically possible.

The shed door creaked open under his hand, groaning on rusted hinges. Inside, it was little better than outside. The walls blocked most of the wind and rain, though the wood floor was rotting and cobwebs hung thick in the corners. The only dry space was the loft above, but even that looked like it might fall down any second. A rust-streaked tractor sat in the middle of the space, listing to one side. Fifty years ago it had been a state-of-the-art farm tool. Now it was junk.

"Bobby?" Jake called, his voice low but sharp.

Silence, then a small voice. "Up here!"

Jake raised the light. Bobby peered over the edge of the loft, soaked to the bone, his brown hair flattened against his forehead. He looked small. Lightning flashed again, illuminating his brother's pale, muddy face—and for a brief second, Jake saw how scared he really was.

Scared, but safe.

"You okay?" Jake asked.

Bobby nodded. "Yeah . . . I guess so. Just a second!" He ducked back out of view.

Jake sighed, more out of relief than frustration. He closed the door behind him to get some respite from the driving rain. Even with his slicker and hat, he was drenched.

The floor squelched under his boots. The smell of mildew and old oil made his nose wrinkle in disgust—from the scent and the fact that the Mendozas hadn't maintained the small barn or anything in it for decades.

Something—a rat, maybe—scurried across a support beam above. Then the loft creaked.

"Here!" Bobby reappeared, holding out a plastic jug and a wire cage. "I didn't want to leave them behind."

Jake frowned as he walked over to the ladder. Bobby was too far up for Jake to just reach out and grab the items. He eyed the ladder. It bowed in the middle, half the rungs dark with rot. How the hell had Bobby climbed that thing?

"Hold on." Jake tested it. The first rung bent. The second cracked under his weight. He reached as far as he dared—then the rung beneath him gave way.

He jumped back just in time, boots sliding. His knee slammed into the ground. The ladder leaned sideways like a dying tree, but remained mostly upright.

Bobby's face paled. "Are you okay?"

"Yes. Be careful."

"Can I drop them?"

"Leave everything," Jake said. "We'll come back—"

"But what if we find Cleo?" Bobby's voice cracked.

"We're not looking for that damn cat, Bobby!" Jake snapped, sharper than he meant. "Whisper Creek has flooded its banks, we have to go the long way home. We don't have time to look for a cat."

Bobby hesitated . . . then dropped the cage anyway.

Jake didn't try to catch it. The metal clanged on the ground beside him.

Then Bobby stepped onto the ladder—and it gave way completely.

"Bobby!" Jake dove forward just as his brother fell, limbs flailing. He caught him hard, the boy's slight weight knocking him backwards. They crashed onto the muddy ground together, Jake grunting as his back hit hard.

They didn't move for a moment.

Then Bobby clung to him.

"I was so scared," he whispered, voice muffled against Jake's chest.

Jake tightened his arms around him. "I know, kid. I know."

But Jake sensed it wasn't just the fall Bobby was talking about.

"You were here alone a long time," he said softly. "That would scare anybody."

Bobby shook his head, breath hitching. "Not that." A pause. "Avery. She was tied up."

Jake's chest tightened. That must have been terrifying for his little brother.

He sat up slowly, pulling Bobby with him. The storm outside raged louder now, wind howling through the cracks in the walls. "I know. Mom knows. We think that the people who went to the Mendozas' house robbed Greg Baldwin and then got stuck in the storm last night."

"I saw one of the men earlier and hid in the barn. I knew Avery was in trouble, but I was so afraid of being seen I hid."

"You did the right thing."

"But what if I could have gotten help earlier? And when the man left, I went to help, but Avery was all tied up in Gianna's room. And there were still people there. We have to get her!"

Bobby was ten, he was old enough to know the truth.

"I talked to Mom before I came here. She went to the Mendozas, and they're fine, but the two people who were with that man you saw, they took Avery."

"It's my fault!" Bobby sobbed.

"You are a ten-year-old kid who hid from kidnappers, Bobby. You got away *and* you got help. You called Ryan, right? I wouldn't have known where you were if you hadn't told him. You did the right thing."

But Bobby was shaking his head, eyes wide and wet. "She saw me, and I ran. I should've stayed. I should've done something. I could have gotten help. I *could* have!"

Jake wrapped an arm around his brother's shoulders and held him tighter. "You did what you had to do. And we're going to find her, okay? We'll get her back."

But his gut twisted. He knew what these people were capable of. They had shot Greg Baldwin and his dog. They were ruthless and likely scared of being caught. Panicked criminals were even more dangerous, like a trapped animal.

At that moment, Jake missed his dad more than ever. He was supposed to be the man of the house now, and he was terrified that something bad would happen to Avery, something that Jake couldn't stop.

His dad had been a rock. He never raised his voice, but a stern look was more effective than a verbal lashing. He never raised his hand, but his quiet, "I'm disappointed in you, you know better," was more effective than a beating. He never held a grudge, his punishments were more instructive than punitive, and he taught Jake everything about farming, the land, the animals.

"It's in your blood, son, like it's in mine. Whatever you do with your life, you'll end up here."

The last time Jake had seen his dad was the morning he died. Jake was driving to school, Avery in the front seat reading—Jake never understood how she could read in the car, but that's what she did almost every morning on their drive to school. Lyla was in the backseat staring out the window, her expression tight, brow furrowed, as if she was trying to figure out the cure for cancer. And Bobby was chattering away about how he and Grandma had seen a fox when they picked blackberries that morning before school.

Jake had turned down Privett Road, past the Coulters' land, down to the small section that his family owned just south of the Coulters, where their cattle currently grazed. His dad was on his horse, riding back and forth to urge the cows east, where it would be easier to divide and load those they planned to sell Wednesday at the auction in Gainesville. Jake was taking the day off school to help—a lot of kids did—and it was one of his favorite chores. Jake was definitely more a cattle rancher than a farmer, while his dad preferred farming. In fact, it had been Jake who'd convinced him a couple years back to increase their cattle because they were consistently turning a profit at market.

Jake honked, and his dad turned to look at them. John McKenna smiled, raised his hand in greeting. Bobby said—though their dad couldn't hear—"Hi, Daddy!" and waved frantically from the backseat. "Jake, Daddy said I can go to market with you on Wednesday!"

Yeah, Jake knew. He wasn't all that thrilled about it. His little brother was excitable and annoying and asked way too many questions.

Jake honked again as he passed, glanced at his dad in the rearview mirror. He was still watching the truck, looking like a giant atop the horse. Jake wanted to be the man his dad was. Strong, hardworking, loyal. He wanted to raise his family here, at Whisper Creek Ranch. They were expanding, and he could build a house for his own wife and kids. Someday.

He pushed aside the memory, which with everything else going on today threatened to bring him to tears, and said to Bobby, "We need to go. You okay?"

"Yeah. We're going to find Avery, right?"

"Yes. Mom talked to Sheriff Perez."

"I called Ryan on the radio because I didn't want to go on our family channel because the bad guys have Avery's radio. I didn't want them to hear."

"That was very smart," Jake said, and meant it. Then he looked down and noticed that Bobby's feet were bare. He hadn't noticed at first because they were caked with mud.

"Where the hell are your shoes?" Jake asked, scanning the shed again. He looked up toward the loft.

"I lost 'em. In the field. When I was running."

No shoes, broken ladder, rising creeks, and more than two miles of back roads between here and the house because they couldn't go home the short way.

A flash of lightning illuminated the old barn, then the thunder hit fast, like a monster closing in.

"We need to go now," Jake said. "Before we can't."

His cell phone wasn't getting a signal, so he took out his radio. "Mom, it's Jake. Over."

A moment later, his mom came on. "I'm here, did you find Bobby? Over."

"Yes. He's here with me. We're not going to be able to go back over the creek. I'm going around the long way, but I don't know how long it's going to take. Over."

"Be safe. Over."

Bobby grabbed the radio. "Mom, where's Avery? Jake said she's missing. What happened?" A second later, he pressed the button again. "Over."

Her answer came right back. "Sheriff Perez is looking for her. They're also looking for the Mendozas' truck. We'll find her. Over."

"I know what the other truck looks like," Bobby said. "It's a black Ram truck with four doors. And it had a Louisiana license plate. I memorized it—223HPW. Over."

Jake hit his brother lightly on the arm. "Wow, Bobby, that was smart."

Bobby grinned sheepishly, then said, "It's only smart if we can find Avery."

The radio beeped and their mom said, "I have a pen, can you repeat that? It's 223 and? Over."

"HPW, over," Bobby said.

"Thank you, Bobby. Be safe out there, both of you. Over."

Jake got up, pulled Bobby to his feet. "You okay walking to the truck?"

Bobby nodded. "Do you think Cleo is okay? Do you think she found a safe place to wait out the storm?"

The cat again. "Yeah, I think she did," Jake said. He opened the door and they stepped out into the driving rain.

CHAPTER TWENTY-SEVEN

"Hello, ma'am!"

The county employee climbed out of his work truck and waved to her. Ellen didn't recognize him, but considering that the county seat was in Gainesville and most of the time they wanted to forget how they neglected the agricultural region of the county, she wasn't surprised. The last time she saw work crews doing anything was nine months ago when they finally repaired Privett Road and the intersection at Orchard that had been in vast need of repair for years. Ellen almost always took the long way to get to town because of the potholes on Privett.

They didn't pave it, that would cost too much according to the local politicians. But they did fill in the holes and level the dirt and gravel.

It would have to be done again this year, and she wondered how long they would delay, if it would be another four or five years.

She nodded. "What can I help you with?" She pocketed the radio and desperately wanted to call Rick with the license plate information that Bobby had given her. "We're kind of busy around here."

"Couple things," he said. He carried a clipboard. "Can I come up to the porch and get out of the rain?"

She nodded and he jogged up the stairs, pushing back his hood when he reached the top. "Damn, it's raining cats and dogs out there," he said with a smile.

"Power's out, but it just happened, so I'm sure you're not here for that."

"No, ma'am. I didn't even know. Is it out just here or at other properties?"

"I don't know, it happened ten minutes ago. We got the generator on, so we're fine." Hurry, she wanted to say. Instead, she stared at him, mentally willing him to get this over with.

He nodded. "I'll call it in, but I don't think anyone will get out here until tomorrow. But if the problem is at the powerhouse, they might get it up faster."

Tell her something she didn't know, she thought, and waited, growing more impatient.

"I'm out checking the status of waterways throughout the valley. The creek that cuts through your property to the east"—he gestured—"has flooded Orchard Lane. I just came to tell you we're blocking off the road at both ends until it subsides."

"I know where it's flooded, and even in the worst years it's not going to flood more than fifty feet from the banks."

"It's for your safety, ma'am."

Jake and Bobby were on their way back, going the long way, which means they had to get home through the intersection where Privett Road met Orchard. That couldn't be flooded—they had just repaired the area last year and put in huge draining culverts to avoid flooding even in storms like this one. But she would warn him. They might have to park at the Coulters and walk through, or go farther north up Privett and go through Travis's place along the back road, then cut through the old path that led to Orchard right across from their entrance. It wouldn't be any safer than just cutting through the intersection.

She just wanted all her kids home as soon as possible.

"Fine," she said. The county would put up a set of traffic barricades with reflective stripes, maybe a flood warning sign. Then they would forget about them for weeks. Par for the course. She and Jake would end up moving them to the side.

He looked down at his phone. "Excuse me." He answered it.

She didn't have time for this.

"If that's all," she said, trying to get him to hurry up.

"I can't hear you—Brian, you there? Damn." He pocketed his phone. "That was my boss. The storm is messing with cell phones."

No shit, she thought, but didn't say.

"Would you mind if I make a call? I just got back from Rock Creek, where we had to put up a barricade—a car tried to make it through and had to be rescued."

Not the first time, Ellen thought. She had barely made it across the road, and that was more than an hour ago. Definitely wasn't a local, because they would know better.

"And," he continued, "I'm supposed to check everything north of here, though I don't know that I'll be able to get through."

She just wanted him to leave, so said, "Fine, but I have things to do, as I'm sure you're aware."

She led him into the kitchen. Penny was sitting in a padded rocking chair in the corner. It was her waiting chair, she called it. When she was waiting for a pie to be done or water to boil. Half the time she dozed off until the timer rang.

She looked tired, Ellen thought. The weather got to her more now in her eighties, sure, but Ellen suspected Penny was just as worried about the kids as she was.

"There," she motioned to the phone on the wall. "You can see yourself out when you're done."

"Thank you, ma'am."

She leaned over to Penny, put her hand on her too skinny arm, and said softly, "Jake found Bobby, they're on their way back."

"Thank the Lord," Penny said with a small smile. "But I have more prayers to be answered."

"Me, too." Ellen motioned to the man in overalls. "He's with the county. They're blocking off Orchard."

"In the middle of the storm?" Penny pshawed. "The signs will be knocked over in the wind." She said that loud enough for the government employee to hear; he just looked at them sheepishly and continued his conversation.

"I'm going to check on Margery. Don't get up, he can let himself out."

Ellen went upstairs and found Margery sleeping, an empty bowl next to her. Good.

She stepped out, closed the door, and texted Rick the license plate information Bobby had memorized. She was proud of her youngest son to have thought of that, but residual fear lingered that he could have been caught and in the same position as Avery.

Rick responded with a thumbs-up emoji, and then Ellen went into her room, where she'd had Lyla lie down after being shocked earlier by the generator.

"Hey, how are you feeling?"

"My arm is almost back to normal, but my fingers still tingle."

Ellen sat on the edge of the bed. "It could have been so much worse."

"Who would do that to us? It wasn't a prank."

"No, it wasn't."

"It was probably the same person who cut into the barn and the reason why the barn is collecting water."

Ellen had thought the same thing.

Only she had also thought, Verdacorp.

She knew Mitchell Robinson was ruthless, but she never

expected him to sabotage her property. Who else could it be? Maybe one of his goons? Like Tom Garza? She had never liked that man.

Tomorrow, she would pound on Mitchell's door and demand answers.

"Jake has Bobby," she told Lyla. "He's fine, they're on their way back, but have to go around the long way."

"It's awful out there, Mom. Do you think they'll get back okay?"

"Jake is smart, he knows what to do."

"And Avery?"

"Rick is looking for her." Ellen felt so helpless, and she didn't know how to make her daughter feel better when she herself was so torn up inside. "I don't know what else to do, I want to go out myself but that would be foolish. The last thing we need is Rick and his people having to rescue me because I got caught up in mud or stranded in the middle of a field."

"Jake said that Ryan was on his way, he should be here by now."

"He may have been turned back at Mule Run. Rick said everything north of there is blocked off."

Which made it weird that the county employee was cutting off Orchard Lane, which was a tiny road off a minimally traveled road. Typical of government, she thought. They had so many ridiculous rules and regulations, most of the farmers ignored them.

She rose, said, "You can sleep in your own bed if you don't mind sharing the room with Margery, or you can stay here and share with me, whatever you want."

"I might not sleep at all," she said.

Ellen kissed her forehead and went back downstairs.

Penny was still in her rocking chair. "Where's the guy from the county?"

"Finished his call and left. Took the cookies I offered."

"Then he's not completely stupid," Ellen said with a slight smile.

She looked out the kitchen window and watched the truck drive off. The license plate was a private Texas plate, not a county exempt plate. Not wholly unusual—she had a friend who worked for the county and she'd drive her own truck for some county business—but on a day like this, she found it odd.

Penny said, "Clive Robertson dropped off a contract for you earlier. They want to trade part of the Baldwin property for the two hundred acres between the Robinson and Coulter properties. Then Travis called, and said Clive came by and gave him a copy, asked that Travis talk to you about it, they need it Sunday night. I put it on the desk over there," she said, gesturing to the small desk under the phone.

"They don't listen!" Ellen exclaimed.

A timer went off and Penny pushed herself out of the rocking chair.

"I can get it," Ellen said.

"Naw, I need to move," Penny said, sounding tired. "Just more cookies. The stew is still warm on the stove for when Jake and Bobby get back, and Millie's shepherd's pie is edible, I have it on warm in the second oven. But I'm going to lie down for a spell, if you don't mind."

Penny got the cookies from the oven and turned it off. She shuffled around and Ellen was worried about her.

"Are you feeling okay?"

She didn't immediately answer.

"Grandma," Ellen said, and looked her in the eyes.

"I just want Avery back home. Is that too much to ask?" Tears welled in her eyes and Ellen hugged her, fighting her own tears.

"No, definitely not too much to ask," Ellen said.

When Penny went down the hall to her room, Ellen called Rick. It took him more than a minute before he answered.

"Sheriff Perez."

"It's Ellen. Any word about Avery?"

"No. I've alerted every deputy, and I've brought in everyone

I can. I alerted state police, the rangers, and every county in a hundred-mile radius. Photo and description of the Mendozas' truck as well as the license plate you gave me. No one has seen them, but there's not a lot of people out there right now. More cops and county work crews than people, to be honest. It's bad out there. Have you seen Ryan yet?"

"No."

"Dammit. LuAnne is panicking, he should be there by now, and he hasn't answered his phone. I tell her the cell phones are hit-or-miss, and lightning took out one of the towers."

"My power's out."

"Half the county is out. Your generators working?"

"Yes, but someone sabotaged our barn generator with copper wire, and the shock knocked Lyla back."

"Did you say *sabotage*?"

"Yes. It's not the first damage to our barn; I was going to file a report tomorrow."

"I'll get over to you when I can. Is Orchard Lane open?"

"West of Whisper Creek should be okay, but someone from the county just came by to tell me they were closing Orchard Lane at both ends."

"Must be even worse than I think, and I think it's pretty damn bad. Please call me or have Ryan call as soon as he gets there."

"I will. Thanks."

She hung up, ate one of the warm cookies, and picked up the folder labeled *Verdacorp Offer for Whisper Creek Ranch*.

She had to do something to get her mind off Avery.

CHAPTER TWENTY-EIGHT

Friday Evening

Travis was drunk. Not so drunk that he couldn't function, but he was ready to call it a night—even though it was only five thirty.

The rain had lessened a bit, but it was still coming down and the wind was picking up.

He checked on Timber, who wagged his tail when he saw him. He cooked up a couple hamburger patties—one for him, and one each that he broke up and added to the dog dishes over their kibble. Timber limped over to eat, a good sign.

On his bun, Travis put a couple pieces of cheese, a thick onion slice, and his grandma's barbecue sauce.

He drank water and popped four aspirin while he ate his burger and thought about what Clive told him earlier. Something was going on with Verdacorp. There was no logical reason that Mitchell would trade eight hundred prime acres of Baldwin's former land for the two-hundred-acre square that was better for grazing than growing.

Maybe he should have sobered up earlier, so he could think about the why.

And what about Monday morning was important? Why did Ellen have to sign before then?

If it wasn't raining, he'd drive over there and look around.

He almost laughed. He'd grown up on this land. He *knew* this land. Until he was eighteen and enlisted in the Army, he had left Cooke County only to play football at neighboring schools. His parents weren't big on vacations or time off—they lived and breathed farming.

There was nothing about that area that should appeal to Mitchell Robinson, except for the fact that it connected Robinson's property to Coulter's.

He rinsed his plate and stacked it in the drying rack. He took the dogs out to do their business, watching carefully that they didn't wander. Timber returned first, and Travis dried him off with a towel and opened the door to let him inside. He then waited for Titan, but he was nowhere in sight.

"Titan!" he called. "Come!"

He counted to twenty; the dog didn't come.

"Titan!"

The German shepherd responded with a bark from the far side of the house.

Dammit, he didn't want to get wet. "Titan!" he ordered in his most commanding training voice.

Titan barked twice.

Resigned that his dog had something to show him—probably a dead animal—Travis shrugged on his rain parka, put up the hood, and walked down the stairs with his cane. He hated using his cane, but the mud was slick and he needed the support. His fake leg was fine for walking around the house or going to the grocery store, but uneven terrain was problematic.

Though it wasn't yet six, the low, dark clouds made it look almost like night. The outdoor lights illuminated Titan, who stood fully alert at the door of his sub-basement.

Was it flooded? He had a pump down there because keeping it dry was always a problem. The doors weren't locked, and they didn't even close fully, but because of the awning his grandpa had built over the stairs, it usually didn't get too much water.

He heard a hiss and thought snake, but he rarely saw snakes on the property.

Please don't be a skunk.

Titan had been sprayed once as a puppy and it was days before he smelled more like dog than skunk.

He couldn't see what captured Titan's attention. "Come on, I'm getting wet." He started back around the house; Titan didn't follow. Instead, he barked again.

Travis went back inside, grabbed his flashlight and a crate. If it was a wild animal, he would trap it and take it out of the area tomorrow. If he tried to shoo it away, Titan would chase it.

Titan was a good dog and mostly well-trained, but he still loved chasing rabbits, foxes, and any critter smaller than him. He didn't kill them, but Travis certainly didn't want to chase his dog in this storm.

He went back outside. Now Titan was lying in the mud, head up, tongue out, tail wagging. He looked like he wanted to play.

Travis shined the light down the stairs.

Two eyes glowed back at him. At first he thought fox, but as he moved the light, he realized it was a black-and-white cat.

A cat trying to bring kittens up the stairs because the bottom landing was flooded.

Three kittens were on the third stair from the bottom and the cat had a fourth kitten in her mouth. She dropped it with the other kittens and went back down. She pulled another kitten from the water and went up three steps.

He didn't know if that kitten was alive. But she didn't go back down, instead watched him while she sat with the kittens.

She was wet, and likely cold and hungry.

He couldn't leave her out here.

"Stay," he told Titan firmly. He hoped he didn't regret this. These stairs were slick stone even when it wasn't raining.

He sat on the top stair and went down on his butt, bringing the crate with him. He was dizzy and his stomach lurched. The whiskey, the hamburger, the rain, sliding down these stairs on his ass. But he did it. One, two . . . seven stairs. The kittens were on the ninth stair down.

The cat hissed at him, but didn't attack.

"You're Cleo, I'll bet," Travis said. "There's a little boy who is going to be very happy to see you."

He reached down and picked up the first kitten. Cleo swiped at him and drew blood.

"Hey, I'm trying to save you and your brood," he said. He got the other kittens and put them in the box. He thought they were all alive, but he couldn't be positive. They weren't more than a day or two old, their eyes still closed.

He tried to reach for Cleo, but she ran back down the stairs.

He brought the crate back up. Getting up was a lot harder than getting down.

He put the crate on the ground under the awning, but the cats were wet and getting wetter. Titan immediately came over to inspect them, sniffing, tongue out, and Travis thought there was a smile on his dopey face.

"You're a strange dog," he said affectionately.

He looked back down the stairs. "Cleo, get up here," he called.

The cat just stared at him.

Well, shit.

Muttering and swearing to himself, he went back down the stairs, sliding halfway down when his fake leg went out from under him. He winced when he hit his knee hard on the stone.

"Damn cat. Come on, meet me halfway."

She just stared at him.

Grumbling, thinking he should have just left the cat to fend for herself, he lunged forward and grabbed her, pulling her tight against him. She struggled, but he had a good grip. She was skinny and frantic, but she was also a mom cat and he hoped she didn't bolt and leave her kittens. If she did, they would almost certainly die tonight because he couldn't make it to the feedstore to get kitten formula for them until tomorrow.

He had to practically crawl up the stairs, the angry cat under one arm, balancing with his other arm and good leg. He collapsed at the top and the cat fought him, hissed, but he held on. He took off his rain slicker while still holding her and quickly shoved her in the crate with her kittens, keeping the jacket over the opening. She hissed, jumped, tried to get out, but he held it firm.

Travis used Titan's strong back to help him get up, then the dog trotted next to him as Travis limped back to the house. His fake leg was crooked and he hoped he hadn't bent the metal attachments. He could probably fix it himself, but if it was broken, he'd have to go to the VA and get a new one.

It took him a good ten minutes to get around to the front of the house, up the stairs, and inside. He put the crate down and closed the door so the cat couldn't escape. He took the rain slicker off the top of the box. Cleo hissed, but didn't jump out of the box. Maybe she was hissing at Titan, who looked in as if he had found his new best friend.

Travis sat in the entry and caught his breath. Damn, he was out of shape. Too much alcohol and not enough exercise.

A few minutes later, he used the wall to help pull himself to standing. He took the crate to the kitchen, opened the pantry, and put it on the floor. The cat would feel safer, he thought, in a small, confined space.

He went to the linen closet and got a towel and an old wool blanket. He brought them back and made a bed for her under the shelf. He then filled a bowl with fresh water, and another bowl with tuna, since he didn't have cat food. He put them next to the new bed and then closed the pantry door. He wasn't worried about the dogs—they wouldn't chase the cat—but he wanted the cat to feel secure.

He picked up his whiskey bottle and poured the rest into a glass. Brought it to his lips, then stopped.

What the hell was he doing?

He had been near exhausted just getting the cat into the house, and he hadn't walked that far. He had to make some decisions. And the first decision was to get his fucking life together.

He poured the whiskey down the drain.

Instead of drinking, he took off his crooked leg, took a shower, and laid down in bed. He picked up the phone and called over to Ellen, to tell her he'd found Bobby's cat.

There was no answer.

He'd try again in a bit.

Travis put his leg back on. Yeah, the metal was bent, but not too badly, and he forced it back into place. It now made a noise when he walked. He'd have to go in and get it fixed, but at least he could get around.

He went to the kitchen, dumped all his alcohol down the drain. If he hadn't been drunk, he probably wouldn't have slipped down the stairs. Or he might have thought of a better way to get that cat and her kittens into the house. Then he cracked open the kitchen window to let in some fresh air—outside it was humid and thick, but it was better than the stale whiskey and sweat that filled the space. He cleaned. Not just the kitchen, but the living room, too, and then he changed his sheets as well. He doubted he'd changed them in a month.

An hour later, after he started a load of laundry, he opened the pantry door and peered inside.

Cleo was in the bed he had made her, four kittens nursing. He looked in the crate. One left. Travis touched it. It was stiff. He hadn't made it.

"Good job, Mama. You're a fighter." He picked up the crate. "I'll take care of this little guy for you. It wasn't your fault."

He left and closed the door behind him.

CHAPTER TWENTY-NINE

Jake had to drive the truck practically at a crawl along the slick, rutted road, one cautious foot at a time. The tires sloshed and slipped in the mud, fishtailing whenever he touched the brakes too hard or tried to accelerate too fast. Twice, the truck dipped dangerously into unseen holes.

The first time, Jake rocked it free by backing up and easing forward, again and again, his jaw clenched so tight it felt like his teeth would crack. The second time, he and Bobby had to shove it out—in knee-deep cold water. Mud sucked at his boots, and Jake didn't want to think about Bobby's bare feet. To his little brother's credit, he didn't complain. Jake's hands trembled as he climbed back behind the wheel, soaked, their breath steaming the window. Jake turned the defrost on high, and put the heat on for Bobby's feet.

He didn't say anything. Neither did Bobby. He wanted to ease Bobby's worried mind, but didn't know what to say. His headache pulsed behind his eyes with every bounce and lurch of the truck.

"We'll get home," he finally said as they started forward again.

"I know," Bobby said. And that was it.

Bobby trusted him, and Jake needed to earn that trust by keeping them safe.

He was even more worried about Avery than about the storm they were driving through. Where was she? Was she safe? Would he ever see her again?

The rain had let up just enough for the wipers to smear the windshield into something that resembled visibility. But as the rain lightened, the wind rose, shrieking through the trees. Leaves and twigs slapped against the glass. A chunk of bark bounced off the hood with a loud *clank* that made Jake's spine jolt straight and Bobby yelp.

He turned down Hopper Bend—Baldwin's road—and managed only a quarter mile before the way was blocked. A massive oak had come down across the road, its limbs sprawled wide, its roots torn up and pointing skyward like claws. Water gushed in the ditches, brown and fast-moving, impassable. The tree blocked one ditch, causing the water to pool there and rise, making it impossible to walk through.

He hadn't been able to go directly home because Whisper Creek had flooded the road; now he couldn't go what they'd always called the long way, basically a four-mile square. Now, he had no choice. He threw the truck into reverse and turned around, tires skidding close to the ditch's edge. He cursed under his breath, jaw tight. The blocked road meant he would have to go miles out of the way, halfway to Rock Creek Road, then cut across a private stretch of land he knew only by rumor and caution.

The Chisum family owned most of the land Jake would have to cross. They weren't always friendly, they were very territorial and mostly kept to themselves. Rumor was they made their living legally from their cattle, illegally from moonshine. They didn't like people coming onto their land, and Jake supposed if they were illegally distilling liquor, that was a reason to be distrustful. Still, his dad had had a cordial relationship with the patriarch of the family, Wyatt Chisum, who had gone to high school with Jake's grandfather.

But today he had no alternative if he wanted to be home tonight, and he hoped they would understand. They were practically neighbors, and they had something in common—neither of them had sold out to Verdacorp. That had to mean something. And tomorrow, he'd come back and bring a peace offering and an explanation. Because when they saw the ruts his truck made in their muddy road, they'll know someone came through and that would make them more distrustful.

When he reached the Chisum's private lane marked only with a NO TRESPASSING sign, he took a breath and told Bobby to keep his eyes open and be ready to hit the floor. He turned and drove in. Nervous, but resolute. The lane was similar to the McKennas' driveway—packed dirt and gravel. But this one was thicker, and while his beams reflected water in the fields, the road itself wasn't flooded.

He braced for headlights, for a shout, a bullet. The land passed in eerie quiet, fields dark and wet, air heavy with rain. He could barely see beyond the hood of his truck because sheets of rain continued to fall. Maybe the Chisums were hunkered down for the night, tending to their own troubles during the storm. He was mindful of cattle—though he figured their herd would have been moved to the highest area of the property, which was the southern half of their acreage.

Then bright lights came at him from the east, right in his driver's side window, nearly blinding him. They were so close and he hadn't seen them approach. They must have driven out here with only their fog lights on or completely blind in order to surprise him.

Dammit. If they made him turn around, there was nowhere he could go.

He slowed to a stop. He made out two pickup trucks with

monster tires, each with spotlights over the cab. Now he knew exactly where he was—the end of the driveway that went directly to their house.

Shit, shit, shit. Bobby looked at Jake, eyes wide.

Jake said, "Be calm, sit still." He kept his hands on the steering wheel.

He saw a man approach his window. He was in a dark gray rain slicker, blending with the dark gray clouds. The man had a handgun, which he used to tap on Jake's window so hard Jake thought it might break.

It didn't.

He had two options—bolt or talk. Running would be dumb. His truck couldn't compete with those two monster trucks, and he didn't know this land. He was heading straight through, but what if others waited on the other end of the road? What if they started shooting at Jake's truck? He *was* trespassing, after all.

He rolled down his window. He was near blinded by the spotlights, but he made out a man in his forties with a long beard and thick mustache, wearing a wide-brimmed, well-worn cowboy hat.

"You're trespassing, son. Turn around, go back the way you came."

"I'm Jake McKenna, and—"

"I know who you are. You're still trespassing. Willfully, I might add. The sign on the road is still up, it's clear what it says."

"Yes, sir, it is. And I'm sorry, but this is the only way I can get home. Orchard Lane is flooded to the east, I tried to go down Hopper Road, but an oak fell and blocked it. Rock Creek is flooded, so this is the only way I can get home."

When the man didn't immediately say anything, Jake continued, "The Mendozas who live on the other end of Orchard from us, they were held hostage by three robbers who shot Greg Baldwin and his dog last night. Now, those people have my sister and I have to get home to help my mother. I'll make it up to you as soon as the storm passes. I'm strong, and I'm good with cattle and horses."

The man walked away without saying anything else, went over to one of the trucks. Jake couldn't see him anymore, nor could he hear what anyone said. His chest grew tight and he wasn't above begging, but he doubted these people would respect him if he begged.

"What's happening?" Bobby whispered.

"I don't know," Jake admitted. "Just sit still, it'll be okay." He hoped.

A full two minutes later, the bearded man returned. "My pa says to let you go through. He says Penny's pecan pies are the best in Texas, was wondering if you'd ask her to bake a few. Maybe bring her over for a visit, Pa says it's been a while."

"They are the best in Texas," Jake said, not quite believing what this man was saying. "I'm sure she'd be happy to."

The man nodded once. "We'll be on the lookout for any strangers out this way. Oh, and call when you plan to bring the pies so we know when to expect y'all. And there's a gate at the end of this here road. It's closed with a chain, but it's not locked. You make sure you close it back up."

"Yes, sir. I know I don't have a right to ask a favor, but could you call my house and let my mom know I'm on my way back? We should have been home an hour ago."

He shook his head. "Phone lines are down. Sorry."

"That's okay, thanks, Mr. Chisum."

"Call me Maverick. I knew your pa. Sorry about his accident."

Jake nodded, rolled up his window, and drove forward. The trucks stayed where they were until suddenly the lights went off and Jake was again in the dark.

"That was stressful," Jake said out loud.

"They didn't seem so bad," Bobby said. "I think it's like Grandma says, some peacocks like to strut their feathers more than others, but they're all just birds."

Jake laughed, and the tension eased.

Ten minutes later, he was at the end of the private lane. There was in fact a closed gate; Jake braced himself against the wind, unchained it, then drove the truck through. He stopped the truck, went back and closed it exactly how he'd found it, fighting the wind the entire time.

When he got back into the truck, he was more exhausted than before, but the rest of the drive should be easier.

Still, when he crossed into Verdacorp territory, he felt the instant pressure in his chest, anger and tension that he knew wasn't good, but he couldn't help it.

Verdacorp had spread its tentacles throughout the valley after their success in the panhandle that made wealthy Mitchell Robinson even richer. Technically, the road wasn't theirs, it was a county road that went through their property, but Jake still didn't like being down here.

It was getting darker by the minute. He hadn't seen the sun all day, but the storm clouds had smothered the light, and there wouldn't be a visible sunset. The headlights barely cut into the gloom. Reflectors mounted on fence posts shimmered in the mist like eyes watching from the brush. The road looked wider than it was, but Jake knew better—one wrong turn and they'd be in the water-filled ditch.

Still, Bobby hadn't said a word since Jack had climbed back into the cab after securing the gate.

Jake glanced over. His brother sat stiff in the passenger seat, arms crossed, knuckles white. His silence was worse than his usual chatter. Bobby was holding his fears and worries inside. He saw the dangers of the road just as Jake did.

Then, at the four-way—no signs, just a crossroads of back roads—Jake spotted something glinting in the ditch.

He eased off the gas. Metal. Chrome. A vehicle. He felt Bobby tense and lean forward.

Jake swung the wheel gently and slowed. The beams from the truck hit the ditch just right and his stomach dropped.

It was a red truck, nose buried deep in the water-filled ditch, the passenger side nearly submerged. The floodwater had crept up to the road, rising fast, swirling around the submerged wheels. The current was stronger than it looked.

But that wasn't what froze Jake's blood.

The license plate was unmistakable, with the blue-and-white wheelchair printed before the numbers.

The Mendozas' Dodge truck.

"No," Jake whispered. "Please, no."

He jammed the gear into park but left the engine running. The heater blasted, but he already felt cold. He turned to Bobby. "Stay put. Don't open the door. Don't get out unless I tell you."

Bobby didn't argue. His wide eyes tracked Jake as he pushed the door open and stepped into the storm.

The wind punched him immediately. The air had taken on a chill and the rain drilled sideways into his jacket. Every step toward the ditch felt like stepping toward the edge of something terrible. He used his flashlight, its weak beam cutting through the dark. He had to look, but he didn't want to see.

The ground sloped down sharply, slick with runoff. Jake slipped once, slid, caught himself against a tangled mess of brambles. His boots hit water, then sank. The ditch was deeper than he'd thought—water up to his knees, rushing past his legs with enough force to knock a smaller man off his feet. And still he went down until he was submerged waist high and the current, churned up by the increasing wind, threatened to sweep him off his feet.

He reached the driver's-side window. Shined his light inside.

Water filled the cab—up past the seats. Front and rear.

No movement.

He pounded on the glass. Nothing.

Jake's heart hammered. He looked carefully, searching for a body. Looking for red hair.

Expecting to see his sister.

She wasn't inside. No one was inside, and he finally let out his breath. It came with a cry of relief.

His sister wasn't here.

Neither were the people who took her.

He pulled himself back up the embankment, then he lost his footing and slipped again, went under, the water swallowing him so fast he almost didn't realize what was happening. He burst back up through the surface, coughing and soaked, flashlight clutched in his hand.

Jake pushed back through the water, dragging himself up the bank, every step a struggle. His clothes hung heavy. He trudged back to his truck through ankle-deep water, which covered the road.

He pulled the door open and climbed in, dripping, shivering.

Bobby turned to him, tears streaking his dirt-smeared face.

"Was she—?" His voice cracked.

Jake shook his head. "No one's inside."

"But what if she's out here somewhere? Walking around? Lost? What if she's hurt? We have to look for her!"

Jake cranked the heat higher. He could barely feel his fingers. "She wasn't in the water. She got out. She could already be at home."

"No, she's not!" Bobby shouted. "Mom would have called on the radio."

Jake slammed his hand on the steering wheel, not hard, but loud enough to make Bobby flinch. "I know!"

The silence returned, hanging heavily in the cab. Jake sat there, hating himself for yelling at his brother.

He swallowed. "I'm sorry," he said. "I shouldn't have yelled at you."

Bobby said, “Me, too.” Then, “I’m scared, Jake.”

“Me, too,” Jake said.

He eased the truck forward, kept the high beams on. Scanning the shoulders. The ditches. The fields.

Looking for Avery. Looking for anything that might give him an idea of where she went, and if she was okay.

He didn’t see his sister.

He didn’t see anything except water and the debris the storm kicked up.

CHAPTER THIRTY

Brock laid the contracts on Mitchell Robinson's desk. "They're all there," he said.

Finally. He was almost done with this man. He couldn't wait to get home and find Sam a doctor.

He didn't like scaring that family, but he did what he had to do. With the money Mitchell paid, he could take time off to plan for the future. Find a job that didn't entail him to put his life—and his family—on the line.

Mitchell was going through the contracts one by one, nodding as he put each aside. Brock watched the rain pound on the deck outside the huge windows. If he never saw another raindrop it'd be too soon.

"Did you have any trouble at the McKenna house?"

"No, sir. She was preoccupied and led me right into the house to use the phone. The Coulter contract was sitting on the desk under the phone. I was discreet, slipped it right under my clipboard. There was so much going on that I don't think they'll even notice it's missing. She'll probably think someone accidentally threw it away or that she misplaced it."

Clive stepped into the room. "Rick Perez is on the phone for you, Mitchell. One of the McKenna girls is missing."

Mitchell picked up the phone on his desk. Brock couldn't hear the other end of the conversation, but he froze when he heard Mitchell say, "Hello, Sheriff, what can I do for you?"

The McKenna girl.

The redhead Rena had taken with her.

Brock needed to be calm. He'd leave her tied up in the Coulter house, they'd find her in the morning. Just like the family he'd left behind. All he wanted was to leave Cooke County tonight, no matter how bad the storm. He regretted taking this job and regretted ever knowing Mitchell Robinson.

Mitchell listened for a long minute, looking straight at Brock. Brock forced himself not to react, and not to look away. "I see, Rick. I'll definitely be cautious . . . Hmm. Yes. Of course. How is Greg?" Brock couldn't read his expression, but Mitchell had a good poker face.

This was fucked. Brock needed his money and he needed to get out of here now. Was Mitchell going to hold this over his head? Was he going to gyp him on the money he owed him?

Brock's fists involuntarily clenched, and he forced himself to relax.

"Let me know what I can do for Greg's girls. Anything . . . Yes, we're hunkered down for the night, good to hear that the flooding seems to be isolated. Thanks, Rick."

Mitchell put his phone down on the receiver. He stared at Brock. "There's a lot you haven't told me," he said, voice low and angry.

"I brought you the contracts. Pay up, and I'm outta here."

"Do you have her?"

Brock didn't respond. He didn't trust Mitchell. Hell, for all he knew he had a recording device under his desk that he could edit to make Brock look guilty and Mitchell innocent.

There wasn't an innocent bone in this man's body.

"Fuck," Mitchell said.

"Pay me what you owe me, and we'll leave tonight."

"What does she know?"

"Nothing."

They stared at each other. Clive looked from one to the other and said, "What the hell is going on?"

Mitchell opened his desk and took out a large manila envelope. He threw it at Brock. "Don't come back."

Brock left without another word.

═

"What the hell, Mitch?" Clive said. "What is going on?"

"Don't play ignorant," Mitchell said. He was angry at Brock Jones for shooting Baldwin and grabbing the McKenna brat, but he had all four contracts back, and that's all that mattered.

He walked over to his fireplace and burned each and every one. He turned, a smile on his face until he saw Clive's expression.

"Oh, please," Mitchell said. "You knew we had to get the contracts back."

"Because your bimbo screwed everything up!"

"I'm sending Nicole to Europe. We're through, she just doesn't know it yet."

"Avery McKenna is *missing*. The police are involved. It's going to come out— Dammit, Mitch, Rick Perez isn't an idiot. He's going to put two and two together."

"How? And even if he suspects something fishy, there is no evidence. None. I paid Brock in cash. I have no connection to him on paper, never been seen with him other than in front of *you*." Mitchell looked pointedly at his brother. "Do I have to worry about you, Clive?"

Clive shook his head. Mitchell took it as a sign he was on board, but his brother was annoying him more than usual.

"Grow a pair," Mitchell said. "This is business. If it weren't for me, Dad would have run the ranch into the ground. As it is, until we launched Verdacorp, we were in the red. Now, we've even exceeded Grandfather's vision. If I didn't save our land, you would be repairing cars down in Dallas for snobs, and you damn well know it."

"At least it would be honest work," Clive snapped.

Mitchell slammed his fist on his desk. "Our father squandered his legacy on booze and women. I saved it. *Me*, not you, because you have no business sense whatsoever." He might have gone a bit too far, so backtracked just a bit. "We make a good team, Clive. I have the business sense that Grandfather had, and you are good with people. They like you."

"You don't. You have no respect for me, or for the people we're screwing over."

"Don't go soft on me now, Clive," Mitchell said, his voice now a warning. "This deal is too important to blow right now."

"Blow? We don't have a deal if Ellen McKenna doesn't sign over those two hundred acres."

"I'm not letting one woman screw this up."

"What are you going to do? You can't force her to sell."

"Then you need to do a better job convincing her to make the trade. I'm giving her the moon, Clive—eight hundred prime acres for two hundred. It's a steal, and I'm not happy about it, but it's the only option on the table right now. You need to get it done."

Did he sound panicked? Maybe. A little. He needed that land. Presley was working on a forgery, but right now, it wasn't good enough. But if Ellen went to court it wouldn't matter—because what judge would think Mitchell was lying when clearly Ellen was getting the better end of the deal? At least on paper.

"I hope this is worth it, Mitchell," Clive said as he opened the door. "I really hope you can live with yourself."

He shut the door firmly. Mitchell hoped Clive didn't do anything stupid.

No, he wouldn't. He was as guilty as Mitchell. And if Mitchell went down, Clive would go down harder.

His phone rang and he wanted to ignore it, but caller ID told him this wasn't a call he could ignore.

"Hello, Jeanne. Just today I was finalizing the menu with the caterer for your fundraiser," he said, putting fake enthusiasm into his tone. "This is going to be your best event yet."

"I've heard," she said. He noticed she was losing her Texas drawl, at least when she wasn't speaking publicly in the district. Five short years in DC was already stripping away her roots. "Perry says we've already brought in eighty thousand, and we're getting more RSVPs each day. I'm thrilled."

"You should be, last year we only raised fifty thousand."

"Thank you for all you've done," she said. "But I wasn't calling about the fundraiser. I trust you and your people. But Davis told me the land hasn't been notarized yet. I can't hold up the bidding on the project anymore. The proposal has to be complete by Monday."

"It's in the process. My proposal stands as I wrote it."

"But the paperwork isn't in order. We're friends, Mitchell, I've really gone all out for you this time, but as I told you last week, I can't ask for another extension."

"I'm not asking for one," he said, his voice calm and cool, but he was seething inside. "I'm not pulling out, the land is mine, I just have to cross the t's and whatnot."

She sighed, spoke to someone on the other end of the phone, which irritated him. If it weren't for him, Jeanne Culvers would never have been elected. She thought running on her grandfather's name was enough to give her the win! Hardly. He cleared the field for her. He raised money for her. He owned her, and she damn well knew it.

But he didn't say that. Instead, he said, "Trust me, Jeanne. You really don't have a choice, do you?"

She didn't say anything.

He smiled without humor. She thought she was the politician? She was nothing but a prop.

"I'll talk to you later. Have a nice weekend," he said and ended the call.

CHAPTER THIRTY-ONE

Friday Night

By the time Avery and Ryan reached Greg Baldwin's house, they were so exhausted, drenched, and hungry they could barely think straight. Avery was severely chafed from walking in wet jeans for miles, and she didn't think that Ryan had fared better, though he didn't complain.

At the beginning of their walk, she'd told Ryan everything that happened; he told her that Bobby had reached out to him because he didn't want to use the family radio channel in case the people who held the Mendozas captive could hear him. Avery was so proud of her little brother, and grateful that Ryan had immediately called Jake to tell him where Bobby was hiding.

But after she finished sharing what happened, they walked in silence. No one passed them on the road, the ditches were filled with water and rising, and by the time they reached Baldwin's long driveway, it was near dark and they couldn't see where they were going. They had no flashlights and no streetlights illuminated the road. But Avery knew this country as well as anyone, and she recognized the straight row of cedar elms that lined Baldwin's driveway.

They turned and headed down toward Baldwin's dark house, careful with each step because of the potholes and deep water. Both of them had sore ankles, and Avery's head still pounded from where Rena had hit her with the gun.

But she was alive, and Bobby was safe, and she was so, so grateful.

"No one's here," she said when they came up to the house. Not even the security lights were on, which told her the power had gone out in the entire area and no one turned on the generator.

"Greg's still in the hospital," Ryan said. "I'm sure his daughters went there, not here. And they won't be able to get through tonight anyway."

Parts of conversations she'd overheard clicked in her head. "Brock, Rena, Sam—they did it. They shot Greg."

"Why would they stay around? They should have left after it happened."

"Because of the storm last night, they couldn't get out, and . . ." Avery thought, trying to pull together all the conversations she'd overheard. "I don't know specifics, but they talked about having one more job. When Brock left the Mendozas, he talked about being back in an hour or two and they'd leave. They promised not to hurt anyone, but . . ."

Ryan gripped her hand. "But you saw them."

A chill went down her spine. "Yeah. They aren't from Texas. Maybe they thought they could leave and hide and no one will know who they are. But they didn't wear gloves, their prints will be everywhere, and the younger guy, Sam, was injured. His blood is all over the guest room."

"My dad always said criminals aren't the sharpest tacks in the box." Ryan tried the door; it was locked. "You wouldn't by any chance know if Greg Baldwin leaves a key lying around?"

She shook her head. "Would your dad be very mad if we broke in?"

"He'll understand. But we'll walk around first, see if anything is unlocked."

None of the doors were unlocked, probably because the police had been here earlier this morning. So Ryan broke one of the small window panes in the mudroom, reached in, and unlocked the door.

They walked in dripping water onto the tile floor and Avery breathed a sigh of relief, even though the house was eerily silent. Not even the hum of an appliance. Except one faint tick of a grandfather clock, the pendulum moving back and forth. She shivered.

Ryan flipped a light switch. Nothing. He tried another. Still nothing.

He walked over to the telephone on the wall and picked it up. "Phone's out, no dial tone."

"I need to call my mom, let her know that I'm okay." Her voice cracked. Avery had been trying not to think about her family as she and Ryan walked here, and fortunately there had been enough to distract her. But now she was so close to home . . . yet it was almost impossible to get there. What if her mom or Jake went out to look for her? What if one of them got caught up in one of the flooded ditches? Or stuck in the mud? Or trapped by one of the many fallen trees? Or what if they knew someone had kidnapped her, because by now they would have gone to the Mendozas, right? Since Ryan had talked to Jake about Bobby being stuck in the equipment shed.

"My mom's probably freaking out," Avery said. "I have to find a way to let her know I'm okay."

"My dad, too," Ryan said. "We need to get out of these clothes, then we'll look for a radio. Baldwin has to have one someplace." He took off his boots and left them in the mudroom. Avery followed suit. She felt weird being here with Ryan. She of course knew

Baldwin's house well and had been here many times, but never alone. Even when she and Lyla fed and exercised his horses when he was out of town, they never went inside the house.

"Um, Greg's bedroom is at the top of the stairs to the right. I'll go to Monica's room." Monica was Greg's daughter and close to Avery in size and shape. They started up the stairs together. "This feels so weird," she muttered.

"Yeah," Ryan concurred. "But what choice do we have? I don't think Greg would mind."

"No, he won't," Avery said. "I really hope he's going to be okay."

They parted ways at the top of the stairs. Avery went to Monica's bathroom, stripped off her clothes, and hung them over the edge of the tub, though she'd probably throw everything out. Her shirt was stained, her jeans torn, even her underwear had holes in it.

She grabbed a towel and dried off. Her skin was cold and raw from the wind and rain; her hair a frizzy mess, her eyes looked bruised. Ugh. The insides of her thighs were so severely chafed they were blistered and bleeding.

She searched through the medicine cabinet and found petroleum jelly. She lathered it on the chafed skin. Though it still hurt, it felt so much better.

Avery opened the dresser, awkward and embarrassed and vowing to send Monica flowers or something as a thank-you and an apology all at the same time.

Monica was a senior in college, but fortunately visited often enough that she still had some clothes here. Avery put on underwear, found sweatpants, which felt much better than jeans against her damaged skin, and a long-sleeved T-shirt that was just a little too big. She brushed her thick, frizzy hair as best she could and then braided it down her back. She slid on a pair of wool socks and they felt amazing, though her feet were still cold, blistered, and sore.

She stepped out into the hall as Ryan emerged from Greg Baldwin's room, tugging at a pair of sweatpants that were far too big on him. Avery grinned as he pulled the drawstrings as tight as possible.

"I feel like a kid wearing my dad's clothes," he grumbled.

She looped her arm in his. "Let's find a radio. I'll look in the kitchen, you look in his office."

They split at the bottom of the stairs. Five minutes later, Avery found a radio in the pantry, oddly behind baking supplies.

"Ryan! Found it!"

He came into the kitchen looking sullen.

"What's wrong?" she asked as she turned on the radio. It came to life; the batteries were working.

"There was dried blood on the floor of this office."

She shivered, then reached out and touched his arm. "I'm sorry."

"They really are bad guys," he said. "They shot him *and* his dog. And they took you." He held her hand, brought it to his lips, and kissed it. She felt him shaking. "All for nothing."

"They didn't take anything?"

He shrugged. "I mean they probably did, I don't know what it was. My dad texted me this morning when I was at school, so I don't have details. He just said something like they made a mess but didn't take his guns, which are right out in the open. But these people had *you*, Avery. They could have killed you."

A chill went down her spine. "They didn't," she said and gave him a hug.

"I'm glad you're okay."

"I'm glad you found me."

He held her, and it felt right. She wished that Jake wouldn't give Ryan the cold shoulder like he'd been doing. They'd been friends, and Jake was treating her boyfriend like a . . . Well, like a jerk. And Ryan was the best guy she knew. They shared dreams, they wanted to share their future.

Everyone said she was too young to fall in love, but she didn't believe them. She knew how she felt—and how Ryan felt. They weren't planning to get married right after high school, but even if they did, so what?

They had a plan: two years at community college—she'd study agricultural business, and Ryan would study agriculture. He grew up in Cooke County but had always lived in town. He didn't understand farming the way she did, and she wanted to learn how to make the farm profitable.

Then they'd get married. She hoped to work the family farm, maybe even be an accountant—she was good at math, and business was mostly math anyway. She wanted it more than Jake, more than Lyla, who only cared about horses. Bobby was still too young to know what he wanted.

But she knew. She wanted what her parents had: roots. And someone to plant them with.

They sat on the kitchen stools and Ryan turned the dials on the older radio to tune it to the emergency channel. The nice thing about the older units was that they were durable; the bad thing was that they could be sensitive to the slightest nudge.

Then he started talking. "This is Ryan Perez, SOS, over," he said.

No response. He nudged the dial a hair.

"This is Ryan Perez, SOS, over," he repeated.

Static. He continued to nudge the dial until the static was sharper, and he repeated his call, adding, "I need to be put through to Sheriff Perez, it's an emergency, over."

"Ryan? This is Sally at county dispatch. Hold on, your dad is looking for you. Don't turn the dial! I'll patch you through. Over."

"Thank God," Ryan muttered. Avery squeezed his shoulder, barely breathing.

A half minute later, Sheriff Perez's deep voice came through the tinny speaker. "Ryan, is that you?"

Ryan grabbed the transmitter mic and pushed the button. "Dad!

It's me! I'm with Avery. I have so much to tell you, but we're safe. We're at Baldwin's place. The power is out and the phone lines are down."

There was a crackle, then his father's voice came in clearer. "Ryan? You're at Baldwin's? Are you hurt?"

"No, we're fine. Just wet and freezing and sore. We couldn't reach Avery's mom. Can you get through to Mrs. McKenna and tell her that Avery is okay?"

"Yes, but tell me what happened."

Avery spoke up. "I was at the Mendozas' house and three people were holding us hostage. Then the man named Brock left, and after, a woman named Rena took me, she was with her brother, Sam, who is really hurt, then she steered us into a ditch when she saw Ryan drive by. She carjacked Ryan, and he saved my life." There was so much more she needed to say. "I can describe all three of them. But someone has to check on the Mendozas! They were tied up in their house."

Crackle. Then, "Your mom was there, they are okay. No one can get into the north valley. Rock Creek is flooded so we can't get in through the east, and Mule Run is flooding so I'm stuck on the south side. But we've got roadblocks on every possible road out of the valley, in case the suspects try to flee. The whole area's boxed in, they won't get out."

"They're in my truck, Dad."

"I'll change the APB."

"They're going to a place on Privett Road," Avery said. "I don't know where, but the only places I can think is either the Sudduth ranch or the Coulters."

Crackle. Silence. Crackle. Avery looked at Ryan. "Did we lose him?"

Ryan pressed the button. "Dad? Are you still there?"

Crackle. "I had a call a couple hours ago from George Coulter. Someone impersonated their youngest daughter—someone who knows a lot about their family. The person pretending to be the daughter said she'd been in an accident and asked them to come down and help with the kids. They left before Mule Run flooded, called me when they realized it was a hoax."

"A hoax? That's so mean," Avery said.

"Coulter thinks it was a prank, but now I'm wondering if there's something else going on. Because we've had a rash of robberies in the area, and maybe the Coulters were next. But I haven't been able to get up there."

Avery was in a near panic. What about her family? "You have to get someone out to my house. What if they go there?"

"I haven't been able to reach your mom because of the phone lines, but I'll keep trying. Not everyone's lines are down, but I guess your area is completely out. There could be downed lines somewhere that we don't know about yet."

Avery looked at Ryan, imploring him. She said, "We have to go."

Rick said, "Stay put, both of you. It's safer where you are. Avery, describe the three suspects to me."

"Brock is tall, like as tall as you are, Mr. Perez. Maybe thirty. Dark hair, beard. Dark eyes. Big. Um, Rena—she, I think, is his wife, something she said when we were in the car. She's maybe the same age, a little younger. Long, dark blond hair. A little taller than me. And Sam is her brother, blond, he's not much older than Jake, I guess. Maybe nineteen or twenty? He was shot and is in a lot of pain and I think he's going to die if he doesn't get help."

Rick said, "I got all that, I'll add it to the APB, and we should be able to figure out who these people are and where they're holed up. Stay put, both of you."

"No!" Avery didn't mean to shout, but she was so worried about her family she couldn't think of anything else. "My mom doesn't even know I'm okay! What if she goes out looking for me? Or . . . What if she thinks the thieves are long gone but they're not? What if they go to my house? I have to warn everyone!" She was about to cry because she felt so helpless.

"Dad," Ryan said, "we'll take one of Baldwin's ATVs over to Avery's. We have to warn the McKennas."

"Dammit, son!" Rick exclaimed. Then, when Avery thought they'd lost him, a crackle and beep brought him back. "Okay, I get it. You listen to me—Whisper Creek flooded Orchard Lane, wiped out the road between the McKennas and the Mendozas. Last report in was that it's still rising. That means it'll flood all the fields in the area. It's nearly dark, and you won't know how deep the water is until you're in it."

"We'll be careful, Dad," Ryan said.

"I'm going to find a way in, if I have to take a damn rowboat across Mule Run. If the weather breaks and lightning passes, we'll send in a chopper. And Deputy Ferris is at the Rock Creek blockade. As soon as he can get through, he'll be on his way, too."

"We'll check in when we reach Avery's house," Ryan promised.

"Ten-four. Be safe. Sheriff out."

CHAPTER THIRTY-TWO

Brock slammed his truck door and ran up the steps to the Coulters' near-dark house, his wet, muddy boots leaving a trail behind him. He hadn't been able to reach Rena, but cell towers were down throughout the region, and he only had one bar on his phone that kept going in and out of service.

The screen door banged shut behind him as he stomped into the old farmhouse. Inside, the only light came from a battery-operated lamp in the living room, where Rena sat on the edge of the couch, her head in her hands.

She looked up when he came in—her face blotchy, eyes red from crying. Her lips trembled as she spoke.

"What happened?" He sat next to her, took her hand. It was cold, even though the house was warm. His heart pounded so hard he almost couldn't speak. "Where's Sam?"

"In bed. He's worse. He lied about his pain, now he can't lie anymore. He needs a hospital. We have to do it, Brock. We have to get help."

"Okay."

But he didn't get up. "What else?" He knew his wife, and he knew that something else was wrong. Then he realized something. "The truck out front—that's not the same red truck from the house."

She shook her head. "I did exactly what you said. I took the redhead, I tied her to the steering wheel. She was fighting me, I hit her with the gun. Out of rage, I hit her because she wouldn't shut up!"

His stomach fell. "And?"

"She complied, just like you said she would if I showed her who was in charge. She drove and then another vehicle was coming toward us. The driver recognized her and I knew we were in trouble. I panicked, turned the wheel, and we plunged into the drainage ditch. The truck started filling with water. I got out, got Sam out and—well, the other driver got out of his truck and I threatened him." She laughed, but there was no humor. "I fired the gun and said give me your car. He did. I left him, left her."

She put her head in her hands and sobbed. "I left her tied to the steering wheel and the truck was taking on water and I just left. I don't know if she's dead or alive. And now Sam—Sam is worse. If he dies, it's karma, for me leaving that girl."

He rose from the couch, his blood cold. Sam would *not* die. "Rena—" he began, but she steamrolled over what he planned to say.

"I cleaned up the mess you made," she said. "The papers. The drawers. I thought maybe if I could undo something—" Her laugh was short, manic. "It didn't fix anything. He's dying. My little brother is *dying* and it's all my fault." She pointed to the phone table. Brock glanced over, spied a Rolodex like the one his grandmother used to have. "I went through their phone book. It's all handwritten. And Ellen McKenna—the redhead's mom? She's a nurse. It says so, right there. A *nurse*. Maybe if we had known—"

"The girl didn't tell us," Brock said, jaw tight.

"Why would she?" Rena snapped. "We tied her up, scared her half to death, terrified her friend. Why would she tell us? We don't deserve the money. We don't deserve anything!"

She stood, paced, wrapped her arms around her body, but she was shaking and Brock didn't know how to fix it, fix her, fix Sam. He wanted to hit something, but was rooted in the center of the living room. Trapped. Frozen.

"Sam—he didn't ask for this. He followed us because he *loves* us. He wanted to help. And now he might—" She stopped, swallowed hard. "He doesn't deserve to die because we were desperate."

Brock's chest ached. He looked toward the hall, toward the dim bedroom where Rena had set up another portable lamp.

"I'll fix everything," he said, but had no idea how. No idea what he could do that would change the deadly course of events that were unfolding tonight.

He left Rena sobbing in the living room and walked down the hall to the bedroom. Stood in the doorway and looked at Sam.

He was curled on the bed, barely conscious. Fever glistened on his forehead, lips cracked, eyes fluttering but unfocused. He looked impossibly young—more like the fourteen-year-old boy Brock had rescued than the man he was supposed to be.

Brock knelt beside the bed. *God, not him. Please, don't take Sam.*

He thought of the day he met Rena—her arms crossed tight over her chest, trying to act like she wasn't shattered after her mom's death. Her dad had been drunk on the porch, yelling at Sam for something. The boy had looked up with silent defiance, his lip still bleeding from an earlier beating.

Back then, Brock only knew one thing: you *did not* hit someone smaller than you. You didn't hurt people who couldn't fight back.

He'd taken Rena and Sam from where he'd found them in rural Alabama when he was working for a jackass who was friends with their asshole dad, and they went to Louisiana, where Brock had grown up, where he knew the land and the people and could survive. It was a rough life, but it was *theirs*. They made it work—until they didn't. Crime had always hovered at the edge of Brock's life like a shadow, he flitted in and out of the life, and eventually, he stepped into it for good.

Robinson paid well. It was easy.

Until it wasn't.

Now Sam, the smartest kid he'd ever known, the one who never complained, who had always looked up to him, was dying. He saw it in his unfocused eyes.

Brock leaned over, kissed his forehead. "I love you, Sam. I'll fix this."

Then he walked back to Rena.

"I'm taking him to the hospital," he said.

She looked up sharply, surprised that he had agreed with her.

He dropped the envelope on the table. "You take this and go home. Sam'll need you when he's better."

"No." Her voice was firm, almost angry. She shoved the envelope back at him. "We do this *together*. I love you. Where you go, I go."

"You don't understand. They'll arrest us. I can't let you go down for what *I* did."

"*We* did it," she said fiercely, grabbing his shirt. "You think I don't know what I've done? I left a girl trapped in a submerged truck during a storm. I *left her*. I'll live with that forever. You don't get to carry this alone."

"The driver, he helped her," Brock said, though he didn't know that, couldn't know that. "You said he recognized her, right? So he helped her."

"If she was alive," Rena whispered.

He didn't respond. Instead, he kissed her desperately, then held her tight.

He said, "Bring the truck right up to the door. Not my truck, the other one, I'd rather have the Texas plates tonight than the Louisiana plates. I'll carry Sam out."

She nodded and disappeared outside.

Brock wrapped Sam in a comforter and cradled him like a child.

He was burning up, murmuring nonsense. As Brock eased him into the backseat, Sam whimpered and clutched his wrist weakly.

Brock leaned close. "Hold on, buddy. We're going to get you help. Just a little longer."

Rena slid over to the passenger seat and Brock took the wheel. The wipers squealed against the glass as the rain pounded and the wind swirled. They headed south down Privett Road, slow and steady. Brock's jaw clenched the whole way, each bounce of the wheels jarring Sam in the back. But he was silent now. Unconscious? Or dead?

The rain had thinned to a mist, but the road ahead shimmered with standing water. Then, without warning, the front of the truck dropped and slammed hard—*thud*—into a ditch and stalled.

"No!" Brock pounded the dash. "God, no!"

He jumped out into knee-deep water. The road had partly collapsed. A shallow sinkhole, the remnants of the last storm, now filled with swirling runoff from the fields.

"Damn it!" he shouted. He could practically feel the water rising up his legs.

Back in the truck, he turned to Rena. "Get in the driver's seat. Put it in neutral. I'll push us out."

"Brock, it's too heavy—"

"Just do it!"

He stomped back through the water, bracing his shoulder against the bumper. The ground was thick, muddy, uneven, but he dug his boots in and shoved with everything he had. He prayed, prayed to a God he had always acknowledged but never counted on.

For Sam. Not me, for Sam.

The tires spun. Mud and water sprayed. The truck rocked, then slowly, miraculously, rolled back.

Brock let out a ragged breath and stumbled to the passenger side. He jumped in as Rena restarted the engine—blessedly, it held.

"Where?" she asked.

"Ellen McKenna's house."

She flinched. "Brock, she won't help us. Not after what we did."

"We're not asking."

Her hands tightened on the wheel.

"For Sam," Brock said quietly. "We have to do this for Sam."

She wiped her eyes, put the truck in gear, and backed up slowly until she could turn around and head north.

CHAPTER THIRTY-THREE

Ellen was going half out of her mind with worry about Avery, but was trying to keep it together for Lyla and Penny. When she was alone in the kitchen, she picked up the phone to call Rick for an update; the line was dead.

Her cell phone had no reception, but that didn't surprise her as much as the landline. She couldn't remember the last time the landline had gone out during a storm. She tried the radio, but all she got was static. The one time she thought she heard a voice, it was gone before she could respond.

And Jake wasn't back.

She wasn't as worried about Jake—he had Bobby, she had talked to them, and Jake wouldn't risk dangerous roads. He would seek shelter and be safe—she believed it.

She had to.

But she was definitely worried about her daughter, taken by strangers, three people who had left Greg Baldwin for dead, who had shot a dog, who were desperate.

They had her child.

She cleaned the kitchen because it was that or pull her hair out. She wanted to go out and look for Avery, but she had no direction to go in. It was dark and far more dangerous now, even though the rain had lightened up. Because flash floods could take out a road or a field without warning. As she cleaned, she prayed hard that Avery would be okay. That she was fine. That she would come home in one piece.

Penny reclined in her easy chair in the living room, her eyes closed. She was an old woman, but she looked too old right now. It wasn't the baking and cooking all day; it was the stress of worry.

"Go to bed, Grandma," she called to her.

"I don't want to," Penny said, stubborn as usual. "Not until my great-grandkids are all home."

Lyla came downstairs with an empty bowl and glass and washed them in the sink. As Ellen put away the sweets Penny had baked that day, she asked Lyla, "How is Margery doing?"

"Tired. She's upset because the phones are down and she can't talk to her sister, but she ate Grandma's stew."

"Hopefully she'll sleep," Ellen said. "That's the best thing for her right now." She had checked her blood pressure when she brought up her dinner; it was steady at 135 over 70. Slightly elevated, but consistent. Ellen was thinking that her initial stress was caused by not talking to her husband on their planned schedule. Then it didn't help that they had driven through the storm.

Still, when the roads were clear, she would suggest that Susie take Margery to the doctor. They could monitor her blood, proteins, urine, everything they needed to make sure that she didn't have a serious condition that could jeopardize her or the baby. And hopefully, she could talk to her husband in the next day or two.

Lyla looked out the kitchen window. "The wind is picking up. Maybe I should check on the horses again. They were so agitated with all the thunder this afternoon."

"They're fine. They have their blinders on, they've been through storms before."

"Where do you think Jake and Bobby are?" Lyla asked.

"Safe," Ellen said, believing it mostly because she had to.

"Do you think Avery is going to be okay? Do you think they got out before Mule Run flooded? Is Sheriff Perez looking for her? And where's Ryan? Jake said Ryan was on his way here, but it's been *hours* and what if he got stuck?"

"Too many questions I can't answer," Ellen said. "The phone lines are down, cell reception is poor, so if Ryan couldn't get through, he may not have been able to call to let us know."

"But he uses a radio and knows what channel we're on. Why didn't he call?"

Ellen had been thinking about Ryan as well, but Avery dominated her worries right now. "I don't know," she said. What else could she say? "I tried reaching Rick earlier, but radios have limited reach, especially when it's raining. There has been some static on the radio, and maybe that's Ryan trying to reach us. Bobby's radio likely needs a recharge."

"But—"

"Lyla," Ellen said and turned to her daughter. "I'm worried, too. I hate being trapped here, unable to do anything. All we can do is wait."

Lyla, who was her least demonstrative child, spontaneously hugged her. Ellen melted into her embrace, surprised at how much she needed the hug.

"I love you, Mom," Lyla said.

"I love you, too, sweetheart."

They finished cleaning up the kitchen together, then Lyla went to sit with Penny in the living room, and Ellen decided to put on a pot of coffee. As it started to brew, she heard footsteps on the porch. Jake and Bobby? Finally!

She ran to the mudroom door, opened it, but no one was there. Her imagination playing tricks. She wanted her boys home and her mind convinced her they were.

Then she heard Lyla scream from the living room and Ellen

ran through the kitchen and dining room and stared at a large, hulking man in the threshold, drenched, with a handgun pointed at her daughter.

He turned the gun to Ellen. "Do not move. Do not do anything, or so help me God, I will shoot someone."

"What do you want?" she asked through clenched teeth.

"My brother has been shot. It's serious. You're a nurse. You're going to save him."

"No," she said. "I know who you are. You have my daughter."

He stared at her. "You save Sam, I'll give you your daughter."

A wave of conflicting emotions ran over her, and it was all she could do to not scream in frustration and fear. Instead, she said as calm as she could, "How do I know she's okay?"

"You don't. But if Sam dies, you'll never see her again."

He didn't break eye contact. Ellen glanced at Penny in her reclining chair, Lyla next to her on the couch. She thought of Margery upstairs, and her unborn baby and the stress this situation would cause. She thought of Jake and Bobby and the fact that they could come home at any minute, walking into this situation completely unaware of the danger.

Quietly, she said, "I'll help."

The man grabbed the shotgun from the corner and Ellen almost sobbed. She had another gun; it was upstairs in her nightstand. Jake had a rifle, but it was probably with him in his truck. But even if she could get to a weapon, she didn't know if she could stop them before they hurt someone in her family. And if she did stop them, there was no reason for them to tell her where Avery was.

She couldn't risk it. It was better to do what they wanted and hope, pray, he wasn't lying.

The man waved to someone behind him. She couldn't see her driveway clearly in the dark mist, but then a woman came in half dragging, half carrying a young man not much older than Jake. She steered him toward the couch, but Ellen said, "On the dining room table," and motioned through the opening. "I need the light and the surface."

She quickly pulled out a tablecloth from the hutch and spread it on the smooth surface. She helped the woman get Sam onto the table. He was wrapped in a comforter that looked familiar, but she couldn't place it. It was the familiar scent that tickled her memory.

But she dismissed that as soon as she saw that the young man was feverish and had a bandage around his abdomen and another around his leg.

"Is anyone else here?" the man asked.

She could lie and hope Margery slept through everything, but if she lied they might hurt someone.

"A friend of mine is sleeping upstairs. She's pregnant, in her last trimester, please let her be."

He shook his head, handed the gun to the woman. "Watch her," he told the woman. "Shoot her kid if she tries anything." Then he said to Ellen, "I'll try not to scare her, but she needs to be down here where I can keep an eye on everyone."

"I need my medical bag," Ellen said, resigned that she was being forced to help these people. "It's in the room with Margery."

He nodded, went upstairs.

Ellen examined her patient. He was pale and clammy. Feverish. His pulse was erratic. "He needs a hospital," she said. "He has an infection, he needs an IV, antibiotics, fluids. He needs—"

"We *tried*, dammit!" the woman barked. "The roads are flooded. We can't get out of this godforsaken valley. Just—do what you can. You're a nurse. Save him." Her voice cracked.

"Rena." Sam's voice was barely audible, a whisper sliding through cracked lips. "It's okay."

"It's *not* okay," Rena said, voice breaking. "I can't lose you, Sammy. Hang in there, she's going to help you." Rena looked at Ellen, her eyes pleading with her even as she aimed the gun at her chest.

Ellen's every instinct screamed to find a way to get these people out of her house. But they had Avery.

And this young man was suffering. No matter what they'd done, she couldn't let him die if she could help.

The larger man came back down the stairs, escorting Margery by the elbow. He glanced into the dining room, then brought Margery to the couch. "This will be over soon," he said, almost kindly. Ellen didn't know what to make of these people. One minute the man threatened to shoot Lyla, and the next he was gentle with a pregnant woman.

Margery looked from Ellen to the strangers, eyes wide, confused and scared.

The man said to Ellen, "I locked your dog in your bedroom. He looks like a good dog, but I can't be too careful."

Ellen nodded, turned to Margery, and assured her that it would be okay. She worried about her health as well as her own family. "They promised not to hurt anyone if I help them."

The man nodded, caught Ellen's eye, then put her medical bag down on a chair next to her. "I'm watching you closely," he said. "I may not know much about medicine, but I know about knives. If you try anything—"

"Just stop with the threats," she snapped. "I'm not going to do anything except try to save this man. He needs a hospital, but I understand you don't want to do that right now. I can make do with what I have in the barn. Livestock-grade ketamine and antibiotics. They're locked in a cabinet. I can be there and back in ten minutes."

"You're not going alone," he said. "You run, your family dies."

"You *have* my family," Ellen said evenly. "I'll come back. I promise."

"How do I know you don't have a gun out there? A radio? A phone? *No*."

"I can't promise he'll make it," Ellen said, "but if there's a chance—*any* chance—I need those meds."

Brock nodded at Rena. "Take the girl."

"No!" Ellen snapped.

"It's okay, Mom," Lyla said, already moving. "Just tell me what to get."

Ellen's gut twisted at the thought of her daughter outside with Rena, but she had no choice. She leaned in close, spoke clearly. "Ketamine's in a blue box. Antibiotics—penicillin and ceftiofur—white vials, red and green caps. Don't forget the flashlight."

Rena and Lyla left, rain and wind blowing in as they went out.

"Is that why you were here earlier pretending to be with the county?" Ellen asked the man. "So that you could case my house and determine whether you could just break in?"

"No," he said.

She waited; he didn't say anything else.

Ellen turned to Margery. "Are you okay? Do you need water?"

"I'm okay," Margery said, her voice shaking.

Penny took one of her hands. "They're not going to hurt us," Penny said with quiet strength, then turned to the man. "Right?"

"No, ma'am. I just want my brother to live. That's all. I'm sorry about the trouble. I just need my family safe. You can understand that."

His voice was almost earnest. Ellen wanted to believe him—but didn't.

"You came here under false pretenses," she said. "You're not with the county. Why? Tell me!"

He hesitated, then said, "You save Sammy, I'll tell you."

"And Greg Baldwin?"

His jaw tightened. "We didn't mean for him to get hurt. He wasn't supposed to be home."

Just like the other robberies this week, Ellen thought. What was going on with these people? Burglars with hearts of gold? She almost laughed at the thought.

Ten minutes later, Lyla and Rena returned, soaked to the bone. Rena held the supplies in a plastic bin. Lyla's expression caught Ellen, wide-eyed, alarmed. But she didn't say anything.

Ellen filed it away and turned back to Sam.

The dining room was the only space with halfway decent lighting and close to the kitchen for sterilizing tools. Ellen ordered Rena to boil a pot of water while she checked Sam's vitals. His fever was of the most concern. She would prefer to have an IV to inject the antibiotics and ketamine into, but she didn't. She would have to make do.

She did the math on a scratch pad and adjusted the dosage of the medication. She prepared three shots.

Once the water was boiling, she slipped on latex gloves and told Rena to do the same, then put her forceps and scalpel into the water and rinsed them with vodka that she had in the cabinet.

Sam's abdomen was taut and warm to the touch—bloated. The wound had started to scab at the edges, but it was oozing pus, dark and foul-smelling.

Ellen injected ketamine into his thigh. His body jerked briefly, then slackened. He was barely conscious when he came in; now he was out.

"He won't feel pain now," she told Rena.

With a second syringe, she injected ceftiofur directly into a vein at the bend of his arm, then followed with a broad-spectrum penicillin.

"You're really gonna cut into him?" Rena asked, pale.

"Unless you want the infection to kill him before you can get him to the hospital." She was more concerned about internal bleeding, and didn't know if she would be able to stop it.

Ellen took a deep breath. She sliced into the edge of the wound, carefully enlarging it to expose the embedded buckshot. Sam moaned, muscles twitching involuntarily under the sedative.

Every pellet she removed came with fresh pus and tissue. She worked slowly, methodically, gripping the tiny fragments with forceps, wiping blood and infection away, whispering to herself with every extraction.

"One . . . two . . . three . . ."

By the sixth pellet, her gloves were slick. Her fingers trembled.

"Come on," she whispered.

The seventh was lodged deep near his liver. She hesitated, then angled her forceps and eased it free. The eighth she nearly missed—it sat just beneath the skin near his navel, and removing it caused a sudden gush of blood.

Dammit, this wasn't good. "Pressure, I need pressure!" she barked.

Rena scrambled to grab a clean towel, pressing it down with shaking hands.

When the bleeding stopped, Ellen poured aluminum sulfate powder generously into the wound—old school, rough, but the best she had. It fizzed as it reacted with the exposed tissue. Then, she packed the cavity with gauze and wrapped the abdomen in layers of clean bandage.

Sam was pale, but still breathing.

Ellen leaned back, sweating, her head aching. It was the best she could do under the circumstances.

"He's unconscious," Rena whispered, leaning over him, eyes red and wild. "Is he still . . . ? Is he . . . ?" She looked up at Ellen, imploring her for an answer.

"Yes, he's alive for now. If he has internal bleeding, I can't fix that here."

Tears streamed down Rena's face. "It's my fault. All of it. I just wanted to help him . . . I didn't mean for your daughter to get hurt. I was scared. I—"

"Save it."

Ellen got up and went to the kitchen. The man followed her, stood in the doorway between the kitchen and dining room where he could see everyone. She pulled off the gloves and tossed them in the trash, rinsed the blood from her arms and scrubbed with soap and hot water.

"You want to help your brother?" she snapped. "Get him to a hospital the minute the rain stops. If you wait, you'll lose him."

She glanced at the man. He still held the gun, but it was lowered to his side. "Is he gonna make it?"

"I don't know," Ellen replied honestly. She showed him the bowl of bloodied pellets. "These were in his gut. There's still a bullet in his leg, but I didn't touch that. Too risky, and it doesn't look infected."

His jaw tightened and he nodded once. "Thank you."

"What's really going on?" Ellen asked him. "You promised to tell me."

"Mitchell Robinson hired me," he said quietly. "No one was supposed to be home. I didn't want to hurt anyone, I sincerely hope Baldwin makes it."

It took Ellen a moment to realize what this man had said.

"Mitchell Robinson hired you to steal from Greg Baldwin?"

"And others," he said.

"What could they possibly have that he wanted?"

"Contracts. They were all signed last week but there was an error in it. He needed the contracts back."

"That makes no sense. If the contracts are signed, they're signed. He's what, stealing them back and then . . . ?"

The large man shrugged. "I don't know. He didn't tell me everything, other than where to go and when the house would be empty. Take the contract, break the computer, steal a couple other things so no one knew what we were really after."

"But most contracts are electronic. There's going to be a record."

"He had someone with the skills to hack into the signing program and delete the clause, and I guess the forged docs were the ones filed in the recorder's office. He just didn't want anyone to come up with a different version."

"Three houses . . ." Then Ellen realized why he was at her house earlier today. "How did you know I had a copy of the Coulters' contract?"

He laughed humorlessly. "Robinson has cameras everywhere. He saw you leave the Coulters this morning, and when I found just a copy of the contract, he assumed that you had the original."

"And you took it."

He nodded.

She had only skimmed the contract and didn't remember the details. Only that George was confident that Verdacorp couldn't exercise any of the mineral rights. She saw a clause related to that, but she couldn't remember it verbatim. But if one of those clauses was removed, it could make all the difference.

"He really wants that plot of land," the man said. "Those acres between his property and the Coulters' property, where he has the right-of-way. Like, desperate."

"And you don't know why he's so desperate?"

"No. I'd tell you if I knew. You saved Sam, I owe you."

"My daughter—" she began when she heard Penny calling for her.

"Ellie? Margery needs you."

"The pregnant woman?" Ellen said to him. "She's showing signs of preeclampsia. If her blood pressure spikes, she and the baby are both in danger. You keeping a gun on her isn't helping."

He said nothing.

Ellen took a moment to compose herself, then walked into the living room, brushing past the man with the gun. He followed.

She took Margery's blood pressure. It was 150 over 80. "Lie

down," she said gently but firmly. "Close your eyes. Breathe slow. In. Out. You're going to be fine."

"Mom," Lyla whispered, kneeling beside Margery, voice low. "Ryan's truck is out front. They came in *Ryan's truck*."

Ellen's blood ran cold.

Where was Ryan?

Ellen touched Lyla's arm—*I heard you*—then rose slowly, heart thudding in her chest.

She turned to their captors.

"Where is my daughter?" Her voice was surprisingly steady. "I did what I promised. Now tell me where Avery is."

Rena looked to the man. "Brock," she said, her voice quivering.

The man didn't answer either of them.

Ellen took a step forward, voice rising. "What did you do?" Her breath hitched. "What happened to my daughter?"

CHAPTER THIRTY-FOUR

Jake slowed as he approached the corner of Orchard Lane and Privett, headlights sweeping across the reflective sheen of the water. County traffic barriers stood in a crooked line, barely visible in the dark, orange cones and sawhorses sagging under the weight of relentless drizzle, reflective circles first bright, then dark. Water pooled thick and black across the road, rippling with the wind. He couldn't see how deep it was, but based on the water at the base of the closest sawhorse, it was about a foot deep. He could drive through a foot of water in his truck, but he didn't know if it was deeper farther down. Probably. The county didn't throw up those signs for nothing.

He cursed under his breath. Home was less than a mile down that road. He could almost see it—lights, dry clothes, warm bed. But not at this risk. Not with Bobby sleeping slumped against the passenger door, arms curled around his ribs. And they couldn't exactly walk when Bobby had no shoes, especially when they couldn't see what they were stepping on.

Jake eased off the gas and kept going straight, then a quarter mile up the road he turned sharply onto a long, waterlogged gravel drive that disappeared into a wall of pines.

Uncle Travis's place.

He hoped his uncle was sober. He didn't want to get into a fight with the man. He already felt bad about their conversation earlier today, when Travis wanted to help and Jake said no.

The headlights bounced as the truck rattled over potholes and splashed in pools of water. He drove through one low spot where the water splashed up and covered his windows. He was lucky he didn't stall out. Then the old farmhouse came into view—porch light on, almost inviting. Jake cut the engine and sat for a moment, watching the flickering light from the kitchen window, willing the rain to stop. It had slowed, but was still falling in a steady mist. What did it matter? He was still wet from getting out when he found the Mendozas' truck—and didn't find Avery.

Jake reached over and gently shook Bobby awake. "Hey, bud. We're at Uncle Travis's. Orchard is blocked off by the county."

Bobby blinked groggily, then looked around. "Uncle Travis?" he repeated.

Jake nodded. "Yeah. Come on, I'll carry you."

Jake carried Bobby up the porch steps. Travis answered after one knock, rubbing his face with a towel, dressed in an old flannel shirt and jeans. He looked alert and clean—he'd even trimmed his beard, which was redder than his brown head of hair. He wasn't the disheveled drunk Jake usually thought of when he pictured his uncle.

"Jake," Travis said with a quiet surprise. "Didn't expect— Come in. What happened? Come, get outta the rain."

Inside, the place was cleaner than Jake had ever seen it, at least since his great-grandmother had lived here. No open bottles on the counter. No smell of stale beer or whiskey. Travis must've seen the look on his face because he offered a small smile.

"Yeah," he said. "I cleaned up."

"You're sober," Jake said bluntly. He smelled coffee now, and bacon and eggs—Uncle Travis always did like breakfast for dinner.

"I am tonight. And hopefully tomorrow." Travis stared him in the eye. "I'm going to try and stay sober. I dumped out all the whiskey, and since there's no getting to the store in the next day or two, it's a start." He glanced at Bobby, "Hey, I heard you were looking for a black-and-white cat."

Bobby nodded sleepily. "Cleo."

"Pregnant, right?"

"Yeah. She ran away during the hailstorm Saturday night. I'm worried about her, so if you can look for her tomorrow?" he added hopefully.

"Well, I think I found her. Look in the pantry, but slowly. Don't spook her."

Bobby's eyes widened, and with more energy than he had since Jake found him that afternoon, he half ran, half limped through the kitchen and then slowly opened the pantry door. He peered inside, then he closed it quietly and turned around, a huge grin on his face. "You found her! She has kittens!"

"Four," Travis said. "She had them at the bottom of the stairs leading to the cellar. And I can't take the credit, Titan found her and alerted me."

Bobby sat in the kitchen chair and said, "I was so worried, but I knew she was a smart cat. I knew she would find a safe place!"

Jake glanced at Travis. The bottom of the stairs wouldn't have been safe during this storm, the cellar had a pump, but with rain like this, it would have deep standing water until the pump could catch up.

"I'm glad I found her in time," Travis said. "You got no shoes on, kid. Look at your feet."

"I lost them in the mud when I was running from the bad woman."

Travis looked at Jake. "What?"

"Long story," Jake said. "Bobby, your feet are a mess." They were caked with mud, appeared to have cuts all over them, and one toe was bleeding quite a bit. Jake was surprised he could walk at all.

"Come on, kid," Travis said, "I'll clean you up."

Jake carried his brother into the bathroom. While Travis gently cleaned and bandaged Bobby's feet, Jake told him what happened that day. He hadn't intended to share, but Jake needed help—and sober Uncle Travis was a lot smarter and more dependable than drunk Uncle Travis.

When Travis was done cleaning Bobby's wounds, he handed Bobby a T-shirt to change into; the faded army shirt went to his knees. Jake carried Bobby to the couch. Timber looked up and licked the air, as if greeting him. Titan jumped onto the couch and lay down with Bobby. Travis spread out an old handmade quilt, and Bobby happily petted Titan.

"I need to call Mom," Jake said. "Cells have no reception right now, and the radio died."

Travis handed him the house phone, and Jake dialed home. It rang once. Then again. And again.

No answer.

Not even the machine.

He hung up and tried again. Same result.

"The lines must be down," Jake said as he hung up, his gut twisted at all the things that could be wrong at his house. "Can you keep an eye on him?" Jake nodded toward Bobby, his voice tight. "I need to go home, but I might have to hoof it part of the way and Bobby is in no condition to walk."

Travis stood. "We'll both go. I'm not gonna sit on my ass when my family might be in danger."

"You sure?"

Travis was already pulling on his boots. The metal around his artificial leg creaked. "Bobby can stay here. Dogs'll keep him company. If we get stuck or have to walk, we can't leave him in the truck."

Travis was right. Bobby sat up, clearly fine with being alone here. "I'll be okay. I know where everything is, and I'll take care of the dogs and Cleo."

Jake paused, uncertain, but both Bobby and Travis seemed satisfied with this decision. He kissed the top of his brother's head and said, "Keep the door locked, don't open it for anyone until we get back."

"Promise," Bobby said. "Titan is a good watch dog, he'll let me know if anything is wrong."

Travis scratched Titan's head. "That he will."

Then Jake and Travis walked back out into the rain.

They took Jake's truck and drove back the way he had come, reaching the county barriers in ten minutes. Rain was picking up again, falling in thick sheets, drumming against the roof of the truck. Jake got out, moved two of the barriers so he could drive through.

The road ahead disappeared into a wall of rain.

Jake gripped the wheel tighter as he cautiously drove down the deeply rutted road, water splashing under his tires. But it wasn't deep—no deeper than any of the other roads he'd been on today, and none of them had been barricaded off. Were they worried about a flash flood? It had happened before. But the thing about flash floods is that they were usually unpredictable, and there were other areas of the valley more prone to them than Whisper Creek. Nowhere did the water reach the top of his tires.

Nothing was right about this.

When Jake got to his driveway, he knew the power was off because the light he and his dad had installed that illuminated the

Whisper Creek Ranch sign was off. The generator at the house wouldn't power any of the external lighting they put up.

He turned off his lights, keeping on only his fog lights.

"What's wrong?" Travis said.

"Bad feeling."

It took all his self-control to drive slowly.

CHAPTER THIRTY-FIVE

Avery and Ryan took one of Baldwin's ATVs across his property to the land bridge that Baldwin had built over Whisper Creek, at the point where it met his property line—or now Verdacorp's property line, Avery thought. It was practically all her mom and Jake talked about the last ten days—Verdacorp buying up land or Jake deciding not to go to college. It had been tense around the house, and Avery wished they wouldn't argue.

Ryan stopped the ATV as the headlights revealed a swollen creek that reached the underside of the land bridge, at the very top of the large pipe culvert that Baldwin had put in to direct the creek into the man-made lake.

"I've never seen it so high," Ryan said. "Is the bridge going to hold?"

In the dry season, the lake always had some water because of irrigation overflow and Baldwin's own system, but during spring it helped with both irrigation and flood control. It was wider than she'd ever seen it before.

They had already had to drive around flooded fields and the lake to reach this point, and Avery wasn't going to be thwarted now.

"Yes," she said, though she didn't know. "It's reinforced with the culvert, horses and ATVs have gone over it hundreds of times." It was wide enough for a small tractor. Though the ATV was idling, she could hear the roar of the fast-moving water.

"Ryan," she said, "go. Now." She was nervous, but she had to get home. She had to make sure her family was okay.

He pressed the throttle and they moved forward slowly. Water splashed up from the creek that looked and sounded more like a river. But they made it across, and Avery breathed easier.

They drove along the higher western bank of the creek, which was a well-packed path. Avery spared a glance across the creek—the eastern fields were flooded, and she knew her mother's beloved vineyard she'd planted with Dad wouldn't survive. She hoped the western plot made it, because she didn't like to see her mother sad.

They came toward the barn from the east, and Avery was surprised the barn lights were out and no one had started the generator.

"Hey, Avery, that's my truck," Ryan said as he released the throttle and they stopped on the far side of the barn, where they wouldn't be seen from the house.

The lights were on in the house, and when Ryan spoke, she realized the vehicle parked next to the porch steps was, in fact, his truck.

Avery lurched forward, but Ryan pulled her back. "Be smart," he said.

"That woman took your truck and now she's here! Why?"

"Shh," he said. "The front door is opening."

Ryan turned off the ATV and they ducked into the barn and squatted in one of the stalls, the one that housed Sir Lancelot, her mom's favorite horse. A minute later, the main barn door opened and Avery heard Rena say, "Hurry."

"I am."

Lyla. Her sister was with Rena.

A flashlight shined around the barn, and Avery instinctively shrank as small as she could. Lyla and Rena went into the small office. Lyla said something, but Avery couldn't make it out. Then Rena said, "As soon as possible, we'll leave. We don't want to hurt anyone. This whole thing just got out of control."

"You can always change your path," Lyla said. "You don't have to do what you've always done."

"You're a kid. You live *here*. You have parents who love you. You have no idea what the real world is like."

Avery strained to hear what Lyla said, but the jangle of keys drowned her out and then they were gone.

Still, Avery waited a minute before speaking.

"They opened the medicine cabinet, I'm almost positive. Rena's brother was seriously hurt, he was shot when they robbed Greg Baldwin. That's why they're here! How did they know my mom was a nurse?"

"Maybe they didn't. Maybe they just got lucky."

"But they came here *specifically*, we're not even off a main road. How did they find us? They must have learned from someone that my mom is a nurse."

"A lot of people know your mom is a nurse. I don't think it's all that strange."

Avery thought, shrugged. It didn't matter how they knew, what mattered was that these people were here and could hurt her family.

"We have to do something," Avery said and jumped up.

He pulled her back down. "Stop and think for a second. They have guns. We don't. My dad can't get up here. No one can. We don't even have a working radio with us."

"But— What if— That's my family, Ryan! I can't sit here and wait for something bad to happen to them."

He was thinking, and so was she. "What if," Avery said, forcing herself to be as calm and rational as possible under the circumstances, "we walk around to the mudroom door. We stay low so they can't see us out the window. I don't think they can hear us over the rain if we're careful. We can sneak in or at least look through a window and see what's going on."

"I don't think that's a good idea," he said, then admitted, "but I don't have a better one."

They determined that the best way to get onto the porch without being seen was to go around the house's north side. The living room and dining room faced the driveway—the kitchen faced south, which was next to the mudroom, which had the door they usually used to avoid tracking dirt through the living areas. The kitchen, dining, and living room were all lit up. But the west side of the house was her grandma's room and the den, where they watched television and used the computer. It was most likely no one was in those rooms, so no one would be able to see them approach if they went around the north and down the west side of the house to the mudroom door.

She hoped.

Though the rain had lightened to a steady drizzle, the wind was fierce, driving the small raindrops into her face as they stayed low and close to the barn and garage. They would have to run across the driveway, but it was so dark now Avery didn't think anyone would notice unless they were standing on the porch looking directly at them.

As they ran, Avery thought she heard something. She hesitated, looked down the driveway and saw fog lights reflecting off the rain, surprisingly close. Ryan pushed her down into the mud and they both landed with a grunt.

Was this one of the bad guys? Maybe Brock, the man who had scared the Mendozas, meeting his wife here? To do something bad to her family? Or . . .

"Ryan? Avery?"

"Uncle Travis?" she said.

Her uncle climbed out of the passenger seat. "I heard you were kidnapped by the people who robbed Baldwin."

She hugged him tightly. "Yeah," she said into his chest. She realized then that the truck was Jake's, and she walked over to the passenger door and leaned in, looked around. "Jake? You have Bobby, right?" She didn't see him in the back. Panic flared. "Ohmigod, he's still out there, he's—"

"At my house," Travis said. "Safe and sound."

"Really?" she asked. "You're sure?"

"Or course I'm sure," Travis said with a smile. "You okay?"

She nodded, as she forced her heart to slow down. "I just— I was so, so worried about him."

"Long story," Jake said. "I wasn't certain we'd get through the flooded road, so thought he'd be safer there with the dogs."

Avery breathed easier, then said, "The woman who kidnapped me is inside with Mom. I don't know who else. We were going to look in through the windows."

"We need a plan," Jake said. "Climb in and tell me what you know."

Ellen stared at Brock and Rena who were still standing in the entry between the dining room and the living room.

"Where is my daughter?" she asked again. "You promised to tell me where you left her."

They looked at each other, then Brock said, "There was an accident."

Ellen shook her head, not believing what she was hearing. "Where. Is. She." When they didn't respond, she pounded her fist against the wall. "I just saved your brother's life, tell me where my daughter is!"

"At the end of Hopper Road, right where it turns to the one-lane county road that goes to Privett," Rena said.

Her eyes burned, her gut churned, but she asked as calmly as possible, "Is she alive?"

"I believe so," Rena said quietly.

"Go get her," Brock said. "I'm not going to stop you. I'm sorry about all of this, really I am."

Ellen wanted to scream. Her daughter was out in the storm after an accident and these people had just left her.

Brock continued. "You get Sam to the hospital tomorrow, okay? And we'll go. We'll leave. And you can get your daughter."

"You won't make it out tonight," Ellen said. "We live in the middle of tens of thousands of acres of farmland. There are no paved roads. Drainage ditches are flooded. Rock Creek is flooded, so you can't go that way, and you'll be lucky to get out to the south, Mule Run that cuts across the valley is also flooded."

"We'll take our chances," Brock said.

"Take me to Avery," Ellen said.

"And leave you there?"

"You know exactly where she is, I don't. Please. Hopper Road is miles long. There are at least six intersections. It's dark. What if I miss her? What if she's wandering the roads? Please!"

"We have to," Rena said to Brock. "She saved Sam. We have to do this."

He looked pained. Ellen didn't give them the opportunity to change their minds.

Ellen ran to the mudroom to get her jacket, and Rena walked over to Sam. He was still unconscious, but his chest rose slowly up and down, up and down.

Ellen said to Lyla, "If he wakes up, inject him with this." She put a premeasured syringe on the hutch. "It's a smaller dose of ketamine and will help with the pain and keep him calm."

Rena kissed her brother on the forehead. "I love you, Sammy. I'm so sorry this happened." She looked up at Ellen, her eyes red and overflowing with tears. "He just did what we wanted. He wasn't part of this, not like Brock and me. Please ask the police to go easy on him."

"If Greg Baldwin survives," Ellen said.

"He wasn't part of it. He was the driver."

"He would still be considered an accessory."

Rena turned to Brock, panic in her sad eyes.

"I don't know that he would survive the drive home," he said to her.

Rena turned to Ellen, imploring her for leniency.

Ellen said, "I'll tell the police exactly what you said. But it's not up to me what they decide to do."

"Okay," she whispered. The woman was exhausted, dark circles under her eyes, and Ellen didn't think she'd slept in the last two days. She had a small tug of sympathy, but it was *very* small. This woman had left her daughter in the middle of a storm. Ellen hardened her heart as she grabbed the extra flashlight and a pocketknife from the kitchen drawer, hoping they didn't see her take the knife. She grabbed the radio off the charger, put it in her pocket.

"You love your kids," Rena said quietly.

"I do. We need to leave to get my daughter. Right now."

They started for the door. Ellen hugged her grandmother. "I'm going to bring Avery home," she said.

Penny nodded, but she was shaking. Ellen hated that these people had scared an old woman.

"Look out for Margery, okay? Call Dr. Patel, I have his personal number in my phone book."

"I wish Sam and I had a family like yours," Rena said wistfully. "Our daddy thought I was his wife and Sam was his punching bag."

It was clear now what this woman had gone through as a child. Ellen didn't like her, she would turn her in as soon as she had the chance, but maybe she understood a little better how she reached this place in her life, how she could put her own brother in danger, how she could abandon Avery to the environment.

Ellen reached out and lightly touched her forearm. "Your decisions now are *your* choices."

Brock said, "I left my truck at your neighbor's house because I thought it might have been identified by the police. I'll take you there, then you can follow me to where the accident happened."

Rena said, "It was my fault. I got scared when I thought someone recognized your daughter, and I created the accident."

"Ryan— You have his truck," Ellen said as she stepped out on the porch, and gestured to the older model Ford F-150. "Where's Ryan?"

"I left him at the accident. With your daughter."

Ellen frowned. They wouldn't have stayed in the middle of nowhere in the storm. They would have walked to a neighbor no matter how far. Found a way to contact her.

Unless they couldn't.

Brock opened the passenger door for Ellen, but she hesitated, trying to think what Avery and Ryan would have done after the accident. If Avery's injuries weren't severe, they would go someplace safe, to a house, to a barn. They'd find shelter if they could. Where depended on which intersection where the accident occured.

"What's wrong?" Rena said.

Before Ellen could answer, a man stepped out from behind Ryan's truck. It was Travis, and he had a shotgun.

"Get away from her," Travis said.

Brock pulled out his gun and Ellen said, "Stop! Please! No more violence."

"Mom!"

Ellen whirled around and saw Avery, Jake, and Ryan running from the backside of the porch.

"Avery!" Relief flooded through her at the sight of her daughter.

Brock looked from the kids to Ellen. He grabbed Ellen and whispered in her ear, "I'm not going to hurt you, but I don't want your friend to get an itchy finger."

"Travis, stand down," Ellen told her brother-in-law.

"I'm not letting them take you, Ellen."

"They're not. They're leaving. Right?" she said to the man.

His fingers squeezed her biceps hard enough to bruise.

"Rena, get in," he ordered.

She climbed into the passenger seat and shut the door. Brock pulled Ellen over to the driver's side. "Open the door," he said.

She did.

Travis held the shotgun on the vehicle as Brock climbed in. Brock then whispered in Ellen's ear: "If you want to take down Mitchell Robinson, I kept a copy of everything. It's in my truck at the Coulters' house." Then he pushed Ellen away from the truck and slammed the door shut.

As the ignition turned, Ellen ran up the porch stairs and hugged Jake and Avery. "They said you were in an accident. I didn't know." She was crying.

She heard a shotgun blast and jumped.

"Travis! No!"

The truck fishtailed as buckshot hit the rear gate. Travis racked the shotgun again and took aim.

"Stop!" she screamed. "No more violence. Not here."

"You want them to get away?" Travis asked, shock on his face.

"The police are looking for them. I know their names, and Rena's brother is here. I removed buckshot from his abdomen, but he's in poor shape. I don't know that he's even going to survive, but because I helped him, they gave me information. I know who hired them. I just don't know why."

Travis lowered the shotgun. The taillights disappeared from view. "Who?"

"Mitchell Robinson."

CHAPTER THIRTY-SIX

As soon as they stepped into the house, Ellen looked around. "Where's Bobby?"

"At my house," Travis said. "We weren't sure we'd be able to get through and we didn't want him walking. He lost his shoes."

"Is he okay?"

"Yes. He's great," Travis said.

"Uncle Travis found Cleo," Jake said. "She had kittens."

"Bobby must be so happy."

"Timber and Titan are with him, the house is secure. He's safe," Travis said. "What is this about Mitchell Robinson?"

Before Ellen could explain, she saw Penny getting up out of her chair after taking a fierce hug from Avery. "You doing okay, Grandma?" Ellen asked, concerned about the dark circles under her eyes.

"I'm tired. But I'm okay." She kissed Ellen's cheek. "I'm proud of you. Now you and Travis figure out how we're going to prove that Mitchell Robinson, that bastard, is behind all this."

Penny hugged the boys, including Ryan, then hugged Avery again. "I'm glad you're back in one piece," she said, then shuffled down the hall to her room.

Ellen turned to Margery. "I'm going to take you upstairs, back in bed. You need sleep."

She got Margery settled, checked her blood pressure again—elevated, but not as high as before—and brought her water. She was asleep almost before Ellen left the room.

She let Whiskey out of her room. He ran circles around her feet and jumped up to lick her. "We're okay," she told him, giving the dog a hug, mostly to reassure herself. She went downstairs. Ryan and Jake were looking down at Sam, who lay on the dining-room table, still unconscious. Travis was checking the bandages she'd put on.

"You did a good job here, Ellie," Travis said.

"Is he going to make it?" Ryan asked.

"I don't know," Ellen said honestly. "I did what I could. He needs a hospital, but until the rain and lightning stops we're not going to get a lifeline out here."

She put a quilt over him, and a pillow under his head. Then they all went into the kitchen. "Travis, I need to get Bobby."

"He can stay with me tonight."

She desperately wanted to see and hug her son, but she knew that going there and back would be foolhardy, especially in the dark.

Travis could see that she was still worried. "I'll bring him home as soon as the sun comes up."

"You're right," she said. "He's safe with you."

"We need to figure out what Robinson is up to," Travis said.

Ellen, Travis, Jake, Avery, Ryan, and Lyla all sat in the kitchen; Ellen took the seat where she could also observe Sam, who was still unconscious on the dining-room table.

She began. "Brock and Rena were hired by Mitchell Robinson to steal the original sales or lease contracts for right-of-way that were signed last week. Coulter, Baldwin, two others. Brock said that there was a clause that shouldn't have made it in, likely something related to what they could do with the land under the terms of the right-of-way. If the clause disallowed mineral rights, then that might explain why Robinson wanted to change the terms. But George Coulter would never have signed it with that clause, so either Robinson was trying to deceive him, or he let him sign the right contract, but planned a bait and switch."

Jake got up and went to the kitchen desk. "I told you that Clive brought over a contract that they want you to sign by Sunday, so they can file it first thing Monday, a trade of eight hundred acres for the two hundred acres between their property and what they leased from the Coulters."

He put the contract in front of Ellen. She hadn't read it yet, and the words were swimming in front of her, she was so tired. The house shook in the wind, and she wondered if Brock and Rena were okay out there. Maybe she should have let Travis try to apprehend them . . . But they were desperate. Brock might have shot her brother-in-law. He *would* have. They had been in survival mode, and while he had also helped her by giving her information, he could have acted without thinking and killed Travis or one of her children.

Ellen couldn't lose anyone else.

"Before he left, he told me there was a copy of everything in his truck that he left at the Coulters' house. I want to go get it."

"Now?" Travis said.

"Yes. What if Mitchell knows he had something? What if he's going to try to cover everything up?"

"Or that criminal was lying to you," Travis said. "While the rain's letting up, the wind is a hazard in itself. When Jake and I were coming out here, a tree branch damn near broke the windshield."

She didn't want to wait, but they were right. She couldn't put anyone else in danger.

"First thing in the morning," she said. "Crack of dawn, I'm going."

"I'll go with you," Jake said.

She almost said no, but just nodded. "Okay."

Dawn was only hours away. Then she started thinking as she glanced at the impossibly generous contract—eight hundred prime acres of farmland for two hundred grazing acres. It made no sense.

"Why *this* land?" Ellen said, holding up the contract.

"I've been thinking about it all day, ever since Clive came by. I might know," Travis said. "Jake, go get the map of northern Cooke County. Your dad always had one in his desk."

Jake nodded, left the room.

"What are you thinking?" Ellen asked him.

"They need your two hundred acres because—if I'm right—it gives them a straight path north. Or, rather, a straight path south."

"You're confusing me," Ellen said, "but I'm exhausted."

Jake came back with the map and Travis laid it on the table.

"First," Travis said, "I've been reading about all of Verdacorp's dealings ever since Mitchell started the company when his dad moved to Dallas. John had been skeptical, thinking they were going to disrupt farming in the area. He was more concerned about price manipulation or exclusive contracts that would force smaller farms out of business."

Ellen nodded. "It's why we started expanding into crops the Robinsons didn't grow, and why we bought the Mendoza farm for the pecan orchard." Though that hadn't gone as well as they had hoped.

Travis nodded. "Then after what Verdacorp did in the Panhandle—acquiring a lot of land, then leasing it back to the farmers for farming but selling right-of-way to the utilities while retaining the mineral rights that they leased to the oil companies for pipelines, John was worried they were going to do the same here."

"But our terrain is completely different than the Panhandle," Jake said. "We're wetter, we've got more diverse farming and a smaller region. Any pipeline is going to greatly disrupt dozens of farmers."

"And there aren't any big oil operations around here," Ryan said. "Just the Sudduths with their four pumps, you can't even see them from the road."

"A couple farms have a pump or two going," Travis said, "but you're right, it's small scale and they're not getting rich off it. You know, Grandpa thought of doing it."

"Really?" Ellen said. "I didn't know that."

"When John and I were little, he hired a surveyor and was going to put one right next to Whisper Creek, within sight of the barn, because there was potential. Grandma put her foot down because she didn't want to see it when she was feeding the chickens. I think that was the only time we ever saw Grandpa Milton and Grandma Penny argue about anything."

Ellen grinned. "And Grandma won."

"She usually did," Travis said wistfully. "Anyway, what Verdacorp is doing here is similar to what they did in the Panhandle, only on a smaller, more strategic scale." He spread out the map, which already had some pencil markings on it and writing in John's small, neat block letters. "John was tracking the land Verdacorp was buying. His theory was that Mitchell didn't actually have a solid plan at first, that he was just buying land to have the land. But when he started pressuring John to sell, John became more invested in figuring out what he was up to."

Travis started reshaping the outlines that John had started. Ellen knew what the pencil colors stood for: green was McKenna land; red was Verdacorp land; and blue was owned by other farmers.

As they watched, Travis nearly doubled the size of Verdacorp land and marginally increased the McKenna land. Ellen saw a shape come to life. It was a strip of land going northeast all the way to the Red River, going southwest all the way to Whitesboro.

"I didn't realize he'd bought that much land," Ellen said. "It's not all farmable, and it's an odd shape."

"Long and narrow, the skinniest parcel is this strip here along US 377. And now I know why."

"Why?" Jake said. "You can't farm like that. He's dividing small farms to the point they won't be able to make a living."

"Because of this." Travis tapped Marietta, Oklahoma, which was parallel to a point on the Texas boundary. "Marietta is one of the biggest natural gas outfitters in the area. And I didn't know why Mitchell had bought into the industry, other than as an investment. There is a network of pipes all over the country, but there's a new facility opening in Plano—and if you draw a line from Marietta to Plano, it goes through Whitesboro—and it goes through all the land that Verdacorp has acquired."

"They're going to put in natural gas pipes?" Ellen said. "That has to cost a fortune, and there are already existing pipes."

"Not in this area. Here's the catch. A bill just passed Congress to invest in natural gas and oil production and distribution in the entire region, from the Canadian border down to the Gulf. The author of the bill is Congresswoman Jeanne Culvers."

No one had to say anything. Jeanne Culvers represented their area, and Mitchell Robinson was her biggest contributor. He held a fundraiser at his ranch every year—Ellen had just gotten another invitation today in the mail, which she'd promptly tossed in the trash.

She got up and looked in the recycling bin in the mudroom. There it was. She picked it up, brought it back to the table.

Ellen had liked Jeanne when she was first elected—she was from Gainesville, had ties to the community, and her grandparents had gone to the same church as Penny and Milton.

But over the years, she had become less accessible and more slimy. John once said that good people go into public office, but the system corrupts them. She wasn't that cynical, but she was getting there. Especially once she learned that Mitchell Robinson was her biggest supporter.

"I'll bet there is some deadline on Monday for funding," Travis said. "If Mitchell doesn't own the land free and clear, with all the rights delineated, he's going to lose tens of millions of dollars."

"But why?" Ryan asked. "Wouldn't he have to pay to put in the pipeline?"

"No," Avery said. "In my current events class we've been talking about infrastructure and economics. The government will either give him the money to do it, or lease the rights and put in the pipes themselves. Right, Uncle Travis?"

Travis nodded. "Yep. If the government decided to put the pipeline in through this area, even if they used eminent domain, it would be years of haggling and lawsuits because most of us don't want it here—it's too disruptive to the land, as John has always said. It would divide parcels and make it more difficult to farm and raise livestock. We could win—there have been cases in other areas where small and medium-sized farms have banded together to avoid eminent domain, often the government just drops it because of PR issues. But if Mitchell, through Verdacorp, owns the land, he can lease it without consulting any other farmers. And that's why this"—he pointed to the two-hundred-acre square of McKenna land that Mitchell was desperate to have—"is so crucial for him. It's either this corner or buying out Sudduth on the other side of Privett, and Sudduth is bigger than we are. So, he came after us."

"That bastard."

Ellen thought about the sabotage of her barn, but before she could say anything, Jake brought it up. "Do you think that Mitchell is behind the sabotage on the farm?"

"What sabotage?" Travis asked. "What's been going on?"

"Someone cut narrow holes in the barn parallel to the gutter, then filled the drainage pipes with expanding foam," Jake said. "So, the gutters flooded into the barn. The entire west wall is wet from the inside, and we lost most of the stored hay. And that's just one of several odd things, but the most obvious because it was intentional."

Ellen reached out and took Lyla's hand. "Someone sabotaged the barn generator by wrapping copper wire around part of the engine. When Lyla tried to start it, she got a shock that was strong enough to knock her down."

Travis looked from Jake to Ellen. "Why didn't you tell me?" He sounded hurt, and Ellen realized she should have said something earlier. "Anything else?"

"Small things, nothing I could say was deliberate until the barn," Ellen said.

Jake nodded. "A couple months ago we lost a week's supply of milk when the refrigerator in the barn went out, and that damaged our reputation with our main customer. And we had to replace it because the circuits were fried. And the cattle got out on Privett Road last month as we were in the middle of planting, so we had to hire a couple extra laborers for a few days—we couldn't delay planting—so Mateo and I could get our livestock back. We lost one who got trapped in barbed wire on the Sudduths' property. I thought I hadn't secured the gate properly. But . . . Mateo wondered if someone was playing a prank."

"That doesn't sound like a prank," Travis said.

"No, it's deliberate to damage our business," Ellen said. "All of it costing money, but not enough so that our insurance would kick in. I can withstand losing the crops—we have crop insurance. But it's the small repairs that are killing me. And if I have to replace the barn, we have a huge deductible, not to mention we have to find a solution for the animals while it's being repaired."

"How can we prove it?" Lyla said.

Ellen didn't know. All she had was the word of two criminals.

"Maybe we can't," Ellen said. "But I can stop him from achieving his goals. He's not getting a square foot of land from me."

"Mitchell has proved that he is willing to break the law to get what he wants," Travis said. "We can't assume anything. I might have an idea."

"I'm listening," she said, because she was out of ideas.

"Clive came over to do the hard sell on me, to convince you to do the trade. What if we go over there tomorrow and, I don't know, try to trip him up. Texas is a one-party consent state, so we can record the entire conversation."

Ellen shook her head. "Do you really think that he would just admit to anything?"

Jake caught her eye. "Mom, do you remember last year when Dad and I were taking the cattle to market and the hitch broke off?"

"Of course I do, that was so dangerous, I could have lost you both, and we could have lost all the cattle. Oh." Now she knew what he was thinking. "You think that was deliberate."

"I didn't at the time, I thought it was old equipment. But Dad was . . . I don't know, he didn't say anything specific to me, but he said something like, things like this don't happen."

She nodded. "It could have been the first time. That was in February, right?" Four months before John's accident.

Her chest tightened. The accident. She caught her son's eye, eyes that looked so much like John's it brought tears to her own. "You think—"

He nodded. "Dad was repairing the roof, but it was an unusual repair. Something that should never have needed a sudden repair."

"Oh, dear Lord," she said, and squeezed her eyes shut.

"Um," Ryan spoke up sheepishly, "maybe you should tell my dad about all of this."

"He can't do anything without proof," Travis said.

"We need to sleep on this," Ellen said. "Travis, can you help me with Sam? I'm going to move him to the living-room couch. He'll be more comfortable."

Travis glanced toward the unconscious man and frowned. "You think he's going to make it?"

"So far, so good, and the drugs brought down his fever. I gave him a hefty dose of two antibiotics."

"I can't believe you helped him."

"Look at him, Travis. Really look at him."

Travis did. "He's young." His voice was soft, understanding.

"Twenty-one. He went along with it because of family. Not all family is like ours."

Travis's face twisted in pain and regret, and he turned damp eyes to Ellen. Her heart went out to him and the gamut of emotions that ran across his expression. "I'm sorry for being a drunk for so long."

"No apologies. All that matters is what you do from this day forward." She reached out and hugged him. "I love you, Travis. John loved you."

He nodded, coughed to hide his emotions. "Love you, too, Ellie."

Between Travis, Ellen, and Jake they got Sam to the couch, where Lyla had put down a sheet and a blanket. They covered him with a comforter and Ellen checked his vitals. "He's dehydrated, but I don't have an IV here. He needs a hospital first thing. I'm going to try to reach Rick on the radio. I couldn't earlier, but now that the rain has mostly stopped, I might be able to."

She turned to Travis. "Will you call me when you get home so I can talk to Bobby before I go to sleep?"

"Phone lines are down, so I'll have him call you on the radio."

"Thank you."

Travis left, and Lyla, Ryan, and Avery pulled out sleeping bags for the family room floor. Jake walked upstairs with his mom. "I hope we're wrong about Dad's accident," Ellen said.

"We're not," Jake said. "And we're not wrong about what Mitchell Robinson did with Verdacorp. He hired thieves who shot Greg Baldwin and his dog. He needs to be held accountable. I'm going to sleep downstairs. That guy might be unconscious, but I don't want the girls and Ryan alone down there with him."

She nodded, hugged her son, then went to her room and collapsed onto her bed, exhausted. But she couldn't sleep.

She pulled out the radio and it took her several minutes before she reached Rick Perez. Travis was right, even though the wind was going strong, the rain had mostly stopped, helping to extend the range of the radio signal. She told him that Ryan was here and safe, and then everything that had happened that evening. Rick said he would get an ambulance or a lifeline out to the ranch as soon as feasible. "But it might not be until morning," he added.

Bobby called on the radio as soon as she was done with Rick. She cried, but tried not to let Bobby know she was crying.

"Mom! Uncle Travis found Cleo! She was trying to find a good place to have her kittens and she did, in his cellar. But Uncle Travis saved her before the cellar flooded, because Titan smelled her and barked. He's a very smart dog. She has four kittens! She let me sit with her in the pantry, but I didn't pet her because I didn't want to scare her. But she didn't hiss, I think she remembered me!"

"I'm sure she did," Ellen said through happy tears.

"And she cleaned all the kittens, because she's a good mom cat. And there are two black-and-white kittens like Cleo, and a gray-and-white kitten, and an all-gray kitten. Well, I think the all-gray kitten might have white paws. Can we keep them?"

"Can we talk about it later? They need to stay with their mom for a while."

"I want to keep all of them."

She laughed.

"The gray-and-white kitten I'm calling River, and the gray kitten is Stormy, because you know, they were born when it was raining. And the black-and-white kittens that look like their mom, I'm calling Panda and Pepper. Because they're black and white, get it?"

"You've given this a lot of thought. Maybe Uncle Travis will want a kitten."

"We can't separate them!" Then he paused. "Well, maybe we can have two and Uncle Travis can have two."

"That sounds like a good idea."

"Uncle Travis just made hot chocolate and grilled cheese sandwiches and I'm super hungry. I love you, Mom! I'll see you in the morning!"

"I love you, too, Bobby."

After he signed off, she let herself cry. Not because she was sad; on the contrary, she was relieved and felt extremely blessed. Her children were safe.

But she desperately missed her husband and always would.

She stared at a photo of John for a long, long time. And then, she closed her eyes and remembered how he used to spoon against her back and hold her. She almost felt his embrace.

Only then could she finally sleep.

CHAPTER THIRTY-SEVEN

Saturday

Ellen had coffee brewing at four in the morning when Jake came down the stairs after showering, dressed and ready for their trek to the Coulters.

"I drove down to the road this morning," she said.

He poured himself a mug and sipped. "All good?"

She shook her head. "I thought it would be free and clear—there's a lot of standing water, though it's not deep. But two of those giant ash trees on the southwest corner? Completely uprooted and are blocking part of the road. We might be able to get around, but the ditches are still filled with water. Think the horses can make it across the field?"

"Yeah, they're used to the terrain. We'll take Clover and Stella. Sir Lancelot might have some trouble if we encounter debris."

She nodded, deferring to her son about anything related to horses.

"Can you saddle up while I check on my patient?"

Jake's face darkened, but he nodded and walked out.

She went over to where Sam was lying on the living-room couch.

He looked like he hadn't moved all night, and she worried that he had died. Though the gunshot wasn't her fault, she felt a pang of guilt that she had done something wrong. But when she went over to him she saw the slight rise and fall of his chest, then his eyes fluttered open. Relief rushed through her. She wanted justice, not vengeance, and was glad he survived the night.

"S-sorry." His voice was a croak, then he closed his eyes.

"You made it," she said. "I'll get you some water."

She went to the kitchen, got a cup with water, found a straw. Brought it back to Sam and helped him drink.

"I. Feel. Crappy."

"But you're alive. As soon as the roads clear, an ambulance will be here to take you to the hospital."

"Where's. Rena."

"She and Brock left last night. I promised to get you to a hospital, and I guess they trust me to do as I say."

He drank some more, then said, his voice still gruff and unnatural, "Thanks." He cleared his throat. "I— They didn't. Mean to. Hurt. Anyone." The last word came out as a sigh and he drifted off again.

She checked his vitals. His blood pressure was elevated but his pulse was steady. She gave him another injection of antibiotics, then let him sleep.

By the time she was done, Jake had the horses out front and she pulled on her jacket and boots and went out to meet him. Sam was in no condition to hurt anyone in the house, but she had woken up Ryan, asked him to stay alert while she was gone. She would have woken up Avery, but Ryan said he was fine and to let her sleep since she'd had a rough day.

It was quite endearing of the kid, Ellen thought.

Ellen handed Jake a muffin, then mounted Stella, a sweet, sturdy Appaloosa they'd had for years.

The wind and rain had stopped, and the eastern horizon was just lighting up, a deep indigo that was a shade lighter than night.

Jake took the lead because he had the spotlight to guide them through the storm-damaged fields.

Her son was a man. It was bittersweet. She remembered when he was a young boy, excited to learn, eager to please, happy as the day was long. He followed John everywhere, absorbing not only his knowledge, but his kind, gentle spirit. She knew all of her children grieved the loss of their father, but it had hit Jake the hardest.

She pulled Stella up to ride side by side.

"Are you okay?" she asked quietly.

"Yeah."

"It's okay to talk about your dad. I miss him, too."

Jake didn't say anything, and she didn't want to push, but he had never talked about losing John. She'd been wrapped up in her own grief for so long and she had never pushed him to talk, then or now.

A moment later, Jake said, "I don't want to go to college. I wanted to be a vet because Dad wanted to be a vet, and when I told him I was going to do it, he was so happy. But if I spend seven, eight years in school, I wouldn't be able to come back. There isn't a great need here, we already have multiple vet practices in the county and it's not practical. Which means I'd have to move to Dallas or Houston or some community that has an opening. I don't want to leave our valley."

"Maybe you can study something else—" she began.

"North Central Texas College has a two-year Equine Studies program," Jake said. "I'd graduate with an AAS in equine science. I've already talked to a counselor and a couple of the instructors and it's exactly the kind of program I want. We can expand here, I can breed horses. There's a market for it, and I love working with the horses more than anything. Especially training horses for cattle ranching. I can make a good living out of it."

Tears burned behind her eyes. She was happy and sad all at the same time. "This is what you want?"

"Yes," he said without hesitation.

"Okay," she said.

He glanced over at her and smiled, relief etched all over his face.

"I just want you to be happy, Jake. I didn't want you to not go to college because you think I need you. I never wanted you to feel obligated or pressured to do something you don't want to do."

"I want to be here; it's in my blood. There's no other place I want to put down roots. Like Dad always said, grow or die. Adding horse breeding to our farm will help us grow, just like the pecans, just like the vineyard, just like the sunflowers."

Jake was right. John lived on in his son, and Ellen felt an odd peace fall over her. She glanced behind her and saw rays of light breaking across the horizon as a thin red line told her dawn had broken.

Twenty minutes later, they reached the Coulters' ranch. They rode around the property to make sure no one was there. It was empty. Brock Jones's big truck with Louisiana plates was parked near the house. He hadn't lied about that.

"Jake," Ellen said, suddenly nervous.

"Hmm?" He turned off the light since visibility was getting better by the minute.

"Brock told me last night that Robinson has cameras everywhere. That's how he knew George gave me a copy of the contract."

"Cameras?" Jake looked around, squinting to see in the distance. "Where? His property line is a half mile away."

"I don't know, but I assume all along his perimeter. So, we need to be quick."

"I'm going to take care of the bulls and chickens since I don't know when I'll be back today. I'll be fast."

"I'll search the truck."

If Mitchell or one of his people were monitoring the cameras now, he'd see her. She didn't know how much time she'd have once he knew. Would he confront her? Would he know what she was doing?

She had to assume he'd know this was the truck of the man he'd hired to steal the contracts. She wanted to leave as soon as possible, but she also wanted the evidence that Brock claimed he had left in his truck.

Ellen tied Stella to the horse rail next to the porch and strode through the mud to the truck. Based on the tracks and mud, many vehicles had come and gone, and maybe she was too late. Maybe Mitchell had already found the evidence. The thought made her sick to her stomach. He needed to pay for what he'd done to her neighbors—and as far as she was concerned, Mitchell Robinson was as guilty as Brock and Rena for Greg Baldwin's shooting.

The truck was unlocked, and Ellen hoisted herself up into the cab. There were no keys in the console or ignition or glove box.

She shined her flashlight around. There was blood in the back, and she shivered, thinking of Sam being shot on Thursday night. She hoped Greg Baldwin survived, because otherwise Sam's life was over. He would be charged with murder. If Greg survived, Sam might get out of prison in ten or twenty years.

Maybe.

She searched everywhere she could think of. There were no copies of anything. No papers. No documents. No contracts. Had Brock been lying or had Mitchell Robinson gotten here first?

She hit the steering wheel. "Dammit!"

Jake approached the open driver's door. "Nothing?"

He didn't sound like he expected a different outcome.

"Mitchell took them," she said.

"Or the criminals lied. Because that's what they do."

Maybe, but Brock had no reason to lie because he was already leaving. He didn't have to say anything to her. She had felt at the time that he was angry with Mitchell for getting him and his family in the middle of this mess and wanted to stick it to him.

Jake walked around to the passenger seat and climbed in. "Okay, he said he had copies of everything—maybe he did. Where else could he have hidden them?"

She thought. "I looked in the obvious places. Maybe under the bed liner?"

"They'd get wet. There's no lockbox."

"Under the seats? I checked, but maybe there's something taped to the bottom?"

They looked under the seats; there was nothing taped to the underside. They looked behind the seats. Looked for seams that had been sewn closed.

"We have to go," she said. "Robinson could be watching us now."

"Hold on," Jake said.

He had pulled up the heavy-duty floor mat, which protected the carpet. The carpet had a seam that shouldn't be there, and Jake said, "Someone cut this." He felt around and pulled out a cracked cell phone.

"It's almost dead, five percent, but there's no passcode."

He flipped through the device, turning it so Ellen could see.

"He took pictures of every contract, I'm assuming these are what he stole," Jake said.

"Take the phone, we'll charge it at home and look at everything more closely. I don't want to stay here any longer."

Mitchell stared at the coffeepot, willing it to brew faster. His housekeeper didn't work weekends. He needed to fire her and bring in a full-time, live-in maid. He didn't like making his own coffee, and he hated cooking.

It was five in the morning and he had slept no more than two hours.

Ellen McKenna needed to sign that damn contract. She needed to give him what he wanted. He was trading far more valuable property for those two hundred acres! It made no sense that she wouldn't take the deal. No sense!

He rubbed his eyes. When the pot was half brewed, he jerked out the pot, drips of coffee steaming as they hit the hot burner. He poured some into his mug, then put the pot back to finish brewing.

If he didn't hear from her today, he would have Presley forge her signature and electronically plant the documents in the recorder's office. He'd bribe the recorder to file the originals. He'd done it before; he'd do it again.

He just hadn't done anything like that to the McKennas. They had never been pushovers, and he hadn't wanted a legal battle.

But by the time they figured it out, the project would already be well on its way, and they wouldn't be able to stop it.

In fact, he'd deposit money in her bank account to "prove" she had taken the deal. On paper, it would be true, and what court would believe otherwise?

Risky, true, but it could work.

"Dad, I was looking at the security cameras last night and that guy you hired was still at the Coulters' house at two in the morning."

He whirled around. His daughter stood there in baggy sweats and a faded T-shirt that read FUN FACT: I DON'T CARE.

"What? What are you talking about?" He had told her over and over that he hated the ridiculous shirts she wore, but she ignored him. The lack of respect annoyed him.

"The guy from Louisiana?"

He froze. Presley wasn't supposed to know about any of that. Well, she knew the big picture, but he had never introduced her to Brock Jones, and the man had only been to his house once. How did Presley know what car he drove?

She rolled her eyes, and that made him snap, "Show some respect."

"Dad," she said coolly, "I think you should—"

"I don't really care what you think, Presley."

She glared at him, eyes narrowed, turned on her bare feet and walked out of the kitchen.

Dammit!

"Presley, you know that's not what I meant."

She didn't come back. Well, shit, another woman in his life who was mad at him.

He'd make it up to her. He was just tired, frustrated, and angry.

If people just did what he said when he said it, and did it *right*, they wouldn't be in this situation.

He pulled out his cell phone, no signal. Damn towers. He took his coffee to his office and called Tom Garza from his desk phone. The man had slept in the apartment over the barn last night because the roads were flooded, but it still took him five rings to answer that line.

"Yeah," Tom said, his voice thick with sleep.

"I need you in my office now."

"Okay," Tom said and hung up.

Clive was standing in the doorway. How did his older brother always look so chipper in the morning. "Who were you talking to?"

Mitchell didn't answer him. He didn't want Clive around for this meeting. It was bad enough he'd already questioned him about Greg Baldwin's shooting. Clive was the weak link, and Mitchell needed to get him out of the house for the next few days.

"I've been ignoring calls from Dad," Mitchell said. "I think he's lonely. Can you go keep him company for a couple of days? Maybe take Presley with you, talk to her about going back to college in the fall."

"Why are you trying to get rid of me?" Clive asked.

"I'm not."

"What's going on, Mitch?"

"Nothing is going on except that Ellen McKenna is a stubborn bitch who hasn't signed the best deal she's going to get in her life."

"Yesterday was stressful. I'll, um, go over this afternoon. See where her head is at."

"I know where it's at. In the sand, ignoring progress and opportunity. I'll talk to her, because you certainly haven't been able to get anything accomplished."

Clive bristled, but Mitchell didn't care.

"She doesn't like you," Clive said. "You'll never convince her to sign. Hell, she doesn't even like me anymore because I've been pushing so hard."

"We're running out of time."

"Maybe you should tell her the plan, offer her a stake in it."

He stared at his brother as if he had grown a second head. "Just go away," he said.

Clive reddened, then left.

Mitchell drank his coffee, now lukewarm, and grimaced.

He needed to think. He had less than forty-eight hours to turn this around. He'd find a way—he had to. Or he'd lose millions of dollars. All the land he bought was practically worthless if he couldn't get that last two hundred acres.

Offer her a stake in it . . .

Never. Not the McKennas. He'd rather offer David Sudduth a stake than anyone named *McKenna*.

He felt hot and cold at the same time. Sudduth would laugh in his face, then bleed him dry. If he knew how desperate Mitchell was, that there were time constraints, he'd make Mitchell pay through the nose.

Tom came in, unshaven, dark circles under his eyes.

"Shut the door," Mitchell said as Tom was already in the process of shutting it. "Lay everything on the table. All the dirt."

Tom sat down slowly. "There's nothing."

"There's always something."

"Not with the McKennas. Not with anyone who works for them. I'm done, Mitch. I'm tired. I'm going home as soon as they open Mule Run."

"You're not done. Do I need to remind you—"

"You don't need to remind me about anything." Tom stood. "The people you hired took the Mendozas hostage. Nearly got Ellen's girl, Avery, killed. I just got word from my buddy in the sheriff's department that she's home, but she was tied to a fucking steering wheel and left in a ditch. She's the same age as my son! Dammit, Mitch, I did shit for you I'm not proud of. I'll tell you this: You come after me, it's mutually assured destruction. I go down, you'll go down harder."

"Do not threaten me, Garza."

"I'm not threatening you. I'm quitting."

He walked out.

CHAPTER THIRTY-EIGHT

The sun had crept up by the time Ellen returned home. Jake had gone in the opposite direction to check on the cattle and make sure they withstood the storm without problems, and she put her horse in the corral to graze and cool down. She'd come back and groom the mare after breakfast.

When she stepped inside the house, she smelled sausage cooking, biscuits cooling, and saw Penny mixing blueberries into her pancake batter. Her wispy white hair was pulled back into her customary bun, a little less perfect than usual.

"What's the damage?" Penny asked.

"Not as bad as I thought it would be. We can take care of a lot of the debris over the weekend, hopefully the water will drain overnight and we'll assess the crops tomorrow. Avery mentioned last night that everything east of Whisper Creek is flooded." Which meant she'd lost half her vineyard, unless it drained quickly. Maybe not a complete loss. But she wouldn't know for a day or two. "Jake's checking on the cattle right now, Mateo's meeting him out there. After Rick comes for our patient, we'll go out and inspect the fields."

Any damage would take a couple days to truly assess, but the bulk of the work before them was dealing with standing water, clearing fallen trees and branches, and getting the driveway repacked. Between the hail and the subsequent storm, the potholes were too deep for vehicles, and too dangerous for the horses.

"Where're Avery and Ryan?" she asked as she poured a fresh cup of coffee.

"Ryan and Lyla are feeding the animals," Penny said. "Avery's still sleeping. I told her to get up, don't know if she even heard me. Travis called on the radio—phone lines are still down. He's heading over with Bobby; they'll be here for breakfast."

Ellen put the cracked phone on her charger. "Brock didn't lie about the evidence. He left this phone behind, and it has copies of all the contracts he stole. I don't know if it's going to help us take down Mitchell Robinson and Verdacorp. There might be more on the phone, maybe a history of calls between them, or an incriminating voice message." That was probably wishful thinking, Ellen thought.

Penny glared at it. "There's a special level of hell for men like Mitchell Robinson."

"Do you think Clive knew?" Ellen had always liked Clive, at least until recently. He seemed to be the opposite of his driven, manipulative brother. Yet they worked together, lived on the same ranch, she didn't see how he wouldn't know what his brother was up to.

"Clive knows what he wants to know," Penny said. "Willfully ignorant, that man."

Ellen checked on Sam; he was still sleeping and had a slight fever, but his pulse was strong. She heard a truck and went outside, hoping it was Rick Perez.

Better. It was Travis, with her son.

She put her mug down on the railing and ran out to greet Bobby. She picked him up out of the passenger seat and hugged him tightly. "I missed you," she said, then hugged him again and kissed him all over.

"Mom," he said, grinning but wrinkling his nose. "Put me down!"

She did, then glanced at his bandaged feet and frowned. "What happened?"

"I lost my boots in the muddy field next to the pecan trees. I'm sorry."

She hugged him again. "I don't care. I only care that you are home and safe."

She picked up him again even though he protested and carried him up the stairs before putting him down. Titan and Timber were in the back of the truck. Titan jumped out, and Travis helped Timber get down. He was limping only slightly and seemed happy to be outside. They ran up the porch stairs, Timber only lagging a little behind, and greeted Whiskey as if they hadn't seen each other in years, and Ellen said, "You know they're going to be filthy when you get home."

"That's fine with me," Travis said, watching the dogs with a smile.

She looked at her brother-in-law and was pleased to see that he seemed happier and more at peace. She didn't know exactly what happened with him yesterday when he decided to stop drinking, but whatever it was, she would support him one hundred percent. She would do everything she could to help him succeed.

They went inside. Penny took one look at Bobby and gave him a fierce hug, then pulled out a chair for him. "Sit," she said, then pulled a cast-iron skillet with both hands from the oven. Her county-famous apple streusel biscuit pie, as she called it. Topped with pecans and brown sugar, it was Bobby's favorite dish.

"Grandma," Ellen said, knowing how much time and energy went into making this meal, the biscuits and sausage gravy, the pancakes, the apple streusel, "you're working too hard."

"I'll take Sunday off," she said and put the streusel in front of Bobby, who grinned ear to ear.

Food was Penny's love language.

Lyla and Ryan came in from the barn laughing about something, and they washed their hands after Penny told them to set the table.

"Avery still sleeping?" Ellen said as she brought bowls of food to the table.

"Let her sleep," Penny said. "I'll keep a plate warm for her."

They were dishing up breakfast—Bobby had already served up a huge serving of the streusel—when Jake and Mateo came in. "The run-in held," Jake said as he washed his hands. "Mateo was already out there checking on the cattle when I got there."

"Jake filled me in on what happened after I left," Mateo said. "I should have come back. I'm so sorry, Ellen. What an awful experience. Are you sure you're okay?"

She nodded. "Don't be sorry. I told you to help the Pritchards. How are they?"

"They now realize they need a rural living one-oh-one class," Mateo grumbled. "But I fixed their generator, and helped secure their barn. They have a flooded basement, so we got all the pumps working. Miriam's over there now helping with their kids and giving advice, I'm sure," he added with a grin.

"Thank you. They're such a nice family; I hope they don't move."

"I think they'll stay," Mateo said. "They seem determined."

Avery came in droopy eyed, poured herself coffee and added a lot of cream and sugar, then sat down and drank it while dishing up pancakes and sausage and biscuits. "I feel like I was hit by a bus," she moaned. She sniffed the air. "Is that Grandma's apple streusel pie?"

"She made it for me," Bobby said with his mouth full.

"I made it for everyone," Penny said, dishing Avery up a bowl.

"What happened yesterday?" Ellen asked her daughter. "You never told me about the accident."

As Avery and Ryan recounted what happened, Ellen wished she hadn't let Rena and Brock leave. Maybe she should have let

Travis shoot them. Rena had intentionally run her daughter off the road and left her trapped in a truck that was filling with water.

She could have died.

"Damn them," Travis muttered.

Ellen caught Ryan's eye. She was too emotional to say anything, and he nodded. Maybe he was, too. "We're sore, but we're okay," Avery said. "We walked to Greg Baldwin's house and borrowed some clothes. Oh!" She put a hand to her mouth. "We broke one of the panes in his back door so we could get in."

"He won't mind," Ellen said, her voice cracking. "I'm just glad you're both here." Glad that her family was alive and in one piece.

Lyla got up. "I need to milk the cows." She kissed Penny. "Thanks for breakfast, Grandma."

And she was gone, doing her chores as if nothing out of the ordinary had happened.

"I'll take breakfast up to Margery," Avery said, making a tray.

"Getting out of cleaning?" Ryan teased.

She smiled flirtatiously and took the food upstairs.

"Let me help you, Ms. Penny," Ryan said and took the pans from the stove to the sink.

Penny looked at Ellen and smiled. "Good boy Avery found," she said, plating up leftovers.

Ellen had nothing to say to that. After hearing about what happened last night on the road, she had a lot of feelings—they had both grown up practically overnight. And Penny was right. Ryan was a good young man. But they were still young.

Travis picked up Brock's phone. "Can I go through this?" he asked Ellen.

"Please do," she said. "I hope you find something on it other than the contracts, but if that's it, maybe we can find a way to use those against him. At a minimum, they should prove that he hired someone to steal them."

Travis sat down with the phone and Ellen and Ryan helped

Penny finish cleaning up from breakfast. Bobby sat at the table, chattering about the kittens, and told Penny what he'd named them and how Uncle Travis had saved them from drowning.

Hearing the story even a second time brought joy into Ellen's heart. She watched Travis as he continued to go through every photo and document and call on Brock's phone. He looked almost like his old self, almost like he was before he returned from the Army missing half a leg.

Except older, wiser, smarter. For the first time in a long time, she thought maybe he had turned the corner on his drinking and self-pity. That maybe, he was ready to return fully into the family fold.

Ellen had just started another pot of coffee when she heard a vehicle in the driveway. Travis jumped up first and went out; Ellen followed. They both relaxed when they saw Rick Perez in his sheriff's Bronco. Behind him was an ambulance.

Ryan ran down the stairs first and gave his dad a hug. Ellen and Travis followed.

"I was going to help Lyla in the barn, if that's okay, Mrs. McKenna?"

"We never turn down free labor on the ranch," she said.

Ryan hugged his dad again and trudged through the mud to the barn.

Travis asked, "Roads clear?"

"Partly," Rick said as he followed Ellen and Travis up the steps and into the kitchen. The paramedics were getting their equipment out, and Rick told them to go in through the front door.

"Rock Creek Road is still flooded," Rick continued, "and there're dozens of downed trees, phone lines still out. I don't think we'll get them fixed until early next week, but cell service seems to have been restored. I got over Mule Run at Privett. The rest of Mule Run is still closed until the water recedes at bit. The ditches were already saturated, not many places for the water to go. Be careful if you need to head to town, because there's standing water and the roads are crap. Even one of my deputies misjudged and got his truck stuck just south of the Rock Creek closure, the eejit." Rick shook his head. "I don't have word from the county yet as to the status of the cleanup. They're probably still assessing. How's your patient?"

"Alive," Ellen said. "But not out of the woods."

"Let's get him under arrest and off to the hospital."

Rick let the paramedics in, and Ellen watched as they checked Sam's vitals and transferred him to the stretcher. She gave them the list of medications she'd given him, and when, and a plastic bag with the shotgun pellets. They seemed impressed, but she knew she was lucky he hadn't died.

When they were gone, Rick sat down for a cup of coffee. "I planned to take Ryan home with me," he said. "But I don't know if I'll be able to get him off the farm right now. I don't know where he gets it. We never had more than a horse and a few chickens."

"Sometimes, you're born into farm life, and sometimes, it's just in the blood," Penny said as she slid over a plate of biscuits and gravy in front of the tired sheriff.

"Thank you, Penny."

"You look like death warmed over," she said.

"It's been a long night," he said.

Travis said, "I'm taking Timber to the vet in Callisburg later today, I can drop Ryan off."

"I'd be obliged," he said. "His truck is in evidence right now."

Ellen straightened and leaned forward. "You found Brock and Rena?"

He nodded, swallowed a bite of biscuit, and washed it down with black coffee. "Three o'clock this morning. They were flooded out at Mule Run and Privett. They didn't cause problems, told me their brother was here and that you saved his life. This was after I talked to you last night. Brock Jones is his name, Rena is his wife, Sam is her brother. From Louisiana. I'm going to interview them when I'm done here, I suspect they have a lot to say. Also, I meant to tell you as soon as I got here but I was distracted. Good news. Looks like Greg Baldwin is going to pull through."

"Praise the Lord," Penny said.

"Are his daughters with him?" Ellen asked.

"Both at the hospital right now. He's one lucky man. Owes his life to your son."

"And what's going to happen to the Joneses?"

"We'll see what the DA wants to do, but they'll both be going away for some time."

"He told me that Mitchell Robinson hired him to steal contracts from Baldwin, Coulter, and two other families."

"Robinson didn't tell them to shoot Greg or hold the Mendozas hostage," Rick said.

"I'm not justifying what they did. I'm saying he can testify against Robinson."

"He could," Rick said, "but you have a thief with a long rap sheet speaking against a wealthy, law-abiding man with roots in the valley."

Ellen snorted. "You know as well as I do that Mitchell Robinson is as crooked as they come."

"And proving it is going to be damn near impossible."

"What if we can?" Travis asked.

"It had better be ironclad. And even then, there's no guarantee."

"Brock Jones told me there was an error in the contracts, and my best guess, based on what I saw when George gave me his contract, is that the owners have the right to approve any land-use changes on the property. The only projects allowed in the contract are for the utility lines. It means Verdacorp can't exercise mineral rights without explicit permission of the original landowner. So, he stole the contracts because I don't think that clause was supposed to be included."

"He'll find a way to get around it," Rick said. "He always has something up his sleeve."

"Rick, there's something you need to listen to," Travis said. He put the cracked phone down on the table. "There are multiple calls between Mitchell Robinson and Brock Jones in the phone logs."

"Who's phone is that?" Rick asked.

"Brock Jones left it for Ellen. It was dead and we charged it."

Slight fib, but *technically* accurate, Ellen thought, if they ever had to testify. Brock had left it for her—in his truck.

Rick frowned, glanced at Ellen. "You know that's evidence."

"Hear me out," Travis said. "The phone log connects Mitchell to Jones. Also, the timing of the calls is very suspicious. Several calls yesterday, Thursday, earlier in the week. I'm still going through the contracts, but they're not going to match what's filed with the recorder's office. Jones took photos of what he stole for Mitchell."

"Maybe, but Mitchell can easily say he doesn't know what Jones is talking about, or that they are fake. He doesn't have to answer any questions. He could even claim that he was robbed. Jones is a career criminal."

"But I found one more thing. He recorded a conversation with Mitchell. I only listened to the first part of it before you arrived."

Rick looked skeptical.

Travis hit an audio app on the phone, and at first there was only some rustling that Ellen couldn't place. Maybe cloth or paper.

"Close the door."

That voice they all knew: Mitchell Robinson.

A rustling of paper. "Those are the addresses and a sample of what you're looking for. But don't just take the contracts. You have to make it look good, like a typical burglary."

"Not a problem. And you're going to make certain no one is home?"

"It's taken care of. I attached the schedule. Stick to it and you'll be clear. It'll be the easiest money you've ever made."

A chuckle. That was Brock Jones, Ellen surmised, though his

voice was calmer and more confident on the recording than it had been last night when he was panicked.

"That's what everyone says, but I don't see you breaking in and doing anything about it."

"Drop the attitude. You already have half the money, just stick to the schedule and call me if you have any trouble. Don't fuck this up."

"No, sir," Brock said.

The door opened and closed. The recording continued. There were voices in the background but nothing that Ellen could clearly understand.

Then a truck door, the turning of an ignition.

"We good?"

Ellen thought that was Rena.

"Yep," Brock said. "Put this in a safe place, just in case he tries to double-cross us."

Then the recording ended.

"Texas is a one-party consent state," Travis said. "This will hold up."

Rick held out his hand. "I'll get this to the district attorney, get his opinion on it."

"You mean Sullivan?" Travis said, shaking his head. "Mitchell practically bought his seat for him."

"I can't do anything about that."

Travis frowned, then sent the recording to Rick, Ellen, and himself before handing Rick the phone. "We're going to trust you with this, but Sullivan had better not screw this up. And hold off giving it to him until Monday."

"Why?" Rick asked.

"I can't tell you that."

"Travis—if you do something illegal, I'm not going to be able to help you."

"It's not illegal."

Ellen had no idea what her brother-in-law was thinking, but she didn't ask him in front of Rick.

"Ellie," Travis said quietly, "tell Rick about the barn and generator."

"Jake and I have noticed several oddities, but we realized yesterday that someone intentionally sabotaged the barn by putting expanding foam into the downspouts and cutting holes into the wall to flood our loft," Ellen said. "We caught it, but not before most of our hay was wet." She told him everything else that had been happening over the last fifteen months, including the most recent—Lyla getting shocked by the barn generator that had clearly been intentionally damaged.

Rick frowned. "You're not saying it was Mitchell, are you?"

"I don't know that Mitchell would have the guts to do it himself," Travis said, "but he would hire someone, and you know it."

Rick considered, nodded. "But you have no evidence."

She shook her head.

"Write everything down that you believe was intentional," Rick finally said. "But I don't know what I can do about it. You might want to get cameras out here. I know it's a pain, and good cameras can be expensive, but it would protect you."

"I'll think about it," she said. The idea of being forced to add layers of security on her farm made her sad. They lived in a safe, rural community and knew all of their neighbors. Cameras . . . Then she thought about Mitchell's cameras. He was watching his neighbors, and that made her doubly angry.

Rick rose, rinsed out his coffee mug, and put it in the sink. "You know I care about your family a lot," he said. "Don't do anything that's going to bite you in the ass. Understand?"

"Understood," Travis said.

CHAPTER THIRTY-NINE

"Are you one hundred percent sure?" Travis asked Ellen again as they pulled up to Robinson's sprawling home.

Day laborers were already clearing the debris from the storm. By tomorrow, Verdacorp would once again look like the spread from *Dallas*.

"I'm sure," Ellen said.

This was their only chance, because Rick was right: if they pushed it and tried to get an investigation into Mitchell Robinson and Verdacorp, he had enough money and friends to fight back hard. He gave money to the county supervisors and the district attorney. He was well known in not only Cooke County, but the entirety of north Texas.

Without hard evidence, they couldn't do anything. And he would continue to sabotage Ellen, likely out of spite because she would never in a million years sell him a square foot of her property.

And for what? Because of the ancient feud between the Robinsons and the McKennas? John had been cordial to Mitchell. He'd had Clive over for a meal on occasion. They did everything they could to bury the hatchet, and Mitchell still wanted to live in the past.

Ellen would not allow him to destroy her family, or her family's legacy.

Travis's plan had to work.

They approached the door. Knocked. Presley answered, looking exasperated.

"You," she said.

"Hello, Presley," Travis said with a smile.

She looked him up and down, rolled her eyes. "Uncle Clive or Dad?"

"Mitchell, please."

She motioned for them to follow and led them to Mitchell's office.

"Dad, Travis and Ellen are here," she said as she opened the door without knocking.

Mitchell was seated at his huge mahogany desk, his back to the wall of windows that looked out at his pool and wide fields. Dozens of people were cleaning up the debris. Ellen wondered how he could afford such a large staff, even if part-time. She could barely afford Mateo.

A wall of trophy bucks and a few more exotic animals—a lion, a gazelle, a full bear in the corner—stared glassy-eyed from all sides. Ellen didn't hunt, but Travis and John used to go out annually, catch a buck, and bring it to a butcher for cleaning, cutting, and packaging. They could eat venison twice a month for a year. But they never displayed their kills.

"Hello," Mitchell said with a smile. He motioned for them to sit. "How did your little ranch fare last night?"

"No serious damage," Ellen said with a smile. She hoped it was pleasant enough, because she was primed to attack.

She sat down, tried to relax.

"Coffee?" he offered.

"No, thank you," she said. "I'm already jittery enough from too much caffeine." She laughed lightly, hoping that would explain her stiffness.

Travis sat in the chair next to her. He glared at Mitchell. So much for being pleasant.

"Travis and I were talking this morning about your trade offer." She held up a folder with her copy of the contract that Clive had left. "We had a few questions."

Mitchell leaned back and gestured for them to sit. "What's there to ask? Eight hundred acres of prime farmland for your two hundred. More than a fair trade."

"Seems that I'm getting a much better deal. I looked at the map. It's eight hundred acres adjacent to my field, giving me full access to Whisper Creek and the lake. So, I don't understand why you want this two hundred acres of grazing land that hasn't grown anything other than winter wheat."

Mitchell smiled. "It connects my holdings. It gives me continuity."

"Well, until the Coulter contract falls apart."

He blinked, his smile wavering.

Before Mitchell could reply, the office door opened and Clive Robinson stepped inside. He was damp from perspiration. He took off his hat and wiped his palms on his jeans. He'd actually been out working or at least supervising the cleanup.

"I thought I saw you drive up, Travis."

Travis nodded. "Clive."

Mitchell's posture stiffened. "We're just discussing the fair trade we offered to Ellen."

Clive sat down on the couch kitty-corner to the desk, said hello to Ellen.

"By the way, did you hear that Rick Perez caught the people who robbed and shot Greg Baldwin?" Ellen asked.

By his expression, he hadn't. "Oh? I assumed they were long gone."

He didn't look them in the eye, and Ellen wondered if he had seen Brock's truck at the Coulter house through his security cameras. Yet . . . he didn't act like he had seen *her* going through the truck, so maybe he hadn't checked.

"They got stuck on Mule Run Road last night," Travis said.

"Well, good. We should all feel safe in our homes. Now, what other questions do you have? As Clive told you, I need this signed before Monday morning. So, if you're ready, I'm happy to make the trade now."

"As I've told you multiple times, I'm not selling you anything."

"I know, that's why I proposed the trade—giving you a very good deal."

"Yeah, not going to do it."

"Then why are you here? You said you had questions, and you're not going to sign?" He leaned forward, hands on his desk, glared at Ellen. "I'll have your land one way or the other. I don't have to play nice."

"Don't you mean you *haven't* played nice?" Ellen said, leaning forward. "I know you hired Brock Jones to rob four families, including Greg Baldwin. He wasn't supposed to be home. You hired a thief to steal contracts that had a clause in them you couldn't abide—how it got in there in the first place, I don't know. A mistake from your sexy little legal secretary, perhaps?"

His face reddened and Ellen continued.

"I have a copy of what Brock stole. You know why? Because I saved his brother's life last night, and he thanked me by telling the truth."

"You . . ." Mitchell cleared his throat. "You can't believe a thief. A person who would say anything to get out of prison."

"Rick is interviewing him right now," Ellen said.

Mitchell leaned back, shook his head. "Oh, Ellen, you are foolish. You think I would leave anything to chance?"

Her heart skipped a beat. They weren't wrong, and she hadn't thought they'd underestimated Mitchell, but maybe . . . maybe they had. She wasn't used to thinking like an unscrupulous rancher.

But they were here, and she had to finish. Travis had a theory, and if he was right, then they had only one chance to take Mitchell Robinson down—at least one chance without relying on the D.A.—a personal friend of Mitchell's—to actually do something about his crimes.

"Like sabotaging my ranch?"

He stared at her and shook his head. "Ellen, you're paranoid. I think you need to stop right now before you say something you can't take back."

Had she seen him glance at Clive? Or was that wishful thinking?

"So many little things, Mitchell. I didn't think much about it for a long time, because farms always need repairs. But there were too many little things. I started to suspect something was up when the cattle gate was unlatched." Not completely true, but she wanted Mitchell to believe she'd been thinking about this for longer than the weekend. "Jake is too responsible to make a mistake like that. And then the brand-new refrigerator in the barn broke, we lost a whole week's worth of raw milk, couldn't fulfill our obligation to our supplier. So, I put a couple of cameras on the barn."

She lied so smoothly it surprised her. But Travis was right, this was the only way she was going to get even part of the truth.

"And surprise, when someone I know came into the barn in the middle of the night . . . and then I find holes cut into the wall above the gutter."

"You're bluffing," Mitchell said smugly.

"There were holes in the wall?" Clive questioned. "What happened?"

Travis said, "Someone we all know cut narrow openings level with the gutter and clogged the drainpipes, so when the storm hit, it flooded the loft."

Mitchell glanced at Clive. "They're bluffing."

Clive didn't know, Ellen realized. His face was a mask of confusion. He might have known about Brock Jones being hired to steal the contracts, but he didn't know about the sabotage.

Ellen snapped, "I'm not bluffing, and when I turn over the tapes to Rick he's going to question Tom Garza and I don't think Garza is going to go to prison for you."

"I fired Tom," Mitchell said suddenly. "He'll say anything to get back at me." Then he said calmly, "Ellen, I would never do anything to hurt you or your family. You know that. This deal"—he touched the folder—"is a godsend for you. You need the land to grow, and I'm practically giving it to you. Sign it, and all your troubles will go away."

He smiled like a snake oil salesman and Ellen felt ill. Mitchell was right—if he fired Tom, whatever Tom said may not hold up. If they even got as far as a jury trial, the jurors may not believe him. This was rapidly getting out of control.

Travis said, his voice low and menacing, "Did you have Garza sabotage the roof, too?" He rose from his chair. "Did you kill my brother?"

"Get out," Mitchell said, rising from his desk. "I'll call security and have you dragged out."

"Mitchell," Clive said, "what did you do?"

"I've done nothing! If Tom Garza did anything, he did it without my knowledge or authorization."

"You didn't fire Tom," Clive said. "He quit. He told me he quit this morning."

"Shut up, Clive!"

Mitchell walked to the door, swung it open. "Get out of here. Leave, both of you. You think you've won? I'll own your ranch by winter. Burn what's left and pour concrete over it. Put in a fucking runway for my plane!"

Clive stepped forward. "That's enough."

"They've treated us like dirt for four generations, Clive!" Mitchell yelled. "Mightier-than-thou McKennas who think they are God's gift to farming. So superior. So fucking arrogant! Verdacorp is the future, and if you don't get with the program, you'll have nothing. Don't you see? Family farms are done. Over. Economies of scale and vertical economics are the only way to profit. By holding out you are only prolonging the demise of what you claim to love."

Clive's voice was quiet. "At what cost? You've lost your soul."

Mitchell's hands balled into fists. "You think they didn't screw Dad every chance they got because he was an idiot? It wasn't until I took over that the Robinson name began to mean something again. And don't look at me as if you're innocent, big brother," Mitchell spat out. "Whose idea was it to get back the contracts in the first place?" Suddenly, he stopped talking.

The room went still.

Mitchell blinked, realizing too late.

"Out! All of you!"

Ellen and Travis left, Clive right behind them.

"I'm sorry, Ellen," Clive said. "I never wanted anyone in your family to get hurt. I didn't know what Mitchell was doing."

"You knew about the contracts," she said pointedly.

With a long face, he nodded. "There was an error in the last four contracts we executed and we had to get them back. No one was supposed to get hurt."

"Tell that to Greg Baldwin," she said. "You're lucky he made it, otherwise you and Mitchell would be accessories to murder."

He nodded solemnly. "I'll do what I can to keep Mitchell from coming after you."

She turned to face him, searched his face. Guilt? Good. But that wouldn't bring John back.

"Tell me you didn't know what Tom was doing," she said quietly as they stood on the front porch. "Please, just tell me the truth."

"Mitchell's a bastard," Clive said, "but I never thought he'd sink that low. I am so sorry."

She wanted to go back and hit Mitchell. Scream at him. Tell him that he had stolen a good man from his family, all out of envy and greed and hate.

But it wouldn't accomplish anything.

Instead, she walked to the truck without saying a word.

Travis followed, silent. Once they were safely inside the truck, he pulled a small digital recorder from his coat and clicked it off. "I hope this is enough."

Ellen stared at the device; jaw tight. "It'll have to be."

Then she cried.

EPILOGUE

Six Months Later

Ellen took her coffee out to the porch as the sun crept up on the horizon. Her thick ceramic mug warmed her hands as she hunched into her warm jacket. The day before Thanksgiving promised to be crystal-clear blue skies for as far as the eye could see. The chilly morning would rise to a respectable sixty-eight degrees by the afternoon.

She loved this time in the morning, while her children still slept, before the animals needed tending, when the birds were just starting to wake up. The peace, the silence, the overwhelming sense of awe.

John should be with her today. He should be with her every day. But it had been nearly eighteen months since he died, and while she would never stop missing him, the raw, stifling pain was gone, replaced by a dull ache that she suspected she would live with forever.

And that was okay. Because for the first time since his death, Ellen felt optimistic about the future.

River and Stormy, two of the four kittens born to the stray cat

Cleo, ran over to her and wound around her ankles. Ellen had planned for them to be barn cats when she brought them home from Travis's at eight weeks old; they ended up being house cats. They slept in Bobby's room but got up with Ellen, coming downstairs as soon as they heard her making coffee. She fed them and they came out with her to the porch. After getting more pets, they wrestled on the porch for a minute, before running back into the house when they heard a truck turn up the driveway.

Right on time, Ellen thought. In fact, Ryan was a few minutes early.

He parked by the equipment shed and crossed the yard over to her, raising his hand in greeting. "Hello, Mrs. McKenna."

"Help yourself to some coffee and a muffin."

"I need to fix the—"

"It can wait. Eat first."

"Is Avery up?"

Then they both laughed. Of course she wasn't.

Ryan went inside.

He was a senior in high school now and he'd joined a school-to-work program where he got credit for interning for Ellen on the farm. He worked four mornings a week from five thirty to ten, then went to school and took his required classes. He had a counselor to whom he provided weekly reports about what he did, and Ellen paid him a stipend. He often came on the weekends, not just to spend time with Avery, but to help—because being a farmer wasn't a nine-to-five, Monday-through-Friday job.

Ellen wasn't sure how comfortable she felt with Ryan and Avery's relationship. On her daughter's sixteenth birthday this summer, he'd given her a promise ring—not officially engaged, but they might as well have been. They'd been inseparable now for nearly two years. Ryan intended to go to college and major in agricultural science, and Avery planned to go to the same college and major in agricultural business. They would return to Whisper

Creek Ranch and build a house and raise their family here on the family ranch. Ryan was far more interested in farming than livestock. They talked about it far too often for Ellen to think it was a passing fad.

Ellen believed in young love . . . she and John had fallen in love at eighteen. But she also knew that farm life was hard, dependent on so many factors completely out of their control. Government pricing. Weather. Environmental factors like disease in plants and animals. She would help Avery and Ryan succeed because she loved them . . . but was grateful that they had a plan that included college and options in case something happened to throw a wrench in their future.

Jake was doing amazing at the community college. He took classes three days a week and came home filled with genuine joy. He shared everything he learned with Lyla, who seemed even more interested in horses than her brother.

Ellen had wanted Jake to experience the world, go away to college, and then make a conscious decision to return and take over the farm. He disagreed. He wanted to grow roots here, and she finally understood. Her dreams were her dreams; she had to accept that her children had dreams of their own.

Lyla came out of the barn and walked over to her. "When did you get up?" Ellen asked.

"I don't know, four? I couldn't sleep, and Gracie is about ready to deliver. Jake told me to get him when it was time."

"I'll come out to help."

"We got it, Mom. I know you have that meeting today with the lawyer."

Lyla went into the house.

Sometimes, Ellen marveled at how self-sufficient her kids were.

Ellen was driving down to Dallas to meet with her lawyer. They had several things to work on.

Verdacorp went bankrupt when Mitchell couldn't follow

through with his deal to provide a continuous route for the natural gas pipeline. The government contract went to another company, and the pipeline wasn't even passing through their valley. Some farmers were furious with Ellen for stopping the deal—they had hoped to get payments for years. Others were grateful because they feared they'd be screwed over or that their land would lose value with the pipeline going through.

Ellen was not anti-progress. The pipeline was going to help all of them by providing cheap, reliable natural gas. But it would be built parallel to the highway, not cutting through farmland. There had to be balance, between progress and protecting the land that fed a nation.

To his credit, Rick went to bat for Ellen and tried to get Mitchell and Tom Garza indicted for property damage, conspiracy, and robbery. Nothing stuck. Tom wouldn't talk, and neither would Mitchell. Privately, in a conversation between Tom and Travis that neither recorded, Tom admitted that he had sabotaged the farm. He didn't admit to damaging the roof that ultimately led to John's fall and death, but he admitted to most everything else. He gave Travis some ideas on how to nail Mitchell, but Ellen didn't know what would happen.

After Ellen played the tape for her lawyer, he filed a civil lawsuit against Mitchell Robinson personally, since Verdacorp was now bankrupt. Just last week his lawyer offered a substantial settlement. Ellen was going to sign the paperwork today.

It wouldn't bring John back. And while she wanted Mitchell in prison, that wouldn't happen . . . at least not right now. There were still investigations going on, and even Congresswoman Jeanne Culvers had been raked through the media coals. People were complaining about her part in giving favoritism to Verdacorp in the pipeline deal, and while she hadn't overtly done anything illegal—that they knew about—public opinion had shifted against her.

Three longtime families had paid a visit to Travis last weekend and asked him to consider running for Congress—specifically in the primary against Jeanne Culvers. They showed him a poll they had commissioned that showed she had a lot of baggage and that he—Travis McKenna, seventh-generation farmer and Army veteran—was the best candidate to take her out.

He said he would think about it.

Another good thing that happened was that Mitchell had moved down to his house in Dallas. Clive was managing the farm, and while he tried to extend an olive branch to Ellen, she refused to take it.

She was done with the entire Robinson clan.

Once the settlement from Mitchell Robinson came through, Ellen would make offers on several pieces of land in the area. She already had verbal agreements with three landowners. Her lawyer was also creating a second LLC for the ranch, this one for Whisper Creek Winery, as well as updating her will. There were so many changes going on she could hardly keep them all straight, but Avery—the business brains in the family—was working closely with Travis to learn the logistics of running a ranch. Travis was taking over the business end until Avery graduated from college, then she would work side by side with her uncle until she felt ready to take over the business reins on her own.

And Travis . . . Ellen wished John could see how well Travis had been doing these last six months. Sobriety was only part of it. He had started his own dog training business, and he had a plan to save the pecan orchard. By next spring, they would have a healthy pecan crop. And maybe even running for Congress . . . that seemed like reaching for the stars, but McKennas never ran from a challenge.

Grow or die . . . Now they were growing in many directions, and if one part failed, they had other parts they could lean on.

For the first time in a long time, Ellen felt they were going to be okay.

Penny came out to the porch. She was using her cane regularly now. Her eighty-fifth birthday was coming up right before Christmas, and she was worried about falling. But her age hadn't stopped her from maintaining control over her kitchen.

"I swear, Ryan is eating for an army," Penny said with a smile.

"We work him hard."

"He's a good boy."

"He is."

"I talked to Margery yesterday when you were at George and Millie's place."

"How are she and the baby?"

"Her husband is coming home next month," Penny said. "It'll be the first time he'll hold that perfect little girl of his."

Margery had delivered a six-pound, two-ounce daughter named Amelia Rose nearly at term. Susie went back to college in September, so Margery was alone in her house.

"When does he have to go back?" Ellen asked.

"He isn't. He'll be stationed permanently at the Joint Reserve Base in Fort Worth."

That was less than two hours from their house in Rock Creek.

"I'm happy for them."

"Margery is over the moon," Penny said. "She, Susie, and the baby are coming for Thanksgiving dinner tomorrow."

"I'm glad. The more the merrier."

"We have the Perez family coming, the Mendozas, the Pritchards and their four kids, Greg and his two girls, and Travis invited his friend Chris from the Army—he's married with three or four kids, I don't remember. Maybe five now."

"I'm sure more will stop by. I'll ask Ryan and Jake to get the tables out of storage. It should be nice enough weather to eat out on the porch. I'll set up the heaters just in case there's a chill."

Penny said, "And I think Jake is bringing a girl."

Ellen froze. "What?"

"He hasn't told you?"

"Told me what?"

Penny just smiled and walked back inside.

Was Jake seeing someone? And why wouldn't he have told her?

Her kids were growing up too fast.

Bobby ran out, screen door slamming behind him, Whiskey at his feet. "Hi, Mom!"

"Where are you going?"

"I want to see Gracie before school! She's going to have a foal!"

"I heard."

He turned around, walking backwards. "Why can't I stay home from school? Why does Lyla get to stay home and I have to go? I can help."

"Because Lyla has straight As and you don't," Ellen said.

"Aw, man!" Then he ran off to the barn.

Avery had her license and drove herself, Lyla, and Bobby to school now that Jake had graduated.

Avery had always been responsible, but she had grown up the most since the events six months ago. She'd helped Gianna convince her parents to let her go back to college—she was now living on campus and attending the University of Texas in Dallas. Carl and Rose were selling the rest of their land to Ellen and had already moved to a small home on the river in Gordonville, close enough where Ellen and the family could visit.

Ellen had a lot of plans, and Travis was helping her make them a reality. Jake wanted to start breeding horses. He was also working on breaking in more work horses, which would also help with chores on the ranch.

John would be proud.

She wished he were here.

Looking at the rising sun, she thought that maybe he still was.

Ellen went inside as Jake and Lyla were getting ready to spend the morning in the barn making sure there were no complications with Gracie's delivery. Jake gave Ellen a spontaneous hug on his way outside.

"Love you, Mom."

No matter how life had tried to break her, she felt whole again.

ACKNOWLEDGMENTS

When I came up with this story, all I knew was that my main character was a widow with kids and she was desperate to save the family farm both from a storm and from bad guys I didn't even know yet. Then came research.

A lot of research.

I have had dogs, cats, chickens, fish, and one very lucky bearded dragon. My great-grandparents had a cattle ranch and farm in Alabama but as a young child, I had no idea how much work went into farming. Living for more than twenty-five years on the northern edge of the San Joaquin Valley, I learned to respect and appreciate my farming neighbors. (A shout-out to Davis Ranch—I miss your fresh produce, especially your corn.) Though I have always wanted to have my own small farm, I haven't done it yet. I know how hard the work can be and some of the challenges, but reading about farming and watching documentaries can get you only so far.

So, first and foremost, a huge thank-you to Bryan Ritthaler. I was so lucky (I'm sure Bryan considers himself lucky as well) that he married my friend (and super-talented writer) Tosca Lee. Bryan and his family have been farming for generations, and not only did he answer all my questions, but took time out of his busy day to talk on the phone. At the end of our conversation where I took pages of notes, he said, "I don't think I helped that much." And I was like, "You saved my bacon!" In fact, he gave me the mantra of John and Ellen McKenna: Grow or die. That one phrase helped me in untold ways.

Clearly, if I got anything wrong about farming and crops, it's all my fault. Equally important in this book was understanding cattle ranching. My son Luke graduated from Texas Tech. His roommate during the last two years was also named Luke (confusing!). Luke Williams was born and raised on a cattle ranch in the Texas panhandle and helped me with all the little details I needed to make Whisper Creek Ranch real—not just for me so I could write it, but, with any luck, for you as a reader. He also saved my bacon—I had a general plot idea for the bad guys, and he explained why it wouldn't work in the area I decided to set the story. Since I didn't want to move the family out of Cooke County, Luke took the time to brainstorm with me and we came up with a believable crime based on a real-life situation near where he grew up. Thank you so much, Luke!

Again, if I messed anything up about cattle, that's on me.

Kelley Ragland at Minotaur is an amazing editor. I have been so incredibly lucky to be able to work with her on so many books, going back to 2012. I think *Whisper Creek* is book number 21 together, but who's counting? (Okay, I am, but I may have counted wrong.) I'm a better writer today because of Kelley's gentle but firm guidance on each and every manuscript. Thank you.

The rest of the team at Minotaur/St. Martin's Publishing Group is also fabulous. Kelley's assistant, Katie Holt, who keeps everything in order; marketing whiz Stephen Erickson and his team who have fabulous ideas and help get my books out to the world; Hector DeJean, amazing publicist; and the fabulous cover designer Ervin Serrano. I stare at *Whisper Creek* in awe; it's an amazing cover.

And always, thank you to Dan Conaway, my agent of sixteen years who will never be allowed to retire; his amazing assistant, Sydnee Harlan, who fits in so perfectly with the team it's like she's been part of us from the beginning; and everyone else at Writers House.

Note to readers: Cooke and Grayson Counties really exist. I tried to stay true to the physical environment as best I could. But I write fiction, so I took a few liberties. I hope the residents of this wonderful part of Texas forgive me.

ABOUT THE AUTHOR

Brittan Dodd

Allison Brennan is the *New York Times* and *USA Today* bestselling author of more than fifty novels, including the Lucy Kincaid and Max Revere series. She was nominated for the Thriller Award for Best Paperback Original Novel by the International Thriller Writers and is a two-time winner of the Daphne du Maurier Award for Excellence in Mystery/Suspense by Kiss of Death. Married for more than a quarter of a century, Allison and her husband, Dan, raised five children, and currently live in Arizona, where they enjoy baseball's spring training and exploring the Grand Canyon.